Books by B. V. Larson:

STAR FORCE SERIES
Swarm
Extinction
Rebellion
Conquest
Battle Station
Empire
Annihilation
Storm Assault
The Dead Sun
Outcast
Exile
Gauntlet
Demon Star

REBEL FLEET SERIES
Rebel Fleet
Orion Fleet
Alpha Fleet
Earth Fleet

Visit BVLarson.com for more information.

Glass World

(Undying Mercenaries Series #13)
by
B. V. Larson

Undying Mercenaries Series:
Steel World
Dust World
Tech World
Machine World
Death World
Home World
Rogue World
Blood World
Dark World
Storm World
Armor World
Clone World
Glass World

Illustration © Tom Edwards
TomEdwardsDesign.com

Copyright © 2020 by Iron Tower Press.

This book is a work of fiction. Names, characters, places and incidents are either products of the author's imagination or used fictitiously. Any resemblance to actual events, locales or persons, living or dead, is entirely coincidental. All rights reserved. No part of this publication can be reproduced or transmitted in any form or by any means, without permission in writing from the author.

ISBN-13: 979-8607475109
BISAC: Fiction / Science Fiction / Military

> *"Too bad there is only one world to conquer."*
> —Alexander the Great, 326 BC

-1-

My hometown was Waycross, in Georgia Sector. Out in the countryside, my parents owned a spread of swampy acres near the Satilla River. I'd taken up residence there in a dim-lit shack on the edge of a bog. The place wasn't much to look at, but it had one of those floating iceboxes and a sagging couch to sleep on. I called it home.

My parents felt a little lonelier now that Etta had moved up to Central City. She was doing fine up there, and I'd been pleased when she'd gotten raises and promotions until she was able to support herself fully.

Naturally, I had no knowledge of what she was actually working on day-to-day. Every project was top secret down in the dungeons underneath Central. Some people might be bothered by that, but to me, it was a familiar state of affairs. Legion Varus, my outfit, often served with strange restrictions and protocols—and almost always without the awareness of the general public.

Although I was officially without a clue, I did have an inkling of what she *might* be doing. It had to do with certain captured enemy technology I'd recently encountered.

After a tremendous space battle had occurred at Eridani 77, better known as Clone World, there had been a whole bunch of wreckage left behind. The Mogwa, Rigellians and the Skay had all left the floating hulks of their dead spacecraft behind. We'd even managed to commandeer a few of the ships from Rigel intact. We'd brought them home with us for study.

I happened to know that Floramel was heading up a research group dedicated to studying those wrecks—and Etta was her top aide.

One day in late spring, a full year after the battle had occurred, my tapper began to buzz. Normally, I would have ignored it as the ID was invalid. There was always some hacking market-bot trying to reach every citizen on Earth, and once in a while they got through. This was probably one of those cases.

But instead of swiping it away and obliterating it from my forearm, I stared at my tapper instead. No one *should* have been able to get to me, not with any unknown ID.

That didn't sound right. The ones that got through always had some kind of cover story, pretending to be a coworker or a friend. It never simply printed *unknown* on the screen.

With a growl of frustration, I paused the ballgame I'd been projecting on my grungy ceiling and made a stabbing motion at my inner forearm.

"McGill here—who's this?"

The tapper glowed, but there was no image. Just a blank screen and some signal-strength data. For a few seconds, no one spoke.

"Ah, dammit," I said, sitting up and ready to jab my big finger at it again, this time striking the cutoff button.

"McGill?" my tapper said.

I hesitated. The best sales bots could be tricky. I'd already given it my name. Maybe it had been waiting for just such a clue. My finger hovered indecisively, and I considered disconnecting rather than saying another word. A good piece of software would just learn from me and use what it gained to trick me again the next time.

"McGill?" the voice asked again. "This is Abigail. Are you alone?"

My finger dropped away along with my jawline as my mouth sagged open. I noticed my tapper's camera had a tiny, gleaming red dot of light on it, indicating the caller was looking at me. She was obviously blocking her own outgoing vid feed, but I supposed that was acceptable. Girls sometimes did that when they were naked or something.

I cleared my throat. "Abigail? Really?"

"Yes. I'm sorry to bother you, but it's been months. Have you gotten a chance to contact Drusus yet—on my behalf?"

"Uh…"

Last year, I'd met Abigail Claver for the first time. She was a lady-Claver, a female who was genetically a twin to Claver himself. She'd displayed an obvious interest in poor old James McGill from the start. That was all six kinds of creepy, but the girl herself had looked pretty good to me…

"Did you forget?" she asked.

Naturally, she'd hit the nail on the head. I'd probably forgotten a few minutes after she asked me. I was the kind of man who never remembered what I'd had for dinner the night before, much less a request from a girl who wasn't in my immediate vicinity.

"No… no, no," I lied. "I didn't forget. I gave it a shot, in fact, right after you asked me. But Drusus never got back to me. He isn't very happy with me right now, you see."

"Why not?"

A slight smile of relief crept over my face. I'd mixed a lie with a truth, and now it was not only convincing, it served to move us right past the part about me forgetting in the first place. Lying is like shooting pool, I always say, it's not good enough to sink the ball. A real master sets up his next shot at the same time.

"I believe it all started," I told her, "when I became admiral of Drusus' fleet and wrecked a lot of his starships and suchlike."

"Oh… but that was a brief situation, and it wasn't in your control."

"That's what I said!"

"He's a petty man," Abigail said. "But I can help you get around his petulance."

"Uh…"

I was squarely back in the danger zone. I hadn't contacted Drusus in any way, shape or form, much less asked him about Abigail. On top of that, Abigail was now on the wrong scent. I'd never heard anyone call Drusus petty before. He was a straight-arrow and whenever he'd gotten angry with me, he'd had a damned good reason for it—including this time.

"What's wrong?" she asked.

"How come I can't see you?"

"Bandwidth," she said. "This connection isn't sanctioned, so I'm using the thinnest datastream I can."

"Huh…" I said. "But I can't even be sure it's you when I'm looking at a blank screen."

She sighed and the rectangle of photo-reactive skin on my forearm flickered to life. I saw a gloomy green sky behind her. She moved a little, and I caught sight of the land—none of it looked like Earth. Wherever she was, she was outside and the landscape was full of wet, black rocks. There was a foamy sea in the background that matched the greenish clouds above.

"Green World?" I demanded. "What are you doing out there? Holy shit, are we talking on a deep-link?"

She made a sound of frustration. "How do you know about this place?"

"I'm what you might call a well-traveled man," I told her. "I don't know where it is on a star map, but I've been there. I met my first Wur on that planet."

Abigail shook her head and laughed. The laugh was nice, her voice was soft, and her hair encircled her face just right. She looked at me with those intense eyes of hers. I could tell there were lots of gears and sprockets spinning behind those eyes. She was a smart one, all right. That meant all kinds of trouble for the likes of me.

"Will you call Drusus again?" she asked. "For me?"

"Uh…" I said. "Could you remind me again exactly what I'm supposed to say?"

"We need help, McGill. We need a connection with Central—with Drusus, if possible. We're rebel Clavers, and we're always being hunted. We need allies."

"Yeah, yeah, I get that. You said something about helping me get through to him. What have you got? I can't go in there empty-handed."

"A trade…" she said. "All right. I'll give you something. Remember the Skay—the ones that were destroyed at Eridani 77?"

"I could hardly forget them."

"Those hulks were so badly damaged they're pretty much useless… but I know where another one is. Here, record these coordinates."

She gave me a list of numbers, and I knew enough about astronavigation to realize they defined a point in space. Imperial coordinates were always based on the center of our galaxy, and so the first several numbers were the same if the location was anywhere near Earth.

"926…" I said. "That's not our province. It's not the frontier zone 928 next door, either."

"No, but it's close—in relative terms."

"Almost next door neighbors…" I said, frowning at the numbers. She would probably have described Waycross and a Martian colony dome as being "close" because they were both in the same star system.

"Take that to Drusus," she told me. "Don't give the information up too easily. Make him beg for it."

"I'll have him holding a stick in his mouth by tomorrow afternoon," I said. "Now, what about my part in all this?"

"Ah, at last," she said with a knowing smile. "My brother assured me you'd help out of kindness. Instead, you promptly forgot. That's why people get paid to do things."

"Well… I didn't want any money. I'd just like to take you to dinner sometime."

She blinked twice and stared. I'd actually surprised her. "Really? We're not even in the same part of the galaxy. I haven't been to Earth for almost a year now, and—"

I raised a hand. "No worries. There's no time limit or anything. Just a promise aimed for a convenient moment in the future."

She dropped her eyes and frowned. "Just a date? A dinner?"

"Yeah, yeah, that's all."

Abigail looked up again, smiling. I had to wonder what she'd thought I'd been asking for. I wasn't that kind of a scoundrel. Sure, I was pretty bad. I was generally considered to be a low man of base principles, interests and habits. But I wasn't the type who pressured people for personal favors they didn't want to give.

"All right," she said. "I owe you a date."

"Okay, so, how do I reach you the next...?"

I trailed off then, mouth hanging open again, as I saw Abigail duck low. The green sky, the green sea and the black rocks all spun, and I could hear a scuffling sound that was very loud as the microphone was banged around.

Then, I heard a clacking sound. A rattling of dull hollow tubes.

"No, no," I heard Abigail say to someone off camera. "I'm not talking to anyone. I'm downloading communications from abroad, that's all."

She was a liar, the same as me. That thought made me smile.

There was more clacking, louder this time, and it seemed like a command. The world spun sickeningly again, and for just a second, I saw Abigail's face as she stabbed her finger at the camera pickup.

"Don't forget this time, McGill," she whispered, and the transmission went dead.

That wasn't what occupied my mind afterward, however. It was what I'd glimpsed behind her that really freaked me out.

Looming there, dark and wet-looking, was something that resembled a lobster. A lobster made of cellulose and standing as tall as a house.

It was one of the Wur. One of their smarter, technical types. Once, out on Green World, I'd met up with a creature like that, and we'd killed it, but only after it had taken down a few of my men in turn.

I stared at my tapper for a time after the call had ended. So, Abigail was living with the Wur out on Green World—wherever that was. That was a shocker.

Shaking my head in bewilderment, I went back to watching my ballgame on the ceiling. I found it hard to get into the swing of the game.

God Almighty, why did I find the most dangerous of women interesting? Worse, why did they tend to like me? We were both moths drawn to the flame, I supposed.

-2-

I made a serious effort to forget about Abigail, and the Wur, and all that stuff. But I couldn't. Not this time. It just wasn't in me.

The next morning, bright and early, I sighed awake and worked my tapper with bleary eyes. I hadn't even gone out to spit on the grass or taken a piss yet, that's how much my mind was preoccupied.

Tapping out a simple message, I communicated with Drusus directly. It was only a text, but I knew it would elicit a response.

Some years back, Drusus had placed a standing order with me, demanding that I report "unusual activity" that was "interesting and alien in nature". If this didn't qualify, I didn't know what the hell did. So I shot him a text, reminding him in a few words of his request and suggesting I might have encountered just such a tidbit today.

Not seven minutes later, as I was stepping into the shower to wash off, my tapper buzzed. The call was from Central, no name given.

Now, you might think it would have been a prudent and reasonable thing for any man to finish his grooming before answering such a call. But this was Drusus we were talking about. He was one of a handful of men with the rank of praetor on my beloved green Earth. There was only one rank higher in the military than praetor—that of consul. That lofty rank was only temporarily given in times of the most dire circumstances, as it gave the office holder dictator-like powers. There had been whispers that if the rank were ever revived and used again, Drusus was probably the man who would get it.

The long and the short of it was that a lowly centurion like me didn't go around snubbing such people. I opened the connection and angled the camera up at my face.

"Centurion McGill reporting," I said.

"McGill? What the hell...?"

It wasn't Drusus. It was Galina Turov, the acting tribune commanding my legion. "Oh... Uh... hi sir," I said. "I'm sorry, I was expecting someone else."

Her face soured immediately. Galina and I had a long and sordid past. We'd shared plenty of sex, violence, backstabbing and even a little loving in our twisted history.

"I see..." she said. "I'll call back when you're alone. But just one thing: why are you contacting Central?"

I blinked. Then I blinked again. My mind generally moves like a snail on a drainpipe, especially when I'm surprised, but several things went off in my head at once.

Right off, I realized she was under the false impression I was entertaining a lady-friend in my place. My first instinct was to persuade her that wasn't true, but my second reaction hit me before I could do so.

How did she know I'd just called Central?

That was the real kicker. I was no stranger to being watched and fooled with in my private life. Galina was one of the worst offenders, having both private and political reasons to keep tabs on me. It still pissed me off when I caught her doing it, however.

"There's no one here, girl. As a matter of fact, I'm about to climb into the shower—and maybe you need to stop spying on my communications..."

Galina squinted at me. She knew me well, and she could tell I was honestly angry.

"Well... sorry about that. There's been a lack of trust between us since Clone World, hasn't there?"

"Uh... I guess so."

"Good to have that out in the open. Now, if you can avoid having a hissy fit, can you tell me why you sent a message to Drusus then immediately stepped into the shower?"

I thought about hanging up. I really did. If she'd been just a smidgeon meaner, or less pretty, I probably would have done it. But I'm a man of simple tastes, so I decided to put up with her bullshit one more time.

"I've learned something interesting. Something Drusus needs to hear about."

Her face brightened. "Ah-ha!" she said. "Just as I thought. You're bored and want to stir up trouble. Well, I've intercepted your transmission and trashed it."

My mouth gaped a little. "How'd you do that?"

"It's new tech. Your tapper had an update recently, didn't it? In the middle of the night some six weeks ago?"

"Not if I could stop it, it didn't."

"Well, you can't stop the priority updates. Not anymore."

"What's this new update do?" I demanded. "It sounds wonderful."

"It is… from my point of view. The new software forces communications along the chain of command. No longer are such protocols mere suggestions. They're now mandatory. No soldier is allowed to communicate with anyone directly if the target is more than two steps in rank above you. When you try, it sends a message to your legitimate commander."

"Huh…" I said, chewing that over. I had the water on by now and started rubbing soap everywhere.

"What are you doing now? James, there's water going over the camera lens."

"I bet so. Soap as well. Let me get this straight, you can't even talk to Drusus directly? Is that right?"

"What are you talking about?"

"Well, you're a tribune, right? And he's a praetor… that's more than two steps." Galina frowned fiercely. I could tell she didn't like that idea at all.

"Hold on a minute," she said. "I'll call you back."

She hung up, and I grinned while I sprayed off and climbed out of the shower. While I was toweling off and climbing into my clothes, she called back.

"This is utter bullshit!" she exclaimed. "Who could have thought of such a stupid scheme?"

I laughed. She was all about limiting people's actions until it affected her personally. "Seems like I'm going to have to come up there in person to deliver my news."

She eyed me critically for a moment. "It's that interesting?"

"I think so."

"Come up here, then. I'll help you deliver it."

I knew what that meant. Galina was hoping my information, whatever it might be, could be credited to her if it was hot enough. She was always on the lookout for a useful tidbit to help her sagging career.

Her tapper began to buzz then, and she eyed it unhappily. "Who...?"

"It's probably Equestrian Woodard," I said. "Isn't he the man two steps above you?

Maybe he wants to know why you're trying to pester Drusus."

"You're right... I have to take this. Shit. Haul-ass and get up here—today." The screen darkened, and I laughed my way out of my front door.

My dad knew something was up. He caught up with me in the garage. "Taking the tram to town, are you boy?" my father asked.

"That's right, sir."

"You're not called-up to serve again or anything, are you, James?"

"Not at all. I'm just looking for a quick road trip. Don't worry about the tram. I'll set her to auto-drive herself home."

He gave me a hug, and I left him there, frowning after me. His obvious distrust made me feel a little guilty. Sure, this really *was* an innocent trip to deliver information. But my folks had been ditched high and dry so often they were sensitive about it.

Arriving at the sky-train station in Atlanta, I gave the tram a kick in the bumper while it dithered about the route home. It finally started trundling back to Waycross.

I boarded the next flight and paid the fare by touching my tapper to a tattered armrest on the seat I chose. We launched fifteen minutes later on a sub-orbital flight, heading northeast. Central was only a few hours away by air. It didn't take long or much money to get there.

Settling in for the trip, I realized I hadn't seen Etta in months. A short flight could be too long when you were busy—or even when you weren't busy. Somehow, I never seemed to get around to making the trip to visit her.

Once the seatbelt light went off, someone came along up the aisle behind me. That was unusual, but maybe the fella had to go to the can or something.

Gazing out the window, I felt a sudden presence in the empty seat at my side.

My instinct was to come around with my arm cocked back for a punch—but I restrained myself. After all, this was a public flight, and maybe someone had been unable to find an empty—

My mind froze, as did the idiot's grin of greeting I wore on my face when I turned and saw who had sat down beside me.

"Hello, McGill," said a cocky voice.

I knew that voice, and I knew that tone. It was Winslade. He was a skinny snake of a man with bony arms and a pinched face that was permanently drawn into a sneer. As best I could figure, the man would have sounded sarcastic while reading a shopping list.

Seeing him was a shocker, as I'd last laid eyes on him while I was killing him back aboard *Legate*, our destroyed transport ship. At that point he'd declared himself a renegade, a traitor to Earth, and an enemy of mine in every sense of the word.

"Winslade?" I asked, my jaw sagging low.

"The one and only," he said. "What's the matter? Are you drunk?"

"Uh... what are you doing here?"

"I'm looking for you. I... I need some help, McGill. I'm not clear on certain facts, and I'm hoping you could explain a few things for me."

Looking back toward the sky-train's oval window, I contemplated the amount of force it might take to propel Winslade through it and out into open space. Hopefully, if I managed to throw him hard enough, he'd stay alive all the way down to the ground that was already a dozen kilometers below us.

"Brain-lock again, McGill?" Winslade asked, totally misunderstanding my mood and thoughts.

Finally, I turned back to him, and my fool's grin once again was firmly planted where it had been before. "Good to see you again… uh… Centurion?"

He winced. He was in uniform, and he clearly had the red crests of a centurion-ranked individual, the same as I wore. At the moment I was in my civvies, but once I got to Central I planned to change.

"Yes," he said. "You noticed that, did you? The small matter of my reduced rank came as a surprise to me as well. I've been demoted two steps. What's equally galling is no one will tell me *why*."

That's when my memory of last year's events began to solidify. The brass had said something about bringing back Leeza and Winslade, both of whom had defected to Claver's rebel army and been killed in the fighting. Clearly, they'd brought him back without his full memories, so he didn't know he'd defected and turned traitor.

Damn, this was going to be a seriously twisted mess to sort out.

-3-

I recalled that an evil man had once said you should keep your friends close—and your enemies even closer.

That was the situation I found myself in right now. A concerned, puzzled Winslade sat at my side, questioning me about the details of the previous campaign.

"So... what exactly *did* happen at Clone World?" he asked me.

"Well sir, I'm sure you'll be briefed when we get to Central," I said, using as friendly a tone of voice as I could muster.

"You're mistaken. I've been alive and wandering the halls of Central for over six months now. No one has given me an adequate answer concerning my status. It's quite frustrating."

"Is that so? And you're really hoping I can help?"

"It's a longshot, I admit, but I'm desperate, McGill."

"How'd you even find me?"

He shrugged his narrow shoulders. "I'm still on the alert lists concerning Turov's schedule. She swiped your name onto her roster today."

"That's pretty thin. Just because she's meeting with me, you first hopped a redeye train down to Atlanta, and then boarded this one headed back to Central? Just to find me?"

"Evidently," he admitted.

"But... why not just call me up? Tapper-to-tapper?"

He lifted his arm, and he pulled back his sleeve. His tapper had foil taped over it. "This may come as a surprise—perhaps you'll even suspect I'm a paranoid schizophrenic—but I think my tapper has been spying on me. Ever since my overdue revival here on Earth, odd coincidences keep occurring..."

I nodded. "You're probably right about that. Don't trust it. If the brass wants to snoop on you, they can do it at will."

Winslade squinted at me. "You know, that's an honest answer. No one else I've met with would give anything other than platitudes and snorts of amusement. But you're a man who's often been the victim of such witch-hunts. That's why I came to you."

I shifted in my seat uncomfortably. I'd never really liked Winslade much. But I'd never liked government spooks getting into people's business, either. I felt the stirrings of an ethical dilemma in my near future.

Clearly, Winslade was in the dark as to the reasons for his newfound status as a pariah. That had to come hard to any man, and it seemed wrong to me on the face of it. The accused should at least know what they've done. That only seemed right.

"Winslade..." I said, coming to a fateful decision, "I'm going to tell you something I shouldn't."

He perked up like a dog sniffing bacon. "What?"

"Don't get too excited, I don't know the whole story—probably not much more than you do. But I *do* know you did something wrong out at Clone World."

"But they said I never made it to Clone World! They said I died in a training incident, and there were complications, and I wasn't revived until we got back to Earth. That's why I don't remember a thing about the campaign. How can I have committed a *faux pas* if wasn't even alive at the time?"

I lifted my hand to slow down his tirade. "Look, I said I don't know the whole story. But what I do know is you pissed off the brass, and they didn't revive you until we got home."

"But what heinous act could be worthy of such treatment?" he asked with pleading eyes.

I gave him a firm shake of the head and lied through my teeth. "I have no idea." He sat back and sighed. "Why tell me anything in that case?"

"Because I believe a man who hasn't committed a crime yet—from his perspective—shouldn't be punished for it."

Winslade nodded slowly. "I can see that—especially from your point of view. You've been in that situation before, haven't you?"

"Quite a number of times. It's just not right. It's like sending police to go back in time to shoot children that are destined to become serial killers someday. It's just not right."

"Hmm... All right. Thank you for the help—what little of it you managed to provide. I'll figure this out, and when I do, I'll inform you of the results. Just as payback."

"That'd be mighty considerate of you, sir—uh... Centurion, I mean." At the moment, we both had the same rank. To the best of my memory, that had never happened before. He'd always been a step or two ahead of me.

Winslade contorted his face into a configuration that was even more sour than usual. For the rest of the flight, he regaled me with his numerous attempts to learn the truth about his predicament. I paid very little attention, but I was impressed that the brass had managed to get the results they'd been aiming for.

The idea had been to revive some of the turncoats from the Clone World campaign and watch them closely. If they had contacts with Claver's agents on Earth, it was reasoned that they would seek to connect with them again and demand to know what had happened.

So far, that angle seemed to be working in Winslade's case. He was like a dog on a hunt. His eyes slid from side-to-side with each sly new thought that entered his brain.

Finally, we landed at Central.

"Can I give you a lift, McGill?" Winslade asked.

"Sure."

For some reason, I'd expected him to summon a private aircar for the trip to Central. That wasn't the case. Instead, he summoned a cab. He paid half the fare and looked at me expectantly.

With a grunt, I shoved my tapper at the pay-module. We were splitting the cost. I supposed that was legit, as we were the same rank now.

The auto-cab lurched into motion once our destination had been chosen, and we'd paid in advance. We were given a no-frills ride to Central. The cab lurched at every navigational shift and smelled of ozone, urine and hot motor oil.

Landing on one of the side-slot platforms, we parted ways, and I entered the building alone. Moments later, I was heading up to the Turov's office. She'd insisted on playing a go-between role. The new software update had forced me to agree.

Naturally, I knew she was angling to take all the credit for whatever my news was about. But I had a simple way to block that.

"Nope," I said, crossing my big arms. "I'm telling my story to Drusus, and Drusus only."

Galina had placed a lingering set of fingers on my arm. Now, she dug in her nails. "Listen to me, McGill. You're not cutting me out of this deal."

"Deal? This isn't a deal. This is a report."

"Fine," she hissed. "Call it whatever you want. But you're reporting to me, or not at all."

My fat thumb reached out and stabbed the emergency stop on the elevator. Galina stumbled and cursed as it screeched to a halt.

"What are you doing?" she demanded.

"I'm reversing this car. I've decided not to make my report today."

"What? You can't do that—you're under orders!"

I shrugged, punching up the lobby on the panel. The floors you could visit were always restricted, but everyone could get to the lobby.

"All right, all right!" she said in exasperation. "You'll come with me to deliver your manifesto in person!"

We got the elevator started in the right direction again, and a few minutes later we reached the top floors of the ziggurat-shaped building. Walking carpeted hallways, we found our way into Drusus' sumptuous office.

Every time I met with Drusus it seemed like his office had undergone a recent upgrade. It had been little more than a tent or a bunker back in the old days when he'd been running campaigns on various worlds. Now, it was quite a bit nicer than that.

Just to begin with, he had an aircar parked in the middle of the place. There was a chimney above the vehicle that could be used as a private exit. In the front, we found a wide foyer and a circle of cushy furniture. Perhaps this area was for VIPs to wait or hold informal meetings. In the back was a huge desk, which I knew converted to a tabletop battle computer at the touch of its master's fingers.

After sharing salutes, Drusus indicated we should be at ease. He stood in the middle of his circle of comfy chairs. He smiled at us coldly and indicated that we should sit down. I took command of the biggest chair in the collection and stretched out gloriously.

"*Damnation*, Praetor! This office is bigger than my folks' house! You're doing pretty well for yourself these days."

"Glad you like it, McGill."

Galina sat opposite me, as far as she could get on the other side of the circle. That made me frown, just a little. I'd entertained thoughts of kick-starting the unofficial side of our relationship later tonight. Such happy fantasies were fading fast.

Drusus took a spot in the middle and leaned forward. "What have you got for me, McGill? Whatever it is, I hope it's good."

"It *is* good," Turov said, leaning forward to match him.

We both glanced at her, but no one said anything. Soon, they were both looking at me expectantly. I grinned like a moron with a candy bar.

Drusus threw up his hands. "Let's hear it then! Time is wasting. I have a staff meeting at three."

Still leaning back, I gestured toward Galina. "Maybe you should start, Tribune."

Galina's face went blank for a second, then a quick tightening of her lips told me she was onto my game. She didn't know squat, but she was here to cash in on the credit. She couldn't very well admit that now.

She struggled, with both of us watching, for a full second. "It's related to Winslade," she said at last. "McGill took the flight up here to Central with him this morning."

Drusus looked at me in surprise. "I was under the impression you two didn't get along. Has he finally cracked? Has he shown us how Claver recruited him?"

They were both barking up the wrong tree, so I decided to help them out a little. "No, sir. Winslade is clueless. He's lost and confused. But I do have something else to show you, check this out."

With a flick of my finger, I tossed the numbers Abigail had given me from my tapper to the coffee table we all sat around. The table lit up as it caught the numbers, spun them around so we could all see them and expanded them up so that each digit was the size of my hand.

Galina's mouth transformed into a tight pink rosebud. She was annoyed that I'd just called her bluff—but Drusus seemed intrigued. He frowned at the digits for a moment.

"Galactic coordinates?"

"That's right," I said.

He eyed me with guarded interest. "These numbers… that's pretty far out. Not even in our province. What's out there?"

"You know how we trashed a few Skay in orbit over Clone World? And how we 'rescued' several Mogwa ships for later study?"

Drusus hesitated. "Those rumors are unsubstantiated, McGill."

"Of course they are. This spot is special like that. This is where another advanced derelict ship exists. According to my source, it wasn't a total loss. It's much more intact than the ones we destroyed."

Both their eyes widened as they considered the possibilities. "An alien wreck?" Drusus asked. "Who knows about it? How did you find out about this information?"

I shrugged. "Let's just say I've been contacted by those who discovered it. They want to give us exclusive access to the wreck."

"And what's in it for them?"

"More importantly," Galina interrupted. "What's to keep us from claiming it and cutting them out of any deal you might have arranged—without authorization, I might add."

Drusus glanced at her. "I thought you were instrumental in bringing this information to light."

Galina looked startled. "I'm only concerned McGill has gone too far. I haven't agreed to anything on Earth's behalf—unlike him."

Drusus narrowed his eyes. He was suspicious of her and with good reason.

I cleared my throat and leaned forward. "Here's the deal," I said. "We've been given information. If it checks out and it's valuable, the source wants to be given diplomatic immunity."

"Diplomatic Immunity? So this is some kind of alien we're talking about?"

"Let's just say they need Earth's protection."

"Huh…" Drusus said, thinking it over. "We'd have to check it out first, of course. But if it's real… a find like this is unquestionably valuable."

"But why agree to do anything for them?" Galina demanded. "We already have the coordinates."

"Because," Drusus answered patiently. "They might have more intel we could use. Informants must be paid and protected, or they soon stop coming to your doorstep."

"All right…" she said, but she was eyeing me again. "But how did you meet these

people? You live in a shack!"

"And that suits me just fine, sirs. Do we have a deal?"

I was looking at Drusus now, looking him in the eye. Slowly, he nodded. "We have a deal. If this works out, McGill… Well done."

"Thank you, sir."

Galina looked sullen. Drusus hadn't praised her at all. He wasn't born yesterday, and he'd figured out the situation between us.

"Someone will have to verify the find," she said suddenly. "Someone will have to go out there before we send any ships into a deathtrap."

"Do you have anyone in mind?" Drusus asked. She extended a painted fingernail in my direction.

Drusus looked at me. "It makes sense. You already know about the find—keeping a tight lid on those coordinates is critical."

"Well, McGill…?" Galina asked me.

"I'll do it," I heard myself saying. "But that's a long, long jump."

"It is. I'll tell the teleport deck to schedule you in."

Sighing to myself, I was dismissed and kicked out of the office. I found myself out in the hallway, wondering what new flavor of Hell I'd just volunteered for.

-4-

Leaving Drusus' office, I made the critical error of letting Galina get behind me. She had been quiet all through the end of the talk with Drusus, and the truth was, I'd kind of forgotten about her.

After all, I'd just signed on for a solid killing or two, possibly a perming if things went wrong. Galina's feelings just weren't on the top of my mind at the moment.

Before we made it to the elevator lobby, I felt a sharp blow to my hindquarters. "Hey!" I said, turning around.

There she stood, teeth clenched, breathing hard. I could tell by her stance she'd just kicked me in the butt. Now, normally that would be hard for a girl of her stature, but I happened to know from personal observation that she could high-kick like a ballerina if she wanted to.

"What's the matter with you?" I asked, idly rubbing a few fingers over my back pocket.

"What do you think is wrong, you oaf?" she demanded. "You made me look like a fool back there."

"How so?"

"By making it obvious I knew nothing about your secret alien arrangements. I'm your superior officer, the tribune of Legion Varus—it's my job to know what my centurions are up to."

"Yeah…" I said, mulling that over. "I guess that's so, but I just wanted to present the deal in the best possible light."

"Why?" she asked, taking a step forward and cocking her head to the left. "Who are these people, anyway?"

As she approached to within kicking distance, I instinctively wanted to cover my privates, but I refrained. It would have looked weak.

"They're friends... sort of."

"Plural? As in at least two?"

Already, I could see the wheels turning in her skull. That was a dangerous thing. I didn't want her or anyone else to figure out who had given me the tip. Everyone at Central wanted to execute any form of Claver on sight. I knew I had to prove the worth of this location if I was to have a chance of getting Hegemony to honor the deal I'd just struck with Drusus. If they found out too early where it came from—well, that was going to lead to trouble all around.

Naturally, I didn't let on that I was concerned about any of these things. Instead, I watched her approach like a snake-charmer working with a fresh-caught wild cobra for the first time. My paranoia was focused on her personally.

"What is it?" she asked. "Afraid I might bite you?"

"I *know* you bite, girl."

This garnered me a fresh frown. "Don't talk like that," she said in a low tone. "This is Central, dammit. We must hide our personal indiscretions—besides, that's all in the past now."

I blinked, but I didn't start whining. If I had a nickel for every time Galina had told me she'd never share my bed again, I'd be an independently wealthy man.

"Okay then," I said with a shrug. "I guess I'll see you in the morning at the launch." Turning away, I approached a bank of elevators.

I heard her hurried steps behind me—but she didn't kick me again. Instead, she fell into step beside me. This took an effort on her part, as my stride is unreasonably broad, even when I'm not trying to walk fast.

Taking a glance down and to my left, I saw she was still fuming. "Is something wrong, sir?" I asked her.

"Of course it is. I've signed onto one of your mad schemes without knowing any details. That's highly stressful for me."

"Oh," I said unhelpfully.

The elevator dinged, and we stepped aboard. This, apparently, was the moment Galina had been waiting for. She moved to face me and wagged a finger in my face.

"Now we're clear of Drusus' cameras," she said.

"But what if he's tapped into the elevator feed?"

"Then he's about to get an eyeful. I'm hereby *ordering* you to tell me who is behind this offer, which you so conveniently brought in from out of the blue. How did you hear about it? Who made the original move to contact you?"

"Uh..." I said, thinking things over. I shook my head at last. "I told Drusus it had to be a secret, and he agreed with me."

"So, you're disobeying a direct order from your tribune?"

"Well sir... I guess so."

"Fine!" she spat out, and she stepped to the elevator panel. She waved her tapper over it like a wand. Immediately, all the buttons activated. That was a cool trick. Normally, only selected options were available to the likes of me, but Galina had higher clearances.

"Uh... what are you doing, sir?"

"I'm redirecting this elevator car to the brig."

"Aw, come on now."

But she did it. She didn't listen to any kind of bullshit I could present, either. Soon, we parked on a floor just under the lobby level. I knew it well.

It was the prison level.

"Jeez, Tribune!" I called out, but it was no good.

Two hogs rushed into the elevator to grab me. I let them take an arm each and walked out with a docile stride.

The moment Galina turned her back, I threw them both on the floor. One guy landed badly, he seemed to be groaning and flopping—his neck might have been broken.

The other hog had plenty of fight left in him. I stood on his throat just to let him know who was boss.

"God dammit, McGill!" Galina said, whirling around. "Get away from that man!"

"He's choking on something, sir. I think we ought to call a corpsman."

24

She stomped up to me and looked me right in the eye. "McGill," she said. "I'm giving you three options. You can tell me what I want to know, or you can be kicked out of Legion Varus *right now*."

"Uh... what's the third option?"

"You can be publicly flogged. That's by the book."

I knew she was right. Old Roman rules for handling insubordination weren't easy-going. Not back then, and not now. In fact, if a whole unit needed shaping up, an officer could order them "decimated" which meant every tenth man was killed. Of course, this wasn't as severe a punishment as it had been in the old days of the Roman Empire. Back then every tenth man would have been permed rather than revived to serve again after execution.

The harsh old methods of discipline still worked in most cases. Another man might have quailed and begged for forgiveness. Unfortunately, that sort of thing wasn't my style.

"I'll take the flogging," I said, shrugging my way out of my shirt.

The hog on the floor got up before anyone walked too far away. He had an electric truncheon upraised in his hand. He was breathing hard and kind of red-faced.

"You seen a doctor lately, hog?" I asked him. "That's an unhealthy sweat you've got going. You might want to get your ticker checked."

Galina grabbed his arm. There was a wicked light in her eye. "Will you do me the honor of flogging this prisoner?" she asked. His face lit up like a kid on Christmas morning.

"I would really appreciate that opportunity, sir," he rasped out. His voice didn't sound quite right, like he'd been gargling gravel or something.

The next hour was unpleasant, but it wasn't my first rodeo. Public flogging had been formalized these days. They had a big leather dummy to hang your wrists on, and loops and straps to hold.

The biggest difference was the well-lit, clean room they did it in. The place was all white and almost surgical. Cameras were all around, some flying on drones. They got every angle, and they broadcast it on the grid so it was captured forever.

All of this was meant to strike fear and shame into the heart of the flogged man. For me, however, there was no hope of that working.

Sure, the whip stung, and my back would be scarred up and burning for a while. But my mamma could have told anyone that spanking me as a child had never been overly effective. In most cases, she'd ended up with a hurt hand and sullen boy who'd most likely learned absolutely nothing from the experience.

After the first twelve licks or so, I took the opportunity to turn my head and look back toward Galina over my shoulder.

There she was, wincing with each blow. In fact, she looked almost as unhappy as I did. Maybe even more so.

Showing her teeth, she sucked in a breath and ordered the gleeful hog to stop after twenty lashes.

"I thought you said thirty, sir," he objected.

"Cut him down. Now."

Shaking his head in disappointment, the hog came near to release my wrists. With a grim smile, I straightened and shed them myself. I'd pulled them loose while he wasn't looking, just in case.

He glared at this, but he wisely took a few steps back, circling the edge of the room. I grabbed my uniform and pulled it on, grimacing a bit.

"That's not sanitary, McGill," Galina said. "You're bleeding through the cloth."

"Yeah... I'll go down to Blue Deck and have someone spray it with nu-skin."

She walked with me out of the chamber, giving me frequent wary glances.

Sometimes, I'd been known to become violent after being abused. It was a character flaw of mine that people were well-aware of.

After I showed no signs of going into a rage, Galina grew bolder. "Centurion McGill, you have been justly punished for insubordination," she told me in a formal tone.

"Sure have, Tribune," I agreed.

"So? Are you willing to talk about your informants now?" I shook my head. "Nope."

All of a sudden, her attitude shifted to anger again. "You animal! How can you be so obstinate?"

"I don't know. Comes natural, I suspect."

Twisting up her mouth, she marched to the elevator lobby. I followed her, making sure to stay behind her this time.

-5-

I soon realized that walking behind her might have been a tactical mistake. She still had the best hindquarters I could recall seeing on a young woman—physically young, that was, as she'd been around for at least a decade longer than I had.

But her body showed none of those decades of aging. She'd always managed to get herself killed every once in a while, just to freshen up her looks. She never updated her body scans, and it had been so long since she'd followed the rules that the bio people had given up sending requests to her. As a result, she looked like a college freshman most of the time.

That's what was troubling me now, I realized. Not only was she a fine specimen, the fact that I'd been with her many times over the years gave me an added surge of interest. By the time we got into the elevator and began the long ride down, I was thinking hard on how I might mend some fences with her. At last, I came up with an angle.

"Oooh…" I said, leaning my head back against the wall of the elevator.

"What is it?" she asked in immediate concern.

I moved my shoulders, which had been resting against the wall, and I made sure I left a big stripe of blood there. "I don't know… I'll be fine, I guess."

She came close and examined me. I wrapped my arms around myself and hung my head low. My butt was against the wall, as if I needed propping up—which I didn't.

"You're going into shock," she said with sudden concern. "Shit..."

She moved to the panel and rattled the buttons, seeking a Blue Deck with an open slot. She called on her tapper and all kinds of stuff, but I didn't really listen. I played the dying, beaten man with ease, having witnessed such behavior any number of times in the past.

When we arrived at the medical center, she tried to help me get off the elevator. She absurdly tried to shoulder one of my arms. I didn't lean on her too hard, not wanting to break her. The key was that she *felt* like she was helping me, that's all that mattered.

"Is this the recycle?" asked an orderly with arms as big around as a normal fellow's legs.

My head snapped up. "I'm not feeling *that* poorly. Just give me some ice water and a flesh printer."

"And maybe a transfusion," Galina added. "Why don't you people ever want to do anything other than run people through grinders?"

The orderly looked at both of us, then he took note of our rank insignias. He soon nodded and backed off. "Right this way, sirs."

Two minutes later I was in a floater-chair, gliding down the blue-white hallways to a private room. Over the next hour, I let a few cute bio girls pamper me. While this went on, Galina stood by the door with her arms crossed and her eyebrows knitted in concern.

Sure, sometimes Tribune Galina Turov hated me. She'd had me killed before, and I'd gotten in a few licks now and then myself. But she also loved me, I think, just a little. We had the kind of complex relationship that was all too common in the legions.

To understand it, you have to contemplate spending decades fighting and dying with the same rough lot of people, then being reborn to fight again. We'd lived like that for so long we barely remembered our old, normal lives.

Some of the scariest old farts, like Graves, had been on active duty for close to a century. As a result, all of the senior legionnaires had sour memories. We all held grudges—but we also cared about each other, too. In a way, normal folks barely mattered to us. We were like a big, dysfunctional family of serial-killers.

After I'd had enough, I staged a miraculous recovery. I stood up suddenly and grinned. "I'm feeling much better. You ladies really can cure a man when you put your minds to it!"

The two bio women—who I'd taken the opportunity to chat up while they worked on me—smiled sincerely. It wasn't often a Blue Deck death-monkey heard praise from a legionnaire.

Galina drew in a sudden breath. "I guess I'll be going now. See you in the morning."

She walked out, and to her surprise, I walked after her. She looked at me with upraised eyebrows. "Aren't you going to consummate with your newfound friends?"

"What? Those kids? Nah," I said, laughing. "I was just passing the time and being friendly."

She shrugged and walked away.

There it was again. That fine ass. Sure, I could go back to the bio girls and give it a shot. I had half a mind to after all the crap Galina had put me through today—but my eyes still lingered, and my heart grew fonder.

I'd always heard that absence was a great inducer of love—but I didn't understand that concept at all. I tended to go for what caught my eye at the moment.

"Hey," I called out. "I'm sorry about going up against you and showing you up in front of Drusus today."

"You're sorry? Now?"

"Yeah, sure. I've had time to think about it. Time to calm down."

"I see..." she said thoughtfully. "Are you telling me that you're finally willing to—?"

"Give up my sources? No, I can't do that. But I can take you to dinner."

"What?"

"Yeah, there's this new place down at Fourth and Century. It's not far from here. Come on."

She stared at me, and her mouth did a little drop, a miniature version of the slack-jawed shocked look I wore so often. "Are you kidding me, McGill?"

"No sir. I would like to make amends."

Galina blinked, and she thought about it. I didn't say a damned word while she made her decision, as I didn't want to startle her. When you've got your prey sniffing the bait and circling the trap, you sure as hell keep quiet.

Finally, she heaved a big sigh. "All right. Show me this place. It better not be Thai food, though. I hate those mixed flavors."

"Hell no! It's barbeque. The best in the city."

She rolled her eyes, but she followed me out onto the streets. I soon forgot about my pain, my supposed state of shock and all the rest of that malarkey.

Unfortunately, Galina hadn't forgotten about the first part of the day.

"You're very healthy looking…" she said, marveling. "You don't seem injured at all anymore."

"Damn straight! I'm all fixed up. That proves my darkest suspicions."

"Proves what?" she asked.

"For starters, it proves bio people are as lazy as hell. They have a million credits worth of equipment in every room, and the only thing they want to do is switch on that box of spinning knives."

Galina gave a little shudder. The best part was she didn't bring up my miraculous recovery any more. That's exactly what I'd been trying to achieve, so I let well-enough alone.

Soon, we sat down to some fine beef. I ordered the tri-tip, while she had a fillet mignon. I hadn't even known they had that sort of thing on the menu, but I didn't object.

A thousand credits later, I managed to keep my pasted on smile in place as I paid the bill. She tried to object, but she let me do it in the end.

We downed a few beers at the bar, where she paid, then she tried to make her exit. "All right, James," she said. "I imagine you've got your reasons for keeping this secret from me. I find that irritating, but I'm willing to let you slide this single time."

"That's mighty nice of you, Tribune."

As we got to the door, she looked at me speculatively. "Where are you staying tonight?"

"Uh… in the dorms, I suppose."

"At Central? Still tight on money?"

"I guess so."

Galina ran her eyes over me again. I stood there and let her make the decision. It was all up to her now. Many less knowledgeable men might figure they could sway a woman at these moments with nonstop chatter. But it really didn't work that way with a tough girl like this one. After I'd made my pitch, she had to decide, and that was that. Pushing too hard at the last minute would be a mistake.

Giving me a smirk, she summoned her aircar with her tapper. She got into the driver seat and revved the engine.

"Goodnight, Tribune," I said, and I began walking down the sidewalk back toward Central. Just for good measure, I rolled my shoulders and scratched a little, as if my healing wounds were bothering me.

The aircar rolled up, and I looked down into the blue-lit interior. "Your back still hurts, doesn't it?"

"Nah," I said.

She shook her head in disbelief. "Get in here, you animal."

That was that. She took me home to her place on the edge of town, and we made love for hours. I was still mildly pissed off about being flogged and all, but she'd soon made up for that in her own special way.

-6-

The next morning we arrived at what they called Gray Deck at Central. It was a large chamber underground in the guts of the building. From here, they launched all kinds of Hegemony teleport missions.

Gray Deck was normally hush-hush and super-secret, but the people there knew me pretty well.

"Taking another unscheduled jaunt into the blue today, McGill?" asked the duty specialist. He was a tech—they were almost all techs down here.

"That's the plan."

"Where are you headed?"

"God only knows."

The specialist shook his head and waved me through after the usual inspection and x-rays. They removed a number of weapons, even ones I thought I'd hidden really well.

"You'll be issued fresh gear inside the vault," the tech said.

"Got it."

After that, Galina went through the same process. They didn't give her nearly the pat-down they'd given me. I suppose a man like me had to expect such unfair treatment after having broken so many rules in the past.

When we stepped into the vault on Gray Deck, we found dozens of busy people setting up a harness in a separate area—in fact, the whole thing looked unusual.

"Uh…" I said, staring at the rig. "That's not our typical gear, is it?"

The harness they were working with and charging didn't look like a normal set of smart-straps, batteries and computer modules. Instead, it resembled a deep-sea diving outfit from the 1890s. Something they would have used to explore the bottom of the sea while pumping air to the lucky diver using a hand-crank.

Even the helmet looked weird. It was a metal sphere with glass eyeholes cut into it. "What the hell is that?" Galina asked.

"Ah, Tribune Turov—and McGill," Graves said. He walked up to us and gave us each an up-down appraisal.

I could tell the simple fact we'd walked in together—both of us exactly seven minutes late—had been noticed. Graves knew that we'd had an inappropriate relationship for years. He'd never approved of it, and today he made that clear once again with his twisted lips and narrow-eyed staring.

Being used to his attitude, we ignored him and stepped closer to the new suit.

"Stop!" A small, female tech rushed us and put her thickly gloved palms in our faces. "No one is allowed to approach this experimental gear."

"It's all right, specialist," Graves told her. "This man is our pilot."

She glanced at Graves, then back at me again. "He's too big. We didn't build this suit with these dimensions in mind."

"You'll have to make adjustments."

"And if I can't?"

Graves shrugged. "Then take it up with Drusus."

She heaved a sigh and waved me forward. A half-dozen techs swarmed over me, and I was ushered into the pit where they had suspended the strange-looking suit.

"How come we're not using a regular jump-harness?" I asked.

"A regular harness wouldn't have the range," the tech lady said. "There's no way it could handle this leap. You're about to travel over a thousand lightyears—you do realize that, don't you Centurion?"

"I guess…"

"This is a prototype. It's what we call a deep-dive suit. Up until now, they've only been used on animals for testing purposes."

"How'd that go?" I asked.

The tech lady shrugged. "Some of them lived. Most were messed up internally. In general, we do better with humans. We've had more experience putting them back together."

I nodded, but I wasn't encouraged. Eventually, I was allowed to approach the harness.

Then, much later, I was allowed to put it on.

The sleeves were tight under my armpits. It was too small, just like she'd said. I had them adjusted out as far as they would go, but they were still going to chafe in combat, if there was any. I could just tell.

But there was nothing they could do about that, as there was only one of these long-range, deep-dive rigs in existence. They really hadn't built it with someone of my size in mind.

Graves gave me the final briefing as I prepared to launch.

"McGill," he said, "I don't know how you convinced the brass to send you off on a one-way suicide mission to an unknown location—but you did it, and now you're going to have to pay the piper."

"That's how I figure it, sir."

"We've got you covered in suit cameras. There is nothing extraneous on this kit but recording devices. Other than that, you've got the teleport module and a huge battery for the flight back."

"So this isn't a one-way system? Like the caster?" He frowned.

"Don't talk about that. Not even here."

"Sorry sir."

"Anyway, the answer to your question is: no. This is a specialized rig that's meant to bring the subject back home again. Now, if for some reason you don't come back... well, I can't promise you a revive."

"Permadeath is always on the menu, sir. What about weapons and other gear?"

Graves shook his head. "Not needed. Unnecessary weight might overload the rig and cause it to fail on the way out—or the way back."

Nodding, I put my rifle on the deck. Graves nodded in approval.

"You've got a good attitude today. That's a nice way for any legionnaire to go out. Luck."

He walked away, and I watched him go with some concern. Thoughtfully, I grabbed a hand-beamer and stuffed it into my suit when the techs were busy looking at their readouts. No one tried to stop me, which was best for everyone involved.

Many sets of eyes stared at me when the big generators began to rev up for the launch. Only one set of eyes looked like they actually cared about the monkey in the funny suit—those of Galina Turov.

The rest of the techs and officers were cold. Some seemed curious, mind you. Others were obviously stressed about my size and the limits of their equipment. But none of them gave two shits for me personally. I was a lab rat to them, the kind that scientists liked to shock to death just to see what the process looked like.

Mentally, I shrugged. This was a situation I'd faced before.

After a few more dull minutes, they were ready to launch. The chamber began to glimmer, then glow blue. The blue grew in intensity, and the light throbbed faster. Soon, the whole chamber was lit up in rhythmic flashes.

All this did seem to me to be a bigger deal than usual. The lights were brighter, the thrumming sound was hitting louder notes. The flashes, as they reached their crescendo, transformed into a gleaming white.

Blinded, I squinched my eyes and gritted my teeth. At last, with a sickening lurch, I was launched out into the unknown.

The trip was... well... torture. Essentially, it felt like I was in an airless void—which technically I was—but I still *wanted* to breathe. The problem with that desire was I didn't have any lungs. I was a ghost, really. A mass of transmitted particles.

The sensation was similar to that of drowning, but without the relief of unconsciousness and death. It went on and on. This trip had to be my longest ever. I'm sure it was a solid twenty minutes or more. A personal record in perceived time for one of these journeys into nothingness.

When I phased back into existence at last, I groaned and gasped the canned air inside my oversized helmet. Doubling over, I almost vomited.

Working hard to get control of myself, I tipped up my head to look around. It wouldn't do to be skewered by some hostile creature or robot the minute I got to my destination.

The scene that met my eyes took my breath away again—in an entirely new fashion.

It appeared to me that I was on the dark side of some moon or asteroid. Overhead, the stars gleamed with fantastic brilliance. The ground around me was as black as coal. It was rugged, with an undulating surface.

Forcing myself to stand straight, I fought to regain control of my stunned mind. The trip, the drowning—all of that was gone now. It had never really been real. I told myself that over and over as I calmed down.

Slowly turning and panning with my suit cameras, I spoke aloud for the sake of the recording. "I seem to be inside a valley of some kind—or maybe it's a crater. There's no sun in sight, but it might be night here. The astronavigational unit is saying the coordinates are right—good job at hitting the target, techies."

Taking my first steps, I walked over the ashy, crunchy ground.

"The gravity is low, and looking down at the deck, it seems there was a huge blast here. It's all charred and covered in soot."

My heavy boots plowed up a glittering storm of ash. The ash was laced with glass and crystallized metals. I supposed that this was debris from some kind of terrific explosion.

Looking up again at the craggy peaks encircling me, I frowned. I was definitely in a bowl-shaped region of some kind. Maybe I was standing at the bottom of a crater, or in the caldera of a volcano.

Walking around, I examined the burnt, slagged ground. There wasn't much that was recognizable. I didn't see any blackened trees or boulders. The world seemed lifeless, but that wasn't too surprising.

So far, I was pretty disappointed. I could have explored any of a dozen crispy planetoids like this one with equal disdain.

"No sign of any cool technology," I said. "Nothing worth anything at all. In fact, I—" Suddenly, I halted. My words and my feet froze in place.

Something *was* here. Something had gleamed. An artificial light of some kind. It was red—flashing red.

Using the bright beams of my suit, I turned the full glare of my headlights in the direction of the red gleam. Whatever it was, I hoped it wasn't too dangerous. Graves hadn't seen fit to arm me properly for this trip. I drew the beamer I'd secreted in my suit and advanced.

Six steps through the dust found me standing over a shape buried in the ash. It was a human shape—the shape of a body fallen in the ash.

Stooping down, I gently touched, then rolled over the body. It was a woman, in a spacesuit. She was frozen solid. The red gleam I'd seen was from her tapper, which had gone into emergency low-power mode.

Looking through the faceplate, I saw there was no doubt of who I'd found—Abigail Claver.

For a second time, I'd found Abigail dead in a hellacious spot. She'd given me these coordinates originally. Had she meant to meet me here, but somehow died before I'd arrived?

I looked around with new concern. The melted structures and the spiked peaks in the distance—they all seemed even more threatening than they had before. Could there be something still alive here—something that had killed Abigail?

I took a moment to examine her. It was difficult given her half-buried state, but I brushed away the ash as best I could. Touching my tapper to hers, I was able to download her latest mind and body scans—at least she might be revivable if I could get anyone to do it for me.

I examined the dark rip in her suit. Something had torn a series of three gouges in her belly. She'd been disemboweled, and she was obviously long dead.

That was enough for me. I stood up and reached for my tapper. I activated my launch sequence. My suit began to glimmer and strobe, lighting up the vast crater I was in like flashes of blue lightning.

That must have made something decide to act.

A *thing* came at me. It had been hiding in the debris, behind the craggy spikes and melted humps in the landscape.

A hulking, panther-like shape approached. It was a creature out of nightmare.

I knew in an instant what it was. It didn't really have a name, but it was powered by muscle and machine alike. Inside its bulk, an artificial brain drove its living body.

I'd met up with this kind of thing before. The Skay had such mixed beasts of metal and flesh living inside them. They were chockfull of odd, deadly monsters.

How had it survived out here in hard vacuum? I had no idea, but it had been built for the task. I could see it was sheathed in black, shiny, segmented armor.

Because we were in vacuum, the monster's rush was silent, but it wasn't any less terrifying for all that. The blue wavering of my teleport rig grew, and I realized I was going to blink out soon.

I almost escaped cleanly, but I changed my mind at the last instant and killed the countdown. A final glance down at Abigail's sad form had made me change my plans. I didn't like the idea of this monster winning so utterly. Was I going to allow it to kill a girl, then chase off the soldier who'd come out to find her? Was I really going to run off like a hen in a rainstorm?

I switched off the pulsing light, drew my beamer, and braced for its charge.

-7-

The creature hit me like a freight train. I was bowled over, rolling and kicking up plumes of that floating ash that covered everything on this nasty world.

While I was down on my back, I managed to get my boots up against its chest. The low gravity helped a lot, because its weight didn't matter much. Kicking up and out, I fired the monster off me and watched it go spinning into the night.

Getting up, I found my suit was blinking and complaining. I was losing air. The creature had managed to claw through my suit and into my flesh. I had a half-dozen gouges on my legs.

Clearly, this was how it had killed Abigail. There was no time to worry about that now, however. The critter was falling back to the surface, and it landed a dozen meters away. Scrambling up, it charged at me again. Although I shouldn't attribute emotions to a machine-minded creature, it seemed kind of pissed off at me.

My hand-beamer was out, and I gave it a few shots. This had no appreciable effect, so I drew my combat knife. Graves hadn't said anything about not bringing a knife.

Sidestepping its charge, I struck for the back of the neck. The thrust would have killed a normal animal—but this was no natural beast. It tried to whirl around on me, but I came after it and wrapped my gorilla arms around its body. I was essentially riding on its back while its claws flashed and gouged.

Sparks flew from the metal surface of the world and the debris all around us. More black, glittering dust swirled up. The grit was like volcanic sand.

Half-falling, half-rolling, I took the creature down. I was on my back again, I'd gotten leverage on it. The thing's claws scrabbled and flashed at the sky. I was doing more than holding a tiger by the tail—I was bear-hugging it from behind. This was the sort of tactic that personal combat vets taught legionnaires about dealing with low-gravity environments.

Unfortunately, my advantage wasn't going to last long. Already, the ferocious bucking body had starred my faceplate. It would never stop struggling, and I couldn't hold onto it forever. The body and throat were too heavily armored to squeeze the thing's life away—so I knew I had to take a chance.

Letting go, I grabbed my knife and thrust. Having been in close contact, I knew how those glossy armor plates moved and shifted. I managed to slide my blade between two plates over the neck, and my knife bit deeply.

The handle was ripped from my hand as the thing scrambled up to its four feet again.

Damnation, I hadn't even slowed it down. I only barely had time to get onto my feet when it came at me again.

A big mouth opened. There were teeth, sort of, in that metal jaw. The thing had been designed in the shape of a saber tooth cat, if I had to put a description on it. Bulky shoulders, four huge paws, and a mouth with metal fangs.

Having only one thing left in my hands, I thrust my hand-beamer into that maw, holding down the trigger.

This had a mild effect. It backed up and shook its head-section. Maybe some part of its flesh had been damaged inside, and it knew enough to retreat for a second.

The gun in its mouth was crushed. Little bits of metal and plastic fell from those jaws.

If my hand had gone in there, I would have lost it for sure.

I didn't remain idle during this momentary pause, however. I sprang forward, got both hands on the knife that was still sticking out of its neck, still lodged between two armor plates, and I levered the blade down. A full quarter-turn later, the head was partly severed.

Grinning and puffing, I backed up. The monster was in trouble now. Its head was hanging at an odd angle, and a freezing, steaming vapor went everywhere. Black droplets that must have served it for blood, or oil—or both—turned into shining black beads in the vacuum of space. They sparkled as they flew away from the stricken creature.

Honestly, I thought I'd won at that point. But I'd underestimated this thing's unnatural vitality. It came at me still, kind of dragging its dangling head. The claws were flexing, and I knew they were still deadly.

"Frigging thing!" I called out to no one, blasting air inside my helmet and steaming up my faceplate. I decided to make the only play I had left.

I'm not proud of it—but I ran. I sprang up into the air, giving the mightiest leap that I could on injured legs. It turned out that was enough to take me about twenty meters up and away.

The thing spun around in jerks. The sensory organs were in that lolling head, and it appeared to be having trouble tracking where I'd gone.

After I came down, I sprang again—and again. Each time, I landed farther from the monster, and though it continued to trot toward me whenever I landed, it was clearly weakening.

Blood loss, confusion, freezing exposure—the creature was in a bad way. Due to the low pressure, the liquid serving it for blood was boiling in its veins now, venting as steam that instantly froze. The monster's soft internals were exposed to the harshest environment ever conceived: open space.

Finally, it sagged down, flopping and kicking. I came close and severed the whole head from the body.

Breathing hard, I let it die, then I thought about what to do next. In the end, I scooped up some samples of the dusty ash, videoed every inch of the creature, and sawed off one of those curved black claws. The tip was like black glass, but harder than steel. I thought the lab people might get a kick out of it.

Then, at long last, I teleported home.

-8-

When I arrived home, it looked like I'd fallen out of the ceiling, but that was an illusion. The techies always targeted an empty region a couple meters above the landing zone. That way, if they missed by a fraction, the traveler wouldn't be merged up with the floor.

To be honest, I thought the crew on Gray Deck was surprised to see me reappear and drop to the deck. Maybe they'd written me off as another permed guinea pig.

"McGill?" Graves asked, coming to stand over me. "You're back early—are you all right, man?"

With teeth-gritting effort, I forced my sore, injured body to stand. The most dangerous place to be in Central was at Graves' feet, unable to get up. That was a sure-fire way to win a trip through a revival machine, no matter who you were.

"Just fine, sir. Raring for more!"

He looked me up and down once, with a critical eye. More than one soldier had tried to escape death by looking fit under his scrutiny.

"What happened to your legs? Are those ice crystals…? No, that's frozen blood. Your suit was breached?"

"Uh…" I said, grinning and not even daring to look down. "It's nothing, sir. I'll be fine with a little rest-up."

He turned to a techie who was ghosting at his elbow. She looked at me the way girls looked at a prize pig at the fair—one that had just shit itself.

"Have Blue Deck send a bio up here," Graves ordered. "Who knows? Maybe he's infectious."

The techie nodded and turned her back to whisper into her tapper.

"Aw, come on, Primus," I complained. "Don't you even want to hear my report?"

"I've got your vids. I've already downloaded them off your tapper. What I'm looking for now is a fit man to continue this exploratory…"

He trailed off and frowned. I'd pulled out the obsidian claw which I'd taken off the monster. Graves eyed it. "What the hell is that?"

"A little souvenir I brought you, sir. A trophy, if you will."

"You found something alive out there? Our reports show there isn't even an active star within a lightyear."

"You don't say? Well, that would explain why it was so damned dark out there. Anyway, I took this off an ornery inhabitant of that dead world."

Graves took the claw and examined it. "Artificial exterior… some kind of crystalline material. Looks brittle."

"It's not, sir. It's as sharp as a razor and as hard as diamond."

Graves nodded, rolling it around in his hand. Then he noticed the meaty part of it, where it'd been attached to the rest of the monster.

"There's no bone inside here—just sinew and muscle. This reminds me of a crab, or something with a hard shell instead of bones."

"That's exactly right, sir. But this crab ran around on four legs like a big dog. I had to put it down before it put me down. It was a killer, sir."

He looked up at me again. "How'd you beat it?"

I gave him a brief description, but before I could finish, I felt blood trickling down my legs. The blood had been frozen before, but now it had thawed out and began to flow. What's more, some of my legs and underparts had begun to burn something awful.

Toughing it out, I grinned. "I found something else out there too, Primus. My contact.

She was stone dead by the time I arrived, but at least I nailed her killer." I indicated the claw in his hand.

"She? Why am I not surprised your 'contact' is female?"

"Uh… I wouldn't know about that," I lied.

In the meantime, the techie had returned. She had a pinched-faced bio with her. "Aw now, I'm feeling fine!" I protested as she approached.

"Submit to examination, McGill," Graves ordered.

With a sigh, I did so. The bio knelt and flashed a light into my ripped-up suit. She began to paw at my thighs, and she sliced away more of the tough fabric with a laser-cutter.

"Hey, maybe we should get a room?" I suggested.

She flashed me a look of disdain. She had her hair wound up in a tight bun—that wasn't usually a good sign.

"He's suffering from exposure, frostbite, and lacerations," she told Graves. "I have to take him back to Blue Deck for amputation surgery."

"Uh…" I said becoming concerned.

"McGill," Graves said thoughtfully, "you said something about nailing the creature in question. But you didn't take your rifle."

"Oh, that…" I said. "I always have little extra protection handy."

Graves nodded, so I turned back to the bio. She was still on her knees and ripping at my thighs again. "I'm having a floater-chair brought down. We'll cart you up to Blue Deck and do some work. You'll live."

"Yeah… but what did you say about amputation? I could do without a toe or two, but I can't serve without a leg."

"I'm talking about your testicles. You're going to lose one—maybe both."

"Whoa!" I said, putting a hand between the overzealous bio and my privates. "I don't know you that well yet, Specialist!"

She flashed me another of her disdainful looks. I got the feeling she did that to her patients all the time.

Suddenly, I got an idea. With me, a sudden idea often turned into sudden action. Call it a character flaw or a strength, it's just how I operated.

"Hmm," I said, picking up the laser cutter she'd put down while she examined me. I lifted it and scratched my neck with the tip. "How does this thing work, exactly—?"

"Centurion! Give me that instrument!"

She reached for it, but while the tip was prodding my right carotid, it went off in my hand. I will swear to the end of my lives, until I meet St. Peter at the pearly gates, that it was an accident.

The cutter took about a centimeter chunk of flesh out of my neck. Just a scratch, really, but unfortunately it had ripped open my most important artery. The one that fed my fool brain.

Everyone looked up in shock and alarm. The bio girl fell back on her ass, throwing her arms and her eyes wide. The techie girl stepped behind Graves, as if she thought I was going to shoot her next.

Everyone freaked out, that was, except for old Graves. He twisted up his mouth and slowly shook his head.

For my own part, I slowly sat down, then I lay down on my back on the deck. A warm flood of blood soon around my head.

"I'm feeling poorly," I managed to say.

Graves stepped up to stand over me. His boots were wet with the blood circling my fallen form. "That was a clear violation, McGill. This revive is coming out of your frigging paycheck."

"I can't live with one nut, sir," I told him in a fading voice. "I need them both."

"I don't know," he said, watching me die without a hint of emotion, other than being annoyed. "If we'd gelded you that first day back at Mustering Hall, we might have saved ourselves a lot of trouble."

Then he laughed. Graves always laughed at his own jokes—probably because no one else ever did.

His laughter echoed through my mind. My body and senses began to shut down. It was the last thing I heard as I faded away and died at his feet.

-9-

Coming alive again was like waking up from a bad dream. I'd never enjoyed the process of birth or rebirth. I guess no one really did.

"Huge… male… died on Gray Deck?" a female bio said in a questioning tone. "What have we got here?"

"A suicide," a male orderly replied, "unusual for an officer."

"Ah, see here? He's from Legion Varus. Those thugs are liable to do anything. Maybe he was murdered, and they marked it down as a suicide to cover."

I blinked and groaned. The groan turned into a hacking cough.

"What's his score?" she asked.

"He's a nine… maybe even a nine-five. An excellent grow."

"See…?" I mumbled to no one. "It was all worth it."

"He's trying to talk," the orderly said. "That's early. A sure sign of a good grow."

"All right, all right. Get him out of here."

The bio people flashed lights in every hole they could find and pronounced me fit for duty. I staggered out and made my way back to Gray Deck.

On the way down in the elevator my tapper beeped. It was my tribune, Galina Turov.

"Hello sir?" I said, opening the channel.

"McGill? What's this I hear about you playing with guns on Gray Deck? You could have shot one of my techs—or worse, damaged critical equipment."

"It was a laser cutter, sir. An unfortunate accident occurred. It was just an accident, and no one else was in danger."

"Enough excuses. There are details to this report and the vids we downloaded that require explanation. Get up here right now."

She gave me the elevator codes, and I traveled to her floor without even having a meal or a shower. It was the kind of thing normal legion people weren't used to, but for a Varus man it was par for the course.

When I arrived at her office door, I wasn't even able to touch it or talk to Gary, her secretary. Her interior door was snatched open and left that way.

"Uh…" I said, walking into the outer office. "I guess I'm going in right away?"

Gary looked annoyed. He waved his hand toward the entrance. I marched past him and a crowd of primus-level officers who were obviously waiting to be seen. Galina probably hadn't shown her nose, as she didn't want to face them and make any excuses.

"McGill just marches in there…" one of them muttered, with her arms crossed angrily.

"What was that, Primus?" I asked, stopping at the door. "I didn't quite catch, that, sorry, sir?"

She glared at me and waved her hand at me like she was shaking out a match that had burned her fingers.

Shrugging, I smiled and ambled into the inner office sanctuary.

Galina was sitting behind her desk today. She didn't look at me as I approached.

Instead, she seemed to be staring at a series of open windows displayed on her glowing desk.

"What seems to be the trouble, Tribune?" I began, but she waved for silence. I immediately looked for a seat to sag into, but she stopped me.

"Stand at attention, Centurion."

Surprised, I did as she demanded. Silently, the door shut itself behind me. I heard a lock snick into place. She had all that kind of stuff automated, and mind you, sometimes it was a little creepy.

Galina still didn't look up. She examined the vids—three of them at once—that were playing on her desktop. I heard my puffing breath and the hiss of canned air from the muffled sound. Suddenly, I knew what she was reviewing.

"That's the recording from my body-cams, isn't it? Pretty cool monster, right? Did you see how I—?"

"Shut up," she said, still not looking at me.

I stood there like a recruit on a parade ground for the next solid eight minutes. Maybe that was her intention—to make me feel like a Boy Scout. Instead, I started daydreaming about that bio girl who'd made the call to geld me earlier.

Something about her and her medical examination had made my mind begin to conjure scenarios of a more pleasant nature. She'd looked all sour when I'd cracked jokes, but that moment when she'd fallen back on her butt in front me, that moment of real concern—she'd looked kind of pretty. Sometimes, a sour woman can show you who she really is if you surprise her, and it could be a good thing.

"McGill!" Galina barked at me. "Are you daydreaming?"

"Huh? Oh, sorry sir. I just popped out of the oven down on Blue Deck, you know. I probably could use a few minutes to—"

"Request denied. Approach."

"Uh…" I said, but I walked up to her desk.

She eyed me like an angry cat. "You found a body on that burnt out husk, didn't you?"

"Oh… yes sir, that I did."

"Who was she?"

"Uh… I don't rightly know, Tribune."

She stared at me for maybe three long seconds. During that time, I tried to look as baffled and ignorant as possible.

"You're lying," she pronounced. "She's the one you went out there to meet. She's the contact who gave you bullshit information, isn't she?"

"I wouldn't call it bullshit, sir. After all, the wreck was there."

"But it was unrecognizable and useless. Even if it was a burnt-out ship, it was in terrible condition. I'm beginning to think you arranged this whole thing as a way to meet her in private."

"Uh..." I said, not quite sure where she was going with this particular delusion. "How's that, sir? She was dead."

"Yes, apparently. But that was doubtlessly a miscalculation on her part. She ran into that last guardian creature and paid for it with her life. It's time to confess, McGill—confess everything."

Thinking that over, I realized that a confession was the perfect way to clear the air.

My mind was coming into focus, and I soon had the tail of what I considered a good idea. "I admit, sir," I began, "that the woman in question was the one who gave me the coordinates to that spot. But she's not like a friend or anything. She was more of an acquaintance."

"I don't believe you—but go on anyway."

"Just so, sir. She came to me and promised alien tech. I reported that to Central, and I was sent out there to see what's what. That's the long and the short of it, sir."

Another staring pause ensued. She sniffed in a sudden breath at the end. "The truth is painfully obvious, McGill. You've been screwing her, whoever she is. She arranged this rendezvous in space—but something went wrong. Now, she's dead and—"

"Hold on, sir, I—"

"No, *you* hold on! Let me guess what you're going to say next. That you're as innocent as the day is long? That you have no interest in attractive young women, as you've had your balls frozen off recently—oh wait, you've got them back now, don't you?"

"Jeez, Galina," I said. "I had no idea you could get so jealous about a dead girl I barely know."

She approached then, moving from behind her desk at last. She walked close, swaying those nice hips, and she stood quite close—within grabbing distance—and peered up at me.

"The trouble is that I do know *you*, McGill," she said. "You would do anything to chase a new piece of tail. It's disgusting."

I reached for her, but she skipped back, avoiding my clumsy embrace.

"No, no, I don't think so," she said.

"Maybe we should have a drink or something."

"Forget it. You're getting nothing in this office. *Nothing*, do you understand?"

"Yeah..."

I hung my head as if ashamed. In reality, I was kind of thinking about that bio again.

She'd wanted to cut off my balls, sure, but she hadn't succeeded, and—

"There is one way you can redeem yourself."

My head came back up. "How's that?"

"You can tell me, right here, right now, who that bitch really is."

I thought that over. They had Abigail's body scans. They even had a trace of blood, maybe, from the claw I'd given to Graves. It wasn't going to take six kinds of a genius to run genetic tests and realize who Abigail was. After all, her twin brothers were the most wanted men in the universe. Hell, we'd fought an out and out war with Claver's clones just a year back.

I shrugged, and I smiled. "Promise you'll have a drink with me?"

"I'll try—if I'm not too pissed off by the truth."

She crossed her arms defensively over her breasts, and I nodded.

"All right then... she's a Lady-Claver. Abigail Claver, that's her name."

Galina's jaw dropped. It almost hit the floor. "Are you shitting me?"

"Nope," I said, and I proceeded to explain. Soon, she understood the situation.

My next instinct was to ask her to revive Abigail—but I didn't. That kind of favor toward this strange woman, one that she'd been hating on jealously just moments ago, wouldn't fly.

I'd have to wait, and Abigail would have to rest uneasily in her grave.

After absorbing the situation, Galina nodded her head. "It all makes sense. Why didn't you admit this earlier? I've been so full of suspicion—everyone has. And then, when I realized you'd met a young woman out there on a dead alien ship—well, my thoughts got away from me."

"So you're not feeling jealous anymore?"

She frowned. "I don't feel jealous about you. Never. That would be madness."

"Sure thing," I said, just as if I believed her pretty, lying mouth.

Galina began pacing around. She did that whenever she was thinking hard. I made myself comfortable on her couch.

"It's some kind of trick," she said. "Some evil new game Claver is playing. It has to be. They came to you, and they showed you a girl, because they know you're an idiot who follows his dick wherever it leads."

"Uh…"

While she leaned her butt on her desk, I took the time to pour us two drinks—after all, she'd promised.

I pushed a drink into her hand, and she considered it for a moment, then drank it and went back to staring at the vids on her desktop. I watched her and half-listened to her monologue. She was talking to herself, really.

After a half-dozen paragraphs and replays of various elements of my adventure, she turned on me suddenly. "That's correct, isn't it?"

"Huh? Oh… Hell yeah! Yeah, sure. You got that part right, I'm certain."

I had no idea what she'd been talking about, but this response seemed to please her, so she went back to farting around with the videos. She speculated broadly on Claver's plans, and the possible evil motivations of Abigail. After a bit, I stopped listening to it altogether it.

At last, she settled her ass down on the seat next to me and let me have her. She was distracted, but she did enjoy the proceedings.

I'll just say it was a damned good thing she'd had her office sound-proofed.

-10-

It was a day later that I was summoned upstairs again. As I was technically on active duty, I was sleeping and eating on Hegemony credits, living in their officer's dorms and eating at their cafeteria. The food wasn't half-bad, and there was always plenty of it.

At breakfast, after I'd polished off one tray and dug into the second, I got a notice on my tapper. Unfortunately, I couldn't disable such notifications while I was active, so they knew I got it, and the clock was running.

"Meeting at 0800 hours, Praetor Drusus' office," I read aloud. "Frig…!"

It was already a quarter to eight, and I would barely have time to make it with the way these elevators ran. I had to shovel what food I could into my mouth and trot for the exit. When I rammed my trays into the recycler, I got a sour look from the service people.

"That's wasteful, sir."

"Yeah, yeah. Summons."

I showed the lady the red text on my tapper.

"Drusus?" she asked in amazement. "You'd better get a move on!"

Waving over my shoulder, I left her and high-tailed it to the elevators. Less than fifteen minutes later, I walked calmly into Drusus' office. Sure, I was actually out of breath and sweating a little, but I hid all that. I marched in like I hadn't a care and took the seat they offered me at his over-sized conference table.

Drusus glanced at his tapper. "On time for once. Well done, McGill."

Drusus really liked it when the trains ran on time. He always gave you a little less time than you needed, and when you met his schedule, you were praised. If you didn't, you were scorned. It was a simple but effective way to get people to hustle.

He waved his hand over the table like a wizard, and the illusion of a wooden tabletop vanished. It was replaced with a hologram of a standing Rigellian warrior. The meter-tall bear-dude seemed to be right there, looking around at us and blinking.

"Gee-zus!" I said aloud, jumping a little in my seat.

Drusus smiled. "Very realistic, isn't it? The resolution on this new table is quite high."

"You can say that again, Praetor." I leaned forward to peer at the devilish figure standing on the table. I was a little creeped out by it.

The furry fighter stood in a combat-ready stance. He was wearing that typical fabric suit of tough material they all wore. The suit was light, but incredibly resilient. It wore like smart-cloth but could stop a high velocity round. In practice, Rigel's soldiers were more mobile but still harder to kill than our heavies in reactive plate.

"What's the greatest difficulty you face in the field when combatting a soldier like this, McGill?"

"Getting through that suit is the hard part. It takes a lot of firepower to penetrate."

"Exactly," he said. "Now, I'll get to the point of this meeting. Why am I showing you this? Because the lab people have been running tests on the samples you brought back with you from the mission coordinates yesterday. Do you know what they found?"

I tore my eyes away from the hologram and looked around the table. Everyone was silent, and they were all staring. They were staring at me.

All of a sudden, I got it: They were all in cahoots. I didn't know what they were on about, but I knew it might not go well for old James McGill, depending on how I answered their questions.

"Uh…" I said. "I found a claw. Are you talking about that, sir?"

Drusus nodded slowly. "In part."

He produced the claw and slid it onto the table. It clattered and rasped. We all stared at it. "This is a very unusual item. Do you know what the sharpest natural substance known to man is?"

"No, sir."

"Glass. Broken glass is brittle, but it has the finest edge nature can achieve—and this claw is sharper. It's also much harder."

I looked at it. We all did.

Drusus then proceeded to throw up some molecular models showing the chains involved in the creating of that sharp edge. I couldn't really follow it. I'd gotten a C in high school chemistry, and that was only because the teacher was being nice.

After a long talk, he got back around to something interesting again. I was fooling with my tapper by then, I'd been poking at it in my lap while I pretended to listen.

"McGill…? McGill!"

"Uh… yes, Praetor! What's the trouble?"

Looking around again, I saw every eye was on me again.

"Think carefully: have you got any knowledge that might shed light on this mystery?" I felt a tickling sensation under my arms. I was beginning to sweat, just a little.

"Yeah, I sure do," I lied. I had no idea what he was talking about, but I had one trick up my sleeve. "That place—that freaky world I found with the dead girl and the glass-armored monster—it was a dead Skay. A burned out hulk, which still has a tiny spark of life left in it."

Their eyes widened. "That's quite a claim, Centurion," Drusus said. "How did you come to that conclusion?"

I'd just played my ace-in-the-hole. My only saving move. I'd never told Drusus or any of them I was going to find a dead

Skay. Abigail had mentioned it, but I'd just called it an alien wreck—a tiny detail that could be overlooked by anyone.

They were creatures of the Skay, strange constructs that operated like antibodies to rid the planet-sized beings of intruders.

"It was that curved horizon," I said with certainty. "It was like I was in a vast bowl, or crater. The roof was blown off, of course, but you could still tell. Then, after I met up with the defensive creature, I understood what I'd found. Remember, I've been inside the guts of a couple Skay before."

Drusus nodded slowly. "That's very interesting, and I think it's correct—"

"It *is*?" demanded Turov suddenly. She seemed amazed.

"Yes. It fits the data—but it isn't really related to what we were discussing."

As I had no idea what he'd been talking about, I pressed on with my new change of subject.

"But it does!" I argued. "You see, the claw, the creature, the dead Skay and Rigel. It all fits. Rigel is aligned with the Skay. They want to kick the Mogwa out of this province. They're our real enemies."

Drusus peered at me for a moment. I was way out on a limb now, but I didn't want to admit I hadn't been listening. The truth was I'd been playing skee-ball on my arm. It was a popular pastime, and I'd gotten pretty good at it lately.

Finally, Drusus nodded. "I think I get your point," he said.

Inwardly, I breathed a sigh of relief. I'd bluffed it through. That had been a tight one, as Drusus was nobody's fool.

"What is his point, exactly?" Turov demanded.

I gave her a look that told her to shut up. What kind of a girlfriend was she if she undermined me at moments like this?

Galina ignored my look and gave her attentions to Drusus instead.

"Rigellian armor is something special," Drusus said. "We all know that. We've captured their suits, but we've learned very little about them. All we are sure of is they must have some kind of unusual manufacturing technique we aren't able to duplicate. It's a critical tech advantage that their troops enjoy over ours in the field."

"Damn straight!" I said, slapping the table. The bear-warrior hologram looked at me and shimmered a little.

"Our techs have been doing serious molecular analysis on this claw," Drusus continued. "It's been determined that the material used here is identical to that used to make Rigellian armor. We're ready to make the connection back to the Skay. We're certain they're the original inventors of this technology. In short, McGill is right. He traveled to a dead Skay and brought back evidence linking it to Rigel."

I was all smiles. There's nothing in this world quite so pleasantly buttery-smooth as being told your insights are right in a meeting of peers—especially when you have no actual idea what's really going on.

-11-

The meeting went on and on after that. Pretty soon, I was stifling a yawn every minute or two. This brought a smirk to Winslade, who had just arrived with a message for Drusus.

"Not getting enough sleep, hmm?" he asked me in a snotty tone. I looked at him, and I noticed he was casting amused glances at Turov as well.

His little act didn't upset me much. Sure, I'd slept with Galina recently. No harm in that, from my point of view. Such fraternization was frowned upon by the legions, but it wasn't against regs.

Galina, however, was actually pissed. "What are you doing in here anyway, Winslade?"

He made a languid gesture toward Drusus, who was reading a private note from Hegemony on his tapper.

Frowning, Drusus looked up at Winslade. "You got Wurtenberger to sign this? I'm impressed."

"Not at all, sir. I'm merely following orders. May I?"

Drusus waved him toward an open chair.

"Wait a moment," Turov complained. "Winslade is joining this committee? These topics are... highly classified."

It was Winslade's turn to anger. "With all due respect, Tribune, I've got every clearance you have. If anyone here is to be considered a security risk—"

"It's fine," Drusus interrupted. "Let's continue. Perhaps you can even be of help, Winslade."

"Ah… how so?"

"Do you know anything about a super-tough substance? An alloy of titanium, silicon and carbon that's laced with collapsed matter for strength?"

Winslade looked confused. "That's what this meeting is about? New types of armor?"

"Yes, essentially." Drusus briefly filled him in on the materials I'd found and how they related to the armored Rigellian soldiers.

Winslade mused over it. "A link between Rigel and the Skay… not the first, and probably not the last. Intriguing. I would suggest we question Claver."

"How? No one even knows where he is."

Winslade's smirk grew, and he eyed me again. "Some of us do. This gentleman to my left, for instance. I've heard that he recently met with representatives sent by the Clavers."

Drusus glanced at me in confusion. He shook his head. "Representatives? Claver no longer has a home planet. We wiped out his clones."

"Not so," Winslade said, lifting a finger. "I've been doing some investigations of my own. Perhaps that's why so many drones and spies have been watching me."

Drusus blinked a few times. That was a tell—anyone who plays poker would have caught it. Drusus knew Winslade was under surveillance.

At about this very moment, I was beginning to get concerned. Winslade was in the mood to talk about things I didn't want people to hear. First off, he clearly knew that I'd slept with Galina recently. Secondly, he seemed to know about Abigail and Claver-X. What was surprising about that was I'd only discussed their recent visit to my home with Galina.

How could he know both these facts? That I'd spent the night with Galina *and* what I'd told her? The answer seemed obvious: he was spying on us. He'd done it before, actually. He'd once used a tiny spy drone that resembled a housefly to video us in a compromising situation.

"You spied on us?" I demanded loudly. "Again?"

About then, Galina caught on. She stood up and put her hand on the butt of her pistol. "You red-assed bastard!"

Winslade jumped to his feet, and Drusus stood up as well.

"Don't kill him," he said. He was eyeing Winslade with great disgust as well. "This new table is very hard to clean."

Winslade puffed his lips into a pout. He took a step back. "I can see that I'm not wanted here. I will report this hostility to Hegemony. Good luck to all of you… whatever your nefarious intentions may be."

He marched out, and no one called him back. Galina relaxed with difficulty. "You see that?" she hissed to Drusus. "I told you he isn't trustworthy. We should perm him before he defects again. Who knows which of us he might take down with him this time around? It could be anyone here."

The group all looked from face to face, but most of them landed theirs eyes on me for some reason.

"Uh…" I said, not quite sure why I was the next scapegoat in line. "Did I miss something?"

"Maybe," Drusus said, "or maybe you're just playing us all for fools… again."

"Not so, sir!" I insisted. "I don't know beans about this situation."

"What about getting a visit from a Claver? Did that happen or not?"

I squirmed a little and glanced at Galina. She was the only one who knew, because I'd told her. There wasn't any help at all in her face. Sensing that I was on my own, I decided to fess-up.

"Yeah… all right. Two of the Clavers came to my house the other night." There were gasps around the table.

"But hold on! Hold on before you draw weapons and fire-squad me. They weren't the kind of Clavers you've all seen before. They were new breeds. Renegades among their own kind who aren't loved by anyone."

I proceeded to explain about the nature of Abigail and her ties to Claver-X. The group found the whole story fascinating, if a little disturbing.

"How does this all connect to our present circumstances?" Drusus asked me.

"That's who that woman was—the body of the girl I found on the dead Skay. It was Abigail. Only she knows more about this special armor, and about how Rigel might be using it."

"Oh!" Galina said suddenly. "I get it now. You want us to revive this evil witch of yours, is that it?"

I shrugged. "If you want to find out more about the armor, I guess you'll have to."

Drusus thought hard for a moment, then nodded. "Call Blue Deck. Set up a priority-one revive."

Galina rolled her eyes and crossed her arms. She wouldn't look at me. She'd always been the jealous type, even if she'd never admit it.

-12-

Abigail was revived within the hour. Afterward, she was allowed to recover and clean up—something I rarely got to do when I was summoned back from the dead.

Instead of waiting for her, the meeting broke up, and I was told to stay at Central in case I was needed to help with the interrogation.

Now, I would be remiss if I didn't point out that I felt an "interrogation" was overkill. Abigail might be a Claver relative, but she'd never been accused of a crime to the best of my knowledge.

I wasn't in charge of the situation, however, so I went down to the brig immediately to make sure she wasn't abused. There, I waited for nearly an hour. The revive took about half that time, then the clean-up and transportation through Central took the rest.

But before I even got a chance to glimpse Abigail, Galina showed up. She put her hands on her hips and glared at me the second she saw me.

"Seriously?" she asked. "You're sitting out in the waiting area like an expectant father?"

"Drusus said he might need me."

"Since when were you so overeager?"

I looked at her, and I had to do a little calculating. After all, Galina was my equivalent of a steady girlfriend, and we'd been involved in our own weird way for years. If she was getting seriously jealous, that wouldn't be good for my future

"You're right," I said, standing up and yawning. "I'm getting kind of hungry. I think I'll go up to the commissary and find some grub."

She watched me closely. As I ambled toward the door, her glare softened to a frown.

"If I see Drusus," I called over my shoulder, "I'll tell him you said it was okay to leave the area."

"You'll do no such thing!" she responded. She was always worried about her rank, and kissing up to higher-ranked brass was her most tightly held policy. "Sit back down and shut up."

I flopped back onto the hard seat I'd just gotten up from and pretended to nod off. Galina sat down opposite me, but she didn't talk my ear off. She was busy pecking at her tapper. She was probably working on something sneaky.

When Graves showed up, he seemed mildly surprised to see both of us waiting there. "The prisoner has been moved to interrogation room five," he said. "Generally, this sort of thing is done without senior officers being involved…" He looked pointedly at Turov.

She looked back at him in a dismissive manner. "You're not a centurion any longer yourself, Graves."

Graves blinked, and he nodded. He looked at me. "Perhaps McGill can conduct—"

"No way," she said. "If we leave it to him there will be a paternity lawsuit for Hegemony to worry about."

Graves chuckled. "Right… Who then?"

Another figure stepped onto the scene. He always seemed to be lurking around Central somewhere these days.

"It's been decided, you might as well all leave," Winslade announced. "I'll be performing the honors personally." He looked and sounded insufferably proud of himself. That wasn't anything unusual for Winslade. He was easily impressed by his own shenanigans.

"Says who?" Turov demanded.

Winslade smirked and showed her the red print on his arm.

"Wurtenburger?" she demanded. "Again you pull strings with the euros? What do you have over that old, fat—"

"Careful, careful," Winslade said. "There are recording devices everywhere."

"Drusus must approve this," Turov insisted. "He's in charge here. Wurtenburger is supposed to stay in Geneva where he belongs."

Winslade shrugged. "Who knows what our beloved members of the General Staff are thinking? The simple fact is that Wurtenberger is senior to Drusus, and therefore—"

"And therefore," Graves interrupted, "you've somehow gotten him to pull that thin veneer of authority over Drusus twice in one day. From a distance, no less. This planet needs a consul to pull the hierarchy together."

Winslade and Turov both looked startled. "A consul?" Winslade asked. "That rank is theoretical."

Graves shook his head. "No it isn't. Back in the Unification Wars, Hegemony was run by a consul. Many think that's why our side won."

The rest of us gave each other alarmed glances. Now and then, Graves gave hints as to his real age. I knew that he'd joined Legion Varus when it had first been formed—but could he be even older than that? Could he have fought to unify Earth? Damn, that was over a century ago…

"I guess it doesn't matter how the order was given," Graves said. "Winslade is in charge. Call me if you need me."

He left, and Turov dithered for a time before she left too. She gave me a jerk of the head, suggesting I should follow, but I lingered behind.

"Winslade," I said, "dealing with Abigail isn't like talking to a normal woman."

He snorted. "Indeed? I guess you would know about that, wouldn't you? Thanks for the advice, but your services will not be needed here tonight. Please leave."

He turned on his heel, was admitted through the cage-like doors, and disappeared. In the meantime, I was left standing in the grungy lobby area.

With a sigh, I walked out. I'd done my best to learn about this "interrogation" to make sure things didn't get out of hand, but I'd failed.

When I got to the elevator lobby, I stopped. There was another person walking the other way, toward the brig. I recognized her immediately.

"Centurion Leeza?" I demanded loudly. "As I live and breathe, what a surprise!"

She looked startled as well. She glanced around furtively for a moment before stopping to talk to me.

"I'm afraid I can't talk long, I've been summoned to—"

"You're a hog?" I asked, all but shouting. I'd just noticed the globe on her sleeve.

Leeza was a hard-bitten woman, a tough fighter who'd originally served in Legion Germanica with the likes of Armel and Claver. Now, she had the blue-green emblem of Hegemony on her sleeve.

"Please don't gloat," she said. "There's no need."

"Uh…" I said, chewing that over. "Gloat? What would I have to be proud of?"

"Very little in my opinion, but it's well known that you were instrumental in my removal from interstellar duty and placement here at Central."

"Well known, huh? Who told you that?"

"Winslade. He's been conducting an extensive investigation into the matter."

"Is that so? And now he's got you going in there to talk to Abigail?"

She blinked. "Who's Abigail?"

I shook my head. "Doesn't matter. You'll find out soon enough. Just tell Winslade that I know the real reason you and he got shuffled. He's not going to get anything out of this prisoner about that. I doubt she even knows you two exist."

Leeza narrowed her eyes at me. She had a pinched face naturally, and when she pinched it up further… well, it wasn't a good look for an otherwise handsome woman.

"*You* know…? You know what happened to me?"

About then, I realized I'd just let the cat out of the bag. I'd managed to act like a country bumpkin with Winslade, but Leeza and all her haughty behavior had gotten it out of me.

"Perhaps I misspoke," I said.

"Perhaps you did. We'll talk about this later, McGill. I really do have to go."

I watched as she walked away. She didn't have the kind of curves I usually went for, being too skinny by half, but she did have a graceful step that I could appreciate.

Riding the elevators down to the street level, I tried to get Galina to take a call on her tapper. She wouldn't do it. I was temporarily blocked, in fact.

Shrugging, I decided to hit some bar and grill-type places on the strip in the city. There were a lot of new establishments these days after the Skay bombing. Most of them had never even poured me a beer.

By the time I reached the first one and had ordered my first mug, my tapper was buzzing. It was Winslade.

I took a long gulp, sighed, and opened the channel.

"McGill? Get back here to Central at once!"

"What seems to be the trouble, Centurion?"

I was reminding him that he'd been reduced in rank. He no longer had direct authority over me, as he had our entire professional careers up until now.

His face twisted up. "You told me you knew nothing about my circumstances!" he said in a hissy voice. I got the feeling he was trying not to be overheard by someone.

"How's the interrogation going?" I asked in conversational tone. "Not even going to deny it, eh? All right then. All right."

He closed the channel, and I had a good chuckle. But then, I started to worry. He'd been flexing some political muscles lately, and he might just be planning to flex them against me.

Getting off the barstool, I guzzled the rest of my beer, paid and left.

-13-

When I got down to the detention level, I knew right off something was wrong.

The first hint was the lighting. Most of the glowing ceiling panels were dark. That was weird, because Central had its own fusion generator, and the lights were pretty much *always* on.

The second thing I noticed was the lack of any guards at the entrance to the detention area. Instead, I found the cage-like door hanging open. On alert, I stalked forward from the elevator lobby to the check-in point. Normally, there would have been a guard here overseeing my admittance, and various scanners would have cleared me for entry.

None of that was happening tonight. Instead, I found the door ajar. I swung it open farther, and discovered what was blocking it—keeping it from closing.

A dead hog lay at my feet. He was a fatty, like most of them, and his fallen body had kept the cage door from closing.

The guard's chest had been blown open by a close-range blast. I'd seen such injuries before. The look of utter shock on the dead man's face, coupled with the fact his gun was still in its holster suggested it had been a surprise attack.

I took his gun, as the guards had relieved me of mine back at the lobby. I lifted my tapper to my lips and sent a voice message to emergency services.

"Trouble in Detention D," I said quietly into my tapper. "You've got a guard down, power failure, and an open cage door."

No one responded. I glanced down at my tapper, tearing my eyes away from the scene, to see that I had no signal.

Now that was *truly* strange. If there was one thing that could be counted on in Central, it was a direct line to the grid. You were always online at Central.

"Shit-fire…" I whispered, staring at my tapper.

I'm not a total moron. I knew I should turn right around and get help—but I didn't want to. I didn't like the idea of allowing someone to break in and do as they pleased down here. Whoever it was, they were probably here to either free or kill Abigail. She was the star prisoner. If I took the time to ride the elevator and get help, I might learn later that I could have helped if I'd moved in right away.

First responders in Legion Varus were taught to attack. To engage. Not to play it safe. Not to allow the enemy more time. Hell, if everything went tits-up, they'd just print out a new James McGill.

Accordingly, I hesitated for less than a second before I shouldered the door open. I stepped over the cooling corpse on the floor and walked inside the detention area.

With the guard's pistol in both hands, I moved down the corridor quietly. I didn't call out to see who was around, or who might need help. I stalked the place, looking for trouble.

It didn't take me long to find it. Two small men walked into the passage way ahead of me. They dragged a third man, who was slumped in their arms like a ragdoll between them.

I thought I knew who the ragdoll was. A second glance confirmed it—yes, it was Winslade. He had a distinctive shape to his wiry body, even when he was limp.

There was no better time to start things, so I popped two shots into each of these little guys. They were headshots, all four, and at least one landed on each. The closer of the two pitched forward and sprawled on the deck. The other went to his knees, clawing at his hip for a gun—then lost consciousness and went down.

I rushed forward, and that's when I recognized the dead men. They were Rigellian bears. I hadn't realized it at first, but I should have. The fuzzy head, perky round ears and nasty-looking teeth.

These humanoids weren't twins to earthly bears, mind you, they were more like little trolls out of legend. For one thing, their fur wasn't even in length or nature. Instead of a lush coat, they sprouted furry tufts of nasty hair in many spots.

The fabric was familiar, as it appeared to be their standard body armor, the stuff we couldn't reproduce. Fortunately, they'd had the hood thrown open, either to breathe or see better. My shots wouldn't have penetrated otherwise. The suits they wore were shiny black, one-piece affairs. Apparently, they could be worn while teleporting. I didn't know how else these guys could have gotten here.

A bolt of real worry hit me as I grabbed at one of their guns—but dropped it. The thing was a smart-gun, attuned to the biometrics of the enemy. It wasn't going to work for me. Worse, any other bears that had heard me shooting would have their hoods up. I couldn't face them with a pistol then.

Winslade was squirming. He'd been abused, but he wasn't dead yet.

"Shut up and play dead," I told him, and I rushed into the room the bears had come from.

To my surprise, I found Abigail there, dressing in a suit that looked a lot like a bigger version of what the bears had been wearing.

"Uh…" I said, watching her pull the black suit over her bare flesh. "Underwear too tight?"

She looked up in surprise. "I thought—I thought it was more of them!"

She shuddered, pointing at the dead bears. While she did this, she kept pulling on her suit and strapping in.

I aimed my pistol at her. "Freeze, Abigail."

She knew by the tone of my voice that I meant it. She stopped moving, and she let her hands relax. Her clothes dropped away, and this revealed some shapely curves. I made an effort not to get distracted.

"These bears came to break you out, didn't they?" I asked.

"Your officials were going to torture me, James. They really were. I had to call for help."

I nodded, but I had no idea how she could have gotten a message out to Rigel, much less how they'd teleported into our most critical facility.

"I believe that," I said, leveling my gun at her. "But I can't just let you pop out of here scot free. You owe me some answers. I went out to that rock you gave me coordinates for."

"The dead Skay?"

"Right. I found you dead out there, and I brought your data back and arranged a revive."

"That's sweet," she said, starting to pull her suit up a little.

I shook my head and twitched my gun. She stopped trying to dress herself. I knew these suits. If they had a charge, they could teleport her out. I also knew they were bulletproof. If she got completely dressed, I'd have to shoot her in the face to stop her.

"I need to go, James," she said. "I really do. Either shoot me now, or let me port out."

"Shoot you?"

"Yes. Did you really think this was the only copy of me around? I need to escape somehow, and death is one of those ways."

I thought about recent rumblings I'd heard about torturing people to find out what they knew, and not even letting the original subject hear about it. Even a Mogwa could be copied, tormented, and recycled while the "real" version sat home on Trantor. It was a grim practice, but Central wasn't above it. In fact, it had happened to me before.

I lowered my gun. "Tell me a few things, then you can go anyway you want."

"Like what?"

"These suits. Where do they come from? Who makes them?"

Abigail bared her teeth. She clearly didn't want to answer. "There's a planet... A place where long ago a neutron star blew up and laced it with collapsed matter. Some of the physics there... it helps with the manufacture of gear like this."

She rubbed at the suit she wore, then she tugged at it. "Can I at least cover my boobs? Or haven't you gotten to stare long enough?"

I realized with a flush that I'd been staring at her. "Uh… okay."

She pulled the suit up some, but she didn't zip it. A bare stripe of skin was still visible, running from her face down to her belly button.

"What are the coordinates of this world?" I said. "Do they make the suits there, or just ship the materials—?"

Abigail walked toward me smoothly. "I can't give you any more details."

There was a sound out in the passages. Someone shouted. The hogs were coming.

Abigail grabbed my gun, and she pressed the muzzle up to her bare chest.

I grinned. "Girl, there's no way you're ever going to get this gun out of my hand."

"I know," she said, and she looked up at me with those big eyes. "Don't let them make any more copies of me, James. Please?"

"Uh…" I said, not sure where this was going.

She couldn't teleport out with her suit open, and my gun was pressed up against her heart. I wasn't sure just what she was—

Bang!

The gun went off in my hand. She'd forced my finger to pull the trigger.

Those pretty eyes glazed over, and she flopped down on her back, deader than yesterday.

-14-

A few moments later, a cavalry of hogs came in the door behind me. They found Winslade, the bears... and Abigail. They were all dead on the floor, even Winslade hadn't survived the experience.

Graves looked at me, then the stack of bodies.

"McGill..." he said. "I almost don't want to ask, but I have to."

"Well sir," I said, waving my hands around. "This all was one big misunderstanding."

He nodded. "That's what I thought." He turned to the hogs. "Arrest him. Question him. When you give up, call me."

The hogs looked baffled, but they followed orders. I left a few of them on the deck, but dispensed no permanent injuries. They took me into a neighboring cell and beat on me for about half an hour. At that point, they abruptly stopped.

Now, I know hogs the way I know my own slice of swamp down home in Georgia.

They all operate in pretty much the same manner. There was simply no way they'd gotten bored yet with trying to interrogate me.

My neck was strapped down to a steel table. My arms were twisted up behind my back, almost to the point of dislocation, and tied that way. Still, I was able to roll my eyes way back up into my skull and get a glimpse of the doorway.

Winslade stood there. He appeared to be indecisive, but I couldn't see his expression from this angle. He was framed by the more brightly lit hallway.

"Fresh from a revive, Centurion?" I asked in a cheery tone.

"That's right, McGill. Now, I'm faced with a dilemma."

"How's that?"

"I know you won't tell them anything—at least nothing that you don't *want* them to hear. Therefore, I could call a halt to it."

"Aw," I said. "Giving boys like these unfortunates a workout is just another public service I provide from time to time."

"I couldn't agree more. It must be deadly dull working down here in a dungeon like this."

The two hogs crossed their arms and nodded their heads.

Winslade glanced at them and dismissed them by making a flicking motion with his fingers. "Take a break, gentlemen," he said. "You look sweaty."

They walked out, and Winslade paced around me.

"What should I do?" he asked. "You clearly broke in here to help—you killed both my kidnappers and even shot Abigail herself, preventing her escape."

"That's exactly right."

"But at the same time, I can't fail to recognize that you admitted to knowing why I was demoted—and that you haven't yet told me the real reason."

He had me there. Suddenly, the situation was clear. Winslade had clout from high-level brass right now. He was using it to find out why the entirety of Earth's military command structure seemed hell-bent on shitting on him.

"Graves knows the truth too," I said. "Why don't you go ask him?" Winslade snorted. "I'd do better to question a carved block of stone."

"Yeah..."

Winslade sighed. "All right. Here's the deal, I'll get you out of here if you let me know what happened out at Clone World."

"You don't care about Abigail? About what this whole commando attack was intended to do?"

He fluttered his fingers at me. "How can I concern myself with such things when I know a great injustice has occurred?"

"Huh... well, okay."

He looked surprised. "It's that simple?"

"Yeah. After what happened today, I don't think your part of the story matters anymore."

Then, I told him the whole story—with a few edits. I told him that he'd turned traitor out at Clone World and gone rogue to help Claver. That he'd wanted a legion of Clavers of his own. Before I was halfway finished, he shushed me up.

"You're saying this to screw me, aren't you? You *know* they record interrogations!"

I couldn't shake my head with my neck strapped down, but I tried. "Nope. That's the honest truth. Just think about it. Think about how everyone has been acting. You had to have done something to earn it."

"Such abuse and mistreatment I've suffered..." he said, pacing around again. "I... I think I believe you. It's a painful thing, but it fits the facts. Actually, I'm surprised I wasn't permed out of hand."

"That thought did come up," I admitted. "But they wanted to see how you contacted Claver, how you were turned by him. The experiment has lasted over a year, now, and it seems to have failed to turn up anything."

"Which should have been obvious from the start! Claver doesn't have a planet any longer. He has no legions, no real power to speak of... In a way, that's informative all by itself. These officers here at Central are diabolical. Turov must be behind this. Graves could never have thought of it. Am I right?"

"Uh..."

"That's what I thought. Say no more—I have to get all the recorded files erased as it is."

He left then, and a few minutes later the goon squad came in and released me.

"No hard feelings, guys," I told them. I stretched my neck and arms experimentally. "You know... I think I might skip my weekly adjustment at the chiropractor this time around. You hogs can work miracles!"

They looked disgusted as they signed me out and slammed the rattling cage door behind me.

I didn't make it far before my tapper buzzed with new orders: I was to report to Drusus by the end of the hour. That only gave me a few minutes for a quick shower, but I took it, and I arrived upstairs with seconds left to spare.

Drusus was alone this time. He met me across his glowing desk. He looked thoughtful.

"Your hair is wet. I was told you weren't killed and revived today."

"That's right, sir. This is good old-fashioned sweat."

He nodded. "You still look fresh as a daisy."

I shrugged. "Just a couple of bored hogs having a bit of fun."

"Listen," Drusus said. "I'm concerned about this attack. I believe you have your share of secrets, but you don't normally do things that might endanger Earth."

"You got the right of that."

"So, what did Abigail tell you before you killed her?" I blinked. That was a mistake. A tell. "Uh…"

"Listen," he said, leaning forward. "You seem to have some kind of weird connection with this woman. That's par for the course for James McGill, but this is different. Our enemies managed to penetrate our defenses—killing guards in the detention center, no less—and they did it with armored suits on. That's right, we've already tested the gear they were wearing. All three of the captured suits are tougher than anything we've got."

I nodded, unsurprised. "I get that, sir. I really do. So, I'm going to tell you what I know."

I repeated Abigail's story about a planet laced with neutron dust, collapsed star matter, as being the source of the enemy technology.

Drusus seemed disappointed. "That's all you've got? No coordinates? Not even a stellar catalog reference?"

"No sir… before she said more, she was dead."

He frowned. "Then we might have to revive her and continue with the persuasion." That was the one thing Abigail didn't want to face. I didn't want her to face it, either.

"There's more, sir," I said, coming up with a half-truth. It was really something I'd been thinking about over the last few days. "The weird world I visited during my last mission was a blown-out Skay, right?"

Drusus nodded. "My techs have confirmed that after poring over your recordings and the scraps you brought home."

"Good nerd-work, sir. But if the Skay defenders had this special type of armor, where did they get it?"

He shrugged. "We assumed that it came from some advanced tech in the Core Worlds."

I waved a finger at him. "Maybe. But the defensive creatures we faced before, back when we battled the Skay at Clone World, they didn't have that kind of armor."

"Hmm... no they didn't."

"We've only seen it from two sources," I said. "One was Rigel itself, the second was out on that dead Skay. What if the two are somehow related?"

"The two bodies in question are almost a thousand lightyears apart, McGill. Thousands of star systems exist in that region of—"

"Wait a second," I said, "what if we calculated the drifting course of the dead Skay, and plotted it backward? What if we checked out places where it intersects with a candidate world?"

It was Drusus' turn to blink. He stood up suddenly. "They should have thought of that. The tech people are too focused on chemical analysis. I'll get them on it right now—stay here."

He stepped away to make a flurry of calls. I got up, found some of his prime whiskey, and poured us each a double. When he returned to the table, he looked stunned. He took the drink without urging and took a swig. I did the same. It was a fine single-malt scotch.

"There's only one multi-star system that the Skay might have drifted through—and it must have been decades ago. It's called Tau Orionis."

"What province is that in?"

"Province 928, the borderland between Rigel and Earth."

"Bingo!" I shouted, and I lifted my glass.

He smiled, and we drank together.

"No more torturing my lady-friend?" I asked him when he was done.

"She has nothing to worry about," he assured me.

We had another glass, and I left the office.

Before I got away from Central entirely, however, Turov caught up with me. I got the feeling she was watching my movements by tracing my tapper. Superior officers in the chain of command could do that.

She'd moved to intercept me in the lobby. "Where do you think you're going, Centurion?" she asked.

I looked wistfully out the glass doors into Central City. It was night now, and the place looked lively. I still had plenty of new bars in town to visit.

"I'm looking for some dinner and entertainment," I said. "You want to join me?"

Galina stared at me for a second, then she uncrossed her arms and loosened her face into a smile. "I certainly do."

Surprised, I walked out into the city with her. We ate, we drank, we danced, and around about midnight we screwed like rabbits back at her place.

Up until that point, I hadn't bothered to ask why she was in such a good mood. To my way of thinking, when a woman is in a loving way, you don't ask why. You just go with the flow. That's what I'd done, but even I harbored some level of curiosity about my good fortune.

"Why, James," she said when I asked her about it. "Don't you know? I was having... well... certain dark feelings. Toward that Claver-freak."

"Oh... Abigail. Right."

"Don't say her name."

"Sorry."

"Anyway, I heard that you killed her. That you stopped her from teleporting and shot her dead. That impressed me."

Suddenly, I got it. How could I be obsessed with Abigail if I'd shot her down? Smiling, I accepted her version of events without an argument or a qualm.

Internally, however, I still felt a bit troubled about how that poor girl had committed suicide right in front of me.

I hoped to meet her again someday. Why? I'm a moth that likes to circle flames, that's the only good way to explain it.

-15-

The very next day, I got a surprise call from Floramel. She wanted me to go on a "special" assignment.

Now, as a matter of religion, Legionnaires know you don't volunteer for jack-squat unless you've got a very good reason. In the recent past, I'd volunteered for such duty, and I'd almost gotten myself permed. I'd done it because Etta had been sucking up all my money for her education, and I'd almost gone broke.

After a few missions, however, I'd been cashed out to the tune of several million Hegemony credits. I surely know that's no big sum to a rich guy, but for a swamp-dwelling soldier like myself, a million credits was nothing to sneeze at. I'd been able to pay for Etta's tram and keep her living in her apartment in Central City where the rents were insane.

Etta knew nothing about my money troubles, of course, and I liked it that way. She just thought I had a big stash from the old days. After all, I was a starman, and such people sometimes had discovered a way to cash-in at some point in their long lives.

Not me, however. I'd never gotten a financial break. Every tin ten-credit piece I'd come by had been squeezed out of someone else's iron-tight fist.

So it wasn't a surprise that Floramel, a lab director at Central, had thought to contact me for her clandestine off-world mission, whatever it was.

"James," she said, "I heard you were in Central City, and I thought I'd give you a call."

"Well, that's a welcome change of heart!"

"I didn't mean that," she said, using that sexy husky voice of hers on me, "but we could really use your expertise on our current project."

I considered. I had to admit her approach was working, to a degree. At least I found myself becoming interested in Floramel, if not her assignment.

"Uh... how about you and I have dinner tonight?" I suggested. "We could talk about it."

She hesitated. We had a history, Floramel and I. She was a lovely lady, if a little too smart, too driven and too straight-arrow for my tastes. "I don't want to lead you on," she said.

"Don't worry about that. I know business is business. We could talk about old times—and new ones."

"Hmm... All right. Where shall we meet?"

Surprised, I gave her the name of a romantic restaurant in midtown. She said she'd be there at six and closed the channel that connected her tapper to mine.

After her sweet face faded from my arm, I whistled long and low. If Floramel had actually consented to a date, she must *really* want my services—as a commando, that was.

The day went by quickly. Heading down to the floors in the mid-one hundreds, I found the training centers. I worked up a sweat in a gymnasium and practiced my marksmanship on a firing range. After a long hard day of fun, I walked to midtown and stepped into the restaurant where I was supposed to meet Floramel. Pre-ordering a bottle of Chardonnay, I waited for her to show up. Overall, I was in high spirits.

That all changed after an hour had passed. I'd already finished dinner, the bottle of Chardonnay, and two baskets of bread. I was getting bored and a little annoyed.

Using my tapper, I tried to connect to Floramel again. It gave me the disconnected icon, which wasn't really a surprise. Floramel worked down in the guts of Central, in the underground labs, and regular commercial network traffic wasn't allowed to reach those floors most of the time.

I'd pretty much figured out she'd decided to stand me up. It wasn't like Floramel to do that—she was a straight-arrow, as I said. She was, in fact, compulsively punctual most of the time.

But... we had a past. She might have chickened because she knew I was going to flirt with her. Maybe she didn't think she wasn't ready to face the overwhelming charm of one James McGill again tonight.

Just as I'd given up and called for the bill, a tall presence came up behind me. Floramel was a tall girl, whispery thin and model-like, with elongated bones and features like the ladies they put on magazine covers. Naturally, I suspected it was her arriving at last.

Turning and forcing a smile, I put on my best welcoming face—and then I froze.

"Etta?" I asked, surprised.

My daughter Etta was a sidekick scientist assistant to Floramel. I'd known that, but I hadn't expected to see her here tonight. In fact, I hadn't expected her at all.

"Daddy... I have to talk to you."

Her voice was hushed, and her eyes weren't looking at me. She wasn't hugging me, either, even when I stood up and put out a circle of arm for her to walk into.

Right off, alarm bells began ringing inside my thick skull. I knew Floramel well, and I knew my daughter even better. Etta had a guilty look on her face.

It wasn't a normal kind of guilt, either. Most young people appear sorry when they've done something they know is wrong—but not my daughter. She looked wary, nervous, and worried she might be caught.

"Girl...?" I said. "Where's Floramel?"

"That's what we have to talk about."

"Well then, sit down. I can order dinner—"

"Not here. Come on."

Sighing, I followed her out of the place after dropping a big tip. After all, I'd spent all night sitting at this table and keeping other diners out in the lobby.

When we were walking down busy streets, Etta finally talked to me.

"You were meeting with Floramel tonight, right?" she asked.

"You know I was. Where is she?"

"She'll be fine."

I frowned. A feeling was beginning to come over me. A not-good kind of feeling.

Way back when Etta was young, I'd brought her home from Dust World. At that point in her young life, she hadn't been... civilized.

She had, in fact, experienced a childhood akin to that of a barbarian from a thousand years ago. She was kind of kid who knew how to hunt and skin animals—or sew up a wound all by herself. But she hadn't been too sharp when it came to the social graces.

Etta had, in fact, attempted to murder some of my girlfriends. Usually they woke up afterwards, but even so, it was plain rude. My father had always said Etta had the devil in her—but only when my mamma wasn't around to hear it.

I stopped walking, and I put my hand on her shoulder. She didn't like that. She didn't like any kind of restraining touch—that was part of what growing up wild did for you.

She lifted her lip a little, but she didn't snarl. Not exactly. A decade-plus of schooling had taught her to fake it. Only a trained eye like mine picked up the signs.

"You went feral, didn't you?" I asked her.

She studied the sidewalk.

"I can't believe it, girl! Just because she's your boss, and I asked her out on a date? I thought you gotten over that kind of thing back when you were twelve!"

"It's not like that, Daddy," she said. "It's not like that at all. I'm here to warn you. They want a candidate to go on a mission—a one-way mission using the casting teleporter."

The newest twist in teleportation technology involved what they called "casting" an individual—or victim, some might say—over a great distance. The advantage was they could watch what the person did when they got there for a good ten minutes or so. The disadvantage was they couldn't bring the person back.

Therefore, in order not to get permed, the individual in question had to make sure they died before the connection broke. That way, the people watching back at Central could safely revive them knowing they hadn't made an illegal copy.

"I've done that before," I said. "It wasn't all that bad."

"You died on every trip!"

"I know, I know. But it worked, and I didn't get permed."

She looked frustrated. "You don't understand. This time, we might not be able to watch you—to confirm your death."

"Uh… why not?"

"Because of the properties of the target planet. Supposedly, it's laced with collapsed matter. I've done the math, and I don't think our connection will stay open. Collapsed matter is like lead, but much more dense. It can't be penetrated by any kind of known transmission."

"Oh…" I said, thinking that over. "So, they want to send someone out on a one-way ticket, but they don't know if they can get them back or not?"

"That's right. We've offered this deal to several commandos. They've all turned us down. Floramel is desperate."

I mulled that over. She *had* accepted a date with me. That was odd on the face of it. Desperation… yes, that might be the reason.

"Okay, okay," I said. "You convinced me. I won't go on any such mission. I promise and hope to die."

"Don't say that."

"But it's funny!"

Legionnaires often put death references into everyday conversation. Laughter is the best medicine God ever created, my mamma always said.

"Look, Dad… you just can't do it. Please?"

"Okay. I don't have to anyways. I don't need the money now."

She gazed at me, and a smarty-pants look came into her eyes. "You don't need the money? But you did before…? That's why you took that shitty mission last year, isn't it? Oh God, I can't believe you did that to pay for my tram. I could have done without!"

I reached out my arm again, and she let me encircle her this time. She put her face against me, just like she was a kid again. Passersby gave us odd looks, but I didn't care.

"Okay now," I said gently. "We got this all sorted out, right?"

"Yes."

"Good... Now, it's time to fess up. Where's Floramel?"

Etta turned away, lifted a hand slowly, and she pointed. I followed the gesture to a tram. It was the very same tram I'd died twice to make payments on.

Etta was pointing at the trunk.

-16-

"Damnation, girl!" I boomed, and she shushed me.

Etta looked contrite, and I knew it wasn't an act, but that wasn't really good enough. Not today.

I bent down a little, so I could whisper harshly to her, the way a zillion parents have done with their children in public since time began.

"You went and murdered your boss? Seriously? Just to stop us from having a date?"

"I didn't know how else to stop her. There are cameras everywhere in Central. I couldn't even make a threat. I had to make my move fast."

That was how Etta's mind worked. She was like a wolf, not a dog. Dogs liked to bark before they bit. They'd get all worked up and carry on. They do that way to let strangers know they're not wanted. They're all about warning people off.

But a real predator, a real killer, operates differently. They don't warn the victim. They use stealth, duplicity—anything to make the kill.

That's how Etta was. Like I said, she wasn't entirely civilized, not even to this very day. No one around her on a daily basis would know it, because she hid her true nature—but I was her father. I knew her better than anyone.

"She's in the trunk of your tram?" I demanded. "Are you crazy?"

"Shhh! I didn't know what else to do."

"Come on," I growled, and I climbed into the driver's seat.

Swerving into traffic, I got a few honks and flipped the honkers off without a glance.

"Where are we going?" Etta asked.

"I can't believe you did this, girl. After all the work I've done to teach you how to live with regular people."

"I know Daddy, I'm sorry. But Floramel... she's kind of a bitch, did you know that?"

"She's your boss. All bosses are irritating. That's how it works."

"Yeah..."

We drove through the city, swerving this way and that until we were in the quieter part of town. I'd taken a zigzagging route on purpose to see if we were being followed. I didn't think we were.

"Where are we going?" Etta asked again.

"Out of town. Up into the eastern heights."

"Where the rich people live?"

"Yep."

I drove on, while Etta apologized and tried to explain. She said she hadn't had a choice, as Floramel was hell-bent on recruiting me for the job. She might even have been willing to sleep with me to get me to do it. That tidbit raised my eyebrows. I hadn't thought Floramel operated that way—but then she'd been a director now for quite a while. Such people tended to get dogmatic.

"What are we going to do with the body?" Etta asked again.

"We're going to get her a new one, that's what."

"How?"

"You've cost me tonight. You've really cost me. Here now, this is where you get out and take the train home. I'll send your tram home on autopilot later."

"I'm sorry Daddy—but don't take the mission, okay?"

"I promise."

She got out, and I drove up the dark hills into the nicest of neighborhoods. Up here was where Turov lived.

I parked out front and thumbed the bell like I was selling robot cleaners. At last, Galina answered.

"What do you want, McGill?" she asked in a sour tone.

That was disappointing. She'd been all hot on me just the other day, but now, she seemed to be having second thoughts.

"Uh…" I said. "I thought maybe we could talk."

"Tonight? I don't think so."

"Come on, Galina. I didn't—"

Her front door popped open. She'd been right on the other side, watching me through the cameras and stewing.

"Are you saying you didn't start chasing skirts the second I was busy? That you didn't take that lab-haunting whore of yours to dinner tonight instead of me?"

My eyes blinked twice in surprise. Then they narrowed. "Are you having drones or spies follow me again? I thought we were over that."

"No, I didn't. I merely examined your tapper activity."

"You can do that?"

She shrugged. "I'm in your chain of command. There have been updates, recently, to your tapper software. Didn't you see the new privacy polices?"

"I don't read those things. I—"

"Of course you don't. People shouldn't be so surprised if they don't read what they're agreeing to."

"It was like twenty pages long!"

She shrugged again and studied the hardwood floor of her house. Her arms were crossed tightly, but it wasn't cold out.

"Anyway," I said, "I didn't have any date with Floramel. In fact… I found her dead." Galina's head snapped up to look at me in surprise. "You killed her?"

"Nope. I just found her dead. I will swear on a stack of bibles and pass ten lie-detector tests on that point."

"No one will ever believe you."

"That's right," I said. "That's why I'm here, and that's why I need help."

She looked down again. Honest-to-God I thought she was going to slam the door in my face. I couldn't even have blamed her for it.

But she didn't. She heaved a real big sigh instead.

"All right. We'll dump the body, and I'll arrange a quiet revival." Her finger came up into my face then. "But you *owe* me after this, James McGill. Agreed?"

"Agreed."

Galina put a plan into action that clearly had been executed before. She rode in the tram with me back to Central, where we slid into a quiet entrance in the back of the building on the alleyways.

There, in what amounted to a garbage dump, a stack of credits were exchanged and a wrapped-up package was taken out of my trunk by a pair of grunting men. They tipped their hats to us. After a bit of fooling with scanners, they tossed the body into a furnace.

After that, I sent the car home and accompanied Galina to the nearest designated Blue Deck. A pair of bio specialists were on hand, waiting.

"Special order?" asked the first guy.

"Yes. Here's the code." Galina touched her tapper to the bio flunky's and data was transferred.

"Okay, the files check out," he flicked his eyes and a finger toward me. "This is the recycle, right?"

"No, no, you idiot," Galina said. "Why would I recycle *him*? I'd leave him permed if I had the chance."

The specialist chuckled and walked away, shaking his head. "Give me forty-five minutes."

"For what I'm paying you? I'll give you half an hour."

The specialist jabbed his thumb back toward the revival chamber, where I knew a sweating, shivering bio-machine was hard at work giving birth to whoever needed it. "But I've got—"

"Dump your current grow," Turov interrupted. "I'm not waiting around for two losers to be reborn."

Shaking his head, the bio specialist finally agreed, and we took uncomfortable seats in the waiting area. A long silence reigned for the next ten minutes or so. Finally, Galina broke the spell.

"A report just came in on my tapper," she said. "The bio-people at the dumping station did a quick scan. They say Floramel's body showed signs of bludgeoning—how did she anger you so greatly?"

She looked at me with honest concern. I didn't know what to say. My well of lies was usually brimming over, but today, I was running dry. Maybe that was because I was covering for someone else.

"I don't know what happened," I lied. "I just found her dead and panicked."

"Three improbabilities in so few words... but all right. I'll let you have your secrets. We all have our secrets."

"True."

Another ten minutes went by, and these seemed even longer than before. Finally, she stood up. "I'm leaving. You will come to my place tonight, and I will tell you how you are going to repay this debt."

"Uh... okay."

Galina left, and I waited it out. After the thirty minutes were gone, plus another ten for the examination and release, Floramel came staggering out of the door.

"She's all yours, hero," the bio specialist said, shaking his head at me. Even he seemed a little reproachful.

Did everyone think I'd accidentally beat her to death? That was just grand.

"James?" Floramel asked. She was unsteady on her feet, so I let her lean on my arm. "What happened?"

"There was an accident of some kind," I said. "They didn't want to revive you right off, but I pulled some strings."

She looked at me with wide eyes. I could tell right off that she, of all people, believed me. "You did?"

"Yeah," I said. "I didn't want to miss our dinner date—but it's kind of late for that now."

"Take me home, will you?"

I did, and I tucked her into bed. She grabbed my hand as I tried to walk out.

"I want you to do a mission for me," she said. "Will you do it? The job pays very well."

I shook my head. "I don't need money. Not anymore, Floramel. You'll have to get someone else."

She threw the covers back on her bed. "Spend the night," she said.

For a moment, I stood there, indecisive. Women have an evil power over a man like me. We just can't pass up such invitations. It's not fair, really. We're too easily manipulated.

But I held firm. I didn't want to take advantage of her, and I didn't want to ditch my promise to Galina or to Etta.

Finally, I shook my head. "You can't go recruiting that way. It's not right. You've changed, girl."

She frowned and looked down. Then she covered up. "So have you." I gave her a chaste kiss on the head and left.

-17-

After spending the night at Galina's place, I got an early-morning buzz on my tapper. "One of your subordinates has been lost in action," I read aloud.

Alarmed, I looked at the time. "Ten-thirty?!"

I dashed for the shower. Galina was nowhere to be found, and I assumed she'd left early for Central. I soon was riding in an aircab toward that looming building.

On the way, I looked into the details of the tapper report that had awakened me. Ghost Specialist Cooper had been reported lost while on special assignment. He was classified as missing in action and therefore ineligible for revival.

"Cooper? Shit…"

He'd taken the money.

That thought came to me, and it wouldn't leave. He must have been their second choice. I don't mind telling you that I was kind of pissed about the whole thing.

When I got to Central, I confronted Floramel first. "How could you?" I demanded. "How could I what? Bludgeon myself to death? I've been curious about that all morning."

"Uh… no, no, no… I'm talking about Cooper."

"The Ghost Specialist? Very regrettable."

She didn't sound like she gave two shits, so I walked up and put my hands on her shoulders. That got her attention. For Rogue Worlders, when you initiated physical contact, you were either intending to murder them or make love to them.

"Is this how events began yesterday?" she asked me. "I can't recall the details of my demise."

I dropped my hands from her like she was on fire. "Why'd you want to send me so badly? Why'd you send *anyone* if you knew it was going to end with a perming?"

She looked troubled. "I had no choice. Hegemony demanded a volunteer be found. I tried to recruit you first because you've survived such things before. You were my only hope for a successful mission. Remember all the earliest teleport missions? I read up on your file. You always came back, even when no one else did. Even when it seemed impossible."

I thought that over. I *had* made it home during those early missions, it was true. Back then everyone else had died, but that was because I'd had a Galactic Key in my possession. Floramel didn't know about that. The device had allowed me to manipulate the teleport suits like no one else could. Perhaps Floramel had thought I could pull off the impossible again.

But… Cooper. I felt bad about that. He'd gone in my place, and I doubt he'd understood the risks, or even gotten laid by Floramel. He'd just wanted the money.

"No one told him the real odds, did they?" I asked.

Floramel looked evasive. That was a new look for her. She was generally very forthright.

"The mission was vital," she said. "It had to be performed by someone. When we invade the target world, the lost soldier can be recovered."

"When? You mean *if* we invade, and that only counts if we find his remains."

Floramel looked down at the deck. She lowered her voice. "All right," she said. "We've both done something wrong this week. I will forgive you, if you will forgive me. Neither of us should mention these events again."

Again, I was floored. Floramel was becoming more like an Earther, meaning tricky and deceitful. Maybe running a government lab for so long had changed her.

Thinking over her offer, I decided I didn't like it. Essentially, I was confessing to her murder. On the other hand, she just wanted to put the whole thing behind us, and this would clear the decks for Etta.

"All right," I told her, "but eventually I'll prove to you that I had nothing to do with your death last night."

She put a hand up. "Please, no more lies."

"No lies. That's a promise."

She shrugged, and she didn't meet my gaze. I could tell she didn't believe me. I suppose, when a man bends the truth as often as I do, this sort of moment had to be expected now and again.

Normally, I would have immediately ratted on the real perpetrator, but I couldn't because it was my daughter. Heaving a deep breath, I forced a smile, touched her arm lightly and walked away. She flinched a little, but not much. Maybe she did still have a thing for me. We'd slept together now and then over the years, and even though there was plenty of bad blood between us, we still had an attraction.

Hitting the elevators, I met up with Etta in the lobby. She looked furtive. "Thanks Daddy," she said, giving me a quick hug.

"Lunch today?"

She shook her head. "I'm working through lunch. We've got to go over some data."

I figured she was talking about data from Cooper's suicide mission. My face soured a little. "All right. Next time."

I left that dank dungeon under Central and headed up to Legion Varus' offices. That's where Galina held court as our tribune. It wasn't such-a-much. There were no ornate doors with gold reliefs. Instead, there was the faded red wolf's head of Varus on a circular emblem stamped on the doors. I opened them and walked in.

Gary was on hand, watching a ballgame. He looked at me with surprise, but without much interest.

"Don't see you on the roster today, McGill," he said.

"The roster for what?"

He smirked. "The meeting you apparently weren't invited to."

I looked toward the inner doors. One led to Galina's office. The second led to the conference room. I chose the second door.

"I wouldn't if I were you," Gary cautioned me.

I put my hand on the touchpad.

Gary shrugged and turned back to his game. "It's your funeral."

"Whose in there?"

"Brass. All brass."

Damn. I sighed and moved to the waiting area. Gary smirked again, and I spent forty-five good minutes playing Boy Scout.

It wasn't like me to play by the rules. But this was important. I had to do things right for Cooper's sake. He'd been screwed over and permed, and it was partly my fault the way I saw it. As he was under my direct command, I had to try to get him un-permed.

When the meeting broke up, I got to see that Gary was right. A parade of serious brass walked out. Among them were both Drusus and Wurtenberger, both top ten praetors.

Galina came out last of all. She was all smiles and nods and ass-kissing to the brass.

When they were gone, however, she whirled to face me. "What are you doing here?" she demanded.

"Well... I'm waiting to see you, sir."

Her eyes darkened. Sure, we'd just spent the night together making loud love, but that wasn't any reason to hang around together at the office. Galina and I generally kept our relationship on the down-low by not parading together in public places. People knew we were a thing, but if you didn't rub it in their faces, they tended to ignore it.

Finally, with a twitch of her head, she indicated that I should follow her. I got up and headed for her office door, but she went into the conference room instead. I followed.

"Uh..." I said, looking around. The walls were all lit up with star charts. The holo-table projected a big image of a strange-looking world. It was greenish—black laced with green.

"This is it," Galina said. "Varus has a new target. It sucks just as badly as every world they send us to. Possibly it's worse than average."

I stared at it. "Tau Orionis?"

Her head snapped up. "How did you know that?"

"Just a lucky guess. I've been taking online astronomy courses, you know."

She narrowed her eyes at me, not believing a word of my lie. "No one can keep a secret in this building... but yes, that is Tau Orionis. We will board our new ship and journey there."

"New ship? Is it the same class as *Legate*?"

Everyone in Varus had loved old *Legate*. That transport was a fine vessel, built to take thousands of troops to the stars in relative comfort.

Galina shook her pretty head. "No, sadly. We've been assigned to the newly commissioned *Berlin*."

"But *Berlin* was destroyed too," I complained. "Worse, it was a battlecruiser to begin with."

"We've modified a Rigellian ship we captured. Remember those vessels? This one has armor-piercing guns."

"The passageways are barely high enough to stand up straight."

She shrugged. "I've got plenty of headroom. The real problem was where to put the troops. They finally added troop modules on the external hull, egg-shell thin domes on the flanks for the troops to huddle in."

"That sounds safe... and comfortable."

"It will be neither of those things. The point is, we haven't yet had time to build our own vessels with armor-piercing cannons."

"Why is a battlecruiser needed at all on this trip out to Tau Orionis?"

She looked at me sidelong. "I really shouldn't be telling you this in a private briefing. The public presentation will be happening on Wednesday. That leads me to why you are here. I don't want resistance on this mission, McGill. Yes, it sucks. Yes, it will be uncomfortable and—"

I put my hands up to stop her tirade. "I'll tell you what. How about I play cheerleader on this one? I'll get the centurions to rally for the mission. Even if it means we're all crammed into a battlecruiser like sardines."

"Really? Why?"

I shrugged. I didn't want to bring up Cooper yet. She wouldn't respond well to that, since I wasn't really supposed to know about his secret scouting mission, any more than I was supposed to know about this one. "I just want to help out, that's all."

She looked me up and down once. "I don't believe you, but I'll accept the help. From this moment forward, you're my cheerleader with the lower ranked officers. To answer your previous question, we need the battlecruiser because this substance, this tough material they make on this planet—well, it takes a hard punch to break through it."

"And we assume their ships may be built with this? To make tougher hulls?"

"Exactly."

I nodded, understanding the logic. "What about the zoo legion? We aren't going to have to share air vents with Blood Worlders, are we?"

"No. There's no room for them. There will barely be room for the human troops."

"Great…"

After that, she went on and on. She gave me a run down on the planet's mass, density, gravitational pull and atmosphere. I soon stopped listening because I'd learned all I needed to know.

Legion Varus was headed back out to the stars. With luck, we'd find Cooper's remains. That was all that mattered.

-18-

Cooper had been sent out to the newly discovered planet by the strange tech known as *casting*, but it hadn't worked perfectly. The connection had broken before he'd died, meaning Earth couldn't be sure he wasn't still alive, no matter how unlikely that was. Therefore, he couldn't be revived.

Despite this complication, they'd gotten enough data from Cooper's fuzzy, short-lived transmissions to know they'd hit the right planet. The mix of crystalline structures laced with collapsed matter was just right. Our target world had been chosen.

"This mission is to remove a key strategic advantage Rigel has enjoyed all along," Galina told the assembled troops as we stood in parade formation, ready to board lifters. "Ever since the first time our soldiers fought with these vicious bears, they've been considered superior to humans. Once we gain the ability to make tough, light armor like theirs, this advantage will be lost forever!"

There was scattered applause in response. I could have told her—actually, just about anyone in Varus could have told her—that the bears were damned tough fighters, armor or not. Still, we appreciated the plan to improve our gear.

While she kept strutting around and speeching, something she loved to do in front of a captive audience, I soon tuned her out. I wasn't even focused on her curves, which were cut just about as perfectly as any woman's could be. Instead, I was thinking about the mission.

This trip into the unknown was for more than gaining useful tech, for me, it was about recovering Cooper. The main obstacle in that regard was finding his remains. We knew where we'd sent him, sure, but unknown planets tended to be large. Even a one degree variance in his coordinates might place him far from our landing zone.

Accordingly, when we finally marched aboard the lifters and took off, I called upon Natasha Elkin for help.

Natasha was the best tech I knew and quite possibly the best tech in Legion Varus. She should have gotten promoted into the officer ranks by now, but she'd been held back due to various discrepancies in her service record.

"Forget it," she said the moment I contacted her, "I'm not going off-script and hacking the external cameras or something. Not today, James."

She always called me by my first name, even though I was her centurion. I let her get away with that mostly because she was a friend and we'd once been intimate—but also because I so often needed her special skills.

"Listen, listen," I began. "I don't need anything against regs. All I want to know is how closely we can pinpoint a set of coordinates using that caster-thingie at Central."

Natasha was quiet for a second. "I don't know what a 'caster-thingie' is, James."

"Oh... right. I forgot, it's a secret. Damn..."

I have to explain at this point that I wasn't forgetting anything. I was baiting a hook and dipping it into the water. With any luck, Natasha would bite.

She had one critical personality flaw. She loved new tech gadgets, especially something that was cutting edge.

"I can only surmise from your random statements that you've had experience with this... thingie?"

"Yeah... maybe."

"And it involves teleportation?"

"Yeah, yeah... but listen: I probably shouldn't be talking to you about this. You aren't cleared for it."

She hesitated again. "Since when has that bothered you?"

"Never has, much…" I admitted. "But you're right. We have to be cautious. I've involved you in advanced projects far too often without going through proper channels. I'll contact Floramel about it."

"Floramel?" she asked, bristling a little. "Why her?"

Since Floramel was a near-human Rogue Worlder, she'd been genetically selected for her scientific know-how. Natasha was jealous about her having her own lab and all. She was also jealous because I'd had an intimate relationship with her, after Natasha.

"Well, she's got the clearance," I said. "She's not as imaginative, and she probably won't help anyway, but—"

"Just tell me what this is about—no wait, I'll meet up with you at the aft lounge."

Berlin wasn't as roomy and comfortable as good old *Legate* had been, but we were doing our best to adjust. In a way, it was kind of cool to be aboard a battlecruiser. But in another way, it was cold, crammed and unforgiving. For the Rigellians, I'm sure this warship had been massive and roomy, but tall humans like me found themselves ducking in every passageway. The external troop pods and even the troops themselves were clearly afterthoughts as well.

Natasha showed up at the lounge in seven minutes flat. When she walked rapidly into the chamber, I hid my grin behind a mug of beer. She was falling for my bait, hook, line and sinker.

She flumped down beside me and ordered a drink. In a hushed tone, she told me what she'd learned. "I looked into your device."

"The casting thingie?"

"Shhhh! Yes. There are some posts about it on the dark grid. There's some speculation on the base technology… That's how I know you're not completely full of shit—this time."

"Uh…" I said, less than encouraged. "How'd you do all that while trotting over here?"

She shrugged. "I multitask. So, let's talk. This is some kind of new, hush-hush teleportation system. I get that. Where do I fit in?"

I heaved a deep breath, and I looked around. I did everything I could to look reluctant. My fish was on the hook, but she had to be sure she wanted that bait before she noticed she was being reeled in.

"It's Cooper. This whole mission—it's all about Cooper, what he found out there."

"They teleported him—almost all the way out to Rigel? That's like a thousand lightyears."

"Give or take, yeah. The trouble is we lost him. He's not coming back unless we find him during this mission."

Natasha looked troubled. "What can I do about it? Do you have the exact coordinates?"

"No. But somebody does. I want to look into it, where we're going to set down—the planned LZ if there is any."

"That's not good enough. We're talking about an entire planet here, James. Let's say I could narrow it down to an area the size of Central City. That sounds pretty good, doesn't it?"

"Sure does!"

"But it isn't. Thousands of hectares… I'd have to figure out a way to trace his body with a sniffer unit, maybe…"

Her mind was already churning. I drank my beer with a new sense of purpose. She was about to convince herself that all sorts of skullduggery was required, and I wouldn't have to do a thing.

But suddenly, in the midst of my next beer—which, by the way, was tasting even better than the first one had—she turned on me with a dark look in her eyes.

Naturally, I had no idea what she'd been prattling on about for the last several minutes. To my mind, my work here had been completed the minute she glommed onto the idea.

"Wait a minute," she said. "Saving Cooper is great and all that—but I need something from you, first."

"Uh… what's that?"

"Get me in to see this casting device."

"I can't. It's back on Earth, inside the holiest of holies in Central. We're lightyears away from there now."

"I know—I mean afterward. When we come home. You have to promise."

I frowned at her. "Saving Cooper isn't good enough? You want perks too?"

"It's not like that."

"Yes it is."

She thought it over. "James, I've been passed over for promotion for months. Almost as many times as you have."

"Huh..." I said, not liking the sound of that. No one had ever talked to me about an imminent promotion—but Natasha was on the inside, effectively. She could read anyone's tapper feed if she wanted to. I knew the techs could do that, and they often did.

"Did you think I planned to stay as a noncom for decades?" she asked. "I'm good at what I do."

"You're the best."

"But I don't move up. I *never* move up. That's because of you and your schemes. You've cost me a lot."

"But I'm entertaining," I argued. "And this is a good cause."

"It is, or I wouldn't even consider helping. All the same, when we get home, you have to get me in to see that casting device."

"Okay..." I said at last, giving in.

We shook hands, downed our beers, and parted ways. She was on a mission now, and when that girl got a task into her head she was all in—like a coonhound combing the woods in springtime. She wasn't going to let go of it for nothing.

-19-

The voyage out to Tau Orionis took three weeks. That was pretty amazing, considering the distances involved. Along the way, we had a fair number of complaining new people to contend with. They weren't happy about the cramped quarters, and neither were their drill instructors. In truth, there wasn't much room to exercise and train in.

We no longer had a Green Deck. Instead, we had a pressurized hold full of junk. They stretched something that looked like canvas over all of the junk—but it wasn't just canvas. It was our best tear-resistant material, called Lot-K, from some company back on Earth. It was the same stuff we used to make uniforms for light-troops and crewmen.

"This cloth is the best we've got," Harris marveled, fingering the fabric that covered the walls, the ceiling and heaping mounds of metal gear. There were all sorts of things hidden under the layered Lot-K tarps, and it really hurt if you fell on one of them.

Harris seemed enamored with the fabric. He naturally liked anything he thought might save his life. Conversely, he hated anything that might threaten it.

"What the hell are we supposed to do in here?" I asked, looking around. The fabric-covered chamber was maybe fifty meters long and half as wide. It came to a snub-nosed point at one end, where the prow of *Berlin* was, and a blank wall at the other. The ceiling wasn't all that distant either. It was maybe ten meters over my head.

Harris shrugged. "Maybe we could each take three of these hills of covered junk—the biggest ones—and put a flag on them. Whoever captures the other team's flags wins."

"All the flags?" I asked.

"Yeah, sure, why not?"

This was the haphazard way Legion Varus planned out our training exercises. We came up with a method of exposing troops to stress, deadly weapons and the thrill of victory. Then we set them loose on one another and picked up the pieces afterward.

"No point making them win with all the flags," I said. "That's just the same as an all-out to the death arena fight."

"Hmm... Maybe four of six?"

I shook my head, looking around. "Five out of six. That will add some strategy to it."

"How so?"

"A cagey commander will fall back to his last two flags, and let the others come at him, gunning them down from cover."

"Maybe," Harris said doubtfully. "Who runs each group?"

This was an important choice. We had enough recruits and space for two squads to face off, fifteen per side plus their noncom leader. People who led such exercises got a chance to show off their skills, and it sometimes led to advancement.

"Sargon vs. Moller," I said.

"Sargon is never going to be an officer."

"You said the same thing about me—and I said it about you."

Harris eyed me sourly. "Okay. You're on. I'll go organize the squads."

"Hold on!" I shouted after him as he moved away. "You're not going to go hand-pick Moller's troops. That's not going to happen."

The truth was Sargon and Harris had a kind of rivalry going between them. Sargon wasn't a respectful veteran-ranked noncom. He was sort of the opposite of respectful, like me.

104

Moller, on the other hand, was strictly by the book. Harris liked her better, and everyone knew it.

"I'd never do such a thing," Harris lied.

He should have known better than to lie to a master, but I didn't bother to call him on it.

"We'll bring them both in here, show them the lay of the land, and let them pick their squads from the pool, one at a time."

"Like we're playing kickball or something?"

"Exactly like that."

He grumbled, but I outranked him, so things went my way. Soon, we had thirty-odd scared-looking noobs in the chamber with us. They eyed the strange tan colored fabric covering everything. A few touched the mountains, but pulled their hands away quickly. Sharp objects, even when covered with Lot-K, weren't comfortable to the touch.

I loudly explained the game to them, and I planted the flags on each of the six equipment mounds. They eyed the whole setup doubtfully—especially Sargon.

"This is bullshit," he said immediately. "I call bullshit, Centurion."

"How's that?" I asked in a mild tone of voice.

Harris was already glowering at Sargon, and Moller was shaking her head. Neither of them liked his tone.

"The two sides aren't even," he said. "The one toward the prow is screwed. They've got one hill right back there in the nose of the ship. The other side is clearly given an advantage. They've got two hills right up against the back wall, which means you've still got to take one of those to win. All you have to do to beat the squad at the prow is push them back to the nose of the boat."

I looked around, and I saw what he meant—but I didn't think it would matter much. Once one of these fights got going, it didn't proceed in an orderly fashion. It would probably turn into a chaotic shit-show mighty quick.

"Fine!" Harris boomed. "The whiner wins! He can have the back end of the boat. Moller will take the prow." Moller looked mildly alarmed.

"But!" Harris continued. "She gets first pick of this litter of retards to fight on her side."

I turned to Moller. "Is that okay with you?"

She nodded. That was Moller in a nutshell. She wasn't prone to speeches or complaining.

"Sargon?" I asked turning to him.

He eyed the recruits for a moment, then nodded. "All right."

"Okay then, line up, troops!" I shouted, and they formed a line along one side of the hull. "Moller, who do you pick to be your first recruit?"

She looked them over critically. "What kind of weapons are we using?" she asked. I was impressed. That was exactly what she should ask before choosing.

Lifting a shock-rod, I flicked it on, and it crackled in the air.

"Shock-rods," I said. "No spear-like shaft to mount them on. No snap-rifles, grenades or combat knives. Just the rods."

The shock-rods looked like an old-fashioned policeman's night-stick. They packed much more of a punch, however, due to their ability to numb limbs and daze anyone who was touched anywhere near the skull with one.

Moller nodded, looked over the group, and chose a rangy-looking, long-armed galoot. He was young with shifty eyes and a reach that would've impressed a gorilla.

The long-armed ape immediately trotted to her side. He picked up a shock-rod and flicked it into life experimentally. It hummed and shimmered, building up a charge.

Moller's strategy was already clear. She was going to recruit people with reach. The first one touched by a shock-rod was usually the man with the shorter arms.

Sargon eyed her man skeptically. He chose a man who was small, light and quick on his feet. He had the build of a soccer player, rather than a basketball man.

The choices went back and forth. As always, when the pickings became slim, they became more choosy. The least athletic recruits went last, shuffling almost in shame to their squad leaders.

"Where are we going to stand?" Harris asked me.

I pointed up to the roof. In the corners—there were really three corners, because the prow came to a blunt point—were cupolas. "I'm going up there."

Harris gave a nasty chuckle. "This is gonna be great! I already feel like Graves, sitting back and sipping a cold one while the men beat each other's brains out down here in the pit."

As the hold had been set to about half-gravity, we were able to jump and climb into our safe zones. Sitting up there, I felt kind of dirty. The troops were going to suffer and possibly die while I watched, and there wasn't anything I could do for them. Normally, I was personally involved in these conflicts, but today there just wasn't room for that many people.

Amid shouted threats and boasts, the flags stood tall, and the two sides faced off. We made them start with at least one heel backed up against the wall. They leaned forward like track stars on their marks. They were both gearing up to race in and grab those central flags first.

Standing up, I waved to Harris. He was tucked into the forward pocket in the prow of the ship. He waved back and nodded. His side was good to go.

"Troops!" I boomed. "It's time to capture those flags! Go-Go-Go!"

With a roar, the two sides rushed toward each other.

-20-

Sargon led his troops, front-lining it all the way. That made me proud. He wasn't a coward. He was all-in. The kind of leader that inspired men in battle.

Moller, on the other hand, was in the middle of her troops, shouting encouragement as they advanced. Rather than charging headlong, she led her troops at a trot. They were bunched up and almost in formation.

The two sides met on the hill of the fourth flag. Sargon's rush had caused him to grab three on the way. The fourth one was really in Moller's territory—but it was going to be a fight.

At the crest of a jangled pile of junk covered in cloth, the footing was treacherous. Sargon met the gorilla-armed man— Moller's first pick. The two exchanged a few feints, then both landed a blow. The long-armed galoot struck Sargon's kidney, it looked like, and a blue-white flash lit up the field.

In the meantime, Sargon had ducked and struck low, going for the knees. His ape-armed opponent went down, shrieking and rolling to the bottom of that jagged pile of junk. Each tumbling spin was a world of hurt, I could tell. By the time he reached the bottom, he was struggling just to get to his knees again.

Sargon plucked the fourth flag and stood triumphant on the top of the junk pile. He held the flag in one hand and his shock-rod in the other. If his kidney pained him, you wouldn't have known it by watching. He was like a king over a domain populated by pygmies. Anyone who dared get close was jabbed with the shaft of the flag, or caught by a glittering sweep of the shock-rod.

All around this center point of the battle the two sides clashed. Most of the struggles were on the slopes of Sargon's hill. Some had flags in their hands, picked up from the hills they'd passed over.

Right then, I realized the exercise wasn't quite going as planned. My tapper buzzed—it was Harris.

"Your men are carrying their flags and using them to whack people!" he complained.

"Your guys are doing the same. No one told them they couldn't!"

"You coached Sargon to play it like this, didn't you?" Harris complained. "Always with the cheating and scheming. You never change, McGill."

Fuming, he disconnected. I shrugged. I hadn't told Sargon to do anything. In fact, I'd made up the rules on the spot. He'd done this on his own, and he'd eliminated the problem of uneven hill distribution. His side had simply run faster. By doing so, they already had a four-to-two advantage in flags.

Unfortunately, I could see that the strain was beginning to show on Sargon. He'd taken that blow to the back, after all, which seemed to be causing him trouble. Having been shocked by rods like this any number of times, I knew that they didn't feel good at first kiss, and it only got worse from there as your numbness and loss of muscle control spread.

After five minutes or so, half the troops were down. Many were rolled up into a painful ball. The rest staggered from shocks and injuries, shouting hoarsely and struggling to battle their opponents. The shock-rods were designed to weaken and exhaust people. The toll was mounting up fast.

Then, Sargon went down. Moller and two of her best recruits had rushed him from multiple sides, transforming his king of the hill dominance from an advantage to a trap. He couldn't defend himself from toe-taps and darting jabs to the legs. His own troops had been pushed back, having acted too independently from the beginning.

When he fell, I stood up and ordered a halt to the contest. "It's over. Moller's squad wins!"

"Say what?" Harris demanded, standing in his own cupola on the opposite side of the chamber. "Centurion, you've got to let them finish! Let her team give Sargon's men a good old-fashioned beat-down!"

Harris had a point. In any normal Legion Varus training, there was no mercy shown by either side. The belief was suffering hardened the troops for the future. After all, aliens weren't known for their kindness and warm consideration.

But I had other plans, so I shook my head. "I don't want them too banged up. We'll repeat this exercise tomorrow—and the next day. Two out of three will determine the winner."

"Holy…" Harris said, and I heard him cursing, but I ignored it.

Sure, I'd changed the rules. Harris would say it was like a kid who'd lost at a game declaring two out of three to be the new standard for victory.

But it was more than that. In reality, the whole fight hadn't lasted long enough. They'd barely gotten warmed up. I planned to have several events over several days, and I wanted all the recruits to be able to participate.

Far from relief, there were a lot of groans among the men. They separated with glowering looks and limped off the field of honor. Shock-rods fizzled and died as they were switched off.

Harris came to complain to me in private later, as I'd known he would.

"That was low, McGill. Even for you, sir."

"It just didn't take long enough," I told him. "We can't have one fifteen minute fight and call that a training."

He eyed me with vast distrust. In battle, I knew he could follow orders and believe in my leadership. But when it came down to games like this, he always suspected I had the worst of motives.

"As you say, Centurion. It's your game, sir."

Muttering, he stalked away. I left the exercise deck, such as it was, and went to our assigned balloon-like module.

The sleeping arrangements were the worst I'd seen since Machine World, where we'd all huddled in freezing, stinking tents. This was similar, but at least there was no icy breeze cutting through the middle of it.

Overhead, a rippling dome of white fabric shifted and glimmered. It was lead-impregnated and all, but I didn't think it was too safe. I mean, sure, we were traveling inside a warp bubble that supposedly nothing could penetrate, but it still felt like we were flying through interstellar space inside a plastic bubble.

"This is bullshit, Centurion," Carlos told me for what had to be the thousandth time since we'd left Earth. "We're all getting an illegally high dose of rads every day."

Now, Carlos was a complainer and loudmouth, but he was also my unit's bio specialist. That made him harder to ignore than usual in this case.

"What am I supposed to do about it?" I asked him. "You want to sleep in the hold next to the warheads? Or maybe inside the exhaust ports? They aren't being used right now."

Carlos only half-listened to me. He was looking up, eyeing the not so distant ceiling which rippled and shivered.

"It's like being inside a big bladder," he said. "A rubbery, shivery bladder that needs to be emptied."

I laughed. "You always were full of piss-and-vinegar!"

He didn't laugh. He stared at me instead. "You know why they think they can get away with this, don't you? Dosing us up with rads? Because they don't expect us to live long, that's why. When this campaign is over, they'll ditch us on whatever craptastic excuse for a planet we're fighting over. When they're sure we're all dead they'll make new copies back home."

Pursing my lips thoughtfully, I nodded. "Sounds about right."

I scratched my cheek. Talk of radiation always seemed to make my skin itch.

Carlos watched the dome overhead. "It's been shivering more than usual. Maybe it's the souls of all those poor bastards who died of heart attacks on your field of honor today."

"Come on. Most of the boys lived. We had only three deaths."

The rubbery roof of our bubble shivered again. A bigger ripple went through it—it was almost like it had folded over on itself like a luffing sail.

"Did you see that?" Carlos demanded, pointing. "Did you see that shit? Tell me you saw that, McGill!"

"Huh…" I gazed up and frowned. That last shiver—it *had* been something new and alarming. After a weeklong voyage, I'd gotten kind of used to our minimal quarters, but this…

A klaxon sounded a few moments later, making us both jump half out of our skins.

"Emergency procedures initiated. All personnel must follow their required paths. All personnel…"

The computer voice repeated itself, and the floor lit up. Dark red arrows stood out on the deck under our boots. That was our color, because we were combat troops. Following the path at a trot, we were quickly joined by a hundred others.

We jammed up at the emergency exit, which amounted to a hatch in the deck. Have you ever tried to get a hundred panicked people through a one-meter hole in the floor? It wasn't pretty.

"One at time!" I roared. "Moller, supervise the escape!"

"Sir!" Moller started grabbing each escaping soldier with her fat hands, then she rammed them into the hole as soon as there was room below.

"You realize that hatch is really an external exit from the hull," Carlos said. "We've been living in a bubble on the outside of *Berlin*."

"I sure do. So what?"

"There's absolutely no way we can all fit inside this battlecruiser. If we're out here for another minute longer, they're going to close that hatch and let us die."

Thinking about that for a second, I couldn't find a flaw in his logic. "You're probably right."

-21-

When about half the troops were down the escape hatch, Carlos' prediction came true. The hatch abruptly closed, snicking shut from the side like a cigar cutter. One man was shorn in half, and another lost a hand at the wrist.

Carlos and I were still standing around on the outer hull at that point. We had fifty-odd people with us. One of them was Moller.

"Centurion," she said without a quaver in her voice. "The ship's full-up."

I nodded. "I figured."

"That's all you're going to say?" Carlos demanded while he patched up the man with the missing hand. The injured recruit was howling something awful, so I squelched his mic with my HUD controls.

"Don't go and piss yourself," I told Carlos. "We're either screwed, or we aren't. Not much we can do about it at this point."

Life in the legions was often glorified by the press. When actors pretended to be one of our kind in a feelie, they especially liked to romanticize space travel.

The truth was, grunts like us hated being aboard ship. When a foot soldier was inside any warship, even a big bastard like this one, you were canned meat. You couldn't do much to defend yourself, and you were just cargo in the eyes of the crew.

That's what we were: irritating, stinking cargo that fussed and ate too much.

"Okay," I said, looking over the group. "Sargon's team made it down—very genteel of you, Moller—and so did all my officers. We'll form up two platoons, Moller you take your people. I'll take the rest."

She organized the troops while Carlos left the one-handed guy behind after giving him a speech about being a "big boy". He soon came and stood at my side again.

"What are we going to do?" he asked.

"We'll gear-up on the off-chance we can be useful. In the meantime, are there any techs left?"

Natasha had escaped, but Kivi was still on hand. I told her what I wanted, and she went to work on it right away. "I can do that," she said. "Natasha isn't the only hacker on this ship."

Nodding, I let her try to get into the network and synch with *Berlin's* bridge channel. These days, the crew operated on different channels than the legion they were carrying. It sort of made sense.

While in space, *Berlin's* captain was in charge of the mission. When we landed, however, the Varus tribune would take over. That was made abundantly clear to Turov after certain misunderstandings occurred during the Clone World Campaign.

The long and the short of it was that Kivi had to hack into the crew's command channels in order to find out what was happening to the ship. The Varus command chain had been cut out and separated.

"Everyone shut up!" she said, closing her eyes so she could focus. "I'm getting lots of chatter... There's been some kind of accident."

"Like hell there has," I said. "Sabotage more like—or an attack."

She put a hand up in my face. I shut up sourly. I knew she was listening to a lot of channels and voices at once, all mixed together, and probably without the best sound quality.

"I don't know..." she said at last, putting down her ear piece. "Something happened to the generators. The power from the main banks has gone down. We've still got batteries and emergency backups, but it's not enough to fight with if we had to fight right now."

"Seriously?" Carlos demanded from behind me. "Why the hell would that make them order everyone to get below decks?"

I turned around to face him. He'd snuck up on us. I would have chased him off if I'd seen he was listening in.

"Some fuck-tard tripped on a cord!" he shouted over his shoulder to the others. Then he turned back to us. "I was shitting myself. I owe the guy who did this a—"

"I'm going to give you a swift kick in the pants if you don't shut up," I told him.

Knowing I was serious, he walked away muttering.

"Is he right?" I asked Kivi. "Is this all just precautionary?"

She was listening in again, eyes clenched. "Carlos is an idiot… but he would be right, except…" She opened her eyes looked up at me in sudden alarm. "James, the warp bubble—we're losing power. They're going to shut it down!"

Her eyes were full of fright, but I didn't get it.

"Yeah, so? We'll go back to normal space right? Is that the worst case?"

"You don't understand. We're standing inside a warp bubble. Only a thin lead-impregnated sheet exists between us and that bubble. If they don't shut down properly, if it dies with an unstable glitch—we'll be fried out here by a wave of electromagnetic radiation."

She looked around at the shivering bladder thing. I did the same.

I finally got it. The Alcubierre warp drive had been only theory a century ago, but it was a reality in modern times. The trick had always been in turning on and off the drive without destroying the ship or irradiating it with so many rads everyone inside died.

The start-up and shutdown were the dangerous parts—just like the takeoff and landing of an aircraft, only worse. The field had to be brought up and maintained in the space around the ship, forming a bubble in which everything seemed relatively stable. Outside of it, of course, space was whizzing by faster than the speed of light.

"Uh…" I said, looking at the shivering rubber ceiling with growing alarm. "Maybe we should find shelter after all."

"There's no point," Kivi said, shrugging. "If this goes badly, they'll know we were all fried. That's good enough. At least we won't be permed."

I frowned fiercely. I would normally get drunk or something. I even kept a squeeze bottle in my private sleeping box for that express purpose. I briefly considered asking Kivi to join me in there. We'd had a thing for each other years back.

But it seemed wrong to be pondering ways to go out with a smile. Not yet, anyway.

"There's something strange about this accident," I said aloud. "In fact, I don't think it was an accident at all. "Why not?"

"Because you said *all* the generators failed. What are the odds of that? All of them dying on us—all at once?"

She stared at me and nodded. "It is strange. They are built to back each other up."

"It could be nine kinds of a coincidence—but I don't believe in crap like that."

She shrugged helplessly. "What can we do about it?"

I pointed at the closed and sealed hatch in the deck. "That's just an external hatch, like Carlos said."

"Yes, but—"

"Let's find another one."

Kivi looked startled. "Outside, you mean? Outside our protective bubble?"

I laughed and hopped up high enough to punch the bubble. It wobbled and shimmied more than before. "It's not protecting anyone today."

"Don't do that, you crazy fuck! You'll rip it!"

Nodding, I flipped out my combat knife. The diamond edge glittered.

"Oh yeah…" Carlos said, walking up to us again. He'd been malingering not far off. I had to give him a pass on that, however, as the bubble wasn't really big enough for anyone to be alone.

"This is what I expected," he said with a sad shake of the head. "Mayhem and death."

I looked at him. "I'm going outside to look for another exit. Are you game to come with me?"

"You know I am, big guy. We're as good as cooked anyway."

"You two are ditching me?" Kivi complained.

"Three's a crowd," Carlos told her.

Before she could launch into an angry tirade, I put up a cautionary glove. "We're probably all dead no matter what we do. There's a chance you'll hear something useful from the bridge crew—or they might even open the hatch to let a few more in."

Kivi twisted up her face, thinking it over. "All right. I'll sit here and wait. They might find a way to squeeze us inside. Or maybe they'll fix the generators before the batteries give out and the field dies. You guys can go fry yourselves together if you want."

"Eggs and bacon, baby!" Carlos said, tugging at my arm. "Let's go do this."

Giving a warning to everyone that they should flip their faceplates down, I walked to the back end of the bubble and made a slit.

Immediately, the air began to hiss out in a gush. After all, the ship was in an empty vacuum. There were some screams as the whole bladder began to flatten.

I stepped out quickly and Carlos joined me. On the far side, I could see Kivi spraying sealant to close the wound we'd made. I could see her face through the faceplate, and she mouthed "luck" inside her helmet.

After that, she sealed the cut entirely, and we stood out in the open.

For some reason, I'd kind of expected to see stars out here. After all, we were standing on a spaceship's hull hurtling through empty space.

But there were no stars. There was only a diffuse white light. It was weird, like we'd stepped out of the world to somewhere else. I knew that I was looking at the interior of the warp field itself.

The hull of the battlecruiser was clear enough to see, however. We paced along over it, looking for more hatches. In the distance, the other bladders were pitched like tents. They were kind of close together, if the truth were to be told. Each unit had its own tent, and there were around a hundred units in a legion.

"It looks like some kind of campground," Carlos said. His radio had automatically synched up with my helmet forming a local chat group. "Maybe we can find that hot adjunct from the fifth—what was her name? Oh yeah, Beverly. If we could cut our way into her bubble and rescue her—"

"Shut up," I told him absently. "Look for an external hatch."

We walked around between the bubbles for a good two minutes, but we saw nothing else.

"I've got bad news to break to you, big guy," Carlos said at last. "We're totally wasting our time. Every hatch has a rubbery white bubble sitting on it."

"Yeah..." I admitted. "Let's go forward, to the gun mounts."

"What the hell for?"

"There's got to be an external hatch on those big turrets. How else would the crew do maintenance?"

Heaving a sigh, he followed me. We clumped along on the hull for a while. Each step rang in our ears as the magnetics took hold and kept us from floating away. There wasn't any gravity or air out here—and nothing much else, either.

After about a five minute walk, my tapper beeped. It was Kivi.

"James, you've only got a few minutes left. A warning just went out for the crew—the field is weakening due to the dropping power levels. If you—"

I couldn't hear the rest. Partly, this was because I was now clumping along at a vastly increased pace over the metal deck. I wasn't exactly sprinting, but I was moving as fast as my automated magnetics could grab and release. I soon left Carlos behind, as he had shorter legs.

"Damn you McGill! Don't ditch me, man!"

I kept going, and soon he howled. "The field is losing integrity!"

I glanced up, and I saw he was right. The field was no longer misty white. It now ran with glassy electric colors. To me, it looked like the Northern Lights in the Arctic Circle. Rainbow arcs flew and silently connected with the deck. At one point, I saw one of the rubbery bubbles blast apart. Dark shapes—probably troops left to die out here—were flung away in all directions.

Hustling and breathing hard, I reached the nearest of *Berlin*'s great guns. Unlike the broadsides on a transport ship, these guns were fully independent. They were big and mean-looking. Each turret had four tubes, a box-pattern of cannons jutting up at the sky.

There was a hatch on the side of the turret. It had a wheel on it. Gripping the wheel, my arms bulged.

More lightening flashed behind me. A sheet of it crashed down, a colorful gush of light and power that would have made any primitive man's guts let go in terror. A whole cluster of the rubbery bubbles were blown apart, leaving only scorch marks on the warship's tough hide.

"McGill!" I heard Carlos call on the radio. Then it buzzed and cut out. When it came back, he was in midsentence. "—leave me out here, you prick!"

The wheel was spinning, I had the hatch open. It was dark inside. Crawling in, I looked back when my boots let go of the deck.

Outside, the universe had gone mad. The surface of the ship was buzzing with random discharges. I could feel the shocks coming through my suit, stinging my hands and my ass—anything that was touching metal.

Carlos was only a few paces away. I could see his face in the flashing, colored lights. He looked hopeful, desperate.

Then another surge came down. This one was like a wave of lightning—a connection point that went on and on, dragging itself like a brief tornado over the hull, destroying anything it came into contact with.

One thing it touched was Carlos. One moment he was there, reaching for the hatch I'd left cracked open, the next, there were only two blackened boots, still clinging by the magic of their magnetics to the hull.

I slammed the hatch shut behind me and spun the wheel.

-22-

The inside of a battlecruiser's turret is never roomy. The dark region I'd taken refuge in was more of a crawlspace than a chamber. Scrambling over thick cables, hanging pieces of insulation and the like, I wormed my way down to another hatch in the deck.

There, I hesitated. After all, I wasn't supposed to be inside the ship at all. I was supposed to be trapped out on the exterior enjoying the lightshow like all the unfortunates I'd left behind.

After about five seconds of thinking it over, I shrugged and spun the wheel to open the hatch. Hunkering inside this crawlspace for the next week or two didn't appeal.

I half fell out and onto the deck below. My entrance was anything but grand, but I did cause a commotion. I'd fallen on a number of people who were huddled in the passage. They were sitting in lines, butt-to-butt, as far as the eye could see in either direction.

Those I fell on grunted and snarled in pain, as I was a big load when I land on a person all at once.

"Gee-*zus*!" called out a veteran with a stern eye. He gave me a sharp punch to the ribs. "What's wrong with you, you giant moron—?"

He broke off, no doubt having caught sight of the twin red crests on my shoulders.

These insignia marked me as an officer.

"Oh… ah… sorry Centurion, sir. Let me help you up. You startled me is all."

"He damn near broke my neck," complained another trooper nearby.

"Sorry about that," I told them as I climbed to my feet and smiled good-naturedly. "My mamma made me wrong. I came out too big, she always says."

"You can say that again," complained the one rubbing his neck.

The veteran gave him a swift kick to shut him up, then turned a false smile in my direction. "Can I give you directions to your unit, sir?" he asked. "As you can see, we're all full-up in this passageway."

He made a grand sweep with his arm, and I couldn't argue. Every boot, butt cheek and shoulder was pressing up against the next guy.

"I'll find my own way, thank you kindly."

Turning in a random direction, I stumped off. I ignored the surprised eyes and darting limbs of everyone I approached. They squirmed and squeezed to get out of my way. No one wanted to have my size thirteen magnetics clump down on top of them. The troops made room, even though there wasn't any.

It took me a good half-hour of stomping around overcrowded decks to find the rest of my unit. Half of Legion Varus was huddling in misery inside *Berlin*, and I could see why they'd ordered the hatches shut after the battlecruiser had filled up.

After fielding a few welcoming hoots and calls from my boys when they saw me, I was greeted by a tall thin woman in a crewman's uniform. She seemed familiar, but it took me a moment to place her. At last, I did.

"Centurion Leeza?" I demanded in surprise. "What are you doing here, girl?"

She peered up at me. She'd been Armel's staffer, sidekick and reportedly even his lover before he'd gone rogue. Despite those almost inexcusable lapses of judgment, I'd found her to be an otherwise intelligent person.

"McGill…?" she asked with surprise almost equal to my own. "I'm an ensign now. I've gone Fleet."

She had a slightly euro accent and attitude to match, but I didn't mind. It was nice to see her alive again.

"Fleet, huh? That's a surprise."

Leeza shrugged. "To me as well. I can't seem to recall signing the transfer request." She studied her tablet, which was linked to her tapper. She shook her head. "There's something wrong, Centurion. You're not supposed to be here at all. You're marked as dead."

She eyed me with a mix of suspicion and curiosity. I got a lot of that look, especially from women.

Ensign Leeza, however, was a special case. Back on Clone World, I'd executed her for treason. She didn't remember anything about those events, fortunately. She'd been revived with a few months of her engrams missing, just like Winslade. I figured now wasn't the time to try to explain anything complicated to her.

"Huh..." I said. "The computer must have made a mistake. I'm feeling fine."

She shook her head in disbelief and poked at her tablet. "How did you get back out of the oven already? No revives have been scheduled until we reach the target planet. There isn't a girlfriend down on Blue Deck I should be talking to, is there?"

"No Ensign, nothing like that. I never even died. I just found another hatch and entered that way, see."

Eyeing me, she nodded after a few seconds. "Of course you did... as I recall, you're a difficult man to kill."

"Trying to get rid of James McGill is almost hopeless. It's like stomping at a rat in your bare feet."

"Okay then, I've edited the roster. You're officially back with your unit and in command. Now, if you'll excuse me."

She moved to brush by, but I gently caught her arm. She frowned down at my fingers like they were snakes.

"Hey, just between us," I said in her ear, "what happened to the ship? It's like a lightning storm is out there sweeping the hull clean. I think the warp bubble is breaking up."

She eyed me in alarm. "You saw that? You should get your dosimeter checked. The radiation—"

"Yeah, yeah. I know all about that. But what happened?"

She slid her arm out of my grip, but she didn't walk off immediately. "There was a power malfunction," she said in a low tone. "The techs managed to stabilize it, but we almost lost the bubble. They say a full, sudden collapse of the field could have destroyed the ship."

"Sabotage?"

"Who knows?" she said, shrugging. "Now, if you don't mind, I have to get back to Winslade and turn in this report."

I grabbed her arm again. This time, she looked like she wanted to cut it off.

"Sorry," I said, letting go quickly. "Just tell me one more thing: Why is a Fleet ensign reporting to a hog like Winslade? And what's he doing aboard *Berlin* in the first place?"

"He's an observer for Hegemony. I understand that he's been posted aboard as part of a watchdog effort—the focus of which is your Legion Varus."

"He must have some new, powerful friends," I said. "I wonder who…" I trailed off as I realized who the friend had to be. "That Wurtenberger guy… He's been playing the part of Winslade's guardian angel lately, making arrangements for him all over. It's like they're related or something."

Leeza shrugged and walked off again, but she hadn't taken a dozen steps before she turned to glance over her shoulder.

I was thumping along right behind her.

"McGill? Is this the prelude to an ill-advised attempt to seduce me?"

"Huh…? Oh… no, no, Ensign! Not that you aren't pretty and all, but I have other goals in mind today."

"Then just where are you going?" she demanded. "Why are you following me?"

"I want to see Winslade. I've got some questions for him."

Shaking her head, she turned away again, and I followed her through the passages.

Frequently, when the hunkering men saw me coming, they groaned in dismay. Leeza could slip through any crack like a ghost—but not me. I was more like a wandering elephant, and every now and then some sorry-ass recruit got a stray appendage stomped flat while he was dozing with his head against a wall.

Some things just couldn't be helped, I guess.

-23-

"McGill?" Winslade said in his least inviting tone. "Seriously?"

Considering all the effort I'd gone through to meet with him in person, I would have figured he'd be more polite about it. But not old Winslade. There was no help for the man when it came to having better manners.

"That's right, Centurion," I said, giving him a smile and offering him a big hand to shake.

He ignored both of these and turned to Leeza instead. "Pass me those personnel reports, Ensign."

She did so, flicking them from her tapper to his.

"Dismissed," he said to her in his usual, kind of snotty tone.

I frowned as I watched all this and saw her slip away into the sweaty crowds.

"Winslade, you've never had the touch with women, have you?"

He gave me a pursed-lip stare. I knew he wanted to order me out of his face already, but he couldn't, because he didn't outrank me. Not today. That part was kind of nice.

"I'm not trying to molest every female that comes within reach," he said, "if that's what you mean."

"See there? That's the source of your problem. You're probably the sort who finds flaws in most of the women you meet. So, you either skip opportunities, or you…"

He stared at me with hostile eyes.

"Uh… just trying to help."

"Mind your own business, will you, McGill?"

"Okay, okay. What I'm really here to talk about is what happened to the ship. Did you know the warp bubble almost collapsed? That would have been a sure-fire way to get us all permed if it had happened."

"What are you going on about?" he said, studying his computer paper.

"Just that. If this ship was lost while in warp this far out… well, they might never find a trace. Not even a burnt streak of molecules unique enough to identify. We'd be just so much interstellar gas out here, and they couldn't revive the legion without a verifiable report on our demise, now could they?"

Winslade pursed his lips and seemed to consider my words. "Well, fortunately, that didn't happen. Now, if you'd be so kind—"

"After giving my thanks to the Almighty for that reprieve, it came to me that there are certain mysteries aboard this ship that might deserve a second glance."

He peered at me, shifting up his eyes away from his computer, but not his head. "Such as?"

"Such as the rare odds of all our generators going down at once. It's not supposed to happen that way, you know. There are fail-safes and all kinds of backups."

"Hmm," he said, tapping his lips with a stylus. "I suppose that you're right, there must be safeguards."

"So, sabotage comes to mind as the likely explanation."

He was looking up fully now, and we locked eyes on each other. I was still smiling, but he wasn't, and no one who saw the two of us would have been fooled for more than an instant.

"Why that?" he asked quietly.

"Because it makes the most sense. Don't you see it? My mamma didn't raise a fool. Those power generators didn't all switch themselves off at once, now did they?"

"What are you suggesting, Centurion? What *exactly* has gotten into that Neanderthal's skull of yours?"

He'd lowered his voice, so I lowered mine to match.

"Just this: you're not supposed to be here, Winslade. You're supposed to be dead, permed back when we dusted off the last of Claver's legions. Instead, you're living, breathing, and bitterly poking around on my legion's ship."

"That's pure speculation on your part, McGill."

"Yeah? We'll see about that. Out here, we're in deep space, and we're in warp. Praetor Wurtenburger can't save your ass. You can't even call on him for help. You remember that."

I turned to walk off, but he called after me. "You should watch yourself, McGill. I gave you a pass earlier because you were honest with me aboard the sky train."

"Gave me a pass?" I demanded, coming back around on him. "What fate did I escape?"

"A grim one, let me assure you. I have friends now, powerful ones. I'd advise you—"

I reached out and grabbed up a wad of his flimsy spacer suit. Lifting him half-off his feet, I noted the lower level troops around us were looking antsy. They didn't know if they should try to intervene or not. After all, we were the same rank. If two officers of the same rank wanted to have a duel, it was acceptable behavior in Legion Varus, just as it had been in Napoleon's army, or almost any other organized force in the past.

"Your friends aren't aboard this battlecruiser, Winslade. But I am. So let me advise you to keep yourself out of trouble for the rest of this voyage."

He glared at me, but he shut up. I put him back on his feet. There was a needler in his hand, but there was a combat knife in mine. We both would have been seriously injured or maybe dead if either of us had gone further.

As I walked away, I tossed a glance or two back at him. He was shaking his head, glaring at me. At last, as I got to the next corner, just about to turn it, I saw him look down again at his computer paper.

That's when I shot him down.

Sure, it was a dirty trick. But I had my reasons. I suspected that Winslade had done something to the ship's power systems. Why, I wasn't sure, but I couldn't afford for the whole legion to go missing in space. I had a daughter to go home to and plenty of women to meet and make friends with. Not to mention countless aliens to kill.

Isn't it worth one man's life, and possibly a slight loss of honor, in order to stop everyone you know from being permed? In my book, killing Winslade by surprise was a no-brainer.

-24-

It's tough to hold a trial, or even an investigation, on a ship so full of soldiers they were sleeping in lockers. But I had to hand it to Graves, he gave it a solid try.

"McGill," he said, confronting me with the same sour expression everyone seemed to be wearing today. "What you did today doesn't qualify as a duel. The old-fashioned word for it is murder."

"I'd call it a duel," I said firmly. "He even drew first. He had a needler in his hand, didn't he?"

"We have a dozen witnesses and camera shots of the action," Graves said tiredly. "You walked away, waited until he looked down, then shot him."

"That's a damned lie, sir!" I boomed in the most convincing tone I could muster. "Sometimes, you just have to be there at the scene."

Graves heaved a sigh. He turned to Turov, the only other person in the office.

Galina's modest office was also her cabin now, and only her high rank allowed her to keep it.

"That's all we're going to get out of him," he told her. "Grade-A Georgia bullshit. I suggest we demote and execute. We can revive him when we arrive at Tau Orionis—or even when we return to Earth. He's supposed to be dead anyway."

"But he isn't," Galina said, eyeing me. "And we can't very well revive anyone, not even Winslade. No one below the rank

130

of primus will get a revive on this ship until we reach our destination. It's too crowded."

Graves shrugged. "So? We'll revive them both when we arrive and leave warp."

"McGill?" Turov asked me, ignoring Graves. "There's one thing you never explained... Why did you do it?"

"I told you, sirs. He had a weapon—a concealed weapon in his hand. I had no choice but to defend myself."

Galina rolled her eyes. "I'm trying to help you, you oaf. Talk to me."

It was my turn to look uncomfortable. After all, any further discussion of what had transpired between Winslade and I lately could become messy. I'd avoided telling them I'd given him hints concerning his past, and why he'd been demoted. Sometimes, people took my blabbing about secret information like that the wrong way.

Heaving a sigh of my own, I decided to come clean—partway, that is.

"He was the saboteur," I said. "The man who damaged the power generators."

Both of them shifted with sudden interest. They'd been bored just moments earlier, but this was information they cared about.

"Proof?" Graves demanded. "Do you have proof of these accusations, McGill?"

"I sure do! Those shifty eyes, that needler in his palm—only a guilty man would react like that!"

Graves crossed his arms and frowned at me. "That's not proof, McGill."

"It is where I come from. He's as guilty as sin, sirs. Mark my words."

"Hunches and intuition do not constitute proof, McGill."

"But the stakes were too high! I *had* to kill him! If I was right, and he succeeded the next time he tried, we'd all be toast. You'd be just a few grams of dust and gas sailing through space, Primus. There wouldn't even be enough left of all of us combined to fill a mason jar."

Graves didn't look happy, but Turov chose that moment to intervene. "You're saying you acted out of an abundance of caution? That isn't like you—rash action is, but not caution."

"I had to save the ship. I had to save us all. You let him stay on ice, we'll see if there are any more mysterious accidents on the way out to our destination."

She nodded. "All right. We'll do just that. We will table the matter until after we arrive at Tau Orionis."

Graves grumbled lightly, and I managed not to gloat. I kept a serious expression on my face throughout, until after Graves had left.

Standing up and reaching for the door, I heard Galina's voice behind me.

"Not so fast, McGill," she said. "Why did you really kill him?"

Turning around, I faced her. She was looking just as suspicious, and cute, as usual.

"Winslade is a snake on the best of days," I told her. "He knows something is up. He knows he died out at Clone World and that he lost his memories. He's not too happy about the demotion, either."

"What I don't understand is how he's gotten the ear of Wurtenberger so quickly. I've been trying to charm that man for years. He's a fat lump of stone."

That made sense to me. I knew that Galina was gifted when it came to gathering high-level patrons. These were usually older, figurehead-types among the brass. Political people who'd gotten their jobs through family and influence. Everyone at that level seemed to like meeting a smart, fast-talking young lady—even the women.

Galina wasn't actually young, mind you, but she looked the part. Often, that was all that mattered. She never let herself get older than mid-twenties. When she did, she arranged to be quietly killed somehow to freshen up her appearance. Some people would do just about anything to keep looking good.

"I could try to find out..." I said.

"How? Interrogation? You've already killed him, you brute. And no, I won't revive him just so you can do it again."

"Okay... but I've got other leads to follow up on."

I was bullshitting, but Galina bought it. She'd had a rivalry going with Winslade for many years now. When I'd first met the two of them, he'd been her lackey. Now, as the years rolled by, he'd come into his own in matters of intrigue and scheming. He no longer operated as a henchman. He had personal ambitions, and he'd learned from the best as to how to achieve them.

"Really?" she said. "If you succeed... I would be grateful."

"How grateful?" I asked, and I slipped an arm around her.

Her eyes widened. "James! We're aboard a packed battlecruiser. Absolutely no one on this ship is getting laid until we reach our destination."

I smiled. "Where there's a will, there's a way."

She glanced around, and I pulled her gently up against me. She was still tense, still pushing me off a little, so I didn't paw at her. She had to choose.

Finally, she melted and put her head against my chest. "I like that you killed him. He's been pissing me off lately."

That seemed like a strange reason to make love, but I wasn't the picky type. I gently kissed her, and soon we were in a clinch. The next hour or so passed very pleasantly.

Outside our door, we could hear people shuffle and occasionally thump into the walls. They were so crowded out there they would have been scandalized to see what was going on in the only private chamber aboard the *U. E. Berlin*.

Accordingly, we kept things as quiet as we could.

-25-

Eleven cramped days passed before we finally reached our destination. I don't think the legion was ever so happy to see a strange sun loom bright and close as it was with Tau Orionis. We were ready to get off the *U. E. Berlin* anywhere we could.

Despite our urgency to invade, when the engineers let the warp bubble fade away we all cringed. We half-expected the ship to blow up or something—but it didn't. *Berlin* slid into far orbit just like she was supposed to.

We arrived at a cautious distance from the central star, some eight hundred million kilometers out. That's about the orbital range of Jupiter back home.

"That reentry was as slick as a hog-pie!" I announced loudly.

Graves and Turov glanced at me. They knew I was hinting around that I'd been right about Winslade. We'd had zero problems aboard since I'd put that snake on ice.

"Project the environment," Turov ordered the navigators.

Captain Merton seemed irritated about this. He was a chunky man with black hair and a round face that always looked like it needed a shave. He'd been our captain aboard *Legate*, and since he'd lost his command they'd given him the captured *Berlin* to tool around in.

That might have seemed like a sweet upgrade for a transport flyer, but Merton also got Varus to go with his new ship. That part he wasn't so keen on. In particular, he didn't like Turov and her power-grabbing ways.

Before his crew could so much as reach for the control boards that displayed data on the central holotank, Merton put up his own hand to stop them.

"I want abstract information only," he said in a commanding tone. "A tactical sitrep. Leave all planets and other contacts displayed in wireframe."

Slowly, Turov turned to give him an awful look. All the way out here to Tau Orionis, she'd let him run his bridge the way he liked. But now that we'd reached our destination, to her way of thinking, she was in charge of the mission.

"Captain," she said in an acidic tone, "perhaps there's some kind of misunderstanding—"

Without even looking at her, he whipped out a scrap of computer paper and held it under her nose. When she didn't take it right off, he rattled it impatiently.

"New orders?" she asked in a deceptively quiet voice. I knew when I heard that voice that she was in an evil mood.

"Nothing new here. These were given to me as we left Earth. They stipulate the exact circumstances under which you are in command on this bridge."

"And what circumstances are those?"

He gave her a slight smile. "No circumstances at all, as it turns out. In brief, they say that while on the ground, you are in charge of your legion. While aboard *Berlin*—I'm in charge of everything. Surely you've noticed we're all still on board?"

She snatched away the rolled up computer paper and glanced at it. "You could have shown this to me earlier."

Captain Merton shrugged his lumpy shoulders. "It didn't apply."

No one was fooled, least of all Turov. The captain had wanted to make sure she couldn't argue about the orders, possibly getting them changed by someone back home. By dropping them into her face at the last moment, he was assured they'd be followed—at least for now.

"All right," Turov said. "I'll leave you to it, then. Alert me when you're in position to drop my troops."

The captain looked surprised, but he didn't argue. He watched her saunter off the deck.

I watched the imagery pouring in now. There was plenty from the sensors, and most of it I didn't really understand.

"Zoom in on the target planet," Merton ordered.

Immediately, sickeningly, a spinning globe grew and soon filled the center of the deck. I gaped at it. The planet looked lovely.

"They make stardust armor on this tropical paradise?" I asked incredulously. "We must have the wrong place."

"It's the right world..." the captain said. He was suddenly in a good mood and willing to entertain my questions. Up until today he'd barely tolerated me on the bridge. I guess that Galina's retreat had uplifted his spirits. "You see those crystalline zones? The regions that resemble shiny mountain ranges?"

"Huh... yeah, I guess. I thought they were reflections off of some ocean."

"No, they're glass-like zones of silicates. Crystals the size of glaciers. They move, too. In any case, those regions have been dusted with compressed matter. That said, most of this world is fairly normal—even pleasant."

"I'll be damned..." I stared as the techs zoomed in for a tighter shot. I could see there was a jungle along the equator, shallow seas with white beaches here and there, and cooler, darker green forests near the poles. Overall, it looked like a nice place to take a vacation.

"We'll make planetfall within forty hours," the captain told me.

"Plenty of time to gear up the troops for the drop."

Captain Merton glanced at me then, frowning. "Don't you want to answer that?" he asked.

"Huh? Oh..."

My tapper was buzzing. There was red text all over it. I'd been so busy eyeballing the new planet I hadn't really noticed.

Turning my wrist so only my eyes could read the messages, I found they were rather simple and direct in nature.

The first one said: *KILL THAT FAT FUCK RIGHT NOW.*

I didn't bother to read the rest. They were all from Galina. Swiftly, and managing not to look alarmed, I slid my sleeve down over my arm to cover my tapper.

"Looks important," the captain said, eyeing me.

"Nah. It's no big deal. It's my birthday today. My adjuncts are throwing a surprise party—but I'm in on it."

"I see..." he said in a monotone. I didn't know if he believed me or not, and I didn't much care.

The captain continued talking, showing me the various features of the planet we were supposed to invade. I found the place captivating, and he seemed to be entranced as well.

We'd both been expecting something nasty, maybe with volcanic action and poison dust kicking up everywhere. But Tau Orionis wasn't like that at all. Apparently, whenever the planet had received its close encounter with a neutron star, it had been a long, long time ago. The special materials we were after had sunk deep into the crust. They'd have to be mined out of those glassy mountains.

All the while we talked and marveled together, my tapper kept buzzing intermittently, but I didn't bother to check the messages. I knew who it was, and what she wanted.

What I was thinking about was the order I'd gotten from Turov. I could do it, of course. Hell, I wouldn't even have to break a sweat. The captain was standing near, and he didn't look like he worked out much or anything.

The trick would be to make it look accidental. The bridge marines, who were staring with interest at the planet, wouldn't get in the way for the initial act. But they would surely throw a fuss over their dead captain after the deed was done.

Would they have to die too? It seemed likely.

I began to frown. After all, Galina didn't really have any right to ask me to do this. I knew she was pissed off and all, but killing this captain on his own bridge—well, it just didn't seem right to me.

"Could I see those orders, sir?" I asked him.

Merton looked at me. He considered me seriously for a moment, then he nodded and handed them over.

I skimmed the document. It was signed by all the right people. A single page in length, the words were clear and to the point. Merton was in command in space, Turov on the ground. That was that.

Handing the slip of plastic back to him, I gave him a salute. "With your permission, sir, I'd like to leave the bridge."

Merton nodded slowly, but he put up a hand when I turned to go. "They told me you were a just man, McGill."

"Uh… they did?"

"Yes. I'm glad to see my information was correct."

"Yes, sir."

"Dismissed."

I walked off the bridge, wondering about several things at once. One thought was foremost in my mind, however: I was going to have to have a talk with Tribune Galina Turov.

-26-

After I traversed through a dozen bump-butt passages, I reached her private cabin and office. She didn't answer when I hammered on the door.

There were plenty of crewmen and troops around. They were slouching all over the deck. Some had rigged up hammocks that hung from the ceiling, the walls—anywhere they could find a little space of their own.

The men were nudging one another and smirking. The women were looking huffy and disgusted. It had been impossible, naturally, for Galina and I to keep our illicit meetings on the down-low. With such a cramped ship and all, I figured everyone aboard knew we were screwing by now.

None of this dissuaded me from thumping that door. I knew she was in there—I'd checked with my tapper.

Finally, the door flew open. The interior was dark.

I hesitated before stepping inside. After all, she'd just ordered me to murder a man, which meant by definition she was in an unpleasant mood.

"Uh... Tribune?" I called out vaguely.

There was no response, so I decided to man-up and avoid all the eye-rolling giggles at the same time. I stepped inside and closed the door behind me.

The interior was seriously dark, and it stayed that way, even when I touched the wall panels. She must have muted the switches.

"Uh…" I said, uncertain, "are you depressed or something?"

"Or something," she said.

It didn't take a genius to realize I might have made a mistake coming here, but I was already in her room, so I figured I might as well go all the way.

"Where do you get off ordering me to murder a ship's captain in the middle of a campaign?"

She didn't answer me right off. My eyes were adjusting to the light—or rather the lack of it. She was sitting at her desk in the dark.

It was the glow of her tapper that had caught my eye. She was fluttering her fingers over it like a pro.

"Huh," I said. "Nothing to say for yourself? You were out of line today, and Merton knew what you told me to do. He stood around like he was curious to find out if I'd do it or not."

Finally, she raised her eyes and touched a lamp on the desk. Soft light filled the cabin. "You failed me today, McGill," she said, flopping back in her chair and sighing. "And yes, in answer to your question, I'm miserable."

"Why's that, exactly? We'll get to Tau Orionis soon enough, and you'll be in charge then."

"It's not just about being in charge, James. It's about influence. About controlling one's own destiny. Today's failure predicts more failure tomorrow."

I snorted. "I'm never in control of my destiny—at least, not often. Not unless I'm willing to go rogue and piss everyone off. I'm a soldier. Most of the time, I get ordered around—to fight, and die."

"Yes… Don't worry about it. You have failed—but others will take your place."

"Others? What, have you been screwing everyone on the deck to get them to play assassin for you?"

Right off, after the words were all the way out of my mouth, I regretted them. It was a rude thing to say, but still, I wanted to know the answer.

I expected her to get mad, but she didn't. She smiled faintly instead. "You're jealous.

Actually involved. I'm flattered—but no, I didn't have sex with you or anyone else on this boring ship in order to kill Merton. I'm not that prescient, unfortunately. I fell into a rage, and I tried to lash out at the cause of my anger, that's all."

A few blinks later, I relaxed some. Galina wasn't screwing anyone, and she didn't seem all that angry. In fact, she even seemed to realize that she'd been in the wrong in this situation. That was a whole bundle of good news for me.

But then I went back over her words in my mind... She'd mentioned others before, and I'd been thinking about her in a personal sense... but she hadn't meant that.

"You've got assassins aboard?" I asked her, "...and you sicced them on Merton?"

She nodded. "Like I said, don't worry about it. Have a drink with me. We'll be landing on Tau Orionis soon."

I considered it. I honestly did—but I couldn't. I excused myself and hurried back up to the bridge.

I was too late. By the time I got there, Merton was dead on the deck. He'd had a heart attack.

"Most unfortunate..." Galina said from behind me.

I straightened up and cast a very suspicious eye in her direction. She ignored this and stalked over the deck like a cat that had caught all six canaries.

"Our brave captain must have been working too hard. Well, he's in for a rest now. I'm assuming command, as has been stipulated by these orders from Central."

Galina stooped and plucked a rattling slip of computer paper from Merton's dead hand.

She straightened again, and she looked around at the rest of the ship's officers. "Oh... that is, unless any one among the flight crew would like to challenge my authority?"

She said this in a voice that was low, and almost sweet—but no one was fooled. They didn't even move. They just stared at her from their posts.

"Good," she purred. "Let's go over our approach vectors. I see that corrections must be made immediately."

Turov took over, and the crew let her. No one else wanted to be left lingering in the revival queue just to make a moral stand.

-27-

Galina and I cooled it after that. We didn't contact each other, not even officially. That was okay by me—except for the poor sleeping conditions.

About forty hours later, I found myself happy to suit up and drop on Tau Orionis. Remarkably, I found myself looking forward to the invasion step—anything was better than sleeping in a locker or a warhead casing.

As my unit had mostly lived, the higher-ups had decided to allow a few revives of key personnel to flesh out my team. Exercising what I considered poor judgment, they'd revived my primary bio-specialist, Carlos Ortiz.

"Still no sign of enemy activity?" Carlos demanded for the tenth time. "For reals, McGill?"

"That's right. They've got an automated drilling rig and some slaves and all, but the tiny garrison from Rigel hasn't even transmitted a challenge to us yet. They're going to be the sorriest bunch of bears this side of the core when we drop and introduce ourselves."

Carlos was all grins and jokes. He loved a weak enemy—who didn't?

Unfortunately, onboard *Berlin*, we'd only had room to bring a single lifter. That meant most of us were going to have to use drop-pods. My unit was to establish a beachhead, secure it, and protect the lifter as it came down with the heavy equipment.

"Where the hell are we dropping, McGill?" Harris demanded angrily. He was suiting up his lights, which were going down in the first wave. He never liked playing the spearhead. The troops in the spearhead tended to die the most.

"Right next to the bear's mining camp, as close as I can tell. We'll be maybe ten kilometers out at first. As soon as we're down—"

"Yeah, yeah, I know the drill. But why don't we just blast that camp to shit from orbit? Why take the risk of fighting the bears at all?"

"Destroying this place isn't our mission. We're here to steal the tech, the planet, and the drilling equipment itself. If we blow up this mining installation, we'll have to start over again."

Harris fumed, but he couldn't find a flaw in the logic. After all, if we'd been sent here to destroy the place, we wouldn't even need ground troops. The camp could have just been dusted off from orbit, and we could have gone home.

Still in a sour mood, he launched his lights down the tubes like the pro he was. One girl hesitated, so he got her attention—then shoved her down the hole. She was gone with a squeak, and although we winced, she didn't get cut in half by the slamming jaws of her drop pod. She remembered her training, spun in her capsule, and was fired down toward the LZ with shocking force and speed.

Once the lights were away, we waited for twelve minutes until they'd landed and sent back the all-clear. The heavy platoons went next, then the weaponeers and support staff.

I went with a heavy platoon. Screaming through the atmosphere, I took the time to read up on the atmospheric composition. Oxygen 24%—a little on the high side, but not enough to be a problem. Nitrogen 69%, and a list of trace inert gases followed. It was damned close to Earth-normal and quite acceptable.

The gravity was around eighty percent of one standard G, which ought to put a spring in every soldier's step. The humidity was fairly high, despite the fact there were only a few small oceans. The land to sea ratio was the reverse of that on Earth, this world was three quarters wilderness.

Approximately four percent of the surface consisted of strange, crystalline zones. From above they looked like glass mountain ranges, or glaciers with no snow on top. We were dropping near the equator, so it was going to be hot.

Drilling in the warmest region of the planet was doubtlessly a choice the miners from Rigel had made. They liked it hot, I remembered. Oppressively so. Their home planet was like a vast jungle.

My drop-pod fell through space, punched into the atmosphere and burned its way at an angle toward the ground. After a harrowing ride, I slammed into the surface. I checked a few readouts—just to make sure I wasn't underwater or something—and popped the lid.

Scrambling out into the sunshine, I was surprised to realize I wasn't in a forest. Instead, the area was clear and open. The terrain was rolling green grass, with a wall of trees to the south, and a strange jumbled region of what looked like broken glass looming to the north.

"That's frigging beautiful," Harris said, walking up to me. "Isn't it? Like massive diamonds the size of mountains."

Staring with him, I nodded.

"That's why we're here, isn't it?" he asked. "Those diamond hills?"

He hadn't been part of the briefings. Our true mission had been classified from the start. "That's right," I told him. "The bears are mining in those cliffs and valleys. We're here to take over."

Harris grinned. "I bet some loose chunks would fetch a good price back home."

"If you don't mind the radiation burns, I'm sure they would."

His face fell, and he went back to shouting at his troops. Half an hour later, five cohorts were down on the plain. Soon afterward, the lifter landed on the grass in a shallow depression. Techs began wheeling out gear.

That's when the first missile landed and killed a full unit on the fringes of our camp.

"Incoming!" Harris roared.

Everyone threw themselves flat. I scrambled toward the lifter on all fours. We couldn't afford to lose it.

"Tell the pilot to take off!" I shouted into my radio. "Lift off—run!"

I needn't have bothered. Either the pilot had already gotten the order, or he'd come up with the idea all on his own. He didn't even bother to roll-up his ramps, or give the troops ferrying gear outside a chance to run.

The big jets flared, and scores of troops were burned to death in a gush of radioactive flame. Those who were carrying gear on the ramps scrambled for safety, some jumping off, others racing inside—as far as I could tell, none of them survived. Those who jumped off were incinerated. Those who tried to make it back into the ship were either crushed as the ramp closed, or fell to their deaths as if the lifter itself seemed determined to shake them off.

Harris rushed to me and grabbed my shoulder. He shook it, and I looked at him. "Did they get a revival machine down? Did they?"

"I think so," I told him.

He went off into a gale of cursing, walking around in a circle and beating his fists on his thighs. "Of all the damnable luck!" he complained.

This wasn't my first rodeo, so I understood his odd reaction. If the legion had left no revival gear behind, the brass back aboard *Berlin* could have called this first landing a failure and marked us down for dead. Now, however, they'd want us to fight to get their expensive machines back. That meant we were in for a rough ride.

"They dropped some pigs at least," I told Leeson. "Steal one and start digging trenches."

Supplies were short and then some. Aboard *Berlin* we'd been cramped, but at least we'd had all the food and gear we wanted. Now, we were in a wide open field of nothing, but we were almost bare-assed naked. We had guns, armor, a ruck full of food and ammo each—and that was about it.

-28-

It was pretty obvious to me that the enemy didn't consist entirely of helpless miners. They were raining down missiles, and it took nearly an hour to get an effective force field up to stop them. In the meantime, they'd managed to kill around five hundred of our five thousand men.

Now, however, we had trenches, a few basic puff-crete bunkers and some thin force shields overhead. Missiles—especially smart missiles—tended to ruin an infantryman's day.

We usually had cover from such basic attacks. Today, we were lucky to have survived long enough to stop the pecking shower of small, smart, AI-guided bomblets that kept seeking anything soft they could find to blow up.

Graves summoned me and his other centurions to his command bunker. As our blood-primus, he was not only in charge of my cohort, but also the entire operation from the frontlines. Unsurprisingly, Turov had decided to remain aboard *Berlin* and supervise our support from on-high.

Graves looked us over stoically. We huddled on benches and circled a shitty-looking battle computer with a big crack down the middle of it. Apparently, that was the best tech we had for the purpose.

"Here's our sitrep," he began. "We started with five thousand dead due to the warp-bubble failure aboard *Berlin*. Those losses are being replaced now, as revivals have begun in earnest on the battlecruiser."

I lifted my hand, gloved palm out—but he ignored me. He didn't even glance in my direction.

"Presumably, over the next few days, we'll be able to add a cohort of reinforcements due to more landings. That's the good news."

My gloved hand waggled, but still it was no dice. Graves just wasn't in the mood to hear any of my pearls of wisdom.

"Analysis of the enemy reaction so far indicates they've got some small, automated defenses. These missiles are coming from a stationary battery in the middle of their camp. The defense is limited, but effective—until now."

He lit up the battle computer, and the crack in it gleamed a jagged white. On one side of the crack were our forces, shown as a series of green cubes. Five cohorts were arranged in a crescent pattern. On the other side of the crack, the enemy mining station was shown as a single red circle. It was rather vague, and we couldn't know much about what we were facing yet.

"We have to assume the enemy has called for backup," Graves continued, tapping the red circle. "We've stopped their defensive action so far, and if that's all they've got, they're doomed. We'll send out probing attacks in the morning to find out, then we'll know more."

My arm was beginning to ache a little. I had been holding it up for a long time now, and the armor was weighing it down. I thought about supporting the arm with another hand at the elbow for support, but I passed on the idea. I didn't want to look like a sissy.

At last, Graves flicked his eyes up and met mine. "We have a question. What is it, McGill?"

"Sir, do we have any revival machines here on the planet?"

"Yes. Three of them. That's not enough, but we're working on replacements for the men we lost to missiles and splats we suffered during the drop. Did you really hold your hand up that long just for—?"

I was waggling my hand again. This time, I used my left, as my right was kinda sore.

"Yes, McGill…?"

"I suggest we hit them sooner than tomorrow, sir," I said. "We can't chance the enemy having more firepower than we expect."

He narrowed his eyes at me. "Like what?"

"I don't know… an underground army, maybe. Or maybe something they can bring in right away."

"We're pretty far out from Rigel. Not as far as we are from Earth, but—what is it now?"

"Primus, sir, what if they have high-tech transportation equipment?"

He stared at me for a second. "That would be most unfortunate. But we've seen no sign—"

"Sir? If I might make an observation."

He crossed his arms and glared at me. "Speak."

All around, the other centurions were beginning to look disgusted. They didn't want to hear me flap my gums, they wanted to hear the primus. Only Manfred seemed interested in what I had to say. He was a rare friend among the officer core for yours truly.

"Have we noticed any kind of spaceships?" I continued. "Anything like freighters, here in orbit?"

"No, obviously not. No warships were found on the station, either."

"Yes sir, and that's a good thing. A real good thing. But… how do you think the enemy is getting all this mining material—all the raw glass-stuff laced with collapsed matter—how are they moving that off-planet? I mean, there must be *some* kind of processing center back home on Rigel, right?"

"Of course. We've always assumed they mine the raw materials here and then ship it home to make the armor."

"Right… so where are the ships?"

He shrugged. "One might have just left. Maybe they only come once a month. What frigging difference does it make, McGill?"

"Uh… just this, sir: what if they're using gateway posts to ship it home? What if they have a lifeline from here, all the way back to Rigel? What if we sit here on our backsides till breakfast only to march into a freshly assembled Rigellian army under that mountain? What then, sir?"

Graves froze for a second. He stared at me flatly, and to me, he looked for all the world like a robot that had just been reset.

Suddenly, he stood up and marched out of the bunker. The rest of the group watched this with upraised eyebrows.

Standing outside on the grassy, windswept plain, Graves spoke to his tapper. We could see him up there outside the bunker, getting a good signal. Due to the wind, we couldn't make out the words.

After a few minutes, he marched back down into the safety of the dark and stood at the head of the broken battle computer again.

"There's been a change of plan," he said evenly. "We're moving out. We're not waiting for dawn. We're going to conduct an all-out assault on the mine in—" here, he glanced at his tapper, "—thirty-one minutes. Get out there, marshal your units. Be prepared to advance at the appointed time. Oh, and don't carry too much gear. We want to move fast."

After that announcement, he shooed us out of his bunker. The centurions poured out, blinking in the sunshine. One of the others slapped me in the breastplate with a set of steel-covered knuckles.

"Way to go, McGill. No sleep. No rest. No gearing or planning. Your unit should take point to make up for your big mouth."

"Huh..." I said, considering it. "That's an unexpected honor coming from you, Winton."

He sneered and moved off. I walked back to my unit's camp wearing a grin and whistling tunelessly. Carlos and Harris got the wrong idea right away.

"I see that conniving smile, Centurion," Carlos said. "Come on, give us the good news! We're being recalled from this paradise, right? No one's home, and it's all a big mistake, right?"

"Nope." I proceeded to explain our new reality, and all their good cheer evaporated.

I didn't care. I'd been right. Turov and Graves had seen it, and now we were going to take action.

Sometimes, it's enough to be taken seriously. You don't always have to get praised for it.

-29-

We marched, double-time, toward the enemy. There was no setup, we barely even lined up. Graves and Turov were clearly so concerned that I might be right—that the enemy might have a direct way to get reinforcements from their home world—that they decided it was too much of a risk to wait around.

At first, there was no sign of resistance. The smart mini-missiles, about the size of wine bottles, kept raining down on our mobile force-domes. They popped and fizzled up there, destroyed by the tendrils of electromagnetism that protected our advancing troops.

"Lame defense effort!" Harris remarked. "If that's all they've got, they're going to be sorry."

I waved him and his lights into the front line. The cohorts had spread out, with two cohorts in the front, one in the middle and two behind. Each cohort was more or less covering a rectangle of ground as big as a couple of football fields, but overall, our formation was roughly circular. This was by design, as it allowed our force-dome to protect us evenly from overhead bombardment.

As we reached the edge of the grassy lands, the ground changed dramatically. Large natural crystalline formations loomed. Some were hundreds of meters high, thrust up at angles to meet the sky. Each mountain, or shard, wasn't transparent, not exactly. You could see a meter or so deep into the stuff. It was like gazing into a massive chunk of agate, aquamarine or a cloudy emerald.

For the most part, the crystals were colored liquid blue or green. There were dark streaks and cloudy white sections. I could only wonder what one of these mountainous gemstones might be worth back on Earth.

"Keep moving," I ordered as men stopped to fill their pockets with broken chunks of colored crystal. "It's just glass. It's worthless."

I was lying, of course. These massive gemstones were semi-precious at least. If anyone managed to make off with a chunk that was laced with stardust, it might even be priceless.

But it was also heavy. I couldn't afford to let my men weigh themselves down—so I lied.

They grumbled, but they tossed aside the pretty rocks they'd picked up. We marched under the shadows of the great crystals. They soon swallowed us up, and we were forced to filter in-between them like ants seeking a picnic.

It was hotter—that's the first thing I noticed. The massive crystals focused blazing twists of light on the rocks between them, and heated them up. The ground smoked in places, and it even seemed to move when—

An explosion crumped nearby, and I saw a single flying body, twisting in the air. The corpse flew overhead and landed in the grassy fields behind us.

"Crawlers!" shouted a soldier up ahead—I thought it was one of Harris' lights.

Someone had found a trip-wire, or a crawling smart-mine. Surviving troops threw themselves this way and that, diving for cover.

Taking cover didn't work too well when the explosives were crawling toward you, seeking targets. Seconds later, a dozen more blasts went off. Our men fell back, some dragging mangled limbs.

"Crawling mines, sir!" Harris said, coming close and breathing hard. He'd already led his lights back to Barton's line of heavies. "They're crawling up right out of the ground to meet us!"

Graves probably would have ordered him right back into the crystals, suggesting he could make himself useful if he could fall on two of them at once—but I'd never been that kind of officer.

"Kivi!" I shouted, making a sweeping wave for the specialist platoon to advance.

The specialists were led by Leeson. They'd been skulking in the rear, holding their belcher tubes and other gear with tense hands.

Kivi rushed to my side, and I ordered her to send in a wave of buzzers and the creepy-crawly drones that looked like centipedes. She released them in a rush, and we watched as they wriggled and skittered into the cracks between the giant crystals.

One second passed. Two more seconds, then *boom*!

First one explosion, then two more, went up in rapid succession.

"What a shit-show this is!" Harris complained. "Helpless miners my ass, they've booby-trapped this place to hell and back."

I had to agree. I reported the contact to Graves, and he seemed unsurprised. All up and down our advancing lines similar stories were flooding in. You could hear the thumps of small explosions and see puffs of sparkling earth everywhere.

"McGill," Graves told me, "this rapid advance Turov has ordered is your fault."

"Huh? How so, sir?"

"We could have spent a full day planning and scouting, but no, you had to go and start a panic."

"That's not really fair, Primus, I—"

"Whatever, shut up. Since you're the one with all the bright ideas, I've got new orders for you. Figure out how to penetrate those crystals and get through the barrier with at least one of your troops left alive on the far side. If you can make it about a kilometer deep, our intel indicates you'll reach the mine entrance itself. We'll set that as the goal line."

"Uh…" I said. "Are these special orders just for sport, sir?"

"Negatory. I'm sending in one unit from every cohort. You just happen to be one of my favorite centurions today."

"That's very comforting, sir. 3rd Unit won't disappoint."

"See that you don't."

He was gone. I flipped my visor and rubbed my face. Just like that, he'd ordered me and my men to die hard and fast. My whole body was already coated with grit and sweat. It was making my whole head itch.

"This is bullshit, McGill," Harris said in a low voice. Naturally, he'd listened in and heard Graves' orders. "You've got to figure a way out of this for us. Just because you—"

"Shut up," I said without anger. I stood and looked along my lines. Three dead in three minutes. At that rate, a kilometer was going to come hard.

"Kivi," I said, thumping on her helmet.

She looked up in concern.

"Are you having any luck detecting those smart-mines?"

She bit her lip and shook her head. "They're very hard to detect. No electromagnetics, no—"

"All right, all right, I get it. Get out more of your little ground-buzzers. All you've got. Program them to thread a single pathway, one-man wide, into that china cabinet of breakables."

Without complaint, she bent to the task. She wasn't a master like Natasha, but she was very competent these days. A decade or two of experience had done wonders.

"Harris," I said, turning toward him. To my surprise, I saw I was talking to his ass. He must have known I was going to assign him a duty next, because he'd suddenly seen the light and begun walking back to his light troops.

"Get back here," I ordered.

He came back with poor grace and glowered at me.

"Your light troops are going to follow the drones," I told him. "When they're all gone, my heavy troops will find the rest of the mines."

"How the hell are we supposed to find these mines?" he demanded.

"I don't care. Tell them to slap the ground ahead with their dicks if they have to. Move out!"

Grumbling, Harris turned away and began abusing wide-eyed recruits. Soon, they were following Kivi's congo-line of buzzers into the treacherous crystals.

Graves called again, demanding to know what the holdup was. I told him we were working on it and would be moving in shortly. He didn't curse at me, but it was a close thing.

Looking terrified, Harris' light troops filtered into the gloom between the crystals, probing each step ahead with their snap-rifles.

-30-

After Harris and his lights had vanished into the maze, I moved in with my heavies. Now that we were marching among them, the huge crystals didn't seem so lovely. They seemed like evil, unnatural mountains. Ghostly, almost.

Explosions, screams and gunfire echoed back to us now and then. Over time, the sounds drew closer, because the light troops were balking and their numbers were shrinking.

"What's the hold-up?" I demanded of Harris, who was having an ever more difficult time whipping his lights enough to keep them marching.

"They're about to break, sir. They need to fall back. We've lost half—"

There was another echoing report—an explosion not too far ahead. A small tinkling wave of glass-like crystal slid down and crashed at my feet.

"—we just lost Fredrickson," Harris continued. "My men are over half gone now. I'm telling you Centurion, they're going to break!"

Using my HUD and my tapper, I confirmed what he'd told me. The 1st platoon was down to fifteen souls.

"All right—stop your advance and stand in place. I've got another idea."

I contacted Sargon and ordered him to lead a group of weaponeers forward. It would be a shame to risk them, but they had much thicker armor than our lights did.

Brushing aside lesser men, Sargon's team marched with confidence among the crystal mountains. They spaced themselves out, six men in clanking metal suits moving deeper into the jagged peaks.

For a time, this worked well. The smart-mines tried to get them, rushing in to detonate on heavy boots and ankles. But their weaponeer's armor held.

"Why didn't you think of this in the first place?" Harris demanded.

"Just be glad I came up with it at all—and be even more glad that it's working. Graves would never approve this if I told him what I was up to. You don't risk experienced men in expensive gear unless you have to."

Several more popping explosions were heard, and we made another hundred meters of progress.

"Uh… McGill? Centurion sir?" Sargon buzzed in my helmet.

"What is it, Veteran?"

"These things are acting funny—different, I mean. They're hopping at us now—trying to hit us higher. Pretty soon, they'll reach our balls."

"Rotate the man in front to the back with each attack—and don't worry about your balls. Gonads are purely ornamental on a weaponeer."

The popping strikes continued, and we marched another hundred meters. We were now easily halfway to the mine entrance. I was beginning to feel the creeping sensation of hope.

Harris was right behind me, studying the feedback and grinning. He was really happy his team wasn't the one being marched into the grinder anymore.

BOOM!

A different explosion echoed back through the glittering canyon we were walking in. This one shook the walls of vibrant crystals. Stalactites rattled and fell from above and shattered among us like bombs.

"Sargon!" I called into my tapper. "Sargon? Report!"

There was a buzzing, and I checked my HUD. There were two red names in his platoon now.

"McGill," I heard him say. "These drones are wising up. They hit us all at once, ten of them at least. That was enough to blow up Bennington and—"

"All right, wait there. I'm coming up with Harris."

"Why do I need to be invited to every fiasco in town?" Harris complained bitterly, but he followed me anyway.

We wound our way deep into the pathways and cracks until we found Sargon's sorry team. Every armored plate they had was scarred and burned. They weren't going to make it much farther.

"Shit…" I said, looking over the scene. "We're more than halfway there. It's not that far, really. A man could run it in a few minutes."

"Not if his balls were missing after the first dozen steps," Harris pointed out.

I looked at him thoughtfully. "Speed… You're right, Harris. That's what we need: *speed*. These things are smart, they change their tactics all the time, but they aren't fast. Certainly not faster than a running man. Harris, gather the rest of your lights. Bring them right up here to the line."

Reluctantly, he followed orders. In the meantime, I had my bio people pull back the wounded.

Oddly, no smart-mines attacked us during this pause. They seemed to be programmed to react only when we were approaching the mine.

"Here's what we're going to do," I said, talking to Harris and the huddled squad of troops he had left. "You guys have done a bang-up job on this mission. You've gotten us halfway to the goal line. As a reward, you're only going to have to perform one more time, then you get to withdraw to the rear lines."

They looked hopeful. That was sheer inexperience, of course. Harris was an old hand, so he was naturally very suspicious.

"What's this about a final task, sir?" he asked.

I explained what I wanted, and the light troopers went from hopeful to horrified.

"We're supposed to run—but not in a single line, Centurion?" one young lady asked me. Her eyes were as big around as an owl's at midnight.

"That's right. You're going to scatter off to the sides. Everyone is to go two hundred steps, count them as you go, all in different directions. After you do that, your job is done. You can turn and run back for the exit. Do anything you want—avoid contact, flee, whatever. Just get back to the rear lines and escape this maze."

"I have to speak up, Centurion," Harris said. "This mission is just sheerly unfair. These troops have gone through a lot. Half of them are dead, but us officers are going to watch these sorry bastards risk it all in a deadly charge?"

"No," I said, shaking my head at him. "That's not how it's going to be at all." My finger raised up and suddenly stabbed at his chest. "You're going with them, Adjunct. Now, move out!"

Part of the key to issuing insane suicidal orders was not letting the troops have too long to think it over. Once I got them moving, they'd be committed, and they'd follow through.

Sure enough, when I shouted: "Go! Go! GO!" at them, slamming my gauntlets together and shoving anyone who looked like they wanted to loiter, they began shambling off in random directions. Even Harris himself, cursing as I gave him a push, raced away to the right.

Soon, the group was mostly invisible, having moved into pools of shade between the countless glacier-like crystals.

Sargon walked up to stand next to me. Together we listened, breathing deeply.

BOOM!

BOOM-BOOM!

Sargon winced. He'd overheard my orders, and he'd expected this result, the same as I had.

"Should my weaponeers advance again, sir?" he asked. "I mean, this is some kind of distraction, right?"

"No, no, hold on for ten more seconds. Tell Leeson and Barton we're about to sprint. Tell them to get their asses up here."

"Sprint, sir?"

I shushed him and listened. I also used my HUD to display the relative positions of the spreading

A few more explosions caused Harris' platoon to shrink further. Most of the names were now clearly red.

"Unit!" I roared. "Advance, double-time!"

The second two platoons rushed forward into the crystals.

"Spread out! Spread out!"

All around me, my panting, half-panicked men raced on separate pathways through the glassy crags. To my mind, some of us *should* make it.

The light troops were coming back our way now. Running like scared jackrabbits, they raced back toward us. People collided and cursed and shoved. Then I saw Harris, he was coming back, looking happy. He'd done his two hundred steps and lived. Was that a grin of relief on his face? I thought that it was.

BOOM!

That explosion was close, very close. I staggered, and glassy shards rained down. Looking around, I tried to figure out if I'd been hit—but I hadn't.

Then I figured it out. Harris lay sprawled in front of my path. He was a twisted bloody mess. The blue-green glassy walls around him dripped gore.

Gritting my teeth, I raced onward. By the odds, we should break through to the center zone soon.

The explosions stopped after we'd gone perhaps three hundred meters into the maze. A few minutes after that, we broke through into the open again. As I'd hoped, the drone mines had chased the lights I'd sent off in random directions, and when my main force rushed up the middle, they couldn't catch up.

Bleeding, cursing and panting, we stepped into a no-man's land. All around us stood tall, cold-looking peaks like ice sculptures. The mine itself was here, and it was a pit in the ground. A crater-like hole dug in the center of the region we'd penetrated.

I thought about the depth of it. Could that be the answer to how this place had been created? Had some kind of asteroid landed here eons ago, a broken-off chunk of something huge and dangerous? I could only conjecture on what had made the crust of this world vomit up these crystals. Or what strange body had struck this world and laced it with collapsed dust, the way our moon had pockets of ice in many craters due to impacts with comets in the past.

I supposed that might be the story, or it might be something stranger still. The wild variation in planets and star systems we encountered as humanity spread through space had never ceased to amaze Earth scientists. Our best xeno-biologists and astrophysicists were still learning more about the galaxy every day.

We walked as a group to the rim of the great mine. At the bottom of the crater, a winding conical pit had been drilled. It went down in a spiral, with a road circumnavigating it seven times. At the bottom of that... I could only see a final splotch of darkness. Maybe it was a tunnel, or maybe it was a kernel of whatever it was they were digging up. I really couldn't tell from here.

Sargon crouched next to me on the rim of the crater. "It doesn't look like the drones are following us," he said. "We left them behind in the crystals."

"Yeah. They're probably programmed to work that maze where they have a big advantage."

"What are your orders, sir?"

I looked around the circle of crystal peaks. I didn't see any other units filtering through—not yet. Right about then, Natasha caught up to us. She came up to me, panting.

"James, James!"

"What is it, girl?"

"I think we've found him. I'm getting an alert message on my tapper."

She showed me a blinking blue block of text, but I didn't get it. Not at all.

"Uh... what's that?"

"It's Cooper! I built a detection system, just like you wanted. It's not only looking for these coordinates, it's looking for aerial DNA traces as well."

"You don't say... where is he?"

We both looked around. Natasha used her tapper like a divining rod, following it around until it beeped louder.

"There. Isn't that—?"

We found some bones with scraps of meat on them. It was a dead man—a dead, naked guy.

"Looks like the Vulbites ate him or something," I said. "They're worse than buzzards."

We checked the corpse and got verification. It was Cooper all right. Lifting my tapper, I uploaded my list of confirmed dead, including Cooper. Then I contacted Graves directly.

"3rd Unit has reached the mine, Primus."

I couldn't help but feel a bit prideful about that report. Graves took a moment before he came online.

"How the hell did you get in there so fast?" he demanded. "The rest of them are bogged down with some kind of explosive drones coming at them."

"Those little things?" I asked. "They're like horseflies. They bite and sting, but it's nothing a full-grown man can't get past."

I saw Graves' face on my tapper, and he rewarded me with a rare smile. "That's a good attitude. I've got new orders for your hard-charging unit: get into that mine and shut it down. Establish full control as quickly as possible."

"Uh…" I said, regretting my boasts. "We've lost a third of our troops just getting here, Primus. To push them to the bottom of a hellhole pit like this one, without support… I don't know…"

"Don't tell me you've gone soft, McGill. You made it through some crystals, but you're not done yet. You and your men can forget about taking showers, smoke-breaks, and watching vids on your tappers. You are hereby ordered to advance to contact, and destroy all opposition. I'll shame the other centurions into joining you as fast as they can. Graves out."

That was it then. I stood up and eyed Sargon and Leeson. Barton walked up, panting a little, and she looked at me quizzically.

With an effort of will, I forced myself to grin. "Faithful officers, I've got some great news!"

All three of them groaned and kicked at the sparkling earth under their boots. They weren't fooled for a second.

-31-

As I rousted my men and ordered them to perform their second death-defying advance of the day, I wondered if I was cut out for higher rank. After all, it took a certain heartless nature to do the job of a primus or above. Even though I was a centurion, I didn't set missions. I might tell a given individual they were on point, but it was quite something else again to order thousands to do or die.

A centurion-level officer could always point upward, passing the blame figuratively as he was simply relaying the demands of the distant brass. Men like Graves, Winslade and others of a similar nature were the norm in the upper ranks. They were a different breed who thought of troops the way a farmer thinks of his herds and flocks. We were a means to an end.

"Up and at-em!" Sargon roared, slapping anyone who dared slouch or hang back. Just moments ago, he'd been complaining in low tones that the men needed a break—but you wouldn't know it by watching him in action. He was kicking ass all up and down the line.

In fact, it seemed like he was pushing them harder than usual. He was getting them to move despite their shock. It was a good policy, so I imitated his strategy with any stragglers I spotted.

Soon, we were up and marching again. There was no immediate opposition, so we didn't linger. We trotted over the rim of the crater and approached the central drilled-down hole. Once there, we didn't stop. We slid down the first of the glittering earth walls that formed spiraling steps.

Still, everything was quiet. There was no gunfire, no crawling mines, no missiles—nothing. With a growing sense of unease, we moved deeper into the ground.

After half-falling, half-skidding down the third step, we finally spotted something. We'd run into a team of miners operating heavy equipment.

The workers were nasty-looking aliens from Rigel. About a meter tall with random tufts of fur, they resembled a cross between a bear and a mythical troll. To say they were ugly would be putting it mildly.

In one way, I was surprised to see these bear-dudes doing their own physical labor. Usually they employed less sophisticated creatures like Vulbites to do menial tasks. But maybe this mining installation was so crucial, so strategically valuable, they didn't trust slaves to work here. They were so busy, in fact, so focused they didn't notice us right away. Perhaps they thought their barrier would keep us out forever.

"Unit," I spoke into my tapper quietly, "advance to the edge of the step. Let's have a look."

My troops bellied up to the edge and aimed their rifles over the side. Directly below us—on the fourth barren, shelf-like section of the corkscrewing roadway—about fifty miners were herding some mighty big pieces of machinery down toward the bottom of the mine.

The big machines were about four stories tall. They had black earth dripping from their forward scoops and saw-toothed plows. These were clearly digging machines, and they seemed semi-intelligent, shying away from their comparatively tiny handlers who paced all around them.

Now and then, one of the big mining machines tried to stray, turning back toward the road behind. But the Rigellians persisted, slapping at the huge tires, flapping their hands at collision avoidance sensors and the like. They wanted to force the trundling mining automatons to move down the long spiraling ramp toward the bottom.

"That's where the mining machines went," Leeson said by my side. "Weren't you wondering where the diggers had gone?"

"Uh… not really. I've been looking for something to shoot."

Leeson made a wry face, but he nodded. "Okay… now what?"

"We'll rush ahead of them a ways, then ambush them. Shoot every bear down, but leave the robots alone. Maybe we can use them to mine this place later on."

Leeson trotted ahead. He ordered his weaponeers to stow their missiles. They were to use belchers set to their widest aperture settings. They were to use broad anti-personnel beams only.

Less than three minutes later, we ambushed them. Screeching in rage, the bears that survived our initial blistering wave of fire rushed under the mining machines for cover.

"That's it!" I called out. "Slide down the cliff and mop up! Sargon, lead the charge."

My Varus men attacked without hesitation. I had to hand it to them, even after a long, long day of violent death, they were still ready for more.

I jumped down with the second wave. We met the miners who were huddled under their confused robotic machines.

Fire ripped loose in both directions the moment my men were down amongst the machines and able to bring their guns to aim under them. The fight wasn't entirely one-sided. The enemy had rivet-guns, which were surprisingly effective at close range. After all, the rivets had to be accelerated to a velocity great enough to punch through puff-crete. Hammering away at us, they drilled holes in armored and unarmored alike.

What was more critical, however, was the suits the miners were wearing. The miners had armor, much like the armor worn by Rigel's soldiers.

I arrived with the second wave to support the first. The bears were taking the worst of it, but they weren't beaten yet. Already, a dozen of my men were down or wounded.

Using my morph-rifle, I put burst after burst downrange aiming at any black-clad fuzzy short guy I could get a bead on.

They retreated under the wheels of their monstrous machines, and we whipped their tails for them as they ran.

"We've got them on the run!" I roared. "Advance!"

We surged forward—but before we could finish them the situation shifted again. All of a sudden, the huge mining machines swung around ponderously and bore down on us.

"They're sending their mining drones at us!" Sargon called out.

It was true. Like a pack of cowboys starting a stampede, these sneaky Rigellian bastards were driving their enslaved machines at our lines.

The big machines lit up, as if activated for digging. Conveyor belts ran, dribbling earth-like spittle. The threshing metal teeth in every scoop and vacuum hose clattered and whirred.

"Throw grenades under those machines!" I ordered. "I don't care if you wreck them!"

A dozen pulsing blue bombs were tossed under the advancing line of giant robots. Treads were blown off, and a few bodies went flying—but still, most of the enemy bots continued to advance.

"Go underneath!" I ordered next, as we were being pressed back against the cliff-like wall of earth behind us. "Take the fight to them!"

We surged forward, dodging shovels and clattering claws that sought to crush us. Some men perished, but many made it under the machines.

Unsurprisingly, there was only a meter or so of clearance under the bots. That was ust enough for a Rigellian bear to stand and walk upright—but not a human. We were bent double, some on their knees, some on all fours.

Despite the fact we had armor and proper guns, there was a vicious fight under those massive treads. The bears, civvies or not, were from a species of apex predators. Not a one of them was a chicken in a fight. They were all vicious, natural-born killers.

Sometimes men were caught by the treads as the milling machines began to wander again, moving in confusion without direction. They seemed to want to go back to work. Now and then, a distracted pair of combatants, man and bear alike, were crushed to pulp by those spinning metal treads.

In the end, however, the bears were defeated. We outnumbered them, and we were better organized and trained. They were only miners, not soldiers.

With perhaps twenty men left alive, I let the mining machines trundle off to do whatever they'd been programmed to do. They left behind a steaming mess of blood, flattened carcasses and moaning wounded.

"We won!" I called out loudly. "Good job, troops!"

There was no chorus of cheers to greet my declaration. Not this time.

Sargon had been right. We'd pushed them too far.

Twenty long, long minutes later, I crawled on my belly and reached the lip of the final step. From here, I was able to peer directly into the black hole at the bottom of the pit-like mine. Curious, I zoomed in using my officer's helmet at full magnification.

That's when I saw it. A shimmer of light in the darkness. A familiar wavering gleam. It was an active set of gateway posts. I'd stake my balls on it.

I contacted Graves immediately and relayed the view. He came online and his face peered up at me from my tapper.

"Good work, McGill," he said. "There's only one mission left for your team to perform today."

I didn't bother asking what the mission was. I didn't bother asking for mercy, either. It would have been pointless.

"On it, Primus," I said. "You can count on 3rd Unit."

Graves nodded. "Godspeed."

Sucking in a deep breath, I prepared my mind and body for the final push. I was exhausted, wounded in a few spots, and numbed to almost everything around me.

But none of that mattered. We had to destroy that gateway before it brought through reinforcements from Rigel.

"McGill!" It was Barton. She was the only one of my adjuncts to have survived the day. She was pointing upward, and I frowned at her, then turned and followed her gesture.

Something was hovering above us. It was like an aircar, but open on the sides. Aboard it were a dozen bears in spacesuits.

I knew several things at once when I laid eyes on those bears. For one thing, these were proper troops, not miners. Worse, they were flying one of those open-air flitters they liked. They were like flying chariots. Mounted on the back of each was a heavy beam weapon—about the equivalent of one of our famed 88s.

Secondly, I knew these bears had come through that gateway I'd just spotted. They'd come from Rigel to reinforce the mining installation.

Lastly, I knew we were doomed.

"Take them down!" I roared, and every gun we had was lifted to a tired shoulder. Beams, pellets and mini-missiles stormed up at the aerial platforms.

But they weren't as easy to take out as they looked. They were shielded, and most of our small-arms fire flashed and spanged into sparks and flashes of plasma. Then the return fire came back at us.

Sweeping beams flooded the battleground. Four of them crisscrossed the mud and the dead. The beams sent a gush of radiation that transformed my men to charred bone and dust before my eyes.

A few seconds later, it was my turn. I was melted down, and I joined my comrades in death.

-32-

"What have we got?" a female voice asked.

"Centurion McGill... from front lines? Says here he got all the way to the frigging mine."

"That's bullshit. They told me no one got through those crystal mountains."

"It's right. Check it yourself."

I tried to open my eyes, but they felt glued together. Someone sprayed liquid in them, and spread them wide. The liquid stung a little, but the blinding light was much worse.

"We all died..." I croaked out. "We made it... but we died."

"Centurion James McGill," the female bio read aloud. "You're a goddamned hero. You know that?"

"I sure as hell am."

The two laughed and worked on me, getting my mind and body fired up. Sometimes, revivals went smoothly. Sometimes they were rough. This one was right down the middle.

I was soon standing, swaying, with a big headache and cold feet. The floor of the bunker was wet and freezing to the touch. They usually kept it refrigerator-cold in revival chambers. It kept the bacteria from growing.

Less than ten minutes into my new life, I was uniformed and slapping doors open. I wandered up muddy steps to the outside world. The sun was up and the day was windy.

All around me, the land looked abused. We'd come here to this lovely planet and dug in, tearing up grassy mounds and leaving black-earth wounds on the surface. Our bunkers and trenches were all like that, fresh-cut and unnatural-looking.

Graves didn't send me a note on his tapper. Not this time. He came to me in person.

"Walk straight," he said. "The men are watching."

Sure enough, there was a small crowd. I didn't get it at first, but after a few cheers and clapping hands, I figured it out—they were there to see me.

"Uh…" I said, blinking in the sunshine. My eyes barely functioned, but my mind was in even worse shape. "What's this about, sir?"

"You made it through. No one else got that far. A few units, copying your rush method, managed to break through the crystal badlands and advance to the edge of the mining pit. There, they were met with those flying platforms. Without heavy weapons… it was brutal."

"They got wiped out? Did they take down any of the aerial targets?"

"Two were downed. Two out of four."

"I wish I'd been there to see that."

Graves gave me a small, cold smile. "A little revenge always does the heart good."

"Yes sir. What now? How are we going to get to that mine with their reinforcements flowing?"

Graves expression changed. He was all stony stares again. "That's what I want to talk to you about. Let's go."

He marched away, and I followed. Around me, the small, cheering group melted. By the time we reached Gold Bunker, it was just me and him again.

Graves walked up to a table that doubled as a holo projector and waved his hand over it. The table glowed into life. "Turov is waiting to talk to you," he said. "She's not in a good mood, and she wants to ask you some questions."

With that less than perfect introduction, Graves gestured. The screen glowed and light loomed up like a flame. The flame took the shape of Galina Turov's upper body. The eyes swept the room, and they soon landed on me.

"McGill..." she said. "You made it so far, but you failed anyway. Now, I have no choice."

"Uh..." I said. "What's this all about, Tribune?"

"It's about your failure. Your *abject* failure. Graves owns some of it as well, but you are the focal point of this disaster." Her voice began to rise in volume and intensity. "How *could* you have come within a hundred meters of those gateway posts and left them intact?"

"Oh... that. Yeah... We never got a good shot at them. The moment we spotted them—"

"You should have taken them out! That's what you should have done, instead, you wasted precious seconds prepping and goofing around, sending loves notes to Graves, here."

I glanced at Graves for help, but he was giving me that stony stare again. He was no help at all.

"Before we could act, those flying gunboats appeared and dusted us off."

"I know what happened," Turov snapped. "I've seen the videos pulled from your tapper. You hesitated, and now I'm faced with a crucial choice."

"What would that be, sir?"

"Whether or not to destroy the mine with an orbital strike."

That took me by surprise. "I thought that was off the table," I said. "If *Berlin* fires into that pit, sir, there'll be nothing left."

"Don't you think I know that?" she demanded. "How could you dream, in your wildest brain-dead fantasies, that I don't know what will happen to the mine if we plug that hole? Obviously, we'll have to rebuild it from scratch. There will be nothing left but a slightly *deeper* smoking crater than we have now!"

"That's about the size of it."

Fuming, Galina began pacing around in circles. The automated camera pickups followed her steadily. As a result, her hologram appeared to be walking in place in the middle of the table.

Graves cleared his throat. Turov stopped pacing and peered at him. "You have something to suggest, Primus?"

"Just that you could contact Praetor Drusus and ask for his advice. Let the top brass take the responsibility, if you don't want it."

Galina started pacing again. "Responsibility… Yes… That is the crux of the issue. I see failure ahead. This mission is no longer viable, due to McGill's failure to act."

"Hey now…" I began, but she ignored me.

"That doesn't matter, of course. The highest officer present must take the blame for any failure, and the credit for any success. Therefore, it's time to do what Deech would do."

"Huh?" I asked. "What Deech would do? You mean start sleeping with Drusus?"

They both twisted up their lips in disgust. "No, you fool," Galina told me. "She would pass the buck, as they used to say. She would make it someone else's fault. No failures were ever successfully pinned on her."

"Yeah, because she screwed—"

"No!" Turov said loudly. "It was because she made sure someone below her took the blame."

"Ah… right. I remember that now. Who have you got lined up to play scapegoat?"

Graves cleared his throat again. "Tribune," he said, "although I am a loyal officer, I would have difficulty—"

Turov fluttered her finger at him. "Not you, Graves. No one would buy that. No, it must be someone people enjoy pinning blame upon."

She gazed at me then, and I recoiled. "Not me, sir! Not unless you want to make me a primus first, so I can get busted back down to centurion again."

"Useless…" she said, barely looking at us. "No, the person I have in mind should be obvious to you both, but still, I can see by your expressions you have no idea. There is no innate talent in either of you for this sort of thing. It's no wonder that you've been passed over for promotion so many times."

With that, she dimmed the screen, and her upper body appeared to sink into the table.

Graves and I were left frowning at one another.

"I didn't like the sound of that," Graves said.

"Neither did I. Any idea who she's talking about?"

Graves shrugged. "The woman has a twisted mind. It could be anyone."

I wasn't so sure of that. She operated very logically, once you understood her motivations and rules of engagement. She didn't do things the same way as others, sure, but that wasn't because she was plain crazy. She was crazy like a fox.

It wasn't until about a half hour later that my tapper buzzed and I knew the truth.

A familiar, if unpleasant face stared up out of my forearm. He sneered at me, and I grinned back at him.

"Welcome back Winslade!" I boomed. "I'm mighty glad to see you up and around again!"

"Put a sock in it, McGill. We both know there's nothing less than unbridled rivalry between us now. "In any case, I demand that you address me by my proper rank and title."

"Uh…"

He lifted his tapper so I could see his shoulders. His hair was still drippy from his recent revive. But his new uniform and the insignia on his shoulders was unmistakable.

"You're a tribune now?" I asked in amazement. "Who did you have to—?"

"Ah-ah!" he admonished, waving a finger at me. "I'm now an acting tribune, and I'm this legion's commanding officer."

"But Graves is our blood-primus," I argued. "And what happened to Turov, anyway?"

"She was suddenly called away to Earth. I've been theorizing as to the reasons for that myself… That's why I'm contacting you. You've long been her confidant. Perhaps we could meet, and you could enlighten me as to the situation here on Glass World."

"Glass World?"

"Yes. The bio-people say that's what everyone has decided to call this miserable rock. Tau Orionis is too wordy, I suppose."

"Uh-huh…"

My mind was reeling, and I struggled to take it all in.

Galina had cut and run. She'd ditched Legion Varus on Glass World and used the gateway posts to return to Earth. Worse, she'd placed Winslade in charge.

What a mean thing to do! Of all the skullduggery, scheming and outright fraud I'd caught her at, this had to be one of the worst examples yet.

-33-

My first meeting with Winslade didn't go all that well. I suppose it was bound to be difficult, given our recent interactions. After all, the final moments of his previous existence had been spent arguing with me—then suddenly dying.

He sniffed as if I stank as I walked into his office. I guess maybe I did, a little.

"Is that what this planet smells like?" he demanded. "A livestock market?"

"Uh… kinda. Really, it depends on what you step in. There are these really big critters, sort of bison-like, that wander the grassy plains just outside our camp. I was watching a few go by before I came to your bunker, see."

"I get the point. Disgusting, and yet appropriate. Just like usual, McGill."

"Huh?"

"Make that huh, sir. Or huh, Tribune."

"Oh…yeah, sure. Sorry Tribune, sir. It takes a bit of getting used to—you getting that kind of rank and all."

Winslade had his skinny arms behind his back, hands clasped together. He was rocking on his heels and staring at me with squinty eyes. I got the feeling he was planning out an evil fate for me.

"You might be wondering why I didn't have you arrested instantly upon assuming command."

I blinked a few times. "Why would you do that, Tribune?"

"Ah, playing the fool again. Very well, I'll explain. During my final moments, you and I were having an argument. Agreed?"

"That would describe it pretty well."

"And then, as we parted ways, I was suddenly shot in the back."

My eyes popped wide. "Really? Is that how it happened? How rude! Did you get some bod-cam vids or security footage to determine the culprit?"

Winslade's sour expression soured further. I wouldn't have thought it possible if I hadn't seen it with my own eyes, as he already looked like he was sucking on a fermented lemon.

"No. There is no conclusive proof, and beam guns are generally untraceable."

"You don't say... but what about—?"

"Shut up, McGill. I know you shot me. What I want to know is *why*?"

"Listen here, sir," I said, putting on the most serious and slightly offended expression I could muster. "I'm going to let this go, but I find it kind of offensive."

"Really? Care to explain that odd statement?"

"Here's how I see it," I began, having worked up this particular fabrication on the way up to his office. "The last time we met up man-to-man, we both considered killing the other guy, right?"

"That has been established."

"Right. We both thought about it, but we passed on the feuding. Now, I can understand how you might still harbor strong suspicions and maybe even some guilty feelings—"

"—as if—"

"—however, I consider what occurred to be a matter of honor satisfied. We came eyeball-to-eyeball and neither of us struck in that passionate moment. Don't you think, that if I'd wanted you dead, I would have made my move right then? I'm not a snake-in-the-grass type, sir."

"Hmm..." he said, looking uncertain for the first time. "That is true. You're an emotion-driven beast. You rarely have a thought that originates above the waist."

"Well said, Tribune. Therefore, in short, I don't know who killed you—or why."

Winslade had studied me throughout this bluffing, bullshit-filled speech. I could tell he was in doubt. I'd planted the seed carefully, and it had taken root in his mind.

Oh sure, he was still pretending he knew the real score—but I knew he didn't. If he had known I'd shot him, he would have arrested me and thrown me into the brig by now.

That knowledge had me working overtime now. To escape justice, I had to act offended at the mere suggestion I'd been involved in his most recent demise.

At last, he made a growling sound in his throat. "Very well. I'll play this charade if you insist—but you owe me!"

"Uh…" I said, not quite following his logic. "All right… I owe you. I owe you because you're right, I was nearby when the heinous act was performed, and I should have caught the culprit red-handed."

He rolled his eyes at me, but I could tell he wasn't certain I was the assassin. That single lie, played to the absolute hilt, was my saving grace.

"Fine," he said. "Let us move on. Can you say why *anyone*—not you, in particular—might have killed me that day?"

"Sure," I said, brightening. "First off, there's the matter of your personality, sir. I'm not one to throw around terms like 'abrasive' lightly, but—"

"Put a sock in that massive maw of yours! What I want to know is why I was shot and left dead for so damnably long!"

I took his question seriously. "At the time of your death, we were experiencing mysterious power outages. We almost lost the entire ship that very day."

He frowned at me. "You're saying people thought I was the saboteur?"

"I'm not saying a damned thing, sir. I'm just making an observation."

Winslade nodded and rocked on his heels again. "I get it. Yes… I finally get it. A group of officers might be involved?"

I shrugged, giving him no input.

"I see... They blamed the warp bubble failure on me, and then they sent you as their ham-handed assassin. Weeks later, mysteriously, Turov and her staff have vanished and put me in charge of this mission, which has rapidly transformed into a flaming bag of excrement. The puzzle begins to take shape."

I shrugged, neither confirming nor denying his claims. They were pretty close to the mark—except the part where I hadn't been the one to plan and execute his murder.

"Hmm... You do realize that I can't trust you now, McGill, yes?"

"I wouldn't say that, sir. You're here, you're in charge. Why would you sabotage anything else at this point?"

"I was talking about trusting you."

"Yeah, but in order for you to trust me, you have to be trustworthy yourself. I think you are trustworthy at this point, so you can trust me not to get in your way."

He brightened. "Ah! Are you proposing the most unlikely of alliances? Seriously?"

"Whenever we work together, that's exactly what it is, sir. And we've done it often."

He eyed me for a few moments, thinking hard. I'd conjured into his slick brain the idea that I was not alone in my actions, that I had a cabal of other officers behind me. That kind of vague worry could cripple a paranoid man like Winslade.

"All right," he said at last. "I'm going to give you a chance. Tomorrow, I'm going to throw your cohort into combat. Your unit will spearhead the legion, which is now nearly at full-strength."

"We're talking about another attack?" I asked in surprise.

"Are your ears functional?"

"Yes sir, but—"

"Excellent. Let me assure you, the attack will be more forceful this time."

"Uh... but what about the crystal mountains? What about the drones? What about the army they're spinning up to defend the mine?"

Winslade pursed his lips, wrinkled his nose and brushed away my words with long fingers. "Never mind about all that. It will be taken care of."

"How, sir?"

"Let's just say that I'm prepared to take more drastic action than my predecessors."

"Uh…" I said, not knowing what to make of that.

"Listen McGill, in order to get back into my good graces, all you have to do is make sure one thing happens during tomorrow's battle."

"What's that, sir?"

"Primus Graves must die."

I stared at him and blinked a few times. Finally, I nodded and agreed. He dismissed me, and I stumped out of his bunker in confusion.

Was Winslade working against us for reals? I couldn't be sure.

Was I really going to kill Graves—or get him killed somehow? I wasn't sure about that yet, either. I'd agreed because otherwise I thought Winslade would have me shot down on the spot.

It's hard to do anything when you're dead, I always say. This way, I at least had some time to think and decide what I should do next.

-34-

The next morning came way too early. I hadn't even come up with a plan yet. I had nothing to go on at all, in fact.

Upon being ordered to prep for combat, 3rd Unit began grousing as usual. There were plenty of bitter glances in my direction, in fact. Word must have gotten out that I'd gone to see Winslade the moment I'd been revived. When an officer visits the brass and then is ordered on a suicidal charge the next morning, well, the troops always get suspicious.

What happened after breakfast surprised me the most of all, however. Instead of being lined up and marched into the crystal mountains—a lifter came down from the sky. My entire cohort was herded aboard.

Launching up into space violently, I felt the G-forces take their toll. The pilot wasn't fooling around. He didn't want to stay inside Glass World's gravity-well for one second longer than necessary.

"What's the hurry?" Harris grunted out next to me. "Is he late for dinner?"

"Seems like," I managed to say.

Leeson, sitting on the other side of me, gritted his teeth and spoke through them without parting his clenched jaws. "I thought we were attacking today. Maybe the plan changed. Maybe Turov got nervous and wants McGill to protect her."

Harris snorted with laughter, but I didn't say a thing. It wasn't general knowledge yet that Winslade had taken over and Galina had left for Earth. Part of me hoped Leeson was right, anyway. Maybe we would get a cush job like guarding the ship's quiet passages.

The ship lurched and slowed several long minutes later. Groaning and massaging our numb limbs, the troops aboard struggled to breathe normally again.

A big green light flashed when we docked, then the klaxon sounded. We were attached to *Berlin's* belly again.

I have to say it was a nice place to be. I felt much more secure aboard *Berlin*, cramped or not, than I did on the windswept plains of Glass World.

As we marched off the lifter, following glowing red arrows on the floor, I began to frown a bit. So did Harris and Leeson. Some of the numbers in the arrows were different. In fact, the number three—indicating our unit number—split off from the rest.

"Why are we going down a different passage than the rest of the cohort?" Harris complained. His eyebrows were beetling with vast suspicion already.

"Isn't this the way to *Berlin*'s crappy little Gray Deck?" Leeson asked.

"Oh no…" Harris said.

All of a sudden, my dopey smile and general sense of well-being was shattered. We were supposed to attack the enemy today, and it looked like we were going to. But, rather than being marched over an open field into the enemy guns, some wise-ass had decided it would be better to teleport us into the enemy nest.

As soon as we got to *Berlin*'s Gray Deck, which was a small, low-ceilinged affair with few frills, our fears were quickly realized. A team of unsmiling techs—Fleet pukes, one and all—began strapping us into teleport harnesses.

"Wait a second," Leeson complained. "These rigs aren't carrying enough of a charge for a return trip—not even at this range."

"Nope," I said.

"A one-way ticket, huh?" Harris asked. "What did you do to piss off the brass this time, McGill?"

"That's Centurion McGill to you, Adjunct," I reminded him.

He grumbled, but he shut the hell up.

Trussed up like chickens ready for the oven, we watched dismally as the far wall lit up. Tribune Galina Turov's face wasn't the one that loomed over us, however. Instead, it was a repugnant, greatly enlarged version of Winslade. His nostrils were each as big as a man's head and a lot uglier.

"What the hell...?" Leeson said.

"You *knew*!" Harris hissed out, rounding on me. "You knew all about this!"

I didn't even look at him. "Eyes front, Adjunct. You're acting like a splat."

This settled him down. He glared at Winslade and avoided looking at me at all.

"Troops," Winslade said, giving us a cold smile, "I'm so glad you're all assembled and ready for action. Today, you have a critical mission. For the sake of security, I wasn't able to tell you previously—but now, the cat's out of the bag. Yes, I'm in charge of Legion Varus from this day forward. The Glass World campaign is my first true command."

There were audible groans up and down the line-up. Moments later, thumps and grunts could be heard as veterans slapped the troops to silence. Winslade had never been well-liked by anyone other than the brass who he worked so hard to schmooze.

The new tribune moved at last. A skinny finger the size of a sapling tree trunk poked up, and for an awful second, we thought he might pick his nose with it. Everyone winced and squinted in horror—but all he did was tap at the side of his nostril. We relaxed a fraction.

"Let me first say that I'm proud to be your commander today. Previously, back on Machine World, I was left in a similarly dire predicament with hundreds of faithful Varus troops at my back. That day, as I know will happen again this time, the legion performed magnificently."

The troops around me were blinking in surprise. They weren't used to getting anything like a pep-speech from this particular officer.

I could recall, however, that Winslade *had* managed to pull it together and take his responsibilities seriously on those occasions when he'd been given a shot to do so. Tilting my head, I made an effort to listen to him for reals.

"We're going to start off with a bang. Rather than fighting our way through that morass of broken glass full of crawlers, we're doing an end-run. A commando team will be transported instantly into the enemy camp. Their mission will be to cause as much havoc as possible."

Here, the scene shifted from Winslade's overblown face to a long-range aerial shot of the mine. Bluish crystals gleamed all around like jewels. In the center, the mine looked like a black pupil of a glittering eye.

The scene zoomed in sickeningly. It transformed into the shots I'd taken from close-in, and the crackling light of the gateway posts was soon visible.

"There!" Winslade boomed with god-like volume. "There is our target! Due to the limitations of *Berlin*'s Gray Deck, the attacking force will be transported one unit at a time. The first unit will be commanded by Primus Graves himself. Every few minutes, with just enough time to suit up and charge, the next unit will be sent. Relentless as waves crashing on a beach, we will take them from the center. With luck, we'll wipe them out."

The scene faded, and Winslade's angular face appeared again. He was smiling for reals this time.

"Is he shitting us?" Harris muttered. "A few minutes is a long time for a hundred men to fight a thousand. We'll be dead before the second wave even hits."

"He knows," I said, and Leeson and Harris both studied me.

"Primus on the deck!" roared a noncom.

That's when Graves made his glorious entrance on Gray Deck. He walked in like a king, and we all turned to salute him.

Eerily, Winslade's face turned as if he could see Graves—maybe he could.

"Ah, here we are. Please, Primus, take over if you would. I have other matters to attend to. I'm sure your men will make me proud today."

"Thank you… Tribune," Graves said.

I got the feeling that using that last word hurt Graves somehow. It wounded him more deeply than any bullet or gouging alien claw could ever do. But that's how it was, Winslade was in charge, and we all knew Graves would follow his orders.

He always did.

-35-

The impossible task before us was daunting, but we lined up next to our launchers anyway. Every man put on his teleport harness and rigged it up, plugging into a prong-like connector on stations that were about a meter apart.

I'd been on several Gray Deck launch-staging areas, but *Berlin*'s version of the facility was tighter than most. We were bumping butts and elbows all over, especially the weaponeers with their bulky armor and missile-launchers.

That had been Sargon's call. He'd rather use the launchers to fire a thundering level of firepower all at once, rather than use belchers which would have to be manually adjusted.

"Belchers have their advantages," he told me, "including more destructive power over time for the weight carried—but sometimes you just want to blow things up as fast as you can. This is one of those times."

We exchanged glances, and I approved his edit to our load-out. Neither one of us expected to live long. In fact, our life expectancy would probably best be measured in seconds rather than minutes once we arrived at the LZ.

"Listen-up, team," Graves said, standing in front of us. He was wearing a harness for teleportation, just like the rest of us—but I noticed he wasn't standing next to one of the stations. His connector was loose and dangling. "We're about to embark on a glorious mission. We're being given the chance to strike a hammer-blow against Rigel. They've always enjoyed superior personal protection. We can't allow them to hold that advantage another day."

A ragged cheer went up from the group. We were kind of edgy, but the pep-talk was a good one. A best-in-class for Graves, actually, who usually managed to depress those who listened rather than inspire them.

"Unfortunately," Graves continued, "in a last second change of plan, I won't be going with the first wave. McGill is in command of this spearhead effort. You'll all make me proud regardless. Good hunting."

My mouth sagged open a bit. I'd been kind of counting on the idea that Graves would come down with us and die. How else was I going to make sure Graves died the way Winslade wanted, if he wasn't with the first wave and I was? I'd be dead for sure in minutes myself.

"Uh... sir?" I called out.

"Yes, Centurion?""

"Who made this last second change of plan?"

He and I eyed each other for a moment. I knew Winslade hadn't told Graves to shuffle up the roster. What did Graves know?

Graves glanced at his tapper. "Time to fly. We'll discuss the issue when we meet again. Do me proud, 3rd Unit."

That was it. He stepped back, even farther from the launching stations. In fact, as the countdown began and the blue light began to rise in intensity and color, I saw him shed the harness entirely.

Was Graves busting a move? Was he going to march upstairs and blow Winslade's brains out? I wasn't sure, but I was sure his actions were out of character for him.

Just before the throbbing light reached its climax, I smiled. If Graves was going to go first-strike on Winslade, well, I wished him all the best.

The distance was so short there was no detectable travel time. For a moment, we were in two places. It seemed to me that I was both aboard *Berlin* and on Glass World. Then Gray Deck faded away a moment later and there was only the surface of the target planet to contend with.

Overhead, I saw a starry night. I'd lost count of the hours on Glass World, which rotated faster than Earth did and thus had a shorter day than the fiction we maintained aboard *Berlin*.

Closer to hand, I next spotted a bustling community of armed soldiers from Rigel. They were spread out, working with digging equipment and haulers that carried vast amounts of sparkling earth.

As I got my bearings, I realized these haulers were carrying the ore between the gateway posts. They seemed to be in a hurry. Could they be pulling out?

"Weaponeers! Advance and take out that portal!"

The bears around us were just beginning to wake up to the fact they were no longer alone. There had to be several hundred of them on the bottom floor of the pit, with the tunnel in the back wall of the whole thing looking like the exposed maw of a massive beast. It's yawning wide jaws encompassed the gateway posts, the haulers—everything.

Sargon didn't have to be given an order twice. A shower of what looked like jets of flame shot up high into the night sky, washing out the stars. These smart missiles, perhaps two seconds into their deadly flight, made a sharp, angular ninety degree turn. They were now aiming down from above into the tight knot of bears and work-vehicles. Accelerating for the kill, they selected their own targets independently and roared downward toward the enemy.

All hell broke loose as the bears realized they were under close assault. They snarled, snatched out their slung weapons and began peppering us with pellets.

The missiles, however, were already on their way down. They slammed into the haulers full of ore. The bears driving them scrambled for cover, but they were caught and blown to fragments. The gateway posts themselves were likewise destroyed. The shock of the strike, so up-close and quick, was such that the enemy was overwhelmed.

"Ha!" I called out over tactical chat. "Nice shooting! The gateway is down and on fire! Well done—"

My congratulations were cut short as the bears picked themselves up and charged us from every direction. They had blood in their eyes. They were rushing us, and only death would stop them.

A vicious close-range firefight broke out. We were carrying shotguns like theirs, and at this range, we could penetrate their armor. The enemy fired the same kind of guns at us, but our gear was like tissue paper in comparison. Men were torn apart, screaming, with a dozen pellets tearing through their bodies at once.

About a minute later I was laying on my back dying in the mud. A bear with a feral snarl on his face stood on my chest, growling and holding up something, something that flapped and dripped and fluttered.

It was my arm, I realized. He'd torn it off somehow and was busy displaying the red crest of my centurion's insignia to his buddies.

It wasn't the arm with my tapper, so I could pick up some of the translation.

"I've got their commander! I demand a boon! I demand—"

That's when I drove my combat knife into his crotch. It was a left-handed move, and a dirty one at that. He'd been too distracted with all the excitement of having torn off my arm.

I don't want anyone to think I'd chosen the bear's gonads as my target out of some misguided sense of spite. It was just the only area I could easily reach. Just try having a meter-tall bear stand on your chest sometime—it wasn't an enviable position to fight from.

My move did, however, end his little speech. He hopped off me, bleeding and grabbing himself. A human would have probably been down and out, but not this bear. He came back and beat me with my own arm. Each thump and shudder hurt—but not too badly, as I was armored.

I was disappointed by his response. I'd partly made a dirty attack in order to gain a quick death. This bear was angry—really angry—but he wasn't cooperating by killing me yet.

Deciding I had to up the ante, I flipped open my visor with my single good hand. I was gratified to see him dance away in concern.

"Dumbass bear-cub!" I shouted, coughed, then grinned.

Snarling, a circle of bears came closer. They snatched away my knife, the last weapon I had. Due to cracked ribs, a broken pelvis and other damage, I wasn't able to get up or really defend myself further.

"You speak. You live. You are my prisoner!"

"Nope," I said with certainty. "I'm Squanto's creature. He owns me. He has for years."

They circled like a pack of humping aborigines, confused and disquieted by my words. "You lie! We own you! You are my—"

I kicked the bear with the bleeding crotch. It was the only play I had left.

His jaws snapped, and I heard fabric tear. It was a nasty bite to the ankle, but I grinned. "Is that all you've got, cub?" I asked. "A human child could kick your ass. Give me a minute to get my wind back, and I'll stand and fight you one-on-one."

My original opponent loomed close. He still had my arm, ripped free from my body and flapping oddly in his grip. His crotch still dripped blood from where I'd gouged him.

I'm not certain, but I didn't think I'd ever seen a bear who was more pissed off than this fellow. Maybe Squanto had been, back when I'd pinned him down and made a fool of him as I rode him in front of the Scupper Queen on Storm World. But... maybe not even then.

"There he is!" I called out. "That one is the chicken-shit who—"

They surged closer, growling, and I kind of figured I'd pulled it off. I'd gotten them into a state of murderous rage. They'd forgotten all about taking me prisoner.

Then, before they consummated my date with destiny, a taller, larger shadow loomed behind them.

It was a man. A tall man with an agile way of carrying himself. His every step was a swagger, and I knew him in an instant.

"Maurice?" I called out, and I laughed until my lungs bubbled around my broken ribs.

"James...?"

It was the one and only Maurice Armel. He had been the tribune of Germanica, then the renegade commander of a legion in Claver's employ.

"What are you doing out here?" I asked him. "Cleaning up bear-scat?"

"Nothing so mundane," he said. He had a French accent and a moustache to match. "I'm here for the same reason you are, my demented friend. I need impenetrable armor for my new army. Therefore, I made a deal with Squanto to supply it."

"Ah," I rasped out. The world was getting kind of hazy now, but I didn't want him to notice. He might try to save me if he knew I was bleeding out. "Help me up, would you? I've gotten banged up a bit."

"I don't think so," he said, and he put a boot on my chest, pressing me back down easily. I was as weak as a kitten now, if the truth were to be told.

From somewhere, he produced a long shaft of steel. I knew it well. He had a thing for skinny swords. This one was called a rapier, I think.

He put the tip of it under my chin, right in through my open faceplate. I made no effort to stop him. He leaned down close, and the bears surrounding us shuffled, muttering dark things among themselves. Their words sounded like clicks and growls to me.

Then, he thrust his sword through my throat, my neck, and I think a few vertebrae in the back before it poked out the other side.

"The coup de grace," he told me quietly. "A debt repaid. I do this thing because you helped Leeza breathe again."

I tried to thank him as I died, but I couldn't do it.

-36-

When I came staggering out of the revival chamber in Blue Bunker on Glass World, Winslade was right there waiting for me.

"So there you are," he said in a prissy tone—come to think of it, his tone was almost always prissy.

"Reporting for duty, Tribune!" I told him, throwing a sloppy salute. My muscles were only a few minutes old, and they still felt kind of rubbery.

"I should have left you dead for all the good you did me. Now, there's no excuse to send Graves into that hellhole. We've broken their supply route and—"

"Uh… excuse me, sir. Are you annoyed that we managed to complete our mission with bravado and unexpected speed?"

"Yes I am, McGill. You see, sometimes there's more to a mission than meets the eye. Sometimes, the real purpose of a mission is unknown—to all but those who are supposed to be bright enough not to overdo."

My frown deepened. I'm not a man who cries and whines about getting killed, but when I do, I at least expect to be treated in a respectful manner. Winslade was failing on this account, and he was beginning to piss me off.

"But I blew up the gateway," I protested. "Just like we planned."

"Yes, yes, yes," he said, walking ahead of my new, recovering body. "That's my point. Graves was supposed to teleport down *first*."

"You'd better take that up with him. He decided not to do that on his own, after you left."

"I'm not going to say anything to him. Otherwise, he might divine my plans."

"He might have already."

He blew out a disgusted puff of air. "Trickery. You and Graves are both using deception against me now, McGill. I'd expected you to employ such tactics against Graves!"

I shrugged. "I don't know what I could have done differently. How was I supposed to—?"

"Think, man! You can't be such a cretin. Since you went first, you should have failed to destroy the posts. At least then, Graves might have been forced to go down with the second wave and do the deed himself. With any luck, he'd be dead right now."

"After which he'd be mysteriously lingering in the revival queue?"

Winslade shrugged his skinny, conniving shoulders. "Well… who knows the vagaries of these revival machines better than you do? Graves might come out a bad grow, or worse, his data could be misplaced."

"That one again, huh?"

"Anything to keep him dead for the time being. As it is, he's a threat to my position. At any moment, Turov's order to put me in command might be rescinded."

"She could do that anyway."

"Ah yes… but if I've proven myself first, I don't really care. Who wants to run a shit-outfit like Varus anyway? I have bigger goals in mind."

Winslade had always been a sneaky snake of a man. He had a scheme for every day of the week, and two for Sunday.

"Listen Tribune," I told him. "I'm rethinking my part in all this. I don't see why I owe you anything."

He looked cagey. "I was wondering when the mule would refuse to pull the cart. Rather than threats and coercion, I'll offer you something you really want."

"What's that?"

"A chance to talk to Abigail again."

My eyes blinked twice. I hadn't expected that. I didn't have any serious interest in the girl, mind you, but she did intrigue me.

"The truth is," he continued, "she wants to speak with you... rather badly. She says you have forgotten again to get her into contact with someone. That you failed to hold up your end of a critical bargain."

I gave my head a scratch at that point. Sure, she'd asked to be put in touch with Drusus. I'd made my pitch, and he'd agreed to port me out to her location. But after all that, and all the dying and confusion...

"The thing of it is," I said, "she led us to this spot, to Glass World, but we haven't secured it yet. Drusus is only interested in gaining access to that body armor at the moment. He'll probably meet with her afterward."

Winslade looked alarmed. "*That's* how we got out here? Why doesn't anyone tell me these things?"

I could have told him he wasn't in the loop because no one trusted him, but that wouldn't have improved his mood any.

He began walking around again and making sweeping gestures with his hands. "Drusus must be mad to follow one of Claver's clones around, especially a female version. It's positively bizarre."

"She led us right here. She helped us find Glass World. I guess to her way of thinking that's good enough. She figures we should be meeting with her now."

Winslade formed an ugly smirk with his lips. "Well? Do you want to talk to her or not?"

"Uh... have you got her aboard *Berlin* or something?"

"Indeed I do. I ordered her revival shortly after taking command of this task force."

"So... she's alive and everything?"

Winslade's nasty smile was back. He lifted a hand and patted my shoulder. I didn't like that, but I managed not to hit him.

"If you'd like to learn more," he said, "you know what you have to do."

By the time I left him, I was in a sour mood. Was I really going to kill Graves?

Something one must understand is that killing somebody else in Legion Varus wasn't considered a heinous crime. Sure, it might get you flogged or demoted, but it wasn't really murder—not exactly.

Getting someone permed, though, that was big stuff. Permadeath was viewed as possibly worse than regular murder had been in the old days before revival machines. If someone was permed, it meant a deep and sincere effort had been made to keep them dead. We had backups everywhere these days, which made permadeath increasingly rare. Many of us had lived so long in the legions we no longer thought of death as lasting forever. It just didn't seem natural to us. Therefore, perming someone was seen as beyond the pale, like burning people alive at the stake. It was an act of barbarism, deserving of the worst kind of scorn.

Just killing someone, however, wasn't all *that* bad. An inconvenience to the victim, sure. A criminal act deserving of punishment, definitely. But Varus regulars died all the time in training and in battle. Because of this overfamiliarity with the process, we dealt with day-to-day murders among fighting men the way they might have dealt with fist-fights in the old days. You got yelled at, you went to the stockades, and you might be shot or flogged yourself. Then it was over, everyone went back to fighting together—hopefully without holding a grudge.

So I thought about it. I could kill Graves, of course, in a number of ways. We lived in spacesuits most of time, and if one of those things sprung a leak… well, it didn't take much to kill a man in space.

But I didn't want to pull something like that just to talk to Abigail. It simply wasn't in me. I decided, therefore, as a man who was both lazy and a liar, that I'd wait it out. I'd bide my time, claiming I was working on the goal—but do nothing.

Who knew? Maybe I'd get lucky, and Graves would fall in a hole or something. In the meantime, Winslade would be off my back.

The following day, I woke up stretching and climbed into the showers. A lot of men didn't like showering in large groups in steamy chambers, but I didn't mind. For one thing, there were girls in there. Nude women lathering up and chatting with glistening skin, well sir, for me that started every day in a positive manner.

As long as you weren't leering in an obvious manner, the girls didn't mind at all. It was normal to them. Some of them even liked to put on a show, stretching and lingering and so forth. Today, a familiar woman by the name of Natasha decided to do just that.

She was a nice-looking girl, and we'd had a fling long ago—well, to be honest, it was more than a fling. We'd been on-again-off-again lovers for years.

"What is it, James?" she asked me as I gawked at her.

Natasha had taken up a spray nozzle right next to mine, and I'd already had my water ding and buzz at me indicating my time was up twice. Being an officer, I was able to override that with a single touch of the thumb.

"Uh…" I said, while she smiled up at me over her shoulder. "I couldn't help but notice how fine-looking you are today, Specialist Elkin. My apologies."

She shrugged and kept smiling. "Is it true that our tribune has left the star system? That she won't be back for the duration of this campaign?"

There it was. Natasha had always felt out-classed by Galina Turov. That was a reasonable thing to be intimidated about. Galina was not only finer-looking than probably any woman in the legion, she was also in charge and possessive over one James McGill.

It occurred to me that I should make a move. I blinked and stared at the way the water was washing the suds off her breasts for a few more seconds, then I decided to give it a go. After all, Natasha might have made a play for me at any time over the last several campaigns—but Galina had always been hanging around. This was a rare opportunity.

"I've got an idea," I said, and she looked at me expectantly.

My idea, of course, involved Natasha and me working together on a private project. She agreed, and we did so later that same day.

The preordained night followed, and I'd forgotten what that sweet girl could be like. She wasn't pushy or demanding. It was glorious.

Still, by morning, I found myself wondering what Galina was doing back on Earth. Thoughts like these contributed to my general suspicion that I was a cursed man.

-37-

The imaginary project I'd dreamt up to work on with Natasha had to do with deep-link transmissions. I'd always wondered if they could be detected or even listened in on. In fact, I'd once made up a bullshit story about such a tracing device to get Centurion Toro, who worked for Claver, to help me escape Clone World.

The device had always been a mere figment to me, but I'd long believed it should be possible. Natasha jumped on the idea and, using my newfound high-level security clearance, she went right to work on it.

The next morning, we ate breakfast together in the mess hall. A lot of people tossed us glances. Women who I'd known intimately tended to watch with twisted-lip expressions of disgust. The men slapped each other and made jokes we couldn't quite hear.

Neither Natasha nor I paid any attention. For my part, this was because I didn't really care. On her side of the equation, Natasha didn't seem to notice.

She was too engrossed in figuring out the problem I'd given her. To tap into deep-link transmissions… the thought was intoxicating to her. As she blathered on about quantum computers and in-phase photons on different planets, I daydreamed about a second night of passion. To my way of thinking, such a pleasant prospect was definitely in the cards if old McGill played them right.

"Last night was nice," I said. "Really nice."

"Yes... yes it was," Natasha said, but she wasn't even looking at me. Instead, she was studying her knapsack computer.

Techs like her weren't limited to a personal tapper embedded in the forearm. Instead, they had larger more powerful machines they carried around in military-grade sacks which were usually slung over their backs.

"James... I want you to look at this transmission pattern and tell me if you see anything unusual."

"Uh... okay."

She showed me the display on her computer. It was backlit brightly, far more than any tapper ever was. Maybe that was because human skin could only echo out a muted level of light, and an honest screen could do much more.

On the display was a series of waveforms and stuff. "Looks like a puddle that someone threw a stone into."

"Exactly," she said, to my surprise. "That's exactly right. This is an image of an intermediate object seen only in the form of a group-resonance."

"Uh..."

"What I mean is, this is a planet showing some ripples due to the passage of a deep-link message."

"What? How's that possible? I thought deep-links weren't actual transmissions. That two computers just studied aligned photons that were connected in some way over a great distance."

"That's right. Both ends of the aligned-photon connection change, and nothing else between them does—except for another set of aligned photons."

"Huh?"

Natasha's face took on a patient, but somewhat frustrated expression. That's what usually happened to people who tried to explain astrophysics or similar subjects to me. "Listen, quantum communications involves connecting two points, making changes to one and then watching changes in the other—regardless of the distance between the two."

"Right, I got that."

"Well... what if there were naturally occurring matches in other places? Like on the surface of a sun, or a reflective ocean on a planet."

"Okay..."

"So, using that idea, I began to trace back data readings. I found a record of recent transmissions between this task force and Central. Using the times and dates of those transmissions, I cross-referenced, screening for abnormalities—"

"Whoa, whoa," I said, putting up a big hand. "Did you use my clearance to get a record of when the deep-link was last used?"

She looked down at her untouched food and gave me a shrug. "Maybe. How else could I get such sensitive data?"

"Damn, girl," I said, digging into the apple and toast on her plate. I left the ham. She needed to eat something.

Natasha continued on, showing me more stuff I couldn't make heads or tails of. At last, she put it all aside. "The point is, the ocean here on this planet... Some of the light reflected by the local water shimmered when the transmission was made."

"Really? You figured that out so fast?"

She smiled. "It was your idea. You should get part of the credit."

"Uh-huh."

Already, I was thinking of Floramel. She'd said something years ago about being able to do this. The lab people at Central were most likely going to take a dim view of the discovery, as they no doubt considered it a state secret.

But then, I got another idea.

"Hey, could you actually translate the transmissions? I mean—listen in?"

"I think I can. And if I'm doing it, others are certain to be doing it as well."

"Hmm... what if you ran those shimmers through a lot of software and played the results?"

Her shy smile shifted into a full-blown grin. "That's what I'm going to do next."

That was Natasha. She'd always been a hacker. Playing buzzer-wrangler for the legions was boring to her. She wanted to break into things and examine them from the inside out.

"What was the date, exactly," she asked, "when Turov first mentioned leaving Glass World to go back to Earth?"

"Uh… the fourteenth I think."

"That was the first time she said anything about it?" she asked. "Just to be sure."

"Yes. Remember that announcement?"

She waved her fingers between us. "No, no. Not the official announcement. I'm talking about when she told *you* about it."

"It was the day before… I think."

Natasha smiled again. I frowned as I watched her work. Was she really going to—?

A moment later, she spun her computer display around for me to see again. "Satellite imagery from the thirteenth. I'm picking up a shimmer."

"What does it say?"

"I have no idea—not yet. I'll have to work on it. Listen… if we could do an experiment, we could come up with a baseline to test against."

"Huh… I'm not following."

"Okay, we transmit a simple message over a deep-link right here. Then, we check to see what the reflections do. If we know what a given message says, we can interpolate what other messages will look like. Then… then we can listen in."

She was so excited her butt wasn't even firmly on the chair anymore. Watching her and nodding now and then, I began to regret my most recent choices in life. Just to get laid, I'd gotten this girl fired up and performing interstellar crimes. It wasn't the first time, and it probably wouldn't be the last, where such things happened.

Fortunately, a klaxon sounded shortly after breakfast was over. The whole bunker lit up with red arrows.

My unit was given new orders—an attack was incoming.

-38-

After we'd made our commando attack and destroyed their gateway to Rigel, it was generally assumed that we could take our time encircling and destroying the enemy formation. After all, they were in a crystal fortress, but without supplies from home, time was on our side. We therefore adopted a siege mentality.

But that didn't last long. For one thing, the bears weren't interested in cooperating.

The first thing that came at us was their flying machines. They had a clear advantage in air support. Their flying machines weren't fast like jets, they were more like helicopters. Very maneuverable, they could land anywhere. That kind of design worked better against shielded troops, as fast-moving aircraft would be damaged while flying through the force shields.

The alien buzzing machines swooped over the crystal hills and flew from several angles at once toward our encampment. The shield we had, designed mostly to stop missiles, failed to halt their approach.

Once inside the perimeter, they began hosing down our trenches from above with rapid-fire plasma turrets. The gunners were armored and shielded, as was the bottom of each airship. Our troops fired back with morph-rifles and other small arms, but with little effect.

"Sargon!" I roared when I reached my designated trench. "Have you tried our mini-missiles yet?"

"No dice, sir. The missiles are jammed or something. They can't lock on these targets."

"Then get out belchers. Man the 88s and tilt them upward. We have to hurt them."

Sargon shouted to his weaponeers. They fired belchers clumsily into the sky. It wasn't a good weapon for the task, however. Belchers were direct line-of-sight weapons. Tagging a dodging flying platform that was armored and firing back down at us proved difficult.

The air raid was brief, but effective. Hundreds of troops were left dead or wounded. We'd only downed two of the fliers in four full minutes of fighting.

When Graves got my report, he wasn't happy. "That's unacceptable, Centurion. Do your men know how to shoot straight or what?"

"I'm sorry sir, the enemy strafed us as we were taking cover. Most of my casualties weren't even in a trench when they were hit."

"That's just great, McGill. When the next wave hits, make sure you're ready this time."

My mouth sagged and my eyes blinked. "Next wave? I'm not seeing—oh wait, here they come."

Fast on the heels of the initial aerial assault, a ground force approached. They poured out from between every crack in the crystal wall ahead of us and spread out. They came at a ground-eating run and boiled over the closest trenches.

"We should have built this camp farther back," Leeson complained. "These little bastards are getting in too close. We should have built a killing field—"

"Well, we fuck-all didn't," Harris interrupted. "No one expected this level of resistance. Centurion, what are your orders, sir? Do we just wait for them to hit our trenches?"

It was a good question. Harris was right, this was our opportunity to help the front line—but I wasn't sure if I should order a counter-assault.

Sucking in a deep breath, I wrapped a gun strap around my left hand and bellowed at my unit over tactical chat.

"Everyone, up and out of your trenches! Advance to contact! We're going to support the front lines before they're overwhelmed."

Normally, good tactical thinking would suggest we should stay put and gun the bears down as they came at us. Unfortunately, our rifles lacked the punch to penetrate their armor, and our shotguns, based on Rigellian designs, had short range. To help the front lines we had to advance.

I half-expected Graves to order us to fall back—but he didn't. Instead, units all along the line were following suit.

The fighting on the front line was vicious. The bears were well-equipped professionals, but so were we. The unit we were moving up to support was also from my cohort. It was Manfred's unit, one of the few officers in Legion Varus who shared my outlook and attitude.

As we arrived, I thought at first that the bears had already creamed Manfred's unit. There wasn't a soul who was still standing in those trenches and firing at the advancing enemy line.

But then, without warning, Manfred's entire unit rose up and let rip with a storm of heavy gunfire. They all had shotguns, and they unloaded them into the guts of the advancing enemy.

At the same time, I urged my own men to rush forward. Just as the bears met up with Manfred's entrenched troops, we got there and fired pointblank. Many had fallen when Manfred had ambushed them, but even more were blown down by my charging line. It helped that Manfred's men were standing in a trench, as we could easily fire over them to nail the advancing enemy.

Often, one blast wasn't enough to stop a bear soldier. He had to be gunned down repeatedly—but at last, he stopped getting up.

After they'd taken something like thirty percent losses, the bears turned and ran. I'm not sure if they were following orders or running for their lives. Either way, we were glad to see their tails instead of their fangs.

Sliding down a dirt wall in Manfred's ditch, I almost fell on him. We sat down in the bottom of the hole, both breathing hard.

"McGill?" he said, marveling. He was a broad, stocky fellow with a Brit accent. "How did you get here so fast—no, wait. Don't answer that. I don't want to be the star witness at your court martial."

"That's the right attitude. What's your unit's status?"

He threw up a tired hand at my question. "You don't really frigging care, and I don't have time to answer."

"Why's that?"

"The next enemy wave is coming," he told me.

"Uh... I think we just drove them back."

He shook his head, drank water and shoved a battle-computer in a satchel toward me. There was a little gore on it, and seeing as it was no longer attached to one of his tech specialists, I didn't ask where he had gotten it.

On the display, which was sprinkled with blood and grime, I saw red triangles representing enemy contacts. They were spreading out in a crescent pattern around our entrenched position.

"First off," Manfred said, "their air assault softened us up. Then they sent a ground force to see if they could get rid of us on the cheap—but they're done playing now. They're encircling and planning to finish us methodically."

I nodded, going over the tacticals. They'd been downloaded from *Berlin*—a clear protocol violation. Only the primus-level officers were supposed to see the state of the entire battlefield.

"You've got good hackers in your unit, the same as I do," I told him.

"Of course I do, mate. You can't get far in Varus without the extra intel they don't want you to have. What I want to know is what we're going to do about this?"

He looked at me with an odd expression. I'd seen it before. Just because, I'd been able to alter the natural course of events now and then, people thought I was some kind of magician.

I shook my head. "I don't know... maybe we could get *Berlin* to use her big guns..."

"That's as likely to splatter us as the bears."

"Sure is." I gave him an appraising glance. Just how committed was he to holding this planet?

"Hold on a moment, you crazy bastard. I didn't say we should be annihilated then revive what's left. That's insane!"

"I didn't say anything of the kind."

Suddenly, Manfred half stood up in his trench. A few bolts struck the dirt where his helmet had been momentarily exposed, so he hunkered back down again. The earth smoked and the melted ground cooled into something that looked like dirty glass.

"McGill," he said through his teeth. "This is total madness! Are you telling me the brass plans to destroy the entire ground force once the bears fully engage?"

I actually didn't know any such thing. But the more I thought about it, the more it made sense. The bears probably didn't have revival machines, and we'd cut them off from their homeworld. That meant a trade of forces was in our favor. We could replace our men—and they couldn't replace theirs.

Manfred went on for some time about my imagined plan of action, but I didn't care, and I wasn't listening. I was thinking of the brass up on *Berlin*.

It was time to contact acting Tribune Winslade.

-39-

I wormed my way, mostly on my belly, back to our next closest trench line. It wasn't our original hash-mark of ditches we'd dug when we'd arrived. It had been abandoned by another unit, so we took up residence within.

3rd Unit was in sorry condition. After fighting to Manfred's trench then back again, we'd taken heavy losses. One out of every three of my men had been lost.

It did my heart good to see that very few of the survivors were complaining. After all, we'd accomplished our mission of keeping Manfred's position from being overwhelmed. Along the way, we'd killed our fair share of the enemy as well.

Catching my breath, I had a chance to think. Immediately and unbidden, an idea formed in my mind. I didn't like the idea. I didn't like it at all, but once considered, I couldn't shake it.

Sometimes a thought occurs to a man which is so monstrous, so heinous in nature, that it's hard to wrap your head around it. Today was such a day for poor old James McGill.

Deciding I wasn't really taking any action, that I'd just *thought* of something evil, I could look into the idea without any guilty feelings. I used the blood-crusted computer that Manfred had let me keep.

Very soon, the idea led to action. I couldn't help myself. Connecting Manfred's rig to Kivi's, I was able to open a channel up to *Berlin*. The big battlecruiser was parked in orbit over our heads, but we'd never seen it with the naked eye. The atmosphere was too hazy.

I spent a few minutes coming up with a good message to hijack Winslade's mind. It had to be short, but impactful. A hook, essentially. Something that couldn't be ignored, even in the heat of battle.

In the end, I sent out just four words in a subject line, and I texted it tapper-to-tapper through the channel I'd managed to keep alive.

I've got the answer.

That's all I said. It was short and sweet, and designed to elicit a response from a curious rodent like Winslade.

Sure enough, my tapper was buzzing a few minutes later. Kivi had watched this process throughout, and she eyed the red print on my arm with concern.

"Aren't you going to answer that, Centurion?" she asked.

"I surely am… in a minute."

The buzzing carried on, and the red print kept flashing and tickling my arm. I took a deep breath and a swig of that sweat-tasting juice they gave us all the time. I grimaced. It was full of protein and a little sugar, but I'd never gotten used to it.

"Is that Graves?" Kivi asked.

"Specialist, move on down the line, please. No listening in, either."

She reluctantly retreated, and I turned on the secure-channel option. Then I answered Winslade's incessant buzzing.

"What is it, Tribune?" I asked. "The bears are setting up to rush us again, and I—"

"Don't you think I know that, McGill? I'm staring at the operational map right now. You aren't sending me private notes as a prank, are you?"

"Oh yeah, that message. I've got the answer, sir."

"So I've gathered. Can you please elucidate?"

"Uh… If you mean explain the answer, I certainly can. But first, sir… is this line *truly* secure?"

Winslade didn't answer right away. Instead, I saw the encryption meter tick up a few notches. He'd typed in some security codes only a higher officer had access to.

"There," he said, "unless Drusus himself has secretly stowed away aboard this overcrowded ship, no one will overhear you. Now, please tell me what you're talking about."

"I've got the answer. I'm talking about how to get rid of these bastard bears... and our other problems."

Winslade's face loomed alarmingly large in my tapper screen. He was leaning close, whispering into his tapper. After a moment, all I could see were his lips, and his wet-glinting teeth. I touched the black-out option so I didn't have to look at that.

"McGill, I'm very busy. Tell me your answer right now, or I'll have you flayed alive."

"Yes, sir. Here's the deal, when they hit us, when they hit us hard—bombard our encampment. Kill everyone down here. Kill the bears, kill us—kill everything and everyone. Later, you can decide who to revive."

Winslade was quiet for a few seconds. "It would solve certain... personnel problems, but it seems extreme," he said, "even for you."

"It is, sir. But I think we're going to lose this fight anyway. If you blow them up with *Berlin's* big guns while their forces are hitting us with everything they've got... well sir, by morning you can drop a freshly revived cohort, and I'll bet you dollars to donuts that we can march right into that mine and take over."

"Dollars? Isn't that currency forbidden? Never mind—don't answer that. Let's stay on point for once, shall we?"

"I'm with you, sir. What do you think of the idea?"

He was quiet for about two seconds. "On the face of it, the concept is insanity itself. I might be court-martialed upon returning to Earth."

"Nonsense, sir! Anyone who wants to stay in the top slot has to give orders that make headlines on the grid back home. Besides, there are precedents, and you'll have won the battle with a single dramatic stroke."

"Such finality..." Winslade lamented. "Thanks for the thought, McGill. I'll have to consider it. Hold a moment."

Turning my head, I saw Kivi had crawled near. I waved her off, but she was insistent. She showed me her computer screen.

The red triangles were advancing now. They'd encircled us, and they were coming in for the kill.

"Uh…" I said. "Whatever you're going to do, Tribune, don't take too long thinking about it. We're about to be wiped out."

Winslade broke the connection then, and six minutes later we were up to our assholes in small, angry bears.

They overwhelmed the forward trenches like Manfred's almost immediately. Their approach was different this time, and ingenious. Knowing they had the advantage when they were at close range, they rushed us in groups of twenty. Each group was a tight squad protected by a mobile force-dome that had a radius of five meters or so. These domes crackled as they swept over the grasses, the fallen dead and the muddy trenches.

We shot at the bears, of course. We even fired point-blank with belchers and mini-missiles, but not even our 88s could penetrate their mobile domes.

Once these bubbles reached our trench lines, the sneaky little trolls abandoned the projector device they were carrying, deployed shotguns and leapt into the trenches.

Then a desperate struggle began. It was hand-to-hand at times, and always bloody. We tore apart the bears with mines, automated turrets, force-blades and our own guns. They did the same to us with their enhanced claws and shotguns.

Each alien was small compared to us, but just like bears back home on Earth, their muscle density was higher than that of a human. They were, gram-for-gram, more than our equals. Couple that with the nearly impossible job of penetrating their armor and, well, we were taking the worst of it.

"Are we just going to wait until they assault our trench, McGill?" Harris demanded.

He was angry and scared, and I couldn't blame him. We'd fired a thousand power bolts each, and I doubted we'd killed a single enemy. They were going to hit us soon and wipe us out. It was as simple as that.

"Tell the troops to prepare to charge," I told him.

Harris looked surprised for a moment, but then he seemed to consider. He nodded at last. "Will do, Centurion."

About a minute later, 3rd Unit got up as one and rushed the trenches that held 10th Unit. We had the fun of at least surprising the bears, jumping into the trench behind them and hitting them in the ass. For a time, I thought we might even kill a whole enemy squad.

Then two more bear squads showed up, and the fighting became grim. Soon, a man could hardly stand up straight on the sliding mounds of bodies. The mud and blood mixed together into a crusty soup.

Taking a blast in the back, I never even saw the bear that finished me. In shock and dying, I pitched onto my face and squirmed there, groaning and struggling just to breathe.

Before I died, however, I managed to roll over on my ruined back. Men and bears walked right over me, but I hardly felt it, or saw or heard them.

Staring straight up at the heavens, I saw the skies light up. It was as if the sun had come up—but it was already high noon on Glass World.

Seeing glowing streaks of fire descend, two sets of four in tight groups, I knew the *U. E. Berlin* had fired her big guns. The bombardment of Glass World had begun.

-40-

When I woke up again, I had no idea when or where I was. I was kind of slow about returning to life, and I felt fuzzy. I could be on Glass World, Blue Deck on *Berlin*, or even back home on Earth a year later. None of these realities would have surprised me.

"Did we win?" I croaked out, but no one seemed to hear me.

"Get him up, push him!" a female bio said.

"He's a centurion—and he's not able to walk yet, Specialist."

"I don't care. I don't care about his APGAR scores or his prognosis. I want him off my table."

I was unceremoniously shoved off the gurney onto the floor. Fluttering my eyes open, I saw other men shared the deck with me. They lay in various states. Some were struggling to their feet. Some were shaking their heads and clawing at their eyes. Others were putting on uniforms—and a few looked dead.

"We can't keep rushing every grow!" the orderly said in hushed voice. "It's going to get worse if we seed the chamber too fast!"

"Shut up," the bio specialist said. "We've got our orders, and we're going to follow them. Recharge the tanks and start the next grow. Keep the juices flowing!"

It took me three tries to get to my feet. Once I was up, I found myself swaying and blinking. It felt like I had the hangover to beat all hangovers.

Then I noticed my toes—or rather, I didn't notice them. I didn't have any toes.

"Aw, dammit!" I complained aloud. "No time to grow me some toes? Do you two clowns know how hard it is to run with no toes inside your boots?"

The bio looked at me. Her face was uncompromising. "You've got fingers. That's good enough to hold a rifle. I suggest you get one, get outside, and shoot down a bear."

"The bears are still coming?"

"They sure as shit are, Centurion," the orderly said.

They went back to work, and I stopped giving them grief. Instead, I studied the troops around me. They seemed dazed and listless.

About two minutes later, I had all the live ones up and hopping. They had on uniforms and boots that made them wince with every step. No one in the whole unit had been reborn with a single toe.

"Stuff an extra sock up there," I ordered. "It helps."

"Just how the hell would you know to do that, McGill?" Barton asked me as she complied.

I looked at her. Years ago, we'd had a fling. Now, it felt like that happy time was a century gone. The memory was a pile of dust in my mind, and I could hardly believe it was real.

"When it comes to double-time revives, this isn't my first rodeo," I admitted. "Suit up people! Walk as straight as you can, and move out!"

At my back nine troops followed, staggering along like the walking dead. They were grim-faced, but they weren't complaining. It was obvious to everyone that'd we'd been shit out of the machines early due to some overwhelming emergency.

It was only as we exited Blue Deck that it dawned on me we weren't on Glass World anymore. We were walking inside titanium walls. We had to be aboard *Berlin*—and if they needed fighting men aboard the battlecruiser, that could only be because we'd been boarded.

"All right 3rd Unit," I said to the nine who were struggling in my wake. "We're in a defensive action. This ship has been boarded, and we're going to repel the invaders."

Grim-faced and wincing slightly with every step, we plundered an armory and moved to where we found troops rushing toward the aft region of the vessel. The crew and the ship's marines looked stressed, and even the Varus people I saw looked dazed and bewildered.

Using my tapper, I sought out a tactical assignment from Graves, my primus—but of course, there wasn't any.

"Winslade…" I said aloud.

Barton, the only one of my three adjuncts who was breathing again as yet, sidled close. "What about Winslade, sir?" she asked.

She said this in a low, suspicious tone. She'd really become one of us after several campaigns. The girl was from Victrix originally, but that pedigree had passed by the wayside as the years rolled by. She now knew the score as well as anybody in the legion—well, almost anybody.

"Nothing, Adjunct," I assured her with a helpful lie. "It's just that without Graves being out of the oven yet, Winslade is next up in the command hierarchy."

"Lord help us…" she whispered, and I kept right on smiling like I didn't even hear her.

Working my tapper again, I contacted Winslade. To my surprise, he answered immediately.

"McGill!" he said, sounding as bright-eyed and bushy-tailed as can be. In comparison, me and my men shambled like zombies. "I'm surprised you're up and around already—but then I did put a priority signature on your revival order."

"Oh… thanks, sir. I'm assuming there's a boarding effort underway? Or is it a mutiny?"

"The former, I'm afraid. The bears must not have liked our successful bombardment on Glass World. They've sent out some patrol ships to fight back. Fortunately, during your brief demise, we managed to destroy the patrol ships. Unfortunately, they managed to reach us with assault modules first. Now, if you don't mind, I've got a situation on my hands and as much as I like to chit-chat—"

"I understand completely, sir. But this isn't a social call. I'm reporting for orders. You're my next-in-line CO."

"Oh... of course... and we'd better keep that fiction alive to cover, hmm? All right, your unit is the only one revived right now from your cohort. You're to support the anti-boarding effort forming up in the aft passages. Report there and follow the orders of Marine Captain Khan. He knows how to defend his ship better than you do."

"Will do, sir... but isn't there some unfinished business between us?"

"What? You've got to be kidding, McGill. We're being boarded. You'll get to see your sweetheart clone the moment this action has been completed—presuming that we survive it. Now, I'll put you in touch with the marine captain in question—"

He broke off, then the channel switched to a round-headed man who spoke with an accent and looked like he never smiled. "McGill? This is Marine Captain Khan. I am the commanding officer of *Berlin's* defenders. You're the Varus leader, yes?"

"That's right, Captain." I'd already decided I wasn't going to call this man "sir" as it would be inappropriate. The rank of centurion was equivalent to a marine captain, even if we were aboard his ship and in space at the moment.

If I'd offended Khan, he didn't show it. He stared at me with all the expressiveness of a block of wood. "The enemy assault shuttles have clustered near the engine chambers in the aft part of the ship. You will stand watch on the bridge, McGill, in case something goes wrong there."

Right off, I knew his game. He didn't want me anywhere near his troops or his engines. He wanted me to play watchdog as far from the action as possible.

"I'm sorry sir," I said without hesitation. "My orders are to accompany you and participate in defending this ship."

Khan didn't answer right off. He seemed to be fooling with his tapper. Finally, he looked back up at me. "Your orders have been confirmed. However, it says here that you are under my leadership. Do you accept this condition?"

"Condition...? Uh... sure."

"Very well. Meet me at the pressure doors leading into Engine Room Three. You will back up my troops as we secure the area."

I opened my mouth to answer, but the screen had gone dark. Khan had cut the connection.

"Rude bastard," Barton said. She was hovering at my shoulder, looking on.

"It's his ship. He doesn't want monkeys destroying his engines. I get all that, but we're not as green in this kind of action as he might think."

After setting my tapper to lead me to the designated meeting point, I led the group at a brisk trot. There were plenty of curses and grimaces from each of my troops as we jogged along. Bouncing on their nonexistent toes was probably the worst pastime my troops could think of at that moment, but it couldn't be helped.

After several minutes of rapid advancement, we reached Engine Room Three and found Khan's troops deployed and preparing to break in through a large sealed door.

"What's on the far side?" I asked, rapping my steel gauntlets on the door.

Khan turned toward me, but there was no handshake, and no heartfelt greeting. There was no greeting at all.

"The enemy is about to breach into the chamber."

"What about the crew inside?"

Khan shrugged disinterestedly. "We will revive them later, assuming *Berlin* survives this assault."

Unable to find any fault with his logic, I opened my mouth to ask about any targets we should be careful not to shoot—but he turned away again.

He had a full platoon with him, at least triple the number of Varus troops I had with me. I hoped this wasn't everything we had to defend the ship with, but I suspected it might be.

"Kill everything that moves," Khan ordered. "Try not to hit the instruments. Blow the doors—now."

"Uh…" I said, but no one was even looking at me.

A marine sapper lit off a charge, and the door burned around the lock. The heat and light was intense, and it flickered like burning magnesium. Finally, the door fell open with a resounding clang.

Inside, we were treated to a shocking sight. All the crewmen were already dead. Many of them were floating in ghastly states of repose. To me, it looked like they'd died when the outer hull of the ship had been breached by our invaders.

On the far side of the engine chamber, which was the size of a basketball gym, the nose of an alien craft poked through the skin of the ship. I could see where drill-marks had bitten into the ship's hull and torn it up. Some kind of sharp point, like a spindle, was lodged in the outer wall of the ship.

As we watched, the tip of this spear point spread open. and we could see it was hollow inside. Without orders, all of us began laying down suppressive fire, aiming into that expanding hole.

The thick walls of the battlecruiser groaned as fantastic forces were applied. Somehow, the tip of the assault ship was still spreading open, widening the breach in our hull. Fortunately, the seal was as yet airtight, so the engine chamber was still pressurized. We all had our visors down anyway, just in case.

Marine Captain Khan turned his head in my direction when bears stopped coming in through the hull breach. The invasion module was still spreading, however, opening up the side of the ship like a pair of pliers in reverse.

"McGill," Khan said, "cover the passageway for me. Marines, advance!"

The marines surged forward and left us behind. I posted my troops all around the open doorway. If Khan wanted to go it alone in there, well, it was his game to play.

Khan and his marines surged onto the deck of the big room. The artificial gravity was disabled, so they immediately began to float. I had to hand it to them, they took this in stride. They'd been trained to switch from gravity to floating and back again.

The mouth of the invasion module stopped opening, which made sense, as it was about as wide as it could get. The nosecone of the device was now spread out like a flower, with sharp angular triangles of metal touching the wall all around it.

In the center was that dark, dark hole. It was black inside, as black as space.

"Grenades out! Fire in the hole!"

Several of the marines lobbed grenades inside. A pulsing blue radiance grew and grew in intensity. Suddenly, the rippling flashes began. These were inevitable, but no less dramatic for that. A few bears came rushing out in the final moments, but they were blown apart and shot down.

After that, the marines seemed to relax somewhat. They'd killed a group of invaders. It appeared that everyone aboard the invasion module was dead.

I wasn't so sure, however. Troops from Rigel were many things, but to my experience, they'd never been easy to kill. It was often difficult to stop them at all once they got rolling.

Suddenly, as the bravest of Khan's point-men dared poke his helmeted head up into the yawning invasion ship, a new monstrosity appeared.

Gliding out of that dark, dark hole, a robot of sorts appeared. It wasn't like normal robots—at least not the ones I was familiar with. It floated, rather than running on wheels or treads. For propulsion, it seemed to have dozens of independently moving nozzles. These were clearly attached to some kind of hot propellant, because you could see jets and puffs of plasma firing out of them at random moments.

The marines backpedalled, and we all opened fire—but it was too late. The thing glided into the chamber and automated turrets spun, raking us all with power-bolts.

The firefight that ensued was brief but violent. Out in the passages, my Varus troops were shielded from the worst of it. Khan's marines were shredded to the last man, including Khan himself.

"Close the door!" I roared, and my men all helped me, putting their backs into it.

The robot examined the dead, distributing killing bursts to any marine that still twitched. But as the door swung closed, it took notice of us and zoomed closer. Its hindmost jets flared, and the numerous cameras and turrets swung toward us, seeking fresh targets.

We slammed the door closed in its face and spun the wheel home. A thousand power bolts struck the interior of the door, sounding like a hailstorm of steel on steel.

-41-

Adjunct Erin Barton and I exchanged worried glances. Whatever that thing was in there—it wasn't going to die easy. You could just tell.

"Winslade?" I called over command chat. "Tribune? Are you there?"

"McGill?" another voice came on. "This is Captain Merton, get off this channel, please. You're not authorized—"

"We've got big problems down here at Engine Room Three, sir," I interrupted. "Some kind of flying robot has chased us out of the module and—"

"Centurion," Merton said sternly, "Marine Captain Khan will deal with this. Please—"

"Khan is dead, sir. His whole platoon is dead. The robot shredded them."

There was a moment of quiet then confused voices talking over one another. In the meantime, the robot had stopped firing on the door, which lessened the noise level considerably. Unfortunately, I got the feeling it hadn't forgotten about us. Instead, smoke had begun to come from the seals around the door.

"McGill!" Barton said. "It's burning its way through!"

"Stand clear, boys!"

"This is Tribune Winslade," a familiar, pissy voice said. "How exactly have you screwed up this mission, McGill?"

"Sir, the invasion pod had some bears in it, but behind the bears was some kind of robot. It's aboard ship now, burning its way out of Engine Room Three."

"Are you suggesting the marines can't handle it?"

"The marines are dead, sir!" I shouted, as I clearly wasn't getting through to them. "The marines are *all* dead, the robot killed them all!"

"Why weren't you in that room stopping it?" Winslade demanded.

Right then, the door kind of... bulged. It was as if something fantastically strong had pushed against it. I had no idea how the robot was doing that—could it be liquefying the door?

"It's breaking out, sir! All defenders need to get to Engine Three!"

I disconnected and ordered my troops to retreat. We set up a firing position at the end of the passageway, aiming exactly one belcher and eight morph-rifles at the oddly misshapen door.

My tapper was blinking red again, but I no longer cared.

"It's coming through," Barton said, and we lifted our weapons, sweating and staring until our eyes stung.

The door burst with a rush of gas and white vapor. A swarm of particles swirled around it, and I realized what they had to be.

"Nanites..." I said, but no one heard me. They were all blazing away, firing everything we had at the advancing monstrosity.

Some of the rocket nozzles were knocked out. Even one of its gun turrets was blown off by a tight-beam belcher strike. But it kept coming.

"It must be armored," Barton said, "it's constructed with the tough stuff from Glass World."

I had to agree, but it didn't matter right now. We had to stop this thing before it wrecked the ship.

The robot released rippling fire. Three of my men were taken out, then I lost my nerve.

"Fall back! Fall back!"

We hustled down to the next door and slammed it closed. Soon, the heavy metal barrier began to smoke and bulge like the last one had.

"James," Barton said, her eyes wide with fear. "That thing is eating the doors. It's using nanites—is that what you said?"

"Yeah. Melting its way through. We can't stop it."

"What are we going to do?"

"We need more men."

Erin shook her head. "They said that they've already landed the rest of Varus—everything we've got went down to the planet. All we've got left aboard are crewmen with pistols and cloth jumpers."

"They'll be mowed down."

She nodded and breathed hard. She looked at me, hoping for answers.

My eyes crawled over our surroundings. The ship's klaxons were wailing—shrieking first high, then low. Yellow flashers spun and bathed the passages in a rhythmic light.

My arm raised of its own accord. "What's that bulkhead? Is that an airlock?"

"That leads into the aft hold, I think," Erin said, following my gesture. "Nothing there but cold storage. Gear, maybe a few maintenance staff."

I activated my com-link and called the bridge again. "Captain Merton?"

"Merton here. Are you done wrecking my engines yet, McGill?"

"Not quite, sir. Listen, we can't stop this thing. It's armored like the bear troops, but with a heavier layer. It's melting through every door and taking almost no damage from our small arms."

"What do you suggest I do, then?" he asked. His attitude seemed to have changed. He seemed to finally be able to grasp that his entire ship was in danger.

"Have you got us on your scanner, sir?" I asked.

"Yes, we're watching you now. It doesn't look good, I must admit."

"See the aft hold door? I need you to open that."

"Are you joking, man? That doesn't go anywhere. You'll be trapped."

"Yes, but if you also open the outer doors after the robot follows us… it will be sucked out into space."

"That's a lot of pressure. You'll probably go with it."

"I'm counting on that, sir."

Merton shut up for a second, then the big bay doors swung open. The hold beyond was full of water vapor and darkness.

"Good luck, McGill," Merton said, and the channel closed.

In a rush, we ran for the hold entrance. By the time we got there, the door behind us gave way. The robot glided in our wake. A few stray bolts chased us, but we were inside and taking cover.

"All right," Adjunct Barton said. "Let's strap ourselves down, entwine our feet in the rigging on these crates—"

I grabbed her arm. She looked at me, startled.

"That's not how it's going to go. We have to make certain that thing is pushed out of here. When the airlock opens, we have to help push it out."

She had wide eyes, but she nodded. She didn't say a word.

"Gentlemen," I said, turning to the rest and giving them a grim smile. "I want to say that you all put up a good fight. It's been an honor to serve, and it will be again someday soon."

"Yes sir," they said in fatalistic voices. Legion Varus people aren't exactly accustomed to death, but they do understand it, and they don't shirk from it when duty calls.

The robot glided in, stitching the room with bolts here and there. We ducked and hid among the crates, suckering it in closer.

Soon, it loomed over our hiding spots. Twitching and lurching with puffs of flame from its independently operating jets, the thing hovered over us and spun. It found Adjunct Barton, and she couldn't get away. It showered her down with power bolts. She was torn apart and riddled with black, smoking holes.

Then, the klaxons began to sound again. More flashers, three of them surrounding the airlock, began to spin. Instead of a gentle equalizing of pressure, the big bay doors suddenly shot open.

The airlock was exposed. On the far side of that were windows that led out into open space. These too shot open a moment later. They'd hit the emergency overrides and forced the computer to open both sets of doors at the same time. A great rush of air flowed out into space.

"Grab it!" I shouted over the howling wind. "Grab on and shove it out!"

Together, we sprang up and grappled with the robot. Two men died right off, having grabbed a gun turret that obligingly shot them full of holes. The rest of us managed to get a grip, and with grunting effort, we shoved the robot into the airlock and beyond.

Breathing in gasps, I could feel a numbness spreading in my guts. I'd been wounded there, but I didn't think it mattered at this point.

With a fantastic effort, we aided the shrieking winds to shove the metal monstrosity out of the ship. Once outside, it began to struggle. It snipped off limbs with pincers. It gut-shot the men that clung to its hulk. The force of the struggle threw the robot and all of us who still clung to it into a tumbling spin.

We hung on. Now and then, we could see the vast dark bulk of *Berlin* behind us. I waited until we were so far from the battlecruiser that I could see it in its entirety. The open door of the hold had been shut behind us as well.

Then, with a sense of relief, I let myself die.

-42-

When I came back to life later that same day, I was in a pretty good mood. After dressing and checking my tapper, I noted I'd been invited to a debriefing. I walked up to Gold Deck with a smirk and a rolling step.

However, once I reached the conference room, one glance told me there wasn't going to be any party hats, cake or even a hearty handshake. Every officer present looked glum and irritable. This irked me, as I'd kind of expected to be treated like a hero. But that wasn't in the cards today.

"Hello, sirs. Centurion McGill, reporting for duty!"

"That's great, McGill. Take a seat, please." Winslade seemed as sour as any of them. This seemed odd on the face of it. After all, hadn't Graves died? Hadn't I saved the ship for the second time in a week? In my opinion, some people needed to get over themselves.

Captain Merton pointed a finger at me, and it seemed to me that finger was a bit shaky. He faced Winslade, showing his teeth. "There he is! There's your man! He's a one-gun wrecking machine."

I was beginning to grasp the situation. The brass had lost too much; they'd been pushed too hard. The robot, somehow, had become my fault.

"Uh…" I said. "If by that you mean I managed to kill that robot, you're absolutely right, Captain."

"Shut up, McGill," Winslade said. "Marine Captain Khan, report."

That's when my eyes first fell on Khan. He'd been sitting at the table the whole time, but he wasn't a flashy man. He was quiet, even somber. In a monotone, he delivered his after-action report. It droned on for quite a while, and I soon stopped listening.

"At that point, I died," he finished up at last.

All eyes then flicked in my direction. Unlike Khan, I was all smiles.

"That's when the real fun began."

They listened with concerned expressions while I explained how we'd lured the robot to the hold and out into space. I kept it short, as this meeting seemed like a huge waste of time to me.

"That's it?" Winslade asked at the end. "No more complications or—?"

"Nope. We jumped on it and rode it outside like a mechanical bull."

Winslade turned toward another officer. I thought I'd seen her before down on Blue Deck.

"Centurion?" Winslade asked. "How are our protoplasm supplies holding up?"

"We've got enough—but we're short on bone meal."

"Can you revive my whole legion again, or not?"

"No sir. We have to request more supplies from Earth."

"Supplies…" Winslade said. "It's always about supplies, isn't it? But it's worse than that. We not only have to regenerate our troops, we'll also have to arm them. McGill left an army's worth of gear down there on Glass World the last time he talked me into performing a mass-murder and worse—the utter destruction of most of my legion's equipment."

"Hold on," I interrupted. "I think I misheard something, sir."

Winslade and I locked stares. "I don't think so. Did you, or did you not, request bombardment from orbit while battling with the Rigellian troops?" As he said this, he fingered his tapper meaningfully. I knew what that meant. He probably had a doctored recording of our discussion ready to go.

Damn.

"Uh…" I said, considering his question. Casting me as the decision-maker concerning the bombing of Glass World was a pretty big risk for Winslade to take. After all, I could confess that the whole idea had been to kill Graves, who was even now conveniently lingering in the death-queue.

But I didn't want to talk about that any more than Winslade did. Winslade still hadn't upheld his part of our bargain, and I wanted no weaseling on that score. I hadn't laid eyes on Abigail since Earth, and I felt she owed me some explanations.

So, instead of blabbing, I smiled. "I did make that suggestion, sir—but I didn't give the order."

Winslade accepted those words sourly as he couldn't argue with them. Finally, he released a big sigh. He opened up a deep-link channel and reported in to Drusus back at Central.

Watching Drusus go over the figures, I could tell he wasn't happy.

"You're going to need *how many* kilotons of gear?" he asked. "This list… this is enough to outfit an entire legion. Do you realize that, Tribune? How did you lose everything?"

Winslade's fingers twitched like they were getting itchy. I knew he wanted to point at me and declare me the scapegoat—but he really couldn't.

"The enemy turned out to be better prepared than we expected," Winslade said, almost whining. "We were forced to exchange assets after destroying their gateway. It became quite… bloody. Now, however, we have easy access to reinforcements while they do not. We'll rebuild and dominate this world."

"Are you telling me it was your strategy to destroy Legion Varus and the enemy together? Why not just hit their army before you even landed?"

"The enemy was building up in secret, inside the mine itself. We didn't wish to dust off the entire mining operation."

Drusus and Winslade had a little staring contest after that. Finally, Drusus nodded.

"All right. You'll get your reinforcements—but not without strings attached. Drusus out."

The connection closed, and the meeting was adjourned. I lingered until the last man filtered out, then I approached Winslade.

"Yes, yes? What is it, McGill?"

"Sir… there's the small matter of our bargain."

"What bargain…? Oh yes, of course." He gave me a wicked smile. "Your lady-friend. I must say, McGill, your libido gets you into the most unpleasant of scrapes."

"Thanks for the constructive criticism, sir."

He snorted and made brushing-off gestures with his hand. "You'll find her languishing in the brig. I'll send word down that you're allowed to visit."

"Thank you, sir."

I turned to go, but he called me back.

"McGill… what do you think Drusus meant by 'strings attached'?"

"Huh? Oh… that. I don't rightly know, sir," I lied. All kinds of bureaucratic nightmares and officer replacement strategies came unbidden to my mind. To conceal these thoughts, I kept an idiot's grin on my face.

This seemed to work. He made that brushing-off gesture again, and I left.

Down in the brig, I was allowed to meet with Abigail at last. She was in manacles, and the sour-faced guards didn't seem to trust either of us. They whispered rude things and stared. This began to piss me off after a while.

Since they were watching and listening to us, I couldn't do more than engage in small talk. After a few minutes, I realized I had to get rid of the guards before we could discuss anything important.

"Hold on just a second, Abigail, please?"

"Certainly, McGill. I've got all time in the world."

Lifting my tapper to my face, I spoke into it in an overly loud voice. "That's right, Tribune, sir. I'm right here with her now, and she's got quite a tale to tell."

For a moment, I pretended to listen to Winslade, even though my tapper was blank. "No sir, I don't think they've touched her—not yet. But she could be covering that up. It's for certain they watch her pee, and all kinds of other indignities, just as we suspected."

My eyes glanced up to Abigail, who was looking mildly surprised.

"Isn't that right, Miss?"

Abigail was no dummy. She caught on to what I was doing right away. That was a good thing, because I couldn't very well get a single private word in edgewise with the guards hanging around.

"Um…" she said. "I suppose that describes the problem."

"Hmm…" I said sternly. "Sounds like you're covering up. This investigation needs to be widened to include—"

Right then, the prison duty-chief came near. His badge said his name was Thayer. "Um… Centurion?"

"What's that, Chief? Anything you'd like to say up front?"

"Did you say something about an investigation?"

I gave Thayer a stern look. "Are you interfering with an official matter? I'll have to make a note of that."

Tilting my tapper toward my eyes, I began working it. The thing was indeed flashing with angry messages from irritated superior officers—it always was—so I pretended to make a note.

Duty Chief Thayer went from curious to worried in a matter of seconds. "Wait, wait," he said. "We want to cooperate in every way possible. There's been no mention of an investigation—and no need for one, either."

I put on a flat, fake smile. "I'm hearing a new spirit of cooperation, Thayer. Is that right?"

"Absolutely, sir. What will make this go smoothly?"

"Just let me interview the witness in privacy and in peace. No snarky guards, who've been threatening the witness in an obvious fashion. No spy devices, either."

Thayer's eyes flicked around the interrogation chamber. He looked worried again. "We're required by Hegemony law to record what goes on in here, sir."

"Video is all right. But no audio—and I'll run a sweep if I need to, be assured of that!"

"Not necessary! We'll let you talk to the prisoner in peace, Centurion."

The duty-chief exited the cell, slamming it behind him. Even through the steel door, I could hear him shouting out in the passageway. His two comedian guards were getting an earful.

Turning back to Abigail, I found her gazing at me with an odd mixture of curiosity and amusement. "That was quite a performance, McGill."

"Call me James. Now, shall we get down to business?"

She frowned and looked around. "Aren't you going to do your spy-sweep?"

Naturally, I had no such equipment. I was mildly surprised that she thought I did. It was testament to the fact she really didn't know me all that well yet.

"Already did it," I declared. "And don't worry, they'll be erasing every record they have with your name on it right about now—just in case something looks bad."

Abigail squinted at me. "You turned a bureaucracy against itself in about thirty seconds flat. I stand impressed. My brothers have misjudged you—as have I."

"Uh... maybe. But let's get to business before they check out my story and come back, shall we?"

"Get to business? What are you suggesting?"

There it was again. She was making eyes at me, like I was going to grab her and ravage her on the spot. I had to remind myself that this woman was as tricky as any I'd ever met up with. Maybe even trickier than I was.

"Look," I began, "I need to know some things. You led me out there to that Skay husk, but you died there. Now here you are, languishing in a ship's brig. That doesn't add up in my book. You've arranged things, step by step, to lead me out here. What I want to know is *why*?"

She shrugged. "You already know. We're working to change the course of our race. To change the way Clavers interact with the rest of humanity. To make amends, we're starting off with a gift. Isn't that the custom between two tribes that have been at war?"

I blinked a few times, trying to absorb that. "You wanted to lead us to this discovery—the personal armor, I mean—so we'll trust you? So Hegemony will deal with you again as traders?"

"That's right. That's all we want."

"Huh..."

We talked a bit more, but that was the important part. The rest of the time she said cryptic things and flirted. At last, I saw an eyeball in the porthole behind me. It looked like Duty-Chief Thayer had finally grown a pair.

Standing up, I nodded to Abigail. "Good to see you alive and well again. I'll see what I can do to get you out of here."

"Thanks... James."

Was that the first time she'd called me by my first name? I wasn't sure, but I thought it probably was.

"Just one more thing," I said. "Did you die out there on that dead Skay on purpose? Just to get our attention—just to get my sympathy?"

She smiled faintly and looked at her hands. "What do you think, James?"

Snorting, I laughed and walked out of the brig. After thinking it over carefully, I went to see Natasha.

She'd been working on hacking deep-link messages for days now, whenever she wasn't face down in the mud of Glass World. She still hadn't managed that, but she had gotten access to the deep-link system. She figured that decoding the messages would have to wait, it would take a serious computer like those back home at Central.

Natasha seemed disappointed, but just being able to gain access to the equipment was good enough for me. With a little bit of cajoling, followed by some serious hacking, I got her to send an anonymous text to Drusus back at Central. She had to secretly use the deep-link for that. We sent it without a trace-back so no one would know who'd sent it. Using that kind of gear without authorization was something that could have landed us in a cell on the same row as Abigail's.

But the message got through to Earth, and that was all that mattered.

-43-

The next day, we were still busy printing out new Legionnaires. We didn't have enough of us yet to land on Glass World, so it became an unofficial day-off for everyone except those poor bastards working on Blue Deck.

I was in the middle of a fine breakfast when the ship's crew in the mess hall became agitated. They all seemed to get a tapper-call at the same time. Bounding up like jackrabbits that had sat on a hornet's nest, they all began scrambling for the exits.

Frowning, I checked my own tapper. There were plenty of red messages, but they were all old ones I'd decided to ignore. Touching the update button so it only displayed messages from the last hour, the screen became as smooth and unblemished as a stripper's butt.

What could be upsetting the crew so much? Whenever there was an emergency, they usually contacted old McGill first.

One slacker was running by me at the rear of the herd, still chewing his breakfast. Instantly, I snaked out a long, long leg with a size-thirteen boot on the end of it.

Purely by accident, I'll swear that to my grave and back again, I hooked the last jackrabbit in the room and brought him down. The ensign went sprawling, so I helpfully snagged his arm and set him back on his feet.

"Damn!" I said, "I'm awfully sorry about that. Is your chin bleeding?"

"It's all right. I've got to go, Centurion."

"Sure, sure," I said, giving him a smile. My big hands didn't let go of his uniform quite yet, however. "Just answer me one thing: what's the big hurry about?"

"Haven't you heard? The praetor's aboard. He's brought a whole posse of brass with him, too. I guess it's a surprise inspection. We've all been ordered to our duty stations. We're supposed to shine up the whole damned ship."

"Ah…" I said, and I let him go.

Ambling out of the mess hall, I headed toward Gold Deck. I was supposed to go to a cohort-wide officers' meeting on Green Deck—which was going to be mighty thinly attended, as most of 3rd Cohort's officers were still dead—but that could wait. The scene upstairs in the command sector promised to be much more interesting today.

When I reached the big pressure doors guarding Gold Deck, I met up with some mild resistance.

"Centurion? Excuse me, sir? Do you have orders to attend—?"

The security puke kept talking, but he was talking to my back. I nodded and waved and smiled as I passed him. He looked hurried and upset anyway, so I figured he couldn't be bothered to mess with a centurion.

Unfortunately, my bluster didn't quite work. A hand landed on my collar. I turned around with half a mind to flatten him.

"I'm sorry sir," he said. "We've got a very important guest today."

"I know all about that. Why do you think I'm up here?"

It used to be a few MPs would be stationed at the command deck exits, and getting past them was relatively easy. These Fleet pukes were different. They weren't part of Legion Varus. Because I was a member of a mercenary legion, they didn't have much more respect for my rank than would any hog running around back home at Central.

All of these new layers of policing were nothing but nine kinds of irritation to me. Looking around, I saw just the person I needed to help me out. It was Duty-Chief Thayer from the brig. He was probably in charge of tightening security ship-wide.

Stepping up to the security man, I dragged the little guy who'd stopped me along for the ride. I did this as if I didn't even feel the grip he had on my bicep, or the chattering he was doing about regulations and such-like.

"Chief!" I called out. "Could you explain something to this man of yours?"

Thayer wheeled and his eyes widened with alarm when he saw me. That was a good thing, as it meant he'd never figured out my investigation story was all bullshit. He still had the yellow gleam of fear in his ratty eyes.

"McGill...? What's the problem?"

I jabbed a thumb at the security man who still had one hand—rather pointlessly, I might add—latched onto my arm.

"Could you tell this man I'm part of an approved investigation? That interfering with my duties could be construed as obstruction of justice?"

The chief showed his teeth, and he quickly turned on his subordinate. The poor man was abusively told to let go and leave his betters alone.

That made me smile. I was finally being dealt with in a respectful manner. A few moments later, I was striding around Gold Deck like I owned the place.

Naturally, I took care to avoid the real brass. They looked stern and many of them knew me. They had no more respect for a sneaky centurion than they did for the stuff they scraped from their shoes after mowing the lawn.

My luck held until I reached the banquet room. Apparently, that was where a big meeting was to be held.

Now, it needs to be said that when a banquet is being held—pretty much anywhere—old McGill was very likely to attend. Sure, I'd just eaten two plates at breakfast, but that was light fare. Eggs, bacon, flapjacks and fruit. That stuff went right through a man by lunchtime, and it was almost ten... Close enough, anyway.

A sumptuous brunch was laid out. There were omelets on special order, seafood caught yesterday and brought through the gateway from Earth, and even a hunk of roast beef you could just see had been cooked to perfection. Damnation, the officers sure ate well when the brass came calling!

"McGill?" a voice I'd hoped not to hear today asked from behind me. It was Winslade, and he really did seem baffled to see me.

Turning with my heaping plate balanced on one big hand, I gave him a nod and a smile. "Hello sir, very nice of the captain to welcome Drusus in such a fine fashion, don't you think?"

Winslade's ferrety eyes drew tight. He put his hands on his hips and sneered at me. "Sneaking in where you aren't invited to steal food again, eh? I don't know why I'm surprised."

I feigned shock. "Sneaking in? Sir, that's a damned lie! I was *invited*. Wasn't I on hand during the deep-link call that kicked-off this visit?"

Winslade shook his head. "Stay in the back, try to hide your absurdly large body, and above all, stay silent. I haven't got time to throw you out."

He stalked off, and I felt pretty damned good. I headed to the dessert trays and picked out a few items for later.

Just then, Drusus arrived. He had a posse in tow, just like the ensign kid had said. Checking carefully, I noted that they were all underlings and Wurtenberger wasn't among them. That was a very good thing, as Wurtenburger seemed to be sweet on Winslade lately. Maybe that was why Winslade had let me skate—he wasn't certain of his position.

Making haste, I moved to the back of the room and hunkered over my food like a lion protecting its kill. People started making speeches, but I was eating, so I didn't hear much of it.

At one point, however, Drusus turned to one of his guests. I hadn't noticed her before, somehow. Maybe that was because she'd stayed seated the entire time—after all, she was gravity-bolted to her chair.

The prisoner was Abigail. She looked dressed up and scrubbed—but I'd know those deceptively soulful eyes anywhere.

-44-

Abigail wasn't wearing an evening gown or anything, but she wasn't in her prison-jumper either. She was wearing civvies, standard fare for a businesswoman on the street.

My jaws stopped clacking and grinding, to the relief of those who shared my table.

"Is she pretty to you?" I asked the guy next to me.

He frowned at me. "What? I don't know... I guess so. She's got kind of a sexy look." He looked down then, almost embarrassed. I'd gotten an honest answer out of him—maybe that was part of Abigail's power. She tended to make you want to speak the truth. There were worse gifts, I supposed.

"Officers of this warship and Legion Varus," Abigail began. "I'm here to offer you a way out of your predicament."

People frowned and glanced at one another. To our way of thinking, we'd pretty much won this campaign. It was almost time to go home after we mopped up on Glass World.

"You have captured the planet and a mining center. That's excellent news," she continued. "Unfortunately, you'll find all the suits of armor stored here will only fit your children. To retune the plant, to retool it to forge material that will fit your larger dimensions, you'll have to—"

Drusus cleared his throat. "Excuse me, Abigail," he said. "I brought you up from the brig as you said you had critical information concerning securing a victory here at Glass World. It sounds to me as if you're trying to make a sales pitch instead.

We aren't interested in trade deals. We've all but conquered this planet."

She looked at him, and she didn't look upset or even flustered. "Praetor Drusus, you're misinformed. The prize here isn't the planet. It isn't even the mine. It's the processing center. The technology it takes to transform stardust into wearable armor—will you concede that your people have no idea how to do that?"

There was some general muttering around the room, but no one argued. Some of the posse Drusus had brought with him were Rogue Worlders. Scientist types who were almost autistic. If they'd heard a word out of place, they wouldn't have been able to keep quiet.

"Very well," Abigail continued. "As I was saying, you've exterminated the defenders of the mine—but you haven't even located the processing center yet. You must capture that and learn how it operates before you can call this campaign finished."

The group began to frown collectively—but not me. I was too busy with dessert. They were serving tarts—little cakes with a fruity glaze on top. Done right, that kind of thing really puts a finisher on a man's meal.

"Where is this… processing center?" Drusus asked.

Abigail smiled. I knew that smile. She had old Drusus by the short ones—or at least she thought she did.

"In return for this critical information, my people would like to enter into a mutually beneficial contract with Earth."

Winslade stood up suddenly, as did several indignant others.

"Never!" he shouted. "We just fought a war with your kind, and we're not going to trust you again so easily."

Abigail shook her head. "So little do you understand... Firstly, the war is over. My people are beaten and in retreat. There are only a few legions of us left."

"One legion of clones is too damned many!" someone called out. I wasn't sure who, but Drusus shushed them.

"Listen, please," Drusus said. "No decisions have been made yet. We're going to hear her out, that's all."

"Thank you, Praetor," Abigail said. "Friends… we're a beaten people. We're a splinter colony of Earth, no longer a rival to your planet. Think of us as you might the people from Dust World or Blood World—any of the planets where humans that vary genetically and functionally from Earth reside. Let's put aside our mutual distrust and recognize we're all one people underneath. In short, let's trade again."

If it came to a vote, I'd say the general consensus would have been a powerful "no way" from the crowd. But this was a military organization, not a democracy or a tribunal. Drusus had the power to make the decision unilaterally.

Wisely, Abigail looked at Drusus and no one else. I felt good about that, because she was at least being allowed to make her case. I'd promised her she would be given that opportunity, and I'd come through, no matter how this ended.

Drusus looked down. He seemed to be mulling things over. At last, he looked up and shook his head.

"I'm sorry. We can't go from a state of war to trading partners in a single step. The reaction of all Earthlings will be as you've seen here. Give me the information you've held back until this point, and I'll let you go home. I'll even order a cessation of all hostilities between our two… ah… factions, let's call them. There will be peace again. Perhaps in time, trade will follow once trust is reestablished."

Abigail chewed her lip. "I need more than that. I need a clear win. In order to shift the mindset of my people, I can't take home a half-measure. They won't follow me if I try that."

"Hmm…" Drusus said. "Are you saying you won't tell us where this processing center is?"

"I can't. It's the only bargaining chip I have."

Drusus stood up suddenly and sighed. "Very well." He turned to the guards, who were malingering in the area. "Take this prisoner back to the brig, and execute her. We'll find the processing center by ourselves."

The room erupted at this announcement. Some clapped, some whistled, some booed. There was a lot of loud talking, and it was anything but decorous behavior.

Abigail looked shocked. She stared at Drusus for a moment, making sure he was in earnest—I could have told her he was.

Next, her eyes sought me out. She found me in an instant, as I was standing tall with the rest of the excited crowd—only taller.

"James?" she called—then the gravity bolt was released, and she was dragged away by a pack of those security goons. They seemed kind of pleased with themselves. Maybe, to their minds, this meant there would be an end to the imaginary investigation concerning her treatment.

Holy shit. I could hardly believe what I'd seen. Wading forward, I pushed my way through the crowd.

Drusus caught sight of me coming. He did a double-take, then he looked slightly disgusted. "McGill...? I hope you enjoyed brunch."

"I did indeed, sir. But my stomach has soured. Are you really going to kill that girl just because she hasn't told you everything she knows?"

"She misled us. Her information was critically incomplete, and now she wants to use that as a bargaining chip. Unfortunately, her kind can't be trusted."

"Clavers always keep a bargain. Besides, if she had told you everything, she'd have gotten nothing for it, right?"

"She has bought peace. Isn't that good enough? Why are you so interested, anyway? I got that mysterious text from you about this trade deal offer over the deep-link—a misuse of government property, by the way—which is why I decided to come and deliver the bad news in person."

"Uh... a text, sir? Wasn't me, I swear it. I don't even like texting."

Drusus looked like he didn't believe me, but he decided not to make an issue of it. "In any case, I'm going back to Earth now. Try to focus on finding the processing center she was talking about. The sooner you do, the sooner the legion can go home."

"But..." I said. "Why do we have to kill her?"

There it was, the question that was really bugging me.

Drusus shrugged. "I'm not perming her, McGill. I'm sure you realize that by now. Dying is how her kind gets around. When they aren't making a thousand down-graded copies of themselves, they commit suicide on a regular basis. Effectively, I'm just sending her home."

"Yeah… but…"

Drusus crossed his arms. "Are you seriously telling me you're involved with this woman, McGill? Is there a single eye-catching female in this galaxy or the next that can't sway your judgment?"

"I must take exception to your generality, sir! There never was a woman born that could do that. Not even my mamma."

Drusus sighed. "Listen, we've mocked up one suit of the new armor—really, it's several bear-sized suits patched together. We can't cut it effectively, but we can fold up a few more and wrap them around a man's chest. Additionally, one torso section covers each leg."

"Uh…" I said. "Sounds like it looks funny."

"It does, but it looks better than a man wearing a squid suit. Tomorrow, you're dropping on Glass World again. How would you like to wear the first prototype suit of armor we've ever put together?"

"Instead of my fitted plate?"

"That's right. It's quite bulky and awkward, and it won't give you full coverage, but it's essentially impenetrable. You want to try it?"

I nodded. "You know I do, sir. But what about a stay of execution? At least until this campaign is over, and we have more time to—"

Drusus dismissed me with a wave. "Enjoy your armor, McGill. In a few years, with luck, you'll all be wearing the stuff.

I stalked away, wondering what I was going to do. My mind was wrestling with the vague beginnings of an idea, and I already had the feeling it was going to be a bad one.

The next day the legion was preparing to drop on Glass World again. The enemy resistance was estimated to be minimal—but I never liked estimates. They weren't as solid as bullets and missiles.

Since I was about to be deployed again, I decided to make a move right off. Once I left the ship, it was unlikely I'd get back in time.

With the air of a man who owns everything he sees, I marched down to the brig. I met up with initial resistance, but after dropping Chief Thayer's name a few times I managed to scare him up.

"I'm sorry Centurion," he told me, without quite managing to look sorry at all. "But the prisoner in question has been executed."

"Executed?" I asked, pretending to be shocked. "In the middle of an investigation?"

The chief almost grinned, but he caught himself. "I'm afraid so, sir. The praetor ordered it done last night."

I nodded and made imaginary notes on my tapper. "Exact time?"

"Uh..." he said, his face faltering a little. Then he gave me the time.

"Method used?"

Frowning openly now, as he put his fists on his hips. "Look, sir—it's over. Whatever complaint was made, whatever—"

"Whatever makes a hog like you think they can just murder someone to make all their problems go away? You see it all the time in the news, don't you? Some fool abuses a woman, then kills her. He would've gotten a few years in prison, but he just has to risk it all and get himself permed to cover his tracks. It's one of the mysteries of the criminal mind, don't you think?"

Security Chief Thayer's eyes squinched up in hate when I called him a hog, but then, as I kept speeching, his expression shifted to alarm.

"No one murdered anyone! It was an execution—and look, McGill, I did some checking around. I haven't been able to get confirmation from anyone that you're on some kind of investigation. I'm beginning to wonder—"

"Did you check with Primus Graves?" I demanded.

"Graves?"

"Yes, that's what I said. He's my direct superior."

"Actually, I tried to, but he's still not been revived yet. That is kind of odd…"

I nodded and made more fictitious notes. "Look, Thayer—I like you. So I'm going to do you a solid, okay? Don't get in the way, here. Graves isn't breathing anymore, even though he should be. A woman who had a legit complaint has suddenly been ordered executed as well. Does any of that seem odd to you?"

"Um… I guess so. But what can I do? The woman is dead. All testimony and evidence died with her."

I shook my head. "Not so fast. Have you got a local router here? Something that uploads to the ship's data core?"

"Of course, but—"

"And you took a medical scan of this female before incarcerating her, right?"

"That's regulations."

I smiled. "Good. Copy that material onto this chip, and I'll be on my way."

Handing him a silvery round disk of what appeared to be smooth metal, I left him frowning at it.

"I'll have to get authorization—"

Grabbing his arm, I gave him a little tug. He stumbled closer to me.

"Chief," I said in his face in a low voice. "This is Legion Varus you're playing with. We don't play by hog rules. Are you hearing me?"

He looked annoyed, but also he looked more than a little worried. Legion Varus had the worst reputation of all Mother Earth's legions. We were known to be a rough lot, a mysterious government-sponsored organization that might be compared to the old time mafia—or a pirate's nest.

"Uh… okay."

That was all he said. Walking out, he came back a few minutes later with the chip in his hand. He dropped it into mine, and I looked at it critically. "This better not be full of porn feelies," I told him. "I'm going to check."

"It's not, Centurion. Just her scans and her engrams. Now… could I ask you to disappear? And not come back?"

I gave him a broad smile. "If this file reads right, you've bought yourself some peace of mind, Thayer."

As I left, he asked me one more question. "McGill? What exactly are you going to do with that data?"

I flipped the coin-like disk in the air and snatched it back again. "I'll think of something," I assured him.

That evening, as we prepped to drop on Glass World again, I had Natasha scan the disk.

"There's a person on here, that's for sure. I can't tell who it is, but the double-X chromosome files indicate the subject is female at least."

"Good enough. Thanks, Natasha."

She looked kind of troubled. She always had been the jealous type, even though we'd stopped seeing each other regularly years ago—decades, maybe. As I watched her face, I knew I shouldn't have slept with her that one time on this voyage. It had probably reawakened old wounds.

She fondled the disk then handed it back to me. "You've had so many women, I wouldn't think you needed to keep a copy of one. Who is she?"

I ignored everything she said, and I managed not to get angry. Instead, I got an idea.

"Let's hang out tonight," I suggested. "After all, we're sure to die in the morning somehow."

She looked happy, and we spent the night. It was just like old times. Almost as importantly, she didn't ask me any more questions about who was on that disk.

-45-

The next morning, true to Drusus' word, I was outfitted in an experimental suit of Rigellian armor. I could tell right off why Drusus had asked me to try it. The suit was clumsy, with gaps all over, and it was heavy. Not being tailored to my shape, it fit like a mass of furs on a caveman. Still, for all that, I thought it was kind of cool, and the other troops were seriously impressed.

The drop started out all right. We lined up a pack of chicken recruits and pushed them one at a time into a rhythmically opening and closing chopper-thingy in the floor. It resembled an open drain—to me, it was so familiar it was almost homey.

Not a single recruit went splat, either. They were experienced now, if not professional. They'd already dropped and seen what could go wrong. In lock-step, each one walked out over nothingness and fell into the chute they were assigned. Moments later, they were screaming down to the surface in a pod that looked mysteriously like a smart missile.

The payload in each missile wasn't a warhead, however. They all held soldiers. Throughout time, humans had gotten better and better at blowing things up—but the universe still needed ground troops to effectively capture an objective intact.

I went down last, following a swarm of white cylindrical pods. At first, we slid through space at an angle. Then we touched the atmosphere and plunged through. The angle was critical here. If you came in at too steep of an angle, you'd go too fast and burn up. If you approached at too shallow an angle, you could bounce off the atmosphere and die in space.

Computers had long since conquered the dynamic math problems required to achieve reentry on any planet you might care to mention. As long as it could be seen and measured, any difficulty could be overcome.

A few minutes later a shock to my boots told me we'd landed. The pod rolled and dirt flew over my external camera pickups—but I thought I'd seen *something*.

Something unexpected.

"Sargon?" I called out, checking my pod diagnostics. Usually, when you landed, you wanted to pop out of your capsule like your ass was on fire. Other times, however, a more cautious approach paid off.

"Sargon?" I repeated.

Sargon didn't answer. My HUD was relayed to the screen in the pod, and I swiped over and over, trying to get it to refresh. It was showing every lifeline in my unit as a flat red streak of color.

That's when a cold thought hit me. Could the readings be accurate, not just dead air? Could they all be dead? *All* of them?

I'd taken the last position in the landing group, but that wasn't unusual for a centurion. Coming in last gave you more intel when you arrived, upping the odds of the commander surviving.

Feeling a little concerned, I checked each of the crappy camera pickups outside of my flying tomb. They weren't perfect. Each was fish-eyed, low res and some were covered with dirt. It was kind of like trying to examine the world using only the external parking cameras on your family tram.

I was lying on my back like a vampire in his coffin, trying to make sure the sun had really gone down before throwing open the lid.

There! Movement, off to my left. What looked like a fuzzy dude with long teeth flashed by. That was the only living thing I saw, and it was a bear—a fucking bear.

I cursed and hissed. We'd landed in the middle of an enemy formation. More of them went by now, rushing past my capsule and even standing on it. I heard the chatter of gunfire.

How could there be so many of them? So many that they'd overwhelmed my unit before I'd even reached the ground?

A group of them approached and encircled my capsule. They had guns out and snarls on their faces. They huffed and clacked and scratched at the exterior. I could have told them that would be useless. This thing was a titanium case, and until I blew the explosive bolts—

A loud whirring sound commenced. It was a saw—a frigging diamond-bladed saw. Already, one of the bastards was buzzing away at the seal. Soon, they'd have a crack, then they'd force it open.

Steeling myself, I decided not to be caught on my back jammed into a cocoon. It just wasn't my preferred way to die.

Gripping my gun firmly, I blew the bolts—all of them, all at once.

The bear with the saw did a backflip off the capsule, thrown clear with the upper half of my pod. Grenades went flying right behind him, all four I carried. They landed all around me in the dirt.

I was gratified to hear some squawks of fear. Then the grenades went off—I'd set them on the shortest-fuse possible. I was still lying flat inside of the capsule, and it rocked gently with the blasts.

The shrapnel and plasma bursts, all going off around my protective cocoon, threw a devil's worth of sped-up debris in every direction, but the pod was only scarred, not destroyed or flipped over.

Rolling out of the pod, I took shelter up against it. My flapping experimental armor slapped and caught on things and exposed me like a pulled-up shirt. I tucked it down, cursing, and put my back to the pod. That provided me with cover on one side, so I focused on the other.

A dozen bear regulars approached. They had their weapons out.

"Human," said a strange gargling voice, the speech their translators always used, "you must surrender. You will not—"

I blasted them. Full-auto, close range, targeting the parts of their bodies that were vulnerable. They were knocked down, scattered and thrown back. Some were grabbing at their nuts. Others were clutching at their eyeholes. I'd gotten in a few licks, but they were climbing back to their feet. Unlike the grenades, which could kill by shock alone at close range, my power bolts couldn't stop them.

Hosing them down as they climbed to their feet and growled, I was suddenly grabbed from behind. Two powerful sets of hands—no, they were paws, really—ripped the morph-rifle out of my grip. These bears were as strong and mean as cat-dirt.

They hauled me up and soon, I was surrounded. We were all breathing hard, and I could tell they really, really wanted to kill me.

"Do not kill!" shouted one of them from the back. "Do not feast! This one is mine!"

An officer approached.

"I surrender!" I said loudly.

"Excellent! Back—back my troops. Yes, this one deserves a thousand deaths, and he shall receive them, but not today."

Squinting, I figured out pretty quickly this wasn't Squanto. He was some kind of captain over the unit I'd fallen into the middle of.

He walked up to me, and he hooked a single curved claw into the hanging layers of armor that surrounded me.

"Taken from our fallen?" he asked.

"Yes. I wear these proudly. They are the skins of all the bears I've killed on this campaign so far. I would be grateful if you gave me seven more—that's the count of dead I see around my capsule."

The captain lifted his black lips. "I will do no such thing, barbarian. You will suffer the thousands deaths of the most hated. Squanto will—"

"I bet he's going to pay you a lot for my carcass, huh? Is that why you won't let your troops kill me? Let me guess, you're going to keep all the money for yourself as well, am I right?"

"It would be best for you to be silent. Justice will be harsh with you—very harsh. But it is justice all the same. I—"

"You sure do talk a lot," I said, "and you're kind of a chicken, too. You think you could kill me, man-to-man? Let's find out. Let's wrestle!"

The captain looked up at me in surprise. "That would be pointless, human. You are a large beast, even for one of your kind. But your muscle density is inferior. It's on par with that of prey animals. You could not hope—"

"You're afraid, aren't you?" I demanded, and I let loose a big laugh. "Come on, I'm just a big pussy human. Give it a shot. We'll use only our hands. Now, take off that armor and kick my ass!"

The bear showed his teeth. Around him, his troops were eyeing one another. They were a warrior culture, and they understood challenges of this kind. I'd seen them wrestle one another on many occasions. In fact, I'd wrestled Squanto a few times personally. They were tough little dudes, I'll give them that.

"Very well, impudent animal," the captain said. "I am to deliver you alive, but there is no requirement that you—"

"You talk too much, pansy!" I roared at him, bending my knees and throwing my arms wide.

Two bears, clinging to each of my arms, were lifted into the air. Up until that point, I hadn't let them know I could do that. They were strong—but they were light, too. Especially on Glass World, which had slightly less gravity than Earth.

Hissing, the bear officer threw back his helmet to fully reveal his snout. That mouth of his was full of fangs, and I was pretty certain he wanted to sink them into me.

At a wave from the captain, the two bears let go of me and dropped to the ground. The group surrounded the two of us, and I gave them a grin that was just as feral as theirs.

Throwing off my helmet to match him, I began to circle. The bear did the same, talking big all the while about how he was going to take a scent-piss—his words, not mine—on my bleeding back after he'd laid me out flat in the grass.

Finally, he charged in as I knew he would. These bears were pretty tough in hand to hand combat. They had their own form of martial arts, and this one was no exception.

I knew that if I let him in close, he might be impossible to dislodge. Therefore, I had to act right away.

As he came near, I pulled my combat knife from my flapping layered armor and swung it overhand. It was a close thing—his arm came up to block at the last instant—but forward momentum was such that he couldn't reverse himself and back off. Instead, he threw himself low.

Unfortunately for him, I have overly-long arms. I chunked the knife down, right into the top of his nasty-ass, fuzzy skull. Gore spat up, and the good captain had been struck dead.

What happened next was predictable and exactly what I'd hoped for: the captain's troops went berserk.

I'd gotten the sense that they hadn't liked me all that much right from the start, but after underhandedly destroying their captain with a trick move, they couldn't contain themselves. They swarmed me like a pack of howling wolves. I was dragged down and torn apart, with fangs ripping out my veins and chunks of meat flying.

I stabbed a few more of them, but they were wearing their helmets, and the blade didn't penetrate. Aw well, I chalked it up as a good death anyways.

Lying in the mud on my back, bleeding out, I stared at the alien sun. I laughed and cursed their mothers.

Then, I died.

-46-

When I came back to life, I wasn't angry or laughing... I was mystified. As soon as I could talk properly, I demanded answers.

The person I demanded them from was Winslade. Fresh from the revival chamber, hardly able to walk and talk straight, I barged into his office.

"Tribune...? What the hell happened down there? I landed in my pod, and my men were dead before I hit the ground. Then I found out why—our LZ was crawling with bears."

"Hmm... yes," Winslade said, sounding quite disinterested. He was going over some kind of Glass World charts on his office battle-computer. "Well, there's no need for concern. Your unit just appeared to have been extraordinarily unlucky. The rest of the troops landed without serious resistance and swept the area clear of your murderers. Once your group was confirmed dead, you were marked for revival."

"That's all fine and dandy. But there are very serious implications here. Those bears *knew* I was landing right there, at that exact spot. What's more, they had orders to catch me and hand me over to Squanto."

"High Lord Squanto? You must be mistaken. He's hundreds of lightyears away, McGill. Please get a grip."

"I'm clear of heart, eye and mind, sir. Someone aboard *Berlin* gave away my drop coordinates. Someone gave that intel to Rigel."

At last, Winslade looked up from his glowing computer. I saw now that he was going over detailed LIDAR readings from Glass World, which showed underground hidden chambers and the like.

"Now listen here, McGill. I don't need to hear that kind of talk. No one aboard this ship is a traitor."

In my opinion, he was almost right. The only traitor I knew of was Winslade himself—but he seemed to be trying to make amends.

"Is Graves still dead?" I asked him, arms crossed.

That got his attention. We eyed one another for a few seconds.

"What are you implying?" he asked at last.

"I'm the only one that knows about that. Maybe you thought you should clean up a little."

"Ah... I see. This isn't a complaint, it's an accusation. Fascinating, the machinations of a simplistic mind."

"You were in command of the operation, and you had all the data. You also have access to a deep-link transmitter—and I'm a loose end."

"All true, I'm afraid. Here's the punchline: I had nothing better to do than to come up with an elaborate plan to put you away. Listen, McGill, if I wanted you permed or otherwise expunged, would I have put in a priority revival order on your sorry excuse for a soul no more than an hour ago? Hmm? Answer me that."

I stared at him, and I blinked a few times, letting his words sink in. He had a point. If he'd wanted to get rid of me, and he'd gone to all that trouble to set me up with the bears—why the hell had he revived me? He could have simply left me languishing in the queue like Graves.

My hair dripped thick fluid, and it splattered on his computer table. Winslade looked disgusted.

"Ew! You're dribbling amniotic fluid all over my office. Go find your villain, real or imagined, on your own time—and for God's sake man, take a shower!"

He threw me out of his office. Muttering, I staggered down the passageways in confusion. I couldn't argue with his straightforward logic. It did seem that Winslade was innocent of this particular crime.

But there had to be *someone* aboard who wasn't...

Going through a long list of enemies, jilted lovers and such-like, I came up with dozens of names. But none of them fit. None of them had the power, the means, or the balls to do this.

Then I came up with one final name. I headed down to Blue Deck and made inquiries.

"Ensign Leeza? Yes, she was assigned here during the voyage, but she's since moved on to other duties."

I got what I could from the bio people and left. I headed to talk to Captain Merton, but his sidekicks intercepted me.

"Centurion? Can we help you?"

I eyed the ship's XO warily. She wasn't smiling at me. Not even a fake smile. Her arms were crossed over her chest, and she looked like she smelled shit.

"All I want to know is where Ensign Leeza has been assigned."

"That's private information. I've got no interest in enabling a Varus stalker, no matter what his rank is."

"I think she's the one that's stalking me," I said.

That got a few surprised glances from the crew people. I let them know that Leeza used to be in the legions, and she had reasons to dislike me, as I came from a rival outfit.

Troubled, the XO swiped through some documents. "The truth is... she didn't report to her duty station this morning. The data core says she's in her quarters. Perhaps we should all go down there to perform a welfare-check."

She summoned a few marines, and we marched down into the bowels of the officers' quarters. Ensigns weren't much above noncoms in rank, and they had to bunk up with each other. Leeza's bunk was on the top, and it was empty—almost.

Being a tall man, I was able to see something in the sheets the others missed. I yanked them free, and something flew. It squelched and flopped on the deck.

"What the hell is that?" demanded the XO.

I squatted and poked at it. "It's a ripped-out tapper. The blood hasn't dried yet, so it was done recently."

The marines drew their weapons and aimed them at me.

"Varus," the XO said, "your kind disgusts me. What did you do with her?"

I snorted. "Don't threaten me with your pellet-guns, boys. I'm a magic man. Somehow, I murdered this woman while I was dropping on Glass World. I probably faked my own death and revival too!"

The XO checked out my story, and she soon found it was undeniably true. "You weren't even on the ship when this had to have happened... All right... What's your theory, McGill? Where *is* Ensign Leeza?"

I stood up and leaned on the bunks. "She's long gone, I bet. She removed her tapper so she couldn't be traced. That's a pretty radical move, even for a woman of her caliber."

"Long gone? How?"

"Let's go down to Gray Deck."

When we arrived and checked the records, we discovered one of the harnesses was indeed missing. After I'd dropped, someone had left the ship—but no one knew who.

"Anyone with a tapper would have been 'ID'ed," I said. "I think we know who left."

"Why would she do such a thing?"

"I have theories. You see, I'm not well-liked on Rigel."

"Really?" the XO asked. "I would have never suspected."

"A real mystery, I know. Anyway, I think she helped someone out, and they gave her a new home. A new life."

The XO frowned. "Rigel hates you that much, McGill? Seriously?"

"Uh... yeah. I did some things... well, I'd be lying if I said I wasn't proud of them, but let's just say, Squanto hates me. He wants me bad."

The XO smiled and unfurled her crossed arms. Taking this as a sign of good will, I asked her out on the spot—but she passed. The marines behind her shook their heads and eyed the ceiling, but I didn't care. A man has to take his shot when the moment is right.

She was, however, flattered. She let me look into the Gray Deck records. After she left, I called Natasha, and we combed through the details. As the XO had approved, the Gray Deck nerds let us do it.

"I've got the coordinates," Natasha whispered an hour later.

"Cool. Copy them, and let's get out of here."

"Um... what do you have stuffed under your shirt, James...? Is that... oh no! No way!"

"Shhh!"

I led her out by the arm, and I kissed her in the passageway. She melted into the kiss, but she still was shaking her head no when we came up for air.

"I'm not going to do it, James McGill," she said. "I'm not reprogramming that teleport harness you stole to send you off to god-knows-where!"

"Who said anything about that?"

"I know you. You'll get yourself permed to figure something out."

I shrugged, unable to deny the truth of her words. "Okay then," I said, plucking the data chip from her fingers. "I'll do it on my own."

She followed me, huffing and upset. "Kivi will screw it up."

"Maybe."

She followed a dozen more steps, getting more upset and jealous all the time.

"All right, damn you. I'll help you kill yourself again, if it means so much to you."

"It does girl, it does."

By morning, her work was done. I woke up in my tiny stateroom to see her putting the final touches on her gizmo.

It was a power-concentrator, a kind of coil powered by splicing into the main lines in the ship's walls. Panels were removed, and fittings were wrapped with countless layers of rubber tape.

"Uh..." I said, looking it over. "Is this safe?"

"No. Not in the least."

Natasha looked down at her hands, and I thought she might be ready to cry.

"What's the matter? You've got a body scan of me. You've got an alibi, and evidence that shows I deserve a revive if I don't come back—everything you need to fix this if it goes wrong."

She shook her head. "James… it's not just that. They're going to kill you. When I see you again, you won't even know what happened. These engrams are too old. You won't be this James McGill—the one I've fallen in love with all over again."

She had a good point, so I didn't argue. I kissed the top of her head, thanked her and hugged her—and then I ported out into the void.

-47-

As I flew through the cosmos, I had certain regrets. The trip was a long, long one. That meant I was traversing a large number of lightyears.

These journeys were never pleasant, but not even knowing your destination makes it worse somehow. Sure, you feel like you're suffocating the whole time anyway, but I'd taken to slowly, calmly counting in my head as I traveled. That gave me something of a measure. The trick was not to get nervous and speed up the count, hoping against hope that doing so would somehow speed up the process.

I'd gotten pretty good at counting, and the speed I counted at generally corresponded, one for one, to a lightyear traveled. I'd gotten a real feel for it over the decades.

One hundred eighty-six.

That's was the count when I arrived, and it didn't give me any comfort. That distance... there weren't too many logical targets at that range. It wasn't far enough to get beyond the frontier Province 928 entirely. That meant I was arriving somewhere in the frontier zone.

It could have been Dark World, which was in the middle of the zone, or maybe even Storm World...

But it wasn't. In fact, before the blue rhythmic light had faded, I kind of knew where I was.

Rigel. It had to be Rigel.

Holy shit... I was six kinds of a moron today if that's what had happened. I'd avoided being captured and shipped off to Squanto—probably in just the manner I'd transported myself today. Those bears that had been so dead-set on capturing me hadn't possessed a ship, or gateway posts. They would have almost certainly pasted a bunch of stamps on my sorry forehead and strapped me up with a teleport rig and sent me to their homeworld if they could have—and now I'd gone and done it for them.

Shit.

I was standing on a deck. A metal deck, with a low ceiling. Just as the count had come to a finish, I'd realized where I must be landing, and I'd ducked low. I was in a fighting crouch, in fact.

It was a damned good thing. Those short-assed bears didn't build their ceilings for giants. Their passages were normally a roomy meter-and-half high. That was plenty of headroom for any native of Rigel ever born—but it would have killed me, had I been standing tall upon arrival.

As it was, my helmet was almost touching the roof of the place. Once, back when we'd captured a Rigellian ship, I'd gotten a scalping that way, and I didn't want to repeat the process.

Breathing hard, I pulled my weapon up and flipped my visor open. Bears breathed air that was pretty heavily oxygenated, the mix being a little richer than Earth's, but that was okay as long as you didn't hyperventilate.

A passage. That's what it was. The gravity was low, so I didn't figure I was on the ground. I was probably on a space station or a large starship. Either way, it was unfriendly territory and then some.

Putting my rifle in front of my face, I moved forward quickly, aiming the gun everywhere I looked. There were no other HUD connections. My tapper was spinning, disconnected. I was off the grid.

Switching into low-emissions mode, I activated my passive recorders, such as my body cams. Who knew? Whatever intel I got today might reach Earth by some miracle. It couldn't hurt.

The worst news of all regarding my situation was the flashing red on my teleport harness battery pack. It had been drained way down. If I'd flown only a few lights, I could have jumped home, but that was out of the question now.

Moving through a series of passages, I searched for an outlet, but found nothing.

"McGill…" I said quietly to myself. "Carlos was right. Your brain is defective. You stepped on your own dick today."

The sad truth was I'd found myself in this sort of situation before. I'm not sure if I suffer from overconfidence, denial or just plain old-fashioned retardation. Whatever the case, I pushed these thoughts down and focused on the mission. I was going to recon the place, looking for a way out the whole time. With luck, I'd pop back home ten minutes from now.

A part of my mind that wasn't in fight-or-flight mode took solace in the fact that I at least had my answer. Leeza had screwed me over, then ported out to Rigel herself. In retrospect, that should have been obvious—but it hadn't been, somehow.

After all, if Leeza had done it, she would have been working for a reward. Who would have paid handsomely for my capture?

The only name I could come up with was Squanto, man's best friend out here on Rigel. I'd done excellent detective work, but then blown it on the final step…

"The contact is dead ahead," I heard a voice say. It was a human female voice, and it was coming over a radio. It still sounded kind of familiar…

Several sets of boots tramped on the metal decks. They were behind me in the last side-passage I'd passed by.

Whirling around, I took a knee and quietly slid back the bolt on my rifle. There was nowhere to run. They were too close behind me, and they would have heard my clanking boots anyway.

"Could you have been followed?" a man asked, and I knew who he was at once. He had a French accent—it was Armel.

The female voice spoke again, but I didn't catch the words.

The first shape walked around the corner up ahead. They had pistols out, and I'd expected them to be Claver types—but they weren't. They were saurians.

That was a shock. I'd been expecting bears, maybe. Or Class-Three Clavers. But saurians? I hadn't seen them lately, except for a few bio workers like that lizard-puke named Raash.

It didn't matter. I opened up on them, firing a spray of power-bolts down the passage. The first two went down fast. They weren't armored, and they only carried pistols. I left them piled on top of one another with one of their thick, alligator-like tails sticking up and thrashing weakly.

For a second, the passage quieted. No one else came around the corner, but I didn't hear any pounding feet, either. They weren't rushing in or retreating.

I took a fresh grip on my rifle—why did your hands always get sweaty and cramped at moments like this? I stared down the sights and tried not to blink.

Then I heard something. A click behind me.

Whirling around, I hosed the passageway with bolts. It lit up like the Fourth of July.

Another saurian had come out of a doorway in the passage. Maybe he'd been checking to see what was going on—bad timing for him.

I turned back toward where Armel had been approaching, but I still didn't see anyone. I stepped over the body in the doorway and into the open door. I tried to close it, but there was about two hundred kilos of lizard in the way. Cursing, I struggled with the door, but then I stopped.

This wasn't any escape route. The door only led into a tiny cabin that smelled like snake-shit. It was a trap.

Poking my head back out into the passageway, I looked and I listened. Everything was quiet. The hum of the big ship was all I heard.

"Armel?" I called out. "I know you're still there."

"*Mon Dieu!*" he said in response. "Can it be true? Has my fortune changed this day? James McGill… to what do I owe the honor of this visit?"

"Uh…" I said, thinking of the monkey-logic that had brought me here. Reflexively, I came up with a poor lie and went with it. "I came to find Leeza. She left the ship, and my bed—I wanted to find out why."

There were a few moments of cold silence. Then, a very angry-looking Frenchman stalked around the corner. He placed his hands on his hips. He had a pistol, but it wasn't aimed at me.

His eyes… they looked a bit insane.

"You take back your pathetic lie, McGill! I demand a retraction, this instant!"

"I could gun you down right now, Armel."

He nodded slowly. "This is true. But it means nothing. I have revival equipment within a few meters of this spot. I rather suspect you do not."

"Uh…" I said. He had me there. Sure, I had the gun on him, but he had a ship-full of lizards and a way to come back to life if he felt like it. "All right," I said. "I'm sorry. I haven't been porking Leeza—that was a dirty lie."

Nodding, he seemed to relax somewhat. He wasn't as tall as I was, so he could almost stand up straight in the passageway.

He crooked his finger at me. "Whatever you are here for, you'd best come with me. The bears will have detected all this gunfire. They're not likely to be as forgiving as I am."

So saying, he turned his back on me and walked calmly back the way he'd come.

I was left crouching in some stinking lizard's quarters. It was dark, and dank, like an animal's den.

I cursed a lot over the next half-minute while I considered my very limited set of options. I checked for power outlets, but naturally, none of them fit my harness.

What had I been thinking, porting out here after Leeza like a lemming jumping off a cliff? What was there to gain from confirming the now-obvious fact she'd tried to sell my ass to Squanto?

Nothing, that's what. But I'd never been accused of overthinking my choices in life.

Today was just another case in point, I supposed. With a long sigh, I slung my rifle and followed Armel.

-48-

An hour later found me sitting around a titanium table with Leeza and Armel. We all had drinks in our hands. I was told it was a fine red wine—but I wouldn't know the difference between a good wine and horse-piss.

Leeza wasn't looking at me. She was looking at her wine glass—or maybe her hands. Armel was in a very different mood. He seemed to think we were in a staring contest. I got the idea he was still feeling jealous and prickly.

I'd always suspected there was a relationship between Armel and Leeza that was way beyond inappropriate. Back on Tech World, when Armel had led Germanica, her unit had been the last to suffer out of the whole legion. Later, on Blood World, she'd served as Armel's personal assistant and had once handed me a sword to duel with him.

More recently, she'd joined him to lead Claver's legions. Now that those legions were defunct, here she was again at his side—and not meeting my eye.

"Isn't this a lovely occasion," Armel said. "Think of it, the three of us sitting in orbit over Rigel, discussing old times. It's positively charming of you to drop by and visit us, McGill."

"Uh-huh," I said. I wasn't really listening to him. He often made snarky speeches. He enjoyed that, but I found it dull.

I was trying to figure out what Leeza's angle was. After all, she'd asked me for help back on Clone World. She'd wanted to leave Armel—or so she said. I'd killed her, gotten her revived and rehabilitated—sort of. She'd rejoined Fleet, and she'd seemed good at her job.

All that part added up pretty well. What I couldn't make heads or tails of now was why she'd gone back to Armel. There were only a few possible answers to that question that I could come up with.

For one, she might have been playing a part the whole time. Maybe after she'd escaped a solid perming on Clone World, she'd bided her time until she could return to Armel. Once she got within jumping distance of Rigel, she'd ported out and returned to him.

That was one possibility. It would even explain why she wasn't meeting my eye. After all, it seemed like she'd sold me out six ways from Sunday, even arranging to have me handed over to Squanto before making her escape to Rigel.

But some things about that story bothered me. As a near-professional liar myself, I thought I could detect the trait in others. All along, over the last few decades, whenever I met up with Leeza she seemed to be on the level. For example, she'd let me go when I was an embarrassment because she owed me one. Evil, duplicitous women who sell you out to be tortured to death by aliens don't think they owe anybody anything.

"Would you like another taste, McGill?" Armel asked.

I glanced down at my wine glass, which was empty. I lifted it and frowned. "Have you got anything stronger? Some of that brandy you used to feed Turov, maybe?"

Both of them froze for a cold second. Then they moved again. I knew that reaction—I'd touched a sore spot. That was what I'd meant to do.

Armel cleared his throat and forced a smile. His thin mustache spread out like a stretching caterpillar.

"Indeed, I might have something a bit stronger that is more to your liking."

He got up, and he went into the next room. A locker creaked as he dug in it. Bottles clinked—Armel always had a lot of bottles.

I took the moment to lean over the table and glare at Leeza. "You sold me out, then you bolted. Here I am playing the fool again. I thought you were in trouble, so I came looking for you."

She finally looked up. Her lips parted, and I realized it was due to shock.

"You came all the way out here because of *me*? I don't believe it."

"I didn't know where you'd gone. I didn't think I'd end up on Rigel."

Armel returned then, and his grin faded as he saw we were both sullen and had clearly been whispering.

Leeza dropped her eyes again. I sat back in my chair and waved my glass at him, gesturing for him to fill it up.

A fine brown liquid poured, and I swigged it. "Now that's real brandy all right! It's not the bootleg kind that people make on ships, either—the stuff that tastes like somebody puked inside a rubber glove."

"Yes… it is real, and it is from Earth. Even a clod like yourself should be able to enjoy it."

I didn't take his unkind words to heart. After all, he was half-suspicious that I'd nailed his girl. Even without that complication, we'd never been besties.

"Okay," I said after a final gulp. "Let's discuss what I can do for you."

"What you can do for me?" Armel chuckled.

"Yes. I need to bargain. I need a charge for my suit. It's already programmed to take me home—and I figure a good turn like that deserves a just reward."

Armel's cheek twitched. It looked like the shortest half-smile on record.

"Do you know what I'm doing out here, McGill?" he asked.

"Uh… yeah. Working for the bears—right?"

"Yes, I suppose that much is obvious. You see, I've been a mercenary for a long, long time. Since before it was in style, one might say."

I waggled my glass at him again, and he pursed his lips before pouring me another dollop.

"I am, therefore, a man who works for the highest payment he can get. I left Earth's service when it was no longer in my best interest to be there. At that time, Claver's legions offered me a better deal—we all know how that turned out, however."

"Yeah..." I said, laughing. "You really shit the bed that time."

His eyes flashed at me, but he kept his tight smile in place.

"Yes... the deal went sour. However, even though Claver's troops proved substandard, the Rigellians liked my services as a commander. They charged me with finding new troops to oversee."

"Ah... that's why this place is crawling with lizards? You recruited a mercenary legion from Steel World?"

"That's right. Remember your first journey to the stars? On that fateful trip, you learned that the saurians wanted to become mercenaries—like Earthlings."

"Huh..." I said, beginning to feel the alcohol a bit. "That's true."

"So, it was rather easy to get ten thousand or so of them to join me out here on the frontier."

"Okay, look Armel, that's all fine and dandy, but since I've determined that Leeza here is not in any trouble, I should be getting back—"

He raised a gloved hand, palm held outward. I stopped talking.

"Indulge me," he said. "After all, I've been an excellent host, no?"

"Yeah..."

"Good. As I was saying, I'm a mercenary, and that means I make critical decisions based on profit."

"Uh... okay."

"Today, I have a unique opportunity to improve my influence here on Rigel. Can you guess how I may accomplish this?"

"Well..." I said, realizing how things were going.

I reached for my rifle. Now, I'm a big man, but I'm also quick. Unfortunately, Armel was already aiming a pistol at my belly. He lifted it into view before I could get my rifle out. I froze.

"Really?" I said. "After all this hospitality? You're going to turn me in?"

"I had hoped that you knew something of interest—but I was mistaken. I've wasted good brandy on you, and over an hour of my lifetime. Unfortunately, I cannot recoup these losses—but I can still profit from your idiocy at following Leeza out here."

"I see..." I said, and I did see.

Armel had talked to me to learn things—maybe he'd wanted to know if I really had slept with Leeza, or if I knew about some kind of grand strategy from Earth. He'd struck out all around on those points.

Armel nodded. "I gave you your life on a recent occasion for helping my lady friend, here. I cannot afford to do this again. You understand, don't you?"

"Oh yeah, you're chock-full of compassion."

For some reason, this struck Armel as hilarious. He began to laugh—but in the middle of it, I heard a singing sound.

Suffering from a sudden shock, he stiffened and stood partway up. Then his pistol clattered on the floor. He pitched forward on his face. His dying eyes locked onto Leeza's. He tried to talk, reminding me of a fish gasping on the bottom of a boat.

Leeza had shot him. She'd had a needler in her palm the whole time.

She leaned toward him as he died, and she gazed into his face. There was a tear running down her cheek—I'd never seen that before.

"I'm sorry, Maurice. I truly am... but goddammit, I told you I was through! You had to go and arrange all this, then you tried to get McGill permed and tortured—it's just too much. I can't take it anymore. I'm going back, even if it means prison."

She turned to me next. I wore a slack-jawed look of surprise and hardcore-ignorance on my face.

"James... I've been charging a harness in the other room. We've got to port out of here *now*."

Armel was looking pretty dead, but he suddenly woke up with a gasp and an unnatural jerk. His gloved hand snapped out and grabbed her wrist.

Automatically, my fist hammered down, and I broke his face. I'd seen that before—facial bones can actually break, you know.

"Hold it!" Leeza said. My second punch was aiming to crush his ear to pulp, but I managed to stop it in time.

She leaned close. "What is it, Armel?"

"Did you...?" he asked in a gaspy whisper. "Did you...?"

His eyes flicked up toward me. They rolled way back into his head so the whites showed, and with blood dribbling down over those staring orbs—well, it was kind of nasty.

"Did I what...? Oh... oh no. I didn't. I mean, *we* didn't. James was just messing with your mind, right James?"

"That's right partner," I said, leaning down, so he could see me. "There was no hanky-panky. None at all. Not that I didn't give it shot, mind you. But she's been colder than a witch's tit in a brass bra ever since I met her. I honestly thought she was... well... never mind."

Armel's ruined face worked for a few seconds. He was trying to say something else. But instead, he gave a little sigh, and he died.

Leeza and I charged up two suits, set the destination, and ported the hell out of there before the saurians could finish burning the door down. It was a close thing, but all they found when they broke in was Armel's messy corpse and some spilled brandy.

-49-

When I arrived back aboard the *U. E. Berlin*, I was in for a shock. Leeza was there—but so was another woman I'd gotten to know recently.

We were standing on Gray Deck, and the two women were having a heated discussion. I walked up, confused and bemused.

"Uh... ladies? What's all the fuss about?"

They turned to look at me. Leeza was standing tall and pissed. Abigail, on the other hand, looked relaxed and snarky.

"Did you bring this treat all the way back across the cosmos for me, McGill?" Abigail asked, pointing a finger at Leeza.

That was when things went badly. Leeza lost it. She was, in her heart of hearts, a legionnaire after all. She took after Abigail with a sucker punch.

To my surprise, Abigail ducked it. That whistling fist only grazed her right cheek. With a grab and a twist, she threw Leeza on the deck.

That didn't last long. Leeza bounced up, hissing. She came in again, going for a clinch.

"What's gotten into you two?" I asked, not knowing what to do. I took a few steps closer, but I didn't grab them. After all, they weren't shooting or knifing each other—not yet anyway. In the legions, it was generally considered rude to break up a fistfight unless one person was just cruelly hammering the other, or it was officer against enlisted. Otherwise, we usually let them get it out of their systems.

"You arranged for McGill to be sent back, didn't you?" Leeza demanded. "I didn't do it, and someone had to. It was you!"

Leeza faked left and punched right. This time, she caught Abigail on the nose. Blood flew.

That seemed to break Abigail's composure. She was no longer calm and collected. Each girl threw an angry flurry of blows. Some landed, some were blocked, but either way, there were going to be some serious bruises and clumps of hair on the deck after this one.

After a bit, they caught onto each other's arms and wrestled, trying to trip each other. They were both breathing hard. No one had a clear advantage yet.

I winced once in a while, but mostly, I enjoyed the show. I didn't really have a cat in this fight, and they seemed pretty evenly matched. As the growls and angry shrieks went on, I found I had to suppress a half-smile that kept creeping up on my face.

At last, Leeza shoved Abigail, and she went staggering back. They both put their hands on their knees and panted.

"That's right, take a breather," I said. "You can't land a hard one if you don't have your wind up."

Leeza glanced at me in disgust. "I don't know why I'm fighting if McGill doesn't even care. James, don't you understand? This twisted creature sold you to Rigel. She's the one that told them the LZ coordinates."

Surprised, I looked at Abigail. "Is that right?"

Abigail glanced at the deck and shrugged. "Sometimes profit has to be taken. I thought you'd understand."

"When? While I was getting tormented by those bastard bears?"

She blinked. "No, no, no—I didn't think you'd *actually* be captured. I arranged for you to die midflight by giving them a teleport harness with a flaw in it. That way, after they captured you, I'd have my payment and they'd have nothing—but it would be their fault."

"She's lying, James," Leeza said. "She sold you to Rigel. She probably figured that she could get you revived somehow back here aboard ship and no one would ever know what happened."

"Huh…" I said, thinking about that. The truth was, I might never learn what had actually happened. Abigail was that kind of sneaky—just like her brothers.

The two women looked at me. "What are you doing here anyway?" I asked Abigail. "I thought you were executed or something."

Abigail gave me another of her little shrugs. "You spoke with Praetor Drusus, didn't you? He gave me a chance to make my case. That was very honorable of you. That was a bargain kept."

"So… after he had you executed, what happened?"

She shrugged. "I returned to Earth. I spoke there with other people who were… more congenial. I managed to get myself officially assigned to this mission," she concluded. "I stepped out from Earth only an hour ago."

"How convenient!" Leeza huffed from behind her. "Right when James is crated and shipped to Rigel, you reappear and act like you belong here."

Abigail turned her back on Leeza. While she was making eyes at me, she reached back to settle her admittedly tousled hair—but I saw she had one long finger flipped out in plain view while she did it. That finger took a slow trip down her hair in the back, and Leeza couldn't have missed the spectacle.

Abigail smiled up at me. "We can sort this out," she said.

That's when Leeza kicked her in the ass—or, to be more accurate, a bit lower than that. That boot tip came up hard from behind, and I could tell from the widening of Abigail's eyes that she wasn't a happy camper.

I could have told her she'd made a tactical error. She was used to being around men—hell, as far as I knew she'd only known various versions of her brothers up until recently. But that might have left her with poor predictive skills when it came to the behavior of rival women.

271

Whatever the case, the fight was on again, and this time it was in earnest. Claws were out, and they were reaching for their knives after thirty loud seconds had passed.

I honestly considered letting them kill each other. Sometimes, it was for the best to let new recruits work these things out for themselves. After all, it wouldn't be anything a bit of flesh-printing couldn't fix.

But I found I couldn't stay neutral. They were making an awful racket, and even I was getting tired of it. Accordingly, I reached out and gently thumped their heads together. It was the sort of thing I did to settle down feisty recruits on the training grounds.

I didn't do it real hard, just enough to send them reeling. They both staggered backward, stunned. Leeza went to her knees, and Abigail puked—but I figured that was from exertion as much as anything else.

Helping the girls stand straight, I plucked their weapons from their hands and belts, dropping them on the deck. Needlers and knives clattered loudly. Then, I walked them both toward the exit.

"What are you doing?" Leeza asked me.

"Taking you two to the brig to cool off. I don't know who's a traitor and who's full of shit—could be both of you. In any case, I'm tired of the whole thing."

"McGill, I don't have time for this," Abigail said urgently.

"No? Maybe you should have thought of that before you shipped my ass off to the bears to make a buck."

"It was a business deal. If you'd actually been transported there, you'd have been revived back here aboard this warship. I saw to it. In fact, you would never have known anything had happened if events had gone as planned."

"Yeah, well, is that supposed to make me feel better? Because it doesn't. In fact, I've got hurt feelings. I was kind of sweet on you, Miss Claver. Now, you've gone and burst my bubble. I might have to go get counseling or something."

She glanced up at me like I was crazy. I gave her back an indignant angry look that would have convinced anyone—except possibly my dad.

"I can't go to the brig now," she said in breathy panic. "I've just become respectable in Earth's eyes. I'll tell you what—I'll share the payment with you. How about that?"

I stopped frog-marching the two women toward the lower decks. "Really? How much is my carcass worth to old Squanto?"

"A million credits," she said. "You can have it all."

"Hegemony or Galactic?"

"Hegemony, of course."

I snorted. "That's a crap payout. You got ripped off, girl. Do you know how much that bear cub hates me? In fact, I'm so insulted by that offer you're going to the brig anyway."

For the first time since I'd met her, she seemed actually alarmed about this turn of events. Her eyes were looking around like she was hoping to see an exit—but there wasn't any. She scratched at my fingers, which were wrapped around her arm, but that was like scratching at an oak branch.

"All right," she said. "Two million. I'll give it all to you."

I made a rude, blatting noise with my lips.

We reached the passageways, and crewmen were giving us very strange looks. But I kept marching, not even making eye-contact with anyone.

"James, really, I can't go to the brig. I'll lose all my credibility with certain patrons. Drusus is already against me. I've worked so hard…"

"You should have thought of that before you tried to make a quick buck out of old James McGill."

"Yes. Yes, I should have. I'm very sorry, James."

"Not good enough."

"I'll make it five million—no, five million *each*!"

I stopped walking. I stood the girls in front of me. They didn't look their best, but Leeza didn't appear to be angry anymore. She looked kind of… greedy.

"What do you think about that, Ensign?" I asked her.

"Ten million," she said. "Each. Or no deal."

Abigail bared her teeth. "All right. You've got it."

I let go of the two ornery women.

"Shake on it," I said.

They both reached out a distrustful hand toward one another. After a moment, they clasped hands and shook briefly. Seeing that, I smiled my first honest smile of the day.

I didn't care much about the money. I'd probably end up giving it to my folks to keep them from aging, anyway. However, I did dare to hope to enjoy some peace and quiet around this ship at last.

-50-

My hopes and dreams of a peaceful night were not to be. Around about midnight, just as I stretched out for some well-deserved shuteye, there was a knock on my door.

As a centurion, I rated a small personal cabin, but that was only because there was enough room aboard at the moment. As the revivals continued, troops would pile up like cordwood until multiple centurions would be stacked into this tiny chamber with me. Still, that was way better than sleeping on the deck, which is what most of our soldiers would have to do when things got tighter.

"What is it?" I called out.

The tapping came again. The knocking wasn't a pounding fist, but there was definitely some urgency behind it. Sighing, I threw my arm over my face to shield my eyes from the light and tapped the walls. The room lit up, and I told the door to open.

Two women stood in the passage outside. One was Ensign Leeza. Adjunct Erin Barton stood behind her.

"Uh…" I said, not quite knowing what was what. "Can I help you ladies?"

"Sir," Barton said, "I found this fleet-type slinking through our assigned quarters. She was checking every room, asking for you. Did you approve of this action as she says, or should I remove her?"

"Huh..." I said, thinking over these two options. "What's the problem, Ensign?"

"So she lied to me?" Barton asked, jerking up on Leeza's arm. That's when I noticed Barton had the smaller woman's arm twisted up behind her. Adjunct Barton could be the stern type when she got riled.

Leeza stared at the deck. "I don't understand why your troops think it's appropriate to treat crewmen this way."

"Because you're on every watch-list there is," Barton told her angrily. Leeza's hair puffed up with each word that was blasted into the back of her head. "You've been relieved of all duties by the captain, and you should be in the brig. In fact, I think I'll take you down there and see if I can convince them to lock you up. I'm sorry to disturb you with this trash, Centurion."

"Adjunct?" I said, sitting up and yawning. "Hold on a second."

With visible reluctance, Barton stopped dragging Leeza away.

"Did you want to talk, or something?" I asked Leeza.

She nodded her head. She was still staring fixedly at the deck. I thought that over, and I even glanced lovingly at my pillow. I could really use some sleep after all I'd been through.

Finally, I sighed and waved to Barton. "It's okay, Erin. I'll talk to her for a minute."

Adjunct Barton didn't look any happier to hear these words. She showed her teeth, nodded, and shoved Leeza into my cabin. Then she slammed the door behind her.

"Sit down, sit down," I said, waving my visitor to the bunks opposite me. The cabin had four bunks, two on each side with a cramped aisle in the middle.

Leeza sat opposite me, but she didn't look comfortable there. She didn't meet my gaze.

"What'd you want to talk about?"

"What you saw out there," she said, "or what you *think* you saw. They're talking about an inquiry. Are you going to testify?"

"Uh..." I said, giving my face a rubdown. "You got a beer or anything? It's hard for me to think at night without—"

Leeza produced a silver flask. I didn't ask her where she kept it. Most mercenaries kept alcohol handy for rough moments. She poured out a couple shots, and I gulped mine.

Not quite knowing how to kick-off the conversation, I started with the most immediate mystery. I figured I could get around to the big stuff later.

"You were knocking on every cabin? Why didn't you just use your tapper? Oh—wait, you ripped it out, didn't you?"

She showed me a scarred arm. "Armel's butchers replaced it. The screen is distorted, but it works."

I nodded. "You used to be in charge of seat assignments on this ship. I would think—"

"Used to," she said. "But the captain has lost all faith in me. He… he disconnected me from the grid, except for emergency incoming messages only."

"Is that why you're moping around here at midnight?"

Leeza looked up. "Not exactly. James, I need your help. I… I've been hiding things—from everyone."

She began to tell me then that she'd suffered some kind of mysterious amnesia. That she couldn't remember almost a year's time in her life. That she'd been revived with a big chunk of her history missing, and she'd forgotten the entirety of the Clone World campaign.

While she confessed all this, I winced a few times. Winslade had undergone that same treatment, and he hadn't reacted well, either. I'd begun to regret having a hand in delivering a serious mind-fuck to both these people.

Sure, the versions of them that I'd known and dealt with had turned traitor. They'd been turned by Claver and his promises of promotions in his clone legions. They were supposed to live forever, get higher ranks and escape Earth's smothering government.

All of that hadn't excused them for treason—but this version of these people had never committed the crime. Was it right, was it moral, to punish a person for something they had no knowledge of doing? They weren't the people who'd performed these heinous acts—not exactly. They were more like twin siblings to those wayward souls.

Worse, no one had ever bothered to *tell* them why they were being leaned on, why they were demoted and kicked around... Winslade had reacted by pulling in some big favors with Hegemony. He was a different man now, in some ways, and the change wasn't for the better.

Leeza, on the other hand, had turned her confusion and mistreatment inward. She didn't understand it, and she seemed to be tormented by it all.

I heaved a sigh. "Listen," I said, "I'm going to tell you something I've been ordered not to. Something that explains all the shit you've been going through for about a year now."

Slowly, her face turned up to mine. She had the light of hope in her eyes. She didn't say anything, but she didn't have to. The hunger for the truth was plain to see.

"Don't get too happy," I warned her. "The truth isn't good. It isn't fair. It's not likely to make your day."

She licked her lips and nodded. "I've already figured that out. Just tell me."

So... I did. I told her the truth, the whole truth, and nothing but the truth. By the end of it, I'd had a second shot of booze, and she'd drained the flask.

She stretched out on the bunk opposite me. I thought she was going to cry or something, but she didn't. She'd always been a tough woman.

"You set this nightmare in motion," she said. "When you executed me and talked them into bringing me back."

"You'd rather be permed?"

"I don't know. It's been rough."

"The woman I talked to out there on Clone World—the one who was a primus commanding a cohort of Clavers—she didn't want to be permed. She called in a favor, an old debt, and I agreed."

She thought that over, and she shook the flask. It was empty. She tossed it on the deck, where it clattered like a dinner bell.

"You're right," she said, sucking in a long breath and sighing. "You didn't start this—I did. I asked for a favor, and you did the favor. It's all my fault."

I laughed, feeling good about having come clean on our strangely twisted fate.

Suddenly, she sat straight up. "It's not *fair*! I've been kissing ass for a year without even knowing why. They've leaned on me in so many little ways…"

"Yeah, that does suck. Now, if you're feeling better, maybe you could see your way to letting me get some sleep. What do you say?"

She looked at the deck again. "I don't have an assigned bunk, McGill. I've got as much space on a steel deck as my butt can cover, that's all. They said it was a mix-up—but I know now it wasn't."

"Oh… well, if you want, you can sleep right there—as long as you promise to shut up, that is."

When you tell a woman to shut up, especially when she's drunk and emotional, she'll do one of two things: she'll either get mad, or she won't hear you. Leeza chose the second option.

"There's something I should tell you now. About how I got back to Armel. Things have been weird on Earth and on this ship for months. When Abigail first contacted me, she told me she would relay anything I wanted to Armel. That she was in contact with him."

Frowning, I propped myself up with an elbow. I had been vaguely wondering what kind of monkey-business she'd used to escape her post aboard *Berlin* and why she was so angry with Abigail.

"Go on," I said.

"She tricked me. She knew more than she was letting on. She got me into communication with Armel, who'd been looking for a way to get me back. In fact, I think he had a bounty out on me, and Abigail took it—just the way she did to make a quick credit piece on your head."

"Hmm… that does sound like a Claver," I admitted.

"So, they gave me coordinates. I stole a harness and ported out. In payment… I gave them the location of your unit's LZ during that last drop. I'm really sorry about that."

I chewed that over, and I found I didn't like the taste. "Girl, maybe you *are* a natural traitor. Did you ever think of that? You did it twice now, on two different grows."

"I know, I know! But it wasn't me, it's not about me—it's Armel. He's bad for me. He's always managed to get me to do whatever he wanted. That's my real weakness."

"So you're in love with him? You sure can pick them!"

I laughed, but she didn't. She stopped talking, and I gratefully fell asleep, assuming she'd done the same.

A bit later—it might have been a minute or an hour, it's hard to tell when you're sleeping hard—I felt a light touch.

Snorting awake, I remembered who was in the room, and I stopped myself from killing her in the dark. Slapping at the wall, I looked at her in the sudden light, blinking.

Leeza was on her knees next to my bunk. She watched me like a cat, and I got the feeling she'd never slept a wink.

"Uh..." I said. "What now?"

"Do you like Abigail?" she asked. "Do you think she's pretty?"

Women loved to set traps for men like that one, but fortunately, I knew the answer. It was reflexive, and practically burned into my brain.

"Hell no!" I lied with gusto. For flavor, I decided that simple denial needed a grain of truth placed on it—like a cherry on top. "She kind of freaks me out, to be honest. She looks too much like her brothers."

For the first time in a long time, I saw Leeza smile. She looked a lot cuter when she smiled. Usually, she had this stern, mean-looking expression on her face—but not tonight.

"Good," she said. "I really, really hate that woman."

"You've got no worries in that department," I lied firmly.

Leeza knew my rep, of course, but she was from outside the legion, so she didn't really know how I operated. I could tell she bought every word I said. It was kind of refreshing. All the female officers in my outfit seemed to go out of their way to tell stories about me—they seemed to have skipped giving this girl "the James McGill talk."

She studied the deck again. "I've been kind of interested in you, James. For years—no, for decades now. Maybe it all started when I found you nude on that pool table..."

I laughed, not sure where she was going with this.

Suddenly, she looked up and dropped her bomb. "Do you like me at all? That way, I mean?"

"Well..." I began, but I didn't say anything else.

She had me. She was looking all cute and happy and almost ready to cry. Sure, I knew she was a dangerous woman—but you just try waving a slice of fried chicken in front of a hound dog. He'll snap for it, every damned time.

I sat up on the bunk, and I kind of expected her to climb on the bed with me—but she didn't. She stayed on her knees and began kissing my legs. Things proceeded very nicely—but after a bit, I became alarmed. I got the feeling Armel had taught this lady to do things his way.

"Whoa, girl!" I said, gently taking her by the elbows and lifting her up on the bunk with me.

She didn't resist at all, and I gave her the best I had in me. She seemed to like that, and the night passed by in very pleasant fashion.

-51-

The very next day, the floor lit up red and klaxons dragged us from our bunks. When I came stumbling out into the cramped passages with Leeza yawning in my wake, there were a few snorts of amusement, but I knew how to fix that.

Slamming my oven mitt-sized hands together repeatedly, I roared for people to "move, move, MOVE!" and soon, the whole unit was tramping to the armory. We outfitted ourselves, checked our gear and loaded our weapons.

Surprisingly, we weren't directed to deploy immediately. I got the feeling others weren't so lucky. The passages were crowded with rushing troops.

For my unit, the arrows led to the mess deck first, where we were given a hearty breakfast. There were real eggs, real bacon, and toasted English muffins. To me, it was all a giant danger sign... The brass never splurged on breakfast without a damned good reason.

Deciding not to worry about it, I ate with gusto and entertained myself with thoughts of my new lady-friend. If I had to die on any given morning, I at least liked to have some good memories of the night before. Last night I'd achieved that goal.

As we finished up our meal the biggest, blankest wall of the mess deck lit up. A briefing began while we were still chewing and gulping the last of it.

The wolfshead emblem of Varus glowed, then split apart. In its place appeared Winslade's leering face. A few people hissed, and I heard Moller slapping and shouting for them to shut up.

"My proud legion," he began. "Today, we've been blessed with a rare opportunity. We're going to rectify our mistakes of the recent past. We're going back down to Glass World, and we're going to do it *right* this time."

No one cheered. In fact, I heard Carlos say something about "rectifying" Winslade himself.

I found it hard to blame my troops. For one thing, no one was too fond of Winslade. For another, we hadn't heard the details yet. Love, joy or horror—any of these could be buried in the details.

Winslade began playing with graphic maps. He showed the same odd, wavery shots of the surface he'd been examining in his office the last time I'd spoken to him. Slowly, he panned through a dozen shots, one at a time. They all looked confusing and mostly the same. It was like he'd given the planet an X-ray.

"See here? This splotch with the lines? That's one of the crystal patches. One of the outcroppings of glass-like material that dots this strange world—but today, these obvious features of the planet don't contain our goal."

He panned down, then to the left. The bumpy imagery swam and blurred. Finally, he seemed to find the spot he'd been seeking. Pointing out a lung-shaped region of darkness on the image, his finger looked like the hand of God.

"There..." he said. "Right there. That's a tunnel complex. It doesn't look like much on this scan, but let me assure you, it is at least ten square kilometers of caverns. They exist about five hundred meters below the surface."

The image faded, and Winslade's face loomed again. There were a few groans and boos. I had to admit, I liked the x-ray better myself.

"That's the only sizeable tunnel complex we've managed to locate. It's our belief that the processing center must be inside that sealed region. There's simply nowhere else it could be."

"Did he say *sealed*?" Carlos asked loudly from two tables over. "What kind of fuckery is this?"

I didn't bother to shout at him, or even to look at him. Moller was already up and moving. She would shorten his dick for him, and I didn't have to even worry about it. I smiled, enjoying the kind of small perk that made it worthwhile to be a centurion.

"It's probably full of lava or something," Adjunct Barton said next to me.

I was mildly surprised to hear her speak. She'd sat right next to me, eating without a word for ten full minutes now. I'd pretended not to notice how quiet she was—which was easy, as I really didn't care.

Erin and I had had a fling a few years back, but that was long over with now. If she wanted to get disgusted every time I spent some time with a new lady-friend, well, that was her problem.

"Nah," I said, "not lava. That would be too quick of a death. That's not how Varus does things."

We continued watching Winslade's presentation. He outlined how, after a careful search, they'd been unable to find any other regions large enough on the planet to house a hidden manufacturing center. He failed to mention that Abigail was the source for the theory that a processing facility existed. That was either because he wanted to take the credit, or because he didn't want us to freak out. After all, we'd spent a year on a campaign to destroy the Claver homeworld. No one in Legion Varus trusted any sort of Claver clone, female or otherwise.

"Lastly," Winslade continued, "we've decided on who will be volunteered for this glorious mission."

A loud groan came up from my unit. Moller and Sargon were looking around sternly, but there were so many people groaning it was hard to assign blame. In fact, I counted myself among them.

Winslade's oversized eyeballs peered at us, and his teeth showed in what I imagined passed for a grin on his face. "I can almost hear the dismay in 3rd Unit—but worry not. Your fears are unfounded. I've decided to send troops from 3rd Cohort, yes—but not your unit."

Blinking and stunned, we looked around at each other. We couldn't believe what we were hearing.

"That's right. The first to go will be 7th Unit, then if needed, the 8th. This is to rectify—"

"—he said it again!" Carlos shouted.

"—what I believe to be an error in Graves' operational strategy. He relied overly-much on the admittedly extensive experience of 3rd Unit. Due to this habit, others in Varus haven't gotten a chance to prove themselves. That practice ends today."

People whooped and cheered. Moller was so happy she didn't even cuff Carlos. More importantly, Erin slapped me on the back, and we grinned at one another. All thoughts of jealousy had vanished in an instant, and I thought she looked her best when she smiled a real, honest smile.

When Winslade's briefing ended, the only thing that 3rd Unit cared about was the fact we weren't going in first. Carlos even came up and tried to hug me.

"McGill..." he said, "I don't know who you had to blow for this—in fact, I don't want to know. I'm just glad you did it, big guy."

I pushed him away, cursing. He was escorted back to his seat by one of the noncoms, and we ate the rest of our meal with gusto.

7th Unit, on the other hand, looked like they were attending their own funerals. They were all out of hoots and hollers today. They'd been fingered for the worst of duties: a teleport-assault mission into the unknown.

I grinned and waved at Manfred, who was their leader and a friend of mine. He flipped me the bird in return, but I kept on waving and grinning.

"Bon voyage, Manfred!" I laughed.

The next few hours were sheer bliss. My troops had been certain we'd be chosen to go on this particular suicide mission. We'd done more of them than any other outfit in the legion.

That was the kind of insidious trap that so often caught a man in the military: success usually bought you more difficult assignments and more pain. Sure, we took pride in our record, but at the same time, we were tired of carrying such a heavy load.

Long ago, we'd been chosen to pioneer the original teleportation commando missions. Since some of us had survived the experience, we'd been called upon again and again. Our very success became a curse, as the brass started to rely on our legendary expertise. The more missions we performed, the more they sent us—the cycle had seemed unbreakable.

Until now. Winslade had stated the obvious: others needed to get a shot at using the equipment. As he didn't seem to believe this mission would be difficult to complete, he had no reason to send his best.

Internally, I had to wonder what other factors his calculations entailed. For instance, I knew he didn't like sharing the limelight with anyone. Maybe he was doing this to cut me down a peg. Or maybe it was just so he could do something differently than Graves, as he'd said.

It didn't matter. I was glad to get out of another death today, regardless of the cause. Never look a gift-horse in the mouth, my daddy used to say.

Whistling a cheerful tune, I marched my people out of the mess and down to the shooting range. Today, we were the only unit aboard that was neither slated to go down to Glass World, nor already dead and waiting in the revival queue.

We shot targets, had a few non-deadly contests of arms, and generally whooped it up. Downstairs, on Gray Deck, sorry platoons of guinea pigs were suited-up, jacked-in and fired into the guts of an unsuspecting planet.

About thirty minutes into our celebration, we saw the lights shimmer. That was the second time around, and it was a sure sign of a power fluctuation. Aboard *Berlin*, that kind of thing usually happened when the main guns were fired, or we went into warp. This time, however, I knew it was because Gray Deck was pulling a lot of amperage. Another unit must be charging up to head down to the planet.

"Another group is porting out!" Carlos told me unnecessarily. "I've got confirmation on my tapper. Want to look at the readouts?"

"Nope," I said, lining up my rifle on an alien holo-target. I released a short burst with a practiced squeeze of the trigger. The bolts sprayed the target downrange, destroying the hulking monster.

"You know what this means, don't you?" Carlos persisted in a lowered voice. "It means the first unit didn't finish the job. They needed back up."

I shrugged and fired another burst.

Carlos, never one to take any kind of hint, subtle or otherwise, sidled closer. "You should talk to Natasha. Something's wrong down there. The techs know about it—they always do."

"Are you here specifically to spoil this fine day, Specialist?"

"Hell no, sir. That's Winslade's job. He's in charge of this legion now, and whatever happens, it's his fault."

He left me at last, and I fired three more bursts, destroying three more targets. Finally, however, I set my rifle down in disgust. Carlos had done his dirty work with all that whispering.

I lifted my tapper to contact Natasha—but I hesitated. The ship shivered again.

A third unit? Only twenty minutes after the last one? Why would they have to send three units…? Could Carlos, that loudmouthed, self-appointed buzz-killer be right?

Instead of making a call, I left the range and headed down to Gray Deck. I wanted to see what was happening in person.

Stepping onto the deck, I noted several things. First off, there were techs tearing around, rushing from one panel to the next. At the far end of the deck, standing at the control panels that did group-targeting, I saw a familiar face.

It was Winslade himself, and he was scowling with unusual ferocity. As I approached, he scolded one of the techs.

"Don't tell me that again! Repeated information is useless!"

"But sir, you said—"

"Get back to your console and fix it!"

The tech specialist wasn't one that I knew. Scowling, she slunk away and began poking at instruments.

Rather than approach Winslade, who seemed like he was in a bad mood anyway, I walked after the specialist. She was better-looking anyhow.

"Hey," I said, "I heard I might be up next. Is that right?"

She looked around in surprise. "That's bullshit—sorry Centurion. Did Winslade send you over here?"

"Uh... no. What's the trouble?"

"We don't know," she said, adjusting touch-controls and gripping her station with one claw-like hand. "They just aren't responding. They can't be found or recalled. I don't get it. The empty zone we sent them into is very clearly visible on LIDAR—they can't be entombed down there."

At the word *entombed*, I became concerned. I stepped up to her panel and ran my eyes over it. I wasn't a tech, but I knew my way around a coordinate system.

I pointed a thick finger at a glowing golden circle of pixels. "Is that the LZ?"

"Yes, of course. We've just sent our third unit there. They haven't responded in any way. None of them have. No radio, no gateway hook-up—they were supposed to configure a gateway to bring down more support. I can't believe it. I guess that they're missing, or something..."

"That's a way's down. You don't think they're suffocating? Or burning in magma?"

"Six kilometers deep is the estimated bottom of the tunnel complex. We've been targeting a much more shallow region. It's only about five hundred meters deep."

"You don't say? You've sent three units down there, all to different spots, but you've gotten no response? None at all?"

She looked at me seriously and shook her head. "The tribune keeps telling us to prep the next group. I... I'm worried we might be perming them."

I could see she was freaked out. I put a gentle hand on her shoulder. "I'll go see what I can do."

She flashed me a grateful smile, and I took note of her name plate for later. After all, you never knew...

Walking away, I soon discovered Winslade again. He was tugging and cursing at a teleport harness.

"Uh... what seems to be the trouble, Tribune?"

He looked at me with a snarl on his lips. "Oh, it's you, McGill. Fancy seeing you down here. Well, if you're looking for another shot at glory, you'll have to wait. We're out of serviceable harnesses."

I looked around in alarm. Sure enough, most of the racks were empty.

"That's a crying shame, sir. I was kind of hoping to solve your problem for you."

"That's not going to happen on my watch. I've had enough of your grandstanding and gloating. Can't you let someone else have a shot at the limelight, hmm?"

"As you command, Tribune."

Turning away, I began to stride off, but I didn't make it six sweeping steps before he was on my tail all of a sudden.

"Just a moment, McGill. Suddenly, this situation strikes me as odd. Here I am, struggling with this teleportation gear, when you just happened to show up asking pointed questions. Why is that?"

"Uh… because I felt the ship shudder three times. Also… the techs are starting to gossip. You won't be able to keep a lid on this for long."

Winslade bared his teeth, but he wasn't smiling. He looked toward a table full of techs. They were whispering and casting glances around—and not just at their instruments.

A skinny fist struck the housing of an empty locker. All the harnesses had been used. "Damn it! One of these techs alerted you, didn't they? Some ex-girlfriend with a connection to Gray Deck? It's always the same story with you, McGill."

"Well sir, if I can't be of any—"

"What did you have in mind? What's your solution? Come, come, I know you have an idea rattling inside that thick skull of yours."

"Solution, sir? Well, I…" I stopped, as I realized I *did* have an idea. It was worth sharing, too, as otherwise these men might be permed. The first group had been led by one of my best friends in the legion, Centurion Manfred. "Actually, I do have a suggestion."

"Out with it, damn you, before one of these nerds uses the deep-link to alert Central."

"You need more harnesses. The only way to get them is to send back through the gateway to Earth for them."

"You think I haven't thought of that? The moment I make such a requisition, the brass back home will know I've lost every harness aboard ship. How will that sound to them?"

"Expensive," I admitted. "All right, what if you try something else? What if you send down one man, rather than a dozen?"

Winslade blinked. "You're volunteering for this duty?"

"I might have to, but I wasn't planning on doing things exactly the same way. You need to know what happened to our people. If we used a different device... that might be possible."

"A *different* device? You mean something other than a teleport harness?"

"Yes."

He frowned at me. "Does such a thing even exist? And what would be the nature of the improvement?"

Naturally, I was thinking of what they called the "casting" device back at Central. Etta had worked on it and used it to transport my butt to Rigel twice. That had supposedly been a spying mission—but I'd turned it into more of a sabotage effort.

"I can't tell you—not exactly. Let's just say it's possible to take a look at what is at a given set of coordinates—not just blindly teleport someone to the spot."

"Ah..." he said, tapping his finger on his pointy chin and looking intrigued. "Normally, I'd assume you were full of grade A manure—but I happen to know you've been used as a guinea pig for experimental technologies before... you say this device can let us see what's happened to our troops?"

"Yes."

"And what is your great interest in this matter?"

I shrugged. "Some of those people are my friends, and they're as good as permed right now. If you let me help, I'll at least get them cleared for revival."

"More importantly," Winslade said thoughtfully, "we'll be able to prove whether the processing center is down there or not. Very well, I'm desperate, so I'll give you my permission to proceed with this hare-brained scheme of yours. What do you need—access to the deep-link?"

"Uh... a little more than that, I'm afraid."

I began to explain, and he didn't like it. But as he had no other plan to complete his mission, he eventually broke down and agreed.

Stepping up to the gateway posts that were standing at one end of the long, narrow Gray Deck, I saw them hum and snap. To me, these things always looked like colorful bug-zappers. As always, it took an effort of both will and self-delusion to step in-between those posts.

Steeling myself, I walked between them and was instantly broken down into my component molecules. A moment later, I stepped out on Earth, inside Central.

-52-

It had been a long time since I'd visited Earth this way. I did it, off and on, for one emergency or another. The usual routine began the moment I arrived.

"Halt! Identify yourself, Centurion!"

A trough-load of hogs surrounded me. Most of them didn't have their weapons out. They were clawing at their holsters and fumbling with the safeties.

"Hell's bells, hogs!" I called to them. "If I'd been in the killing mood, I could have waxed the lot of you with my morph-rifle right here."

I shook the gun at them, and they glowered back at me.

"I repeat: identify yourself and state your business, Centurion," their leader said. He was a fancy-looking hog with some brass on his sleeves. The insignia marked him as an adjunct—but he wasn't a *real* officer. No hog guard, in my opinion, warranted that much respect.

Still, he *had* been the first guy to draw his weapon. That impressed me, so I nodded to him and smiled.

"I'm James McGill of Legion Varus. I'm here on orders from Tribune Winslade."

"Do you have those orders, sir?"

As the hog had not yet offered up any kind of insult, I flicked my finger over my tapper. My orders, hastily tapped out by Winslade back aboard *Berlin*, flew across the room and landed on the hog's tapper so he could read them.

"Looks legit. We'll escort you to the lobby, sir."

I proceeded to tell them I needed no escorts, but they didn't listen. They tailed me up from Central's version of Gray Deck to the street level. There, they left me on my own.

Taking a moment to enjoy Earth's sights and sounds, I walked outside. The day was warm and sunny. I immediately considered going out and getting myself some lunch in town.

I took my first step in that direction, in fact, before I stopped myself and frowned. No… no, no. I couldn't afford to go down that rabbit-hole of endless distractions. I was likely to end up in a bar, then at some lady's apartment…

"Manfred might be permed…" I said to myself. "Maybe he's trying to scratch his way out of that tunnel like a rat in a cage right now."

With new-found determination, I did an about-face and marched back into Central. There were options, at this point. I could have gone to see Drusus, or Galina—but I didn't want to do that. If they knew I was back on Earth, all kinds of uncomfortable questions would be asked. None of us wanted to hear those answers.

Instead, I headed back down into the depths below Central. My clearance was good enough to get me down to about floor minus one hundred—then I got stopped.

They had a checkpoint down there. You had to get off the original elevators, pass through a clearance center with full identity-scanning robots aiming guns at your face, then take another set of elevators down deeper into the lab complex.

The trouble was I didn't have those clearances. At times, I had been allowed down here, so my info was in the computers. Unfortunately, I was flagged as off-Earth, not performing a clandestine op for the labs. Some smarty-pants computer put those two things together and beeped "NO ADMITTANCE, PLEASE STAND BY".

Naturally, my instinct was either to bust past the robot, or to do a spin and head back to the elevators before some fresh pack of hogs showed up to irritate me further. Under normal circumstances, I would have chosen one of those two options.

But this wasn't a normal day. I needed to get past this toaster without sending up any alarms. Gritting my teeth, I lifted my tapper and contacted the only person I knew could help me—and who might actually do it.

"Hey, baby-girl," I said, giving Etta a broad grin. "Look who's back in town! I was just in the neighborhood, and I thought I'd drop by to grab some lunch."

She frowned at me, and she blinked a few times. "Dad? Aren't you off-world right now?"

"That's a funny story. I'll tell you all about it, if you just come up to… checkpoint X-ray-five and tell this robot I'm harmless."

"You're… you're here? In Central? Checkpoint X-ray… that's almost down to my level."

"Don't I know it! What are the odds? I figured since—"

"Dad, I'm working."

"I know, honey, I know. I'm working too."

I gave her a serious look, and she sighed. "I'll be up in a minute. Don't break anything, okay?"

That was disrespectful, but I didn't get angry. I pasted on a smile and waited for the brat. It took some nerve for her to act like I was burdening her with my poor judgment. Hadn't I just covered for her, getting her out of a misdemeanor murder? That had taken some pull, and some imagination, and back then her emotional state had been just as frazzled as anything I'd ever seen.

While I was waiting and stewing, an ugly, fat-assed hog showed up to give me a talking-to. Fortunately, before things got heated, Etta reached the scene. She showed her clearance, flicked me a visitor badge, then fast-talked the hog into settling down.

"This isn't regular procedure," the hog complained. He looked like he'd never smiled in his life, nor had he ever smelled anything better than a summertime outhouse. "You can't just give tours down here, I don't care who you are."

"I know, I know," Etta said, giving him the charming bullshit smile I would have given him in her shoes. "But he's worked down here before. We're looking at… a new mission assignment."

She gave him a meaningful look, and the hog checked his records. I had, in fact, volunteered and been paid for a few hellacious journeys into the dark that were associated with the casting project.

"Hmm... it does say you've worked here... but also says you're supposed to be off-world right now."

It was my turn to do some bullshitting, so I stepped right up. "That's right, Veteran," I said. "That's the whole point, if you get my meaning. I'm supposed to be someplace else... in a hurry."

He peered at me for a few seconds, then he seemed to get it. This whole lab section was dedicated to clandestine teleportation experiments, after all.

"Oh... I get it. All right, go on through. But you keep an eye on him, Missy. There are some strange notes in this man's file."

Apparently, this dumbass hadn't noted we had the same last name. I took no steps to enlighten him. When you get what you want, you don't keep on talking, that was my motto.

Smiling and brushing past his bulging gut, I followed Etta into an echoing passageway. Down this far underground, everything seemed to be quieter and more deserted. The place was kind of creepy, if you asked me.

"Dad, what is this all about?" Etta hissed at me after we rounded the first corner and were beyond the sight of the staring, frowning hog.

"Damn, was that guy fat or what?" I laughed. "What are they feeding the guards down here? You wouldn't think sipping coffee all day and eating—"

"Dad, come on. I got you through security, and now I want some answers."

"What? Can't a father come visit his little girl without being suspected of the worst motives?"

She was squinting at me, and it made me a little sad to see that. After all, a dozen years ago she would have bought anything I said. Her daddy had been perfect, and above reproach. Since those happy days, she'd learned there were often unsavory details hidden behind the story I represented to the world—about almost everything.

"Come on, Dad. You're freaking me out with this fast-talking routine. Have you killed somebody? Somebody important, I mean?"

"Not for hours and hours," I said truthfully. "Okay... listen, I'll give you a hint... I need to use the casting machine."

That threw her for a loop. "What? Are you crazy? It's not even online now, much less available for some military op."

"What if I had orders from the very top?"

That slowed her down. "The top? You mean, like Drusus? I don't know—I'd have to talk to Floramel about it."

"Uh... not quite that high."

I showed her the orders on my tapper, and she snorted rudely. "Winslade? He can't approve anything down here! If he ordered you to dig a latrine, I'd question—"

Lifting a hand, I tried to shush her. She backed away, instantly annoyed. She had a temper that was almost as bad as her mother's.

"Look..." I began, and I tried to explain the situation. I naturally embellished and talked as if the lost legionnaires were girl scouts kidnapped in an alley.

She listened, and she didn't even roll her eyes much, but at the end, she sighed deeply. "I can't do it. There's no way. No one will approve this kind of op on short notice."

"Well... how about if we did it without approval?"

Etta stared at me, and her mouth dropped open in surprise. It did me proud, seeing that. It had to be something in her daddy's genes. Her mamma Della never reacted to anything with a sagging jaw. In fact, she hated to see me do it.

"Are you kidding? I can't just—"

"Hey," I said, "this is a family request. It's a real emergency, I swear. A lot of good people are gone and technically permed. But if there's no way you can do it, I'll understand. Just say the word, and I'll drop it, and I won't even mention saving your ungrateful bacon and covering up that rage-kill on your boss."

"Shut up about that!"

"Absolutely. It never happened. My word is my bond, and I never saw what you did to that girl when she—"

She grabbed me, and I was surprised at the grip she had in those fingers. They dug into the skin of my bicep and there were claws at the end of all five.

"Come on," she said, "but if this costs me my job, I'm not living in Grandma's farmhouse. You have to pay for my apartment for life, dammit."

"Uh… yeah, okay."

I was thinking about the money I'd made recently doing a few tricks for Abigail. She'd promised me five million credits a short while back. Maybe I'd need it after all.

-53-

Etta took me into a quiet sub-station. I'd expected to see a big, glowy ball of energy spinning and trying to escape its force field, but instead, it looked like a drab office.

There was half a donut on the desk, so I ate that while she worked at her computer. After a few minutes, she turned around and shook her head.

"I've looked up these coordinates, Dad... do you trust whoever gave them to you?"

"Sure do."

"Well... they're below the surface of a planet in the Tau Orionis system—do you realize that?"

I blinked a few times stupidly. I didn't think she'd be able to figure that out so fast. "That's exactly right," I said, giving her my most reassuring smile.

"That's where Cooper vanished. He was permed, Dad."

She stared at me with hard eyes, and I realized my bullshit smile wouldn't do the trick this time.

"That's exactly right," I repeated. "But look, the coordinates are pretty far off from where Cooper landed. You see, he splashed down right in the middle of... uh... a special geological region. I'm not going there."

"You're sure? The casting system didn't work for Cooper. We got a few numbers back, but we couldn't get full video."

"That was because of the collapsed matter," I explained earnestly, pretending I knew what I was talking about. "Where I'm going, there's none of that stuff."

She sighed and turned back around. "Okay, I've done all the math." She waved toward a stack of numbers. They were jumping through hoops and parading in lines with funny squiggles that looked like musical notes or something.

"Those numbers look good to me, honey. Let's do it!"

She handed me a chip, but she didn't get up and lead the way to the lab. "There's a problem—I can't get you into the casting device. There's lots of security, and you're not on the list today. They won't be fooled by any fast-talk. These guards don't even have a sense of humor."

"Hmm…" I said, thinking that over. "Have you guys got a deep-link handy?"

It was Etta's turn to look surprised, but she led the way to a long-distance comms booth. I'd figured they must have a unit. After all, if you're doing experimental transmissions to distant star systems, it only made sense that the staff would be able to talk to someone at the far end to find out if a given experiment had worked or not.

Sitting in the booth and shooing her out, she frowned at me. "Don't go calling any girlfriends, Dad. Every minute on this thing costs thousands of credits."

"Don't you even worry about it!"

After she left, I hooked my tapper to the deep-link and made a call. It took a few tries and lots of rings, but Abigail answered at last.

"Hey, smart lady!" I began.

"I don't believe it... You're calling to flirt over a deep-link? What are you even doing on Earth?"

"Let's make a deal," I said. "You do me a favor without asking any more questions, and you can keep the millions of credits you owe me."

She thought that over. Her eyes lit up, but she was on guard. "What *kind* of favor?"

I explained what I needed, and she snorted with amusement. "Is that all?" she asked sarcastically.

"It surely is. I happen to know that you Clavers have agents below decks here at Central."

"And upon what would you base these bizarre suspicions?"

I smiled. I'd gotten to know Abigail. She pretended like she was constantly dealt bad cards by the universe—but I knew better. She was dealing them to herself.

"When you were a prisoner here at Central, do you recall how those two Rigellians appeared and tried to drag you away?"

"I certainly do. You were instrumental in saving me, but this is hardly the time—"

"Hold on," I said. "Those two bears shouldn't have been able to teleport in here—I checked. You realize, don't you, that if they could do that, they might as well deliver an A-bomb into the midst of our complex. Central is shielded from stuff like that."

"Then the shield must have failed that day," she said stubbornly. "As to your deal, I—"

"Hold on, hold on," I said. "Let's follow this logical thread for a minute. If those bears didn't teleport all the way out here from Rigel to kidnap you, then they must have popped in from somewhere closer. Right here in town, maybe. Or even from somewhere else inside Central. Am I right?"

Abigail squirmed. "Is this some kind of blackmail, McGill? It's really not necessary—and it's not going to get you what you want."

"I just had another thought… maybe Claver-X doesn't even know about this! Maybe this is *your* secret op."

She blinked at me. "What are you fantasizing about? If I dare to ask?"

"I recall that recording of your voice, playing over and over, sobbing. It was placed to be conveniently found along with your DNA at Dark World. No one knows how that could have happened. No one—not even your countless brothers. But… what if you did all that to yourself?"

She stared at me with a different look on her face. It was a new look, a wary look. "You're talking crazy, McGill."

"Yeah, I sure am. I'm mentally challenged, and you can take that to the bank. But let's talk about other things."

"Like what?"

"Like how I could forget about two bears coming in here to fake a kidnapping, or you setting up your own kin to feel guilty. All I need is a little help from your damned network."

"It isn't doable. I'd have to burn valuable assets. I'm hanging up."

"You can do that. But you'll be a few million credits poorer, and since I know about your power to penetrate our defenses at Central, I can't very well stay silent. Maybe even more importantly, after I get done making calls on this deep-link machine, all your brothers are going to know what you did to wrap them around your little finger for the last decade. Damnation, girl! Everyone in this galaxy will be thinking of you as a traitor by midnight!"

Abigail eyed me with distrust, the way a long-tailed cat stares at a rocking chair. "All right. Your baseless conspiracy theories might damage my reputation, I'll admit. For the sake of our friendship, I'll submit to this ham-handed blackmail—but don't make a habit of it, McGill."

"Outstanding! Seems like we've come to an agreement. Now, hack into Central and put me down on some nerd's day-planner. I need an appointment on the casting project agenda, pronto!"

After a bit more threatening and cajoling, I got her to pull some strings. During this operation, the door to the booth cracked open and an exasperated Etta looked over my shoulder.

"Daddy? You're in here talking to some girl? Seriously?"

"Uh…" I said.

She put her hands on her hips and scowled at me just like her mother. "Where is she located? Did you know the Galactics tack on a surcharge if it's over a hundred lightyears out?"

"I think she's local," I lied. "Mars base, or something."

Both of them rolled their eyes at me, but I didn't care. The wheels were finally rolling in my direction at last.

I hung up on Abigail. By the time we got down to the next layer of security pukes, I was magically added to their list of personnel who were permitted to enter their holy sanctum. Down in the vaults, past all the yellow and black warning signs that said you weren't supposed to eat anything in case it was radioactive or worse, I located and consumed a stale pizza. In the meantime, I watched as Etta input all her hieroglyphic calculations into the consoles. Then she made a hundred small adjustments to the projector machines that created whatever kind of plasma field controlled this lightning in a bottle. I was bored sick just watching her do it.

But, after a few minutes, the big blob of light began to throb and spin.

"I've still got to go through naked, right? You haven't improved that part?"

"I'm afraid so."

"Listen, you need to record it all. Forward it to whoever you think is right—Winslade out at Glass World, if everyone is dead and revivable. Others, if you see something weird."

"This whole thing is weird, Dad."

"Don't I know it." I stared at the spinning blob of light while I stripped down. Soon I was ready to walk into it with my balls in the breeze.

"Do I still have to die?" I asked her, without looking away from the anomaly. "To get back, I mean?"

"Unless you find some other way out, you must die inside the ten to twenty minute window. After that, the connection will randomly break. If the death isn't witnessed—you'll be as permed as the rest of them."

"You're all love and biscuits, girl," I told her. "Wish me luck!"

"Luck, Dad…"

Then, I stepped into that twisting light, and my body was disintegrated. I don't think there was as much as a single, half-burnt hair left behind.

-54-

After suffocating for about fifteen minutes, I finally arrived. Gasping, doubling over and almost puking up my pizza, I slowly lifted my head to look around.

My heart slowed and I stared in wonderment. There were crystals down here. Huge formations of them, but they were different than the bigger glacier-like peaks on the surface. These were more multi-faceted, like clustered gemstones. They hadn't been worn down and polished by centuries of rough weather.

After a minute of blinking in amazement, I wondered why it was, exactly, that I could see these lovely natural formations. Then I saw some lights laying on the gritty floor of the cavern.

Creeping forward, I reached for the nearest of them—but I stopped.

The source of the illumination was a number of suit lights. They were all down low, shining up brightly. That's what had lit the gorgeous candelabra ceiling.

There were dead men all over the floor of the cavern. Their chest lights and headlamps were still on, shining up from where they lay in repose.

Instantly aware there had to be something deadly in this cavern, I hunkered down and crawled—moving as quietly as I could, from one body to the next, looking for an officer. If I could get a recording of his tapper, it would list all the dead and wounded.

With any luck, Etta was still watching me from afar, recording my experiences. I was too far down to use some normal form of communication, like radio signals. Five hundred meters of dirt, rock and crystals tended to interrupt such things.

But Etta's connection to me used quantum-entanglement. It was a trick of physics that had to do with the harmonic phasing of light signals in two different places, and it worked regardless of distance or intervening obstacles. It was kind of like the deep-link boxes themselves.

At last, I found a dead officer. It was Centurion Manfred. He was a fireplug of a man who I'd been fond of since we'd first met. Unfortunately, he was deader than a doornail. His chest plate had been ripped off and his guts torn out behind that.

Gritting my teeth, I grabbed his tapper and touched it to mine. A circular waiting signal spun… and spun some more.

I wanted to curse, but I didn't dare. Could his batteries be low? I had to wait for the data to be transferred, and waiting around while you're expecting sudden violent death isn't fun at all.

While I waited, I lay there on the cave floor and smelled dust and blood. My nostrils caked up, but I didn't dare cough, sneeze or even wheeze. Instead, I just listened.

The cavern wasn't entirely dead quiet. There were cracking sounds—and some rustling. After a time, I thought I could tell where the rustling was coming from.

At last, the whirling wait symbol faded and the download was finished. I felt relief. With any luck, that information had been transmitted home. My comrades were no longer permed.

My next thought was a powerful one: why wait around naked to be killed by whatever terror had killed Manfred and his troops? Clearly, one nude McGill wasn't going to amount to a hill of snot against an enemy that could take out so many trained troops.

Thoughtfully, I found Manfred's combat knife and drew it. One thrust, that's all it would take, and my work here would be done.

I felt like doing it. I really did... but then I heard that rustling again, and I became curious. If I could just take a peek at the inhabitants of this deathtrap, so much might be explained.

Creeping on my belly, I slithered over corpses and sharp stones toward the sounds. Sure, it hurt, and I was soon leaving a blood-trail behind, but I didn't care. This McGill had never been meant to last long.

After a few minutes—a total of eleven since my arrival, according to my tapper—I located the source of the sounds.

Two posts were being assembled and adjusted. The creatures doing it were as familiar to me as the posts themselves—they were Vulbites.

My teeth bared themselves. I hated Vulbites. I don't think there's a man alive who's met up with them that doesn't feel the same way.

There's just something about hulking centipede-like creatures that can rear up and stand as tall as a man that makes my skin crawl. Hell, I didn't even like the foot-long kind that crept around my swamplands sometimes. Those pygmies were disgusting enough—but these monsters? They were a hundred times worse.

For perhaps a minute, I used my tapper to record what I was seeing. I was still flat on my filthy belly, aiming my arm at them and gripping my knife in my other sweaty palm. They were clearly assembling a set of gateway posts, probably to get in or get out of this secret cavern.

Something shuffled near while I did this. I froze, pretending to be dead. Some of the bodies near me had been stripped anyway, so it wasn't a stretch.

Not even daring to move my head, I looked around with rolling eyeballs. I had no illumination sources on me, being buck-naked. Maybe that was why they hadn't noticed me before. I imagined platoons of teleport troops from Gray Deck had come in shouting orders, flashing lights and aiming guns every which way. None of them had come in like a lone commando—except me.

But I was discovered despite my best imitation of a possum. Shuffling, slithering, rasping and tapping feet—

Vulbites had lots of feet, and you could hear them all when it was real quiet like it was now.

The strange thing was that I couldn't actually *see* the approaching Vulbite. I could hear him, and I more or less knew which direction he was approaching from—but I couldn't spot him, despite the shining lights of the dead.

Then, as he crept closer, I caught on—he was wearing a stealth cloak.

Long ago, when we'd first encountered this technology, the Vulbites had been using it. Although the Vulbites were more primitive than humans in most respects, they did have a few excellent tricks. One of them was a cloth-like bag they could drape over themselves that bent light around it.

Once I'd realized this I started looking low—looking for tracks. I spotted his trail immediately. I waited until he crept close, then I sprang up and rammed my knife home—over and over.

Where are the vital spots on a Vulbite? I'd never taken that course in xeno anatomy, if there even was one. Deciding to make sure, I gave him a dozen thrusts—then a dozen more.

Puffing breath out through cracked lips, I must have looked like a savage from days gone by. A naked warrior with a blade in my hands.

Stooping quickly, I tugged at the stealth suit. If I could only get it off him, I could put it on, and—

There was an odd sound, and it seemed to me that I pitched forward. My face was suddenly in the same dirt and slimy mud the Vulbite had created with its own pooling life fluids.

How had I fallen? My legs—I couldn't feel my legs. I was feeling kind of sick, actually. My vision…

Then I saw the second Vulbite, and the third. They shuffled up, like the first one, but they'd thrown back their stealth suits. They stood over me, and one of them had a huge sword of the type I'd seen them use before. The sword ran with dark blood.

Gasping and sucking up grit, I died then, but not before I realized in sick horror that they had chopped me in half, somewhere around waist level.

It could have been they'd cut the legs out from under me, or maybe that they severed my spine and belly—it was hard to say.

Regardless of the details, I was as dead as yesterday.

-55-

I woke up with the shakes. I had the willies—I could tell. Sometimes, a death was a rough one, even for a man as experienced with the process as I was.

"What's wrong with him?" demanded a gruff voice. "Is he pissing himself or something?"

"No sir," the bio said. "Maybe you should come back later, after he's recovered. Sometimes there's a residual reaction to the circumstances—"

"Not with a Varus man! Stand back. Give him some air—leave his arms alone! He can stand, you'll see."

"Graves...?" I said, and I coughed. It felt to me like my lungs were still full of cave grit. I'd sucked in a mouthful during my final moments... but it was only residual fluids from my rebirth.

"There you go! You see? McGill is fine. Stand back, I'll get him off the frigging table myself."

Blinking in surprise, I found myself hauled up by strong hands. I knew those hands, it had to be the uncompromising touch of Graves. He'd never been a gentle, caring man.

A few shuffling steps later, I turned my head toward him.

"What's happening?" I asked, unable to focus my eyes.

"Stand straight and walk out of here," Graves demanded. "Or you'll be dead again."

That worked on me. I was coming together, getting my mind and nervous system into some semblance of order. Graves' warning helped give me the boost I needed.

Standing as straight as I could, I glanced over my shoulder and nodded toward the bio people I could only see as blurs. "Thanks, gentlemen," I rasped out. "I'll be just fine."

"Maybe you'd like to have a shower first?" one of them asked hopefully.

"Nah. I'll do that later. The primus here seems to be in a hurry."

"That's right," Graves said. "I've got orders. Let's go, McGill."

Something soft hit me in the face. I almost dropped the mass with my numb, grasping fingers, but I managed to hold on. It was cloth—a uniform.

Graves was already done coddling me. I hobbled after him, struggling to pull on the clothing while it stuck to me. The smart-straps felt for one another like blind, groping snakes.

Once we were out in the passages, I managed to catch Graves by the shoulder. "I feel like I missed something, sir," I said to him.

"Yeah… you missed two somethings—two lifetimes. You've been coming out as a bad grow. Twice in a row, and if I don't miss my guess, that was number three I just interrupted right there."

I glanced back at the swinging doors that led into the Blue Bunker revival chambers. "Those frigging ghouls. They recycled me *twice*?"

"That's my guess. But don't blame them. Blame Winslade. He had me on ice for more than a week—or did you already know about that?"

"Uh… that's news to me, sir," I lied. "Let me express my heartfelt condolences. No one deserves to linger in limbo like that. Nobody."

Graves looked at me and nodded. "That's what I thought. You knew. Everyone knew. Bunch of bastards…"

I didn't say anymore because he was, of course, correct. There's no point to piling on further lies after the truth is well known, it only pisses people off. Instead, I chose to change the topic.

"Any idea why Winslade might want to play the bad-grow shuffle with me?"

"He's under oversight now. Something happened back at Central, a report came in. That report was lost, but there were new orders with it that stuck. Winslade was ordered to seek my advice on tactics, and to stop screwing around out here. He has to finish this mission, and he wants it to be a win. He was also ordered not to keep anyone else from being revived."

"Uh… okay. So… he's been killing me on and off every hour or so?"

Graves laughed briefly. "Nah. He's trickier than that. He brings you to life once a day, then offs you with some kind of bad-grow bullshit, and then puts you at the back of the queue."

I blinked at him stupidly. I could see his craggy face now, and it looked darkly amused.

"So… like… I've been dying for three days now?"

"That's about the size of it. Someone sent us your file from Central, along with proof that those troops we sent into Hell on Glass World are dead. You'd think that would be accounted as a good thing, but you've been popping out and dying again on Blue Deck like some kind of demented jack-in-the-box ever since."

He seemed to think this was funny, but I failed to see the humor in it. In fact, I was feeling kind of pissed off.

I reached out and grabbed Graves by the arm again. He gritted his teeth in warning, like a snarling dog. Graves liked his personal space.

"Hey," I said. "How about you and me get a little payback?"

He narrowed his eyes and chewed that over. After a moment, he shook his head. "Winslade deserves the worst, but he's still our commanding officer. I won't be involved in any plot, or—"

"Nah, nothing like that!" I said. "I'm thinking more like… you know… short-sheeting his bed or something. Something funny."

Graves eyed me with vast distrust. He knew me well. "McGill, I'm not going to do anything against regs. I'm not—"

"Don't worry about it, Primus," I said brightly. "You don't have to do a damned thing… except, maybe, give me a few permissions I don't already have."

He looked at me with the hardest eyes in the legion. "We're talking about a practical joke, here?"

"That's right! I swear it, as God Almighty is my witness!" I raised a hand, palm out, and smiled big.

He shook his head. "I know I'm going to regret this, but I'll listen—just listen, mind you, to whatever cockamamie scheme is floating inside that skull of yours."

"That's all I can ask for, Primus. That's all I ask."

After that, we walked across the camp, and we talked. In the meantime, I dropped certain elements of my report into his ear, about the Vulbites, the gateway posts I'd seen, and our dead units in the cavern below.

Graves seemed surprised by all of it. "First of all," he said, "how in the living hell did you get down there and learn all this?"

"Uh… that's classified, sir."

He snorted, but he kept listening. After a time, he became concerned. "This explains what he's doing. Winslade has been setting up for another assault—a big one. He wants to overwhelm the Vulbites this time."

Graves marched across the grassy encampment to a bunker where there was a lot of activity. I followed in his wake.

We met up with Centurion Manfred on the way. "Hey!" he shouted at me. "Is that really James McGill, out of purgatory already? What's becoming of this legion?"

We clasped hands, and he leaned close. "Did you get me out of that cave? That's what I heard."

I gave him a nod, and he grinned.

"Thanks, mate. Thanks for all of us. If there's anything I can ever do—"

"As a matter of fact, I've been planning a surprise party for our CO. Would you like to be on the refreshments committee?"

Manfred glanced over at Graves, who scowled, but didn't say anything. Then he slid his eyes back to meet mine. "Put me down for a kegger. You know I'm good for it."

"Excellent."

Graves and I moved on, me still following Graves. We were heading toward Gold Bunker, where the commanders worked and lived.

"That's how you do it, huh, McGill? Personal favors. Loyalty among officers rather than strict discipline. None of this meets the smell-test."

"Sometimes a man's gotta do what a man's gotta do, Primus."

Graves didn't look at me, but he did give a small nod. He'd had enough of Winslade's shit for one lifetime as well.

Unfortunately, we were greeted at the doors by an armed guard. "Sorry sirs, Primus Graves, you're allowed in—but not McGill. No one is to enter today who's under primus rank."

"No problem at all, Veteran," Graves said. "McGill, wait for me right here."

Like a dog that had been told to sit, I loitered at the entrance while Graves went inside. After about twenty minutes, he came back out empty-handed.

"He's stuck in there like a tick in a dog's ear, huh?" I asked.

"That's about the size of it. I'll guess we'll have to—"

I pulled Graves aside. Again, he almost snarled at me when I touched him, but I didn't care. "Sir, just hang on—I've got an idea."

Contacting Manfred, I requested some special gear. He laughed and said he'd bring it. Then I called Natasha and asked for a favor. She complained—she always did. But she did it. When I saw Manfred was maybe a hundred meters away and marching in my direction, I sniffed at the air.

"Do you smell smoke?"

The veteran guard at the entrance shuffled uneasily and glanced back at the door he was guarding. Nothing seemed amiss.

Moments later, the fire alarm went off. People started coming out of Gold Bunker and wandering around blinking at the sunshine in confusion.

"I don't see any fire, or smoke, or nothing," the guard grumbled.

Sniffing the air experimentally, I shook my head. "I have to disagree. There's definitely smoke in the air."

Manfred and his fire brigade arrived then at a trot. They wore special gear including hoses and packs. They brushed past the startled guard. "Come on McGill, get a move on!" Manfred called to me.

Stern-eyed, I rushed inside. The veteran didn't know what to make of it.

Once inside, the fire alarm stopped. Manfred stayed at the entrance.

"How long can you stand here and cover for me?" I asked him.

"Until some jackass tells me it was a false alarm and orders me to get out."

I nodded. "Okay, but take your time about leaving."

Marching through the passages alone, I passed lots of brass and their staffers. They gave me odd looks, but I kept on moving, never meeting their eyes. A man who appears to know his business can often brush by bureaucrats—just try it sometime.

-56-

My plan was straightforward. Winslade and I would somehow get into a heated disagreement, and I'd leave him in the revival queue for a while.

Games like this, where one man killed another in the spirit of friendly rivalry, were always frowned upon in the legion, but they happened often enough. The thing that would set this practical joke apart from other similar misconduct in my past was the fact Winslade and I were now two full levels apart in rank. That meant the action I was contemplating wasn't just another high-spirited prank. Technically… it was an assassination.

But I didn't care. My blood was up, and I wanted some revenge.

Unfortunately, when I got to his office Winslade wasn't alone. Worse, he spotted me immediately.

His face twisted into a smile of recognition. "Ah, McGill," he said. "I wondered when you would turn up. Meet my compatriots."

Here, he waved with a flourish to indicate two unsmiling, burly men that stood on either side of him. Winslade's smile grew as I eyed them.

I knew right off I'd been caught red-handed. Winslade had been alerted somehow. He knew I was alive and coming to find him. He hadn't been fooled by my fire alarm, and now he felt he was in charge again.

"A pleasure I'm sure, boys," I said. "Did you want to talk or something, Tribune?"

"Indeed I do. Please, come this way." Winslade spun on his heel and walked toward his office. I hesitated, but the two guards closed ranks around me to form an escort.

I considered punching them and shooting Winslade in the back right then. I honestly did. But I knew that would lead to violence and death all around, and it would give Winslade a good reason to forget about me until we returned to Earth. There, I'd probably be court-marshalled.

No sir, it was time to play it cool.

"Tribune?" I said to Winslade's back, hatching a new plan even as I was marched into his inner sanctum. "I hope you didn't get the wrong idea about Graves and all."

Winslade glanced over his shoulder with an arched brow. "Not at all. How could I have mistaken the signs you gave me? I'd have to be a cretinous fool."

"Uh… right. But what I meant was that I didn't tell Graves anything about your… well, you know."

Winslade halted in his doorway. Inside his office, over his shoulder, I saw a grav-bolted steel chair and chains. He had been scheming all right.

"You didn't tell Graves anything because there was nothing to tell," he said with a sidelong glance at the meatballs that were holding onto me.

"That's exactly right, sir. It wasn't strange at all that he was dead for so long. His name just didn't come up in the queue, I'm sure of it. These decisions are automated and precalculated by the best computers. In fact—"

"*Shut up*, McGill," Winslade said dangerously.

Again, he glanced at the men at my sides. I got the feeling he knew they liked Graves better than they did him—just about everyone did—and he didn't want to do any explaining right now. "Sit him in that chair and bolt his wrist to the floor."

The hog-like guards did as he ordered, but I saw them frowning as they did it.

"Don't worry about me, boys!" I said. "I've got this. It's all a little game that Winslade and I like to play. We go back, don't you know, way back."

Winslade slapped me one, and I found it surprisingly painful. That's when I noticed he had a crackling shock-rod in his hand.

With numb, bloody lips, I grinned at him. "Don't tell me you're sweet on Abigail."

That made him blink. "What?"

"Abigail. You know, that lady-Claver who—"

"Yes, yes, of course. I know who you're talking about, you oaf. What are you suggesting about her?"

"Well… you know. When a lady takes a shine to a man such as myself, sometimes others become jealous."

Winslade laughed aloud. Flecks of spittle flew from his lips.

"As if! That witch is all yours, McGill. If she jumps into your bed, you'd best jump out, mind you. She's the worst of the clan as far as I can tell."

That threw me off a bit. My barb had not landed at all. Worse, I'd say Winslade was accurate in his assessment of Abigail. That meant it would be hard to bullshit him on the topic.

Immediately, my thinking shifted, and I took a whole new direction. That's the benefit of living in a flexible state of mind. One can go where the wind blows when necessary.

"Perhaps there's a misunderstanding," I said, watching him as he took out a series of what looked like dental instruments. "What I meant to say was we've had dealings, and not everyone appreciates it when others get a better bargain than they've gotten themselves."

"Hmm…?" Winslade said. He wasn't even paying attention. He kept pulling things out, and then he began prodding on my arm. That was kind of alarming, because he wasn't trying to cause pain, or anything so simple. Instead, he seemed to be focused on my tapper.

"Mind if I ask what this is all about, sir?"

"Not at all. You've got a set of recent memories I find troublesome. Those memories are going to be extracted from your tapper, and from the legion data core. When I'm done with that, I'll send you back to the revival chamber none-the-wiser."

"So... you don't really want to question me or anything like that?"

"No, no need. I just don't want some details to be passed on—"

"You mean, like talking to Central about what I saw down there in the Vulbite chambers?"

He flashed me a look of annoyance. "Exactly. My tactical efforts must be pristine. Sheer instinct and military genius shall guide me—not some farcical teleportation suicide mission made by one James McGill."

By this time, he'd poked a few needles with wires attached to them into five spots around my tapper. I supposed he planned to fry it or something.

"That's a sheer relief, sir," I said. "When the people back at Central want my report explained, ignorance will be a gift for me. Sheer bliss. Please proceed."

Winslade did so for a few moments, but then he stopped and frowned. "What do you mean: when they want an explanation? What report? There isn't any report, that's the point. You died down there and you're being revived here now. That's the end of it, once I make certain adjustments to your memory."

"Well... things might not work out that way."

"Why not?"

"On account of the fact I've already reported on the incident in full. Both to Graves, and to everyone back at Central."

Winslade glared at me. "You fancy yourself a masterful liar, McGill, but the truth is you're nothing of the kind. You're full of sewage."

"Not so, sir! Not this time, anyways. You see, it has to do with the nature of the casting device."

"The what?"

"The, um... well, it's classified. But you *do* realize they transmitted my person out from Central to Glass World, right? And you realize that they saw what I saw while I was there, in real time?"

He stared at me. The casting project was top secret, and he naturally had no inkling of how it worked.

"That's right…" I continued. "That's how it works, see. They use it to spy on Rigel and places like that. Unfortunately, they can't get the test subject back again. All they can do is fire a lone, naked man to a location. He plays spy, and then he gets himself killed after ten minutes or so. That's what I did, see, I—"

Winslade released a howl of fury. He threw his tray of instruments across the room. They clattered and rolled around on the deck.

A split-second later, the two hog-like guards threw the door open. They bared their teeth and their hands were on their pistols. They looked around at the blood, needles and shock-rods. What must have left them baffled was my grin and Winslade's grimace of rage.

"Is there any trouble here, sir?" they asked.

Winslade was so pissed he seemed to be having trouble speaking, so I filled in for him.

"He's okay," I said. "He was just having a little trouble reaching the kind of release he likes during our little sessions, see—"

Winslade slapped me in the face again with his crackling truncheon. "Shut up, McGill!" he said in a very unpleasant tone. He turned to the guards. "Get this sack of excrement out of here!"

"Uh…" the two men said, eyeing one another and me uncertainly.

I was grinning ear to ear with one swollen eye, and I figured it was throwing them off a bit.

"So…" said one of them, "you're finished doing… whatever?"

"Get him out of here!" Winslade repeated.

The guards stood me up, causing the needles and wires to pop out of my arm with a rippling effect. Blood ran down to my fingertips and splattered the deck, but I didn't pay any heed. After all, I was still alive. Even better, Winslade was pissed about it. All in all, I accounted this adventure as a good one.

"Just a second!" Winslade called from behind me. "Escort McGill down to Gray Deck. He's going to command the next assault team."

"Thanks for the vote of confidence, sir!" I called back to him.

When we were safely out of earshot, I had a private word with the guards. "You see that? It takes *serious* dedication to your CO to get a command spot in this outfit, boys. I hope you're taking notes."

The guards looked disgusted, and I could tell they hated Winslade that much more after seeing these strange behaviors of his. I grinned happily as they dragged me off to Gray Deck.

-57-

Winslade did indeed make me point-man on the next assault. My entire unit—surprised and wide-eyed with alarm—was tossed into harnesses and fired down at the Vulbite deathtrap without so much as a briefing.

The room began glowing and throbbing blue as our helmets synched up

"This is bullshit, Centurion!" Harris complained bitterly on command chat. "Total bullshit! What did you do, take a crap on Winslade's bed again?"

"In a manner of speaking, yes," I admitted. "But that's all piss off a duck's back at this point." Using my HUD, I switched to tactical chat, hitting the whole unit. Around us, the chamber was already beginning to pulse and waver. "Troops! Listen up! We're about to teleport into a cave network. The cave is full of Vulbites and dead legionnaires. The enemy will be stealthed, so look for footprints in the dust—most of you know the drill. Make Varus proud!"

A few troops hooted, but not many. The light had reached its peak, and we were vanishing, leaping through space in the blink of an eye.

A moment later, we were in a pitch-black cave. At our feet were scattered bodies. Almost all of them were human.

The lights from the dead legionnaires had mostly gone out by this time. It had been a few days, and the batteries had run down.

Scrambling to switch on our own lights, we illuminated the caverns. I couldn't help but suspect we were making the identical mistakes those who had preceded us had made.

"The dirt!" Harris roared. "Look down, fools! If these bugs are coming, you'll see the dirt sink down."

"Watch the roof, too," Barton added. "Vulbites can climb and drop in the middle of us."

She was right, and I saw everyone looking around with panicky lights flashing this way and that.

"Hold on," I said. "Barton, your troops will watch the roof. Harris, put your people on the outer perimeter with force-blades extended. Prod every rock and take a cut at the air before you step forward. Leeson, keep your auxiliaries in the center to back up anyone who gets hit."

"Roger that, sir," Leeson responded.

Tense, moving at a snail's pace, we stepped over the dead and advanced into the monstrous cavern. After a hundred paces, we'd encountered nothing.

"Hey, lookie here!" Leeson called out. "Isn't this you, McGill? You're buck-naked, man."

I walked over to him and saw a grisly scene. I was cut in half, never a pretty sight.

"At least you got a couple of the bastards first," Harris said, joining us.

"Yeah…" I said. "Funny they didn't take the bodies—or the suits."

A few paces away, we found the gateway posts I'd seen them setting up before. I examined them, but they seemed to be inoperative. "Natasha! Kivi! I need a tech."

They both came running. The girls knelt and looked over the equipment, but after a few minutes, they straightened up again.

"It's cold," Kivi said. "This unit hasn't been running for a day or two."

"That's right," Natasha said. "It looks like the Vulbites escaped."

"Aww," Leeson said. "That's such a shame. Winslade wanted us to come down here and die just like the rest, didn't he? He'll be so disappointed to see you're still breathing, McGill, won't he?"

I nodded, eyeing the gateway posts. "They were evacuating the place. Bugging-out the last time I saw them. Let's look around."

We searched the caves, and we did find a number of puff-crete pads. Every indication was that heavy equipment had once rested there.

"They've pulled it all out," Leeson said. "We gave them too much time."

"Natasha," I said, turning to her. "It's all up to you. Can you tap into this thing and find out where they went?"

She shrugged. "I can try."

Natasha began to hack, and Kivi helped her. Natasha was the real master at this kind of thing, and both of them knew it. In the past, such knowledge had been annoying to Kivi, but she seemed to accept it today. They worked together as a team, and I was glad to see the change.

"I don't know," she said after several fruitless minutes. "They aren't using standard galactic coordinates. I don't know where it goes."

"But if you flipped it on, it would still link up with the same destination, right?"

"Maybe... wait a minute, James. Don't even think about that."

But it was too late. I was thinking hard already.

"Turn it on," I ordered her. "Kivi, set up some buzzers. Let's see if they can travel through and get back."

"Even if they can, it isn't proof a man won't be permed," she told me.

"I know that. Just do it."

They worked for a few minutes, and we had to chain together some batteries from our harnesses to provide power, but at last, the gateway posts glowed into life.

That's when I got a surprise. Graves walked up behind us. He had another unit with him, and he seemed to be personally leading it.

"There you are, McGill," he said.

"Nice to see you rated special treatment today," I told him with a smile. "I thought I was the only one."

"What did you do to Winslade?" Graves demanded, his face angry and his rifle held to his chest.

"I just told him the God's-honest-truth, sir! Nothing more, I swear it! Can I help it if a man is allergic to the truth?"

Graves shook his head and looked even more annoyed. I briefed him further on the situation, and he agreed glumly that Winslade had sent us down here out of spite.

"All right," he said. "So we're screwed if you can't get that gateway working, is that it?

I blinked at him. "Well, we can't find out where they took the processing equipment anyway."

Graves laughed. "That's not the problem, McGill. There's no way out of here, haven't you figured that out yet? We haven't got enough power to port out using our harnesses—they're all drained."

"That's true," Natasha said. "The batteries were charged only enough to pop us down here on a one-way trip."

"But… what if we won?" I asked. "What if we'd found the processing equipment?"

"It's all up to him," Graves said, pointing a gloved finger upward as he was talking about the All-mighty himself—but I knew he wasn't. He was talking about Winslade.

"Uh… you mean that to perm us all he has to do is leave us here to rot?"

"Now you've got it," Graves said. "The way I figure it, he did the math. If we found the processing center, we should have enough power to escape and report the good news. After all, wouldn't a processing center have to have a power plant to operate?"

"Yes…" Natasha said, walking up and joining the conversation. "And these packs, even the ones on the dead soldiers—they're all out of juice. They've been running lights, rebreathers and air conditioning for days."

My eyes looked back at the dead behind us. A few suit-lights glimmered, but not many. It took a lot of power to teleport, even one harness used a lot of power to activate.

"That dick," I said, "I didn't even realize… he can leave us down here if he feels like it."

Graves indicated the gateway posts. "Right there, that's your answer. Our ticket home. All we have to do is redirect them to the battlecruiser, or even back to Earth. Can you do it, Elkin?"

Natasha shrugged. "I think I can get them working, but I can't redirect them. They're Rigel-made. They don't have a standard interface, or even software I can understand. We'll be working against time, anyway. Running them will take a lot of power, and we're using up what we've got with every passing minute."

Graves went into immediate action when he heard this. He walked among the two units worth of troops and ordered everyone to shut down all non-essential systems.

While he did that, I turned to Natasha. "You can't reprogram the posts?"

"I don't think so, the problem is they're built to synch-up with a certain set of posts just like these—not our brand. They're not compatible with galactic units."

I suddenly got it. She'd tried to link the gateway to another set of posts we knew about, but they wouldn't connect. And we didn't know where Rigel had their posts.

"We can't risk changing anything," I said. "We have to go through right now and test them."

"James—"

"Switch them on."

She shook her head. "I'm not going to. I'm not having you walk through. We can send drones. We can—"

"What's the damned point, girl?" I asked. "It doesn't matter. We have to go through them in force the minute we turn those on, before they can react. They won't be expecting it, and there's never going to be a better moment than right now. What if they dismantle the far end? We'll be stuck down here forever."

Natasha touched my arm. "Winslade might send more men. He might send a rescue team."

"Sure. That's why he made sure we ported down here with near-empty batteries. He's got the best of intentions."

She pursed her lips, unable to argue further. Everyone knew Winslade could be pretty wicked when he felt like it.

Calling for Harris, I hand-picked a team. Cursing and snarling, they geared up and stood ready. Harris looked at me like I was dog shit on his boots, but he didn't try to talk me out of it. He knew better by now.

Graves came along and saw what we were doing. He nodded in approval. "I can see you've figured out what my next order was going to be. That's the way to take the initiative, McGill."

The gateway sputtered, buzzed, then glowed into life.

"It doesn't like our power frequencies," Natasha explained. "But I think it's working. The indicators say it's connected—to somewhere."

Nobody gave me a goodbye kiss, not even Natasha. Graves tossed me a salute, at least, before I marched my team in-between those glimmering posts.

There's something different about traveling into the unknown. Teleporting in any form often terrified people who were new to the process, but for me, the gateways were the worst. If you let your mind dwell on the complete insanity of what you were doing, a man might even balk before stepping through.

In this case, we didn't even know where we were going to end up. Well sir, I'm here to tell you that's a special kind of demon to face up to.

The only good thing about using gateway posts was the more or less instant nature of the process. I will forever hold the opinion that gateways are entirely different animals when compared to teleport suits, although most find the gateways easier to deal with. One reason, I supposed, was that while teleporting you were somewhat aware. That semi-awareness felt pretty freaky to many folks. You typically spent about a second in limbo for each lightyear traveled, unable to breathe, but conscious.

Not so with the gateway posts. When you stepped into that bug-zapper, you were disintegrated—I don't care what the techs call it—and later reassembled someplace else. With teleportation, there was a feeling of being in a strange, altered state, while with the gateways, well, you didn't exist at all for a time. I preferred the former.

As a natural outcome of this experience, the hardest part was taking that actual fateful step. Many people say it's like parachuting off a cliff, or out of an aircraft. But to me, it's more like stepping into the maw of a volcano, trusting some nerd who's patiently assured you they'll build a new James McGill at the summit of another volcano on the far side of the planet.

Steeling myself and showing none of my concerns, I marched into that disintegration field like I was taking a stroll down Main Street. I didn't glance back to see if my troops were following me, or give them orders to do so. Instead, I presumed they *would* follow my example. Sometimes, that kind of leadership worked best.

Stepping out on the far side, I was surprised I wasn't gunned down or chopped apart immediately. The place was actually kind of quiet.

Two gateway posts hummed behind me, and I soon was bumped in the butt by the next guy. I'd naturally paused to have a look around.

Stepping aside and yanking the heavy trooper forward, I admonished him to seek and destroy. He did so after only a split-second of wonderment

The chamber wasn't occupied, but it *was* freaky. Hanging from the ceiling were suits—bear-sized suits. They hung like empty water skins all over the roof, which was natural and uneven.

Running my lights this way and that, I thought maybe I was looking at another cave. Could it be we'd been transported to some other dank cistern in the guts of Glass World?

Then, I noticed something different. It was the ceiling, between the hanging suits. It was shiny and sparkling, like a frosted spider web that covered the earth.

Then I knew. I'd seen that kind of formation before. We were inside a Vulbite hive. A tunnel complex where they lived in semi-darkness and tunneled deep into the crust of the planet.

More importantly—we weren't on Glass World any longer.

-58-

Long ago, I'd fought on Dark World, a strange planet occupied by the Vulbites. As far as we humans knew, it was their homeworld.

Most of the Vulbites living there dwelled underground. They lived like termites, or ants, in vast mounds that were hollow inside and sometimes as deep as five kilometers below the surface.

Then there was the roof... that's what really convinced me. The roof of the tunnels wasn't just earth, which wouldn't be strong enough to hold the fantastic weight of a Vulbite hive. The dirt was infused with resins—probably spit of some kind—that came from the Vulbites themselves. I knew the look of it, and the feel of the gravity here on this planet...

"This *is* Dark World..." I said to myself, almost whispering the words.

I'd been on the Vulbite home planet a few times before. It was there that I'd found Abigail's body the first time. It was there that I'd met up with Vulbite cities, rather than just fighting them in arenas on Blood World.

More importantly and recently, I'd been shown the planet by Claver-X. He'd done so as if imparting a great gift of wisdom. He'd shown me how the Vulbites and the bears from Rigel were rebuilding their space factory to churn out ships and annihilate Earth.

"McGill!" Harris said, shaking my arm. "Snap out of it, Centurion! We're inside some kind of tunnel. This is no way out!"

I looked at him. He was worried, angry and aiming his rifle every which-way.

"We're fine," I said. "There's no one in here right now."

"It's some kind of storage room," he said, not hearing me. "It must be."

"Yeah. They store finished suits here—but where is the factory that spins these amazing pieces of armor? Go find it."

"Yes sir," Harris grunted, and he advanced into the room.

He led a full squadron of troops which fanned out, shining their lights everywhere.

"Remember, watch for stealthers," I called out.

Carlos was our bio and the only non-combatant in the squad. I grabbed him and spun him around.

"Holy shit!" he said, wide-eyed. "Damn, McGill, I thought you were a Vulbite jumping on my back or something."

"Nah. They'd never eat you first, they don't like their meat to be so well-marbled."

"Har-dee, har, har," he said. "If I'm such a fat-ass that not even these bugs want to—"

"Listen up," I said, halting his tirade, "I want you to go back through the gateway and tell Graves we've reached a Vulbite underground hive on Dark World. He can decide what he wants to do next."

Carlos brightened. "You're letting me out of purgatory? Wow, man, that makes me feel kinda sorry about all the things I said about you today. All of the other days, too. It was especially uncool of me to—"

I kicked him in the ass, which sent him staggering. I was wearing heavy armor, and he wasn't, so he got the message instantly. He rushed back through the gateway. Hearing that familiar buzz and snap—it was enough to make a man's skin crawl.

"Couldn't take Carlos anymore, huh?" Harris asked me. "I don't blame you. This chamber seems to be clear by the way, sir."

"Let's search these side-tunnels next. There has to be more to this place than this."

"Good idea," Harris said, then he proceeded to stand there, looking warily around over the sights of his rifle.

After considering giving him a kick in the ass as well, I pointed toward the nearest exit. "Take a team down there. Probe every hole, no more than a hundred meters down."

"What? Are you serious? I thought you were reporting this find to Graves and waiting for back-up."

"That's an order, Adjunct."

Harris grumbled, but he moved off and angrily dragged a few of his subordinates with him. All of this might have been considered a breach of discipline in most legions, but old Varus lived by special rules. We allowed griping, as long as orders were followed. This was partly because assignments in hellholes like this one so often led to violent death. It was generally believed that troops who could be assigned to suicide missions over and over again ought to be able to at least complain about it.

I didn't have long to wait. Harris and his sidekicks came rushing back out of the first tunnel like panicked gophers.

"McGill!" Harris called in a harsh whisper. "They know we're here! I saw them forming up a team about fifty meters that way."

"Two men, stand to either side of each hole. Blast them when they come through!"

They rushed to follow my orders. There were seven holes, however, almost too many for one squad to cover. I took the center, watching all of them at once.

Harris whispered over tactical to everyone. "Mouths shut and lights out! This is it, people!"

The chamber dimmed and soon the only light was coming from the coruscating colors of the gateway posts. Silver, pink and teal, the posts gleamed in the dark. There was nothing we could do about that other than shut them down, which I didn't want to do.

There was a spate of cursing and gunfire near one of the tunnels. Each of the tunnel openings was only about a meter in diameter, and something had popped out on our side, surprising two trigger-happy humans.

The Vulbites were quickly cut down. They flopped and oozed for a moment, then everything quieted.

"Do you think—?" Harris whispered to me, but I never heard the rest of it.

The bodies were yanked back down into the depths. The troops fired down into the darkness again, like panicked kids, but I knew they weren't hitting anything.

"Conserve ammo," I said calmly.

The firing stopped. Everyone was breathing in puffs, eyes staring until they stung. No one said a word.

Inside our suits, it began to get hot. Dark World was a tropical planet, and even this far down it seemed humid and close.

"Where the hell is Graves?" Harris asked me on command chat.

"Maybe he figures his chances are better on his side of the gateway."

"He can't do that! That's abandonment, and it's pure bullshit!"

I opened my mouth to tell him to shut up again, when the situation suddenly changed. A female regular in armor over to my right suddenly pitched forward onto her face. After a moment, I realized her legs had been chopped off just below the knees.

"Stealthers!" I called out on the general channel. "Hose down every tunnel!"

Rapid fire burst out everywhere. Caught from two sides, Vulbites screeched and lashed out. Two more troops died, but then the Vulbites retreated, dragging away most of their dead.

"How many did you see in that cavern, Harris?" I asked.

"I don't know… maybe thirty?"

I counted the tunnels again. There were seven, and Vulbites were sprouting out of all of them. I estimated there had to be at least a hundred of the enemy, with more joining them all the time.

There wasn't a chance we could survive this for long. Soon, we'd be down to one man per tunnel. After that, we wouldn't be able to cover them all. In short, we were doomed.

Walking among the hanging suits, I plucked several from the ceiling. They appeared to be sticky and covered in a foamy mess.

"That's disgusting, sir," Harris told me.

"Yeah?" I threw a suit at him, then another. I began plucking down more. "These are partly processed. We're taking them back for analysis."

"Back through the gateway?"

"Yep."

Eagerly, he set about grabbing every suit he could. There was another rush by the Vulbites, and we lost three more of our guys. Soon, there would be more tunnels than we had men.

"We're bugging out on three," I said. "One, two…"

Before we could rush for the gateway, however, it began to sizzle and pop. Troops began coming in, with Leeson in the lead. The buzzing and popping was continuous. A full squad of reinforcements had soon assembled.

"It's about damned time!" Harris shouted as Leeson's team advanced. "Help us guard these holes!"

"Vulbites?" Leeson asked.

"What do you think?"

Leeson ordered his group forward, and soon the all the entrances were guarded again. We waited tensely for the next wave.

"Why are we guarding seven tunnels?" Leeson asked. "Let's block-up some of them."

"We're out of grenades," I told him.

"I brought some of my sappers." Leeson soon had two men breaking out explosives kits. They had drone-driven automatics, the kind that could crawl and optimally place themselves for coordinated detonation.

Leeson pointed at the various entrances. "If we close all of these, they'll just tunnel a new one. But if we give them one easy route, they'll keep using it, and we can keep popping them every time."

I nodded. "Do it. Seal six of them."

His sappers quickly placed crawlers on the ground near the holes and pecked out instructions on their tappers. The drones buzzed away and vanished.

"We'll seal each tunnel up tighter than a duck's ass," Leeson assured us.

Carlos, who had come through with the reinforcements, gave me a puzzled look. "Um… what's so tight about a duck's ass, McGill?"

"I guess because it's in water… you know."

"Figures you'd get it!" Carlos laughed and shook his head like I was the biggest hick on Glass World—which may or may not be true.

Normally, I'd have become annoyed with him, but he'd brought through desperately needed help, so I gave him a pass.

"We've got two wounded," I told him. "Patch them up."

He hustled away and a moment later a familiar cry went up. "Fire in the hole!"

The dirt under our feet jumped, and dust shot out of six of the openings. A roar of crashing earth met our ears.

Just in case, I posted one man at each of the six caved-in tunnels and circled the rest around the last, and largest, opening. Everyone took up their positions and waited.

We breathed and sweated. No one talked for about a minute.

At last, the Vulbite rush came. This time they weren't fooling around. They led their charge with a throng of tiny robots.

I recognized these devices in a moment. They were the same little drones that had suicided on our boots back on Glass World.

We showered them with bolts, but a few got through. One man was left howling, but he shut up about thirty seconds later when he bled out.

"They've called up reinforcements as well," Harris surmised. "They'll be sending in armored bears soon. We can't just sit here in the dark until they wipe us out. There are too many of them."

His words were unwelcome, but they were also damningly correct. No one watching this struggle unfold would come to the conclusion that we were winning. We were under siege, and it was only a matter of time until we were overrun.

"I'm going back through the gateway," I said. "Leeson, you're in charge until I get back."

"The centurion is bugging out!" I heard someone whisper over an open mic.

"That's not true!" I boomed, turning on them. "I'm going to get more help, just like Carlos did. But this time, I think we need someone with brains."

Wishing them luck, I stepped between the gateway posts and vanished.

A moment later, I walked into the underground vaults on Glass World. Graves was surprised to see me.

"Did you find a way out, McGill?"

"No, but I found these."

Graves immediately stepped up to me. "You've found something?"

I held up a rack of bear-sized suits we'd pulled from the sticky ceiling. I grinned hugely, like I'd discovered spun gold.

He frowned at them, poked at them, then batted them out of my hand. They crumpled on the chamber floor.

"What the hell is this crap?" he demanded. "That's not a factory, or a documented process. That's a few more bear suits. We've got plenty of those!"

"Not so, sir," I said picking one up and dusting it off. "See these crystals? The whole suit sparkles with threads like silk. These suits are incomplete. We think the Vulbites make the suits, sir. They do it like they're spinning cocoons."

"What do you take me for, McGill? Are you saying these moron bugs can make some kind of spider webbing that turns into armor?"

"Sort of.... yeah."

Graves picked the suit up and examined it closely, poking at it. Then he called for Natasha to examine my find.

"This *is* different," she admitted. "It's a half-processed suit. They're made in layers, fine layers, then we believe they're cured with heat. This suit hasn't been cured yet—and yes, it does look like spider-silk is holding it all together.

Baffled, Graves toyed with the suit. "What kind of machine does this?"

"There's no machine involved, Primus," I said. "At least, none that we can find."

"I think he's right," Natasha said. "I would guess the Vulbites sit and spin these suits out, one layer at a time. They secrete a kind of sticky silk that adheres to the stardust. After many coats, the fabric becomes a solid cloth. With curing, it's an almost impenetrable armor."

Graves looked down at the suit, then at all of us. "It's shit then. This whole mission was a waste. We can't get the Vulbites to do this for us."

"Huh…" I said, looking over a suit and thinking hard. "I've got an idea, sir. But you're not going to like it."

He looked at me with squinting eyes. "I already hate it—but I know we're going to have to try. Just tell me the bad news. No bullshit for once, McGill."

"Sir, I never bullshit you. I give you the straight and narrow. I wouldn't be able to sleep at night otherwise."

"It's that bad, huh?"

I nodded. "Yeah… worse, probably."

He sighed, and he looked defeated. Then I started to explain. I sugar-coated it, and I grinned real hard, and I blew sunshine at him like there was no tomorrow—but it didn't really work. When I was finished, both he and Natasha looked like they wanted to puke.

-59-

Less than an hour later, we took every trooper we had and every scrap of equipment we could find through the gateway to Dark World.

Now, on the very face of it, that seemed downright crazy. I had to give that point to everyone who brought it up. Why leave Glass World entirely? What if more troops came down from Winslade? What if he made a big rescue effort, and they found we were all gone?

The trouble with that hope was that it wasn't going to happen. The numbers were all on the table, and the math was clear. Winslade had decided to bury our sorry asses. He had rid himself of everyone who'd been pissing him off lately. That included me, Graves, Manfred, and all our loyal troops.

What an easy win it was for him. He could return to Earth and mark us down as permed. Sure, he'd failed the mission, but at least he didn't have to worry about my big mouth, or Graves with his seniority in the legion.

I knew what he was bucking for. He wanted Varus. He'd decided to grab control of the outfit months ago, as far as I could tell. He'd gotten Wurtenberger to back him somehow and Galina had never really wanted to run Varus in the first place.

With Graves and me out of the way, it should be smooth sailing. Becoming the tribune in Varus wasn't a hard post to get, after all. No one important really wanted the job.

By the sick look on the faces of those who I talked to about it, I figured they agreed with my theory.

"Assuming we're screwed anyways," I told them as we had a huddle in the Vulbite chamber, "we might as well go for broke."

Graves grunted in disgust. "If I could think of another path—of anything remotely plausible—I'd go with it. But I can't. Therefore, you have the ball, McGill. God help us all."

"Amen," Harris added.

He and all the other adjuncts were circled around us, forming the huddle. They all looked like someone had flushed their goldfish. If I'd been a sensitive man, I might have felt insulted by their obvious lack of faith. Fortunately, I knew my plan was the only play we had, so I didn't care what they thought.

"Adjunct Leeson," I said, turning to the shorter, stockier man. "This first part is going to rely most heavily on you and your sappers. Natasha has used her lidar kit to locate hollow spaces nearby. Below us and a bit to the north, we've located a large open chamber. That's our goal."

"McGill...?" Natasha said nervously. "There's no guarantee that we're going to find anything there. This complex is huge. There are chambers—"

I put my hand up to stop her negative talk. "I know all that, girl. We're not betting on horses here. We're making the one move we've got left, and yakking isn't going to get it done."

She formed a tight line with her lips and nodded. She moved away and used her equipment to pinpoint the best drilling spot she could find.

"Remember," I called after her. "We don't want to run into any other tunnels. We have to get there clean and by surprise."

She didn't answer, she just went to work. I nodded like she'd given me a thumbs-up and turned back to the rest.

"Primus, all the rest of the team has to do is keep the Vulbites out of this chamber for as long as possible."

"There are more enemy troops pouring into this region every minute," Leeson said. "We've killed a thousand at least. They just pull the bodies out of the tunnels and send in fresh troops and drones. If we kill a hundred to one, we're still doomed eventually."

Graves worked on his tapper, going over action reports. "Our casualty rate is too high," he said. "We've only got an hour, maybe two, before we're overwhelmed."

I grinned and slapped my gauntlets together loudly. "That long? That's excellent! I never figured I'd be given that kind of time—thanks for the good news, gentlemen."

They gave me sour looks, but they didn't shoot me down. They knew they were witnessing my ham-handed effort to raise morale.

We split up and went to work after that. The sappers began drilling their way into the floor where Natasha was squatting and scanning. She squawked about not having located the perfect path yet, but I brushed her aside.

"You'll see better once we've worked our way down a few meters," I assured her. "Specialists, proceed!"

The sappers worked their drones like pros. These digging machines weren't as big and efficient as pigs, but their little self-propelled units could burrow through anything softer than puff-crete. They were supposed to be used to dig under a wall or other obstacle then blow themselves up.

Instead of planting explosives, the sappers used the drones to worm their way into the packed earth and loosen it up. A team of men with powered armor and folding shovels then began scooping the old-fashioned way in their wake. Soon, the place smelled of oil and ozone. The whining sounds of drones filled the cavern.

The work proceeded at a steady rate, and I began to believe we might just pull this off—or at least that we had a chance. About twenty minutes later, however, the Vulbites reminded us that they had brains of their own.

"The roof!" Sargon called out loudly. "They're breaking through!"

The Vulbites, unsurprisingly, were faster diggers than human sappers. They'd chosen a similar strategy, and they ripped open the top of the chamber overhead.

The space up there was hung with half-cured armor suits, which fell with a splattering of dirt once the breach opened wide.

A Vulbite trooper, losing his grip, dropped into the chamber with us. Then more fell behind him. The whole mess landed right on top of the gateway posts.

What followed was an eye-opener. All the times I'd ever walked through those posts, I'd always approached by stepping from one side or the other, walking forward through the field at a steady rate.

The falling Vulbites had unwittingly taken a different approach. One of them fell right on top of the field, from a vertical angle, rather than walking through it.

The long and the short of it was the field cut the Vulbite in half. The buzzing nimbus sent a center slice of him—his guts, I supposed—to the far end of the connection. A wet splatter must have arrived and oozed all over the floor back on Glass World.

At our end, two wriggling halves of the hapless Vulbite, each about a meter long, flopped and twisted on either side of the posts.

If the enemy had been human, they probably would have balked at that point—but these guys were bugs. The rest dove in, some dying horribly on the gateway, others crushed by their falling comrades. It rained Vulbites, and many of them were hurt or killed immediately—but they kept on coming.

By this time, half the human troops in the room were aiming upward. We released a firestorm of bolts at the ceiling. The glassy roof smoked and bubbled.

Vulbites fell even faster. Some of them got off shots of their own, striking down a few of my soldiers, but that was rare. For the most part, it was a slaughter.

Still, the rush continued.

"Jumping Jesus!" Adjunct Leeson called out. "If they keep coming, they'll suffocate us with sheer bodies!"

In the end, his prediction didn't come true. Instead, something much worse happened.

One or more of the Vulbites fell out of the roof and dropped right on top of the upstanding gateway posts. As the aliens each weighed a hundred kilos or more, the post was knocked down, trampled, and crushed. One of the posts, I saw, had broken in two.

The glimmering light of the field that was our only connection to the rest of Legion Varus flickered, buzzed, and went out.

We were cut off now, I knew. Cut off and sealed in this underground hellhole—probably forever.

The chatter of gunfire continued, and a few more men lost their lives struggling with the attackers that were falling out of the ceiling. After about a hundred Vulbites had died, however, the attackers stopped coming. Maybe they'd decided it wasn't working—but in my opinion, they'd already done their worst.

Grabbing up a big wad of Leeson's tunic, I pulled him close. "Adjunct!" I roared in his face, using that deeper, threatening voice a man my size can reach at times. "Send all your drones down that chute! Blow that tunnel open, blow it deep! Now!"

Leeson looked both sorrowful and scared. "I'm sorry, Centurion. My sappers have used up all their drone charges."

"Then wire them up with dumb bombs. Have them crawl to the bottom and blow themselves up. Use overloaded power-packs, force-blades—I don't care. Make that hole another ten meters deep—you've got five minutes before I perm you myself."

I set him back on his feet and let him go. He hustled to his team and began kicking tail. They rushed with him, hustling like fresh recruits with a noncom on their heels.

Natasha was my next target. She was working on her computer, as usual, and I pulled her around to face me.

"Is the gateway as trashed as it looks like it is?" I demanded.

She nodded. Her face looked wet, like she was about to cry or maybe had wiped away tears already. "I don't know what to do, James. We're—we're trapped down here. No one will ever find us."

"You let me worry about that, girl. Just gather up what's left of the equipment and haul it with us."

"With us? Where are we going?"

I pointed down at the tunnel mouth in the floor. A booming series of flashes came up from the bottom of it.

"Down there. That's where the Devil lives, and we're going to find him."

It took seven long minutes, but at last, the sappers broke through. Leeson had gone down the hole with them, leading by example. The last thud shook the floor of our chamber, and some troops lost their footing.

"Leeson?" I called down over the smoking rim of what now resembled a crater. "Are you okay down there?"

Only one of the sappers crawled back up to us. "Adjunct Leeson is dead, Centurion," he told me. "He set a charge without a timer—we're out of timers."

I nodded. "Did you break through?"

"Break through to what, sir?"

"To that big hollow area we've been trying to reach for nearly an hour!"

"Um.... No."

I dragged him out of the hole and pushed him aside. He staggered away from me. I got down on all fours and crawled inside the slanting tunnel. A few troops called after me, but I ignored them. I had to see the situation firsthand.

It was dank and dark down here. Dust was everywhere, and I had to flip my visor down to breathe. Squirming deeper, all the way to the end, I shoved Leeson's flopping body out of the way.

Smoking dirt, a few dribbling sands coming down from above—the whole tunnel looked unstable, and I thought it might collapse on me at any moment.

Calling back up to the top of the hole, I demanded a weaponeer with a belcher be sent down. Instead, a clanking, rolling cylinder came to rest against my boots. Grunting, I reached back and dragged it forward.

It was a belcher. Angry, I almost shouted at my troops, demanding to know why the weaponeer was too chicken to come down himself.

But then, I checked the rosters. All the weaponeers were dead.

With a shrug, I set up the weapon and cranked the aperture down to a tight beam. Years ago, I'd been trained to use these things. They were kind of clumsy, but versatile and tough. They rarely failed to operate. More fancy gear like smart missiles and the like could be jammed, packed with dirt and damaged just by banging them around, but not belchers. Say what you like about workhorse-level gear, it got the job done in the end.

Using the shoulder-mounted cannon like a drill, I aimed it downward and began releasing short bursts of energy. The tunnel filled with vaporized rock and my suit began to heat up—but I kept firing. The key was to avoid damaging the unit by holding the firing stud down too long. Heat was the biggest enemy, as the muzzle could become white-hot in seconds.

Pulses of energy won the day. Each pulse, lasting maybe half a second, dug a hole the size of a man's skull out of the rocky earth. Applying the weapon like a jackhammer, I managed to get sixteen pulses out of it before the energy cell ran dry. I roared for a fresh cell until someone rolled it down on top of me. I ejected the old energy cell, tossed it aside, and went back to drilling.

All in all, it took me about eight minutes to blow a hole through the floor into the vast chamber directly below it. I could only surmise that the roof of the lower chamber had been built with stronger materials. It was dense, tough, and hard to dig through.

I'd come to respect the efforts of Leeson and his sappers. Sure, they'd failed to reach the bottom, but they'd given it their all.

Unfortunately, when I finally broke through, I did so with all the sheer idiocy and lack of foresight the Vulbites had shown a few minutes earlier when they'd clawed their way through our ceiling.

The irony of the situation, along with a number of regrets and foul curse words, ran through my mind as the bottom of the tunnel gave way and I fell, ass-over-tea-kettle, into the pitch-black unknown.

-60-

I landed with a crash on top of a pile of dry, crunchy pods. At first, I thought I'd smashed my armored ass down on a stack of skulls—that's what it felt and sounded like. But after some rolling and swearing and looking around, I modified that perception.

It was a pile of shed carapaces. That's what Vulbites did when they grew bigger or when they died: they left behind a tough brownish shell. It was like the shell of soft crab, tough and leathery rather than hard and brittle.

But my weight and the apparent dryness of the stack caused them to crunch and split apart. Being partly hollow, they also broke my fall.

I stood cautiously on a mountain of carapaces that was perhaps five meters high. I looked up at the hole the ceiling.

"Everyone! Jump down the hole!"

The response didn't come back immediately. Finally, Graves got on the line.

"What have you found, McGill?"

I panned around my suit cameras and relayed the view back to him. The chamber was large, much larger than the one I'd come from. There were mounds of carapaces here and there, some even bigger than the one I'd fallen into.

"What's the point of going down there?" Graves demanded.

"We have to go somewhere, sir," I told him. "At least there isn't any sign of more Vulbites down here... yet."

Graves declared me to be six kinds of a retard, but at last he ordered the troops to follow me down. I had to scramble out of the way as they came rappelling into sight on ropes. Some just jumped, or threw gear down. Others used the few floaters we had with us to carry the wounded. These slid off to the sides of the cavern, the riders whooping until they came to a rest at the dusty bottom of the cave.

Graves and I soon stood on open ground. "So... this is it?" Graves asked me. "You worked your ass off and lost an officer to get down here. At this point, I'm less than impressed."

"Let's search the place, Primus."

We walked the perimeter as our troops frantically tried to set up a defense in case the Vulbites came through the ceiling again.

"McGill," Graves said. "I have to give you an 'A' for effort—but this is pretty hopeless. We've managed to dig down into a lower chamber, one that's even more empty and pointless than the first place we walked into. You do realize that sunshine and fresh air are above us, right? Not below?"

"That's not what I'm looking for, sir. The Vulbite billions are above us as well. Even if we did dig our way out of here, we'd never survive."

"So... why did we come down here? To prolong the inevitable? To give the men a sense of activity, rather than hopeless despair?"

I looked at him closely. "It's not like you to talk this way, Primus. Like a defeatist, I mean."

Graves straightened up and scowled at me. "I'm no chicken-shit crying on your shoulder. But I smell a perming, here, and I want to know if you've got anything in that head of yours that you're not sharing."

I nodded. "I understand. I did have a plan—but it's been blown. I'd hoped that we'd find a queen, or something we could bargain with."

"Right... our only hope then is Natasha. She wrapped up and brought down those damaged gateway posts. Maybe she can power them up and—"

"Sirs!" shouted a younger recruit. He was one of Barton's light troopers—a rare breed at this point of the campaign. Most of his fellows had died.

Looking his way, we saw him frantically point at a pile of trash that was... moving. At first, I thought it might be some kind of earthquake. Then I realized it had to be Vulbites, digging their way into the chamber from underneath one of the big piles of loose carapaces.

Then when something reared up out of the piled dead hides, a third thought struck me: one of shock. Whatever this thing was, it was *big*. When I say it was big, I mean it was bigger than a jugger. It was more like the size of a tree-form Wur.

As the head and body broke through, rubbery Vulbite carapaces slid away from it in all directions. That's when I realized what it had to be.

The creature was segmented, brown and shiny. The outer skin rippled, and the body was exceedingly long. It had been buried under the biggest mass of carapaces, like a snake hiding under a mass of eggshells.

The body was much longer than it was tall. I'd seen her kind before, and she made me think of dragons found in the depths of the earth. If anything had ever looked like a dragon uncoiling in its lair, it was this Vulbite queen.

Black, intelligent eyes swept over us. All of the fifty or so rifles we had left aimed at her in fear and disgust.

"Hold your fire!" I boomed. "Don't harm the queen—not if you ever want to see home again!"

A few shots rang out, making the monster rear up higher, like a pissed snake. Noncoms ran among the jittery troops who had disobeyed, kicking their feet out from under them and shoving their faceplates into the ground. In Legion Varus, when an officer told you to cease-fire, you did so immediately, or you might get shot yourself. In this case, there were only a few ass-kickings to be distributed.

"Can we communicate with it?" Graves asked me as the queen tilted her great head this way and that. She had to know she was surrounded and vulnerable.

"Damn straight I can! No lady has ever been born, be she alien, beaver or bug, that I couldn't talk to!"

Graves eyed me with very little trust, but he nodded just the same. "Go for it. Ask her out or something."

I advanced toward the beast. It watched me with black jewel-like eyes the size of basketballs. Ever seen a magnified picture of an ant or something? She was that kind of ugly, with face-horns and twitchy mouth-parts—the works.

Natasha quickly approached me and stood in my shadow. "James... what are you doing? You can't tame this thing."

"I'm not trying to. I'm trying to communicate, girl. Help me out."

She worked her tapper and her computer, fanning through a thousand dialects and translation apps. At last, she found something that sounded *clicky*. It was kind of like the sounds something with a lot of feet makes when it runs across your kitchen floor.

"What are you saying to it?" I asked.

"The basics. We're friends, we won't harm—"

I reached and grabbed the computer from her hands. She complained, but she let me take it without too big of a fuss. She seemed all shuddery just being so close to this monstrous Vulbite.

Quickly, I connected to her translation app and tapped out a message on my tapper.

Queen Vulbite, I told her, *you are a prisoner. Cooperate fully or you will die. All your eggs will die. All your larvae will die. All your children of every kind will die.*

The queen rotated the great head, looking at me with first the right eye, then the left. At last, she spoke. The translator talked for her.

You are food-things. Food must not threaten the Source.

"Uh..." I said, chewing that over. I switched the translator app into audio mode so I could talk instead of tap. "What's this about a source? What source are we threatening?"

"I am the Queen. I am the Source."

"The source of what?"

"The Source of Life, idiot-talking-food-thing."

There it was again. I tell you, I've never managed to have a cordial discussion with an alien being of any kind that didn't end up with them calling me a dummy. I'm not sure why that was, but it was true.

"Listen up, we can kill you anytime we want to. You get that, right?"

"Again, the food-thing improperly threatens—"

"You shut the hell up, queen-bug. You're nothing now. You're lower than hog-shit as far as we're concerned. We'll burn you down, slice you up, and eat you for steaks!"

"Um... McGill?" Natasha hissed, tapping on my shoulder. She seemed upset with the way I was talking to the Queen, but I didn't care. We didn't have time for niceties.

"What you describe is inconceivable. You are a food-creature. I'm here to consume. You must—"

Bending down, I picked up the belcher I'd dug my way through the roof with. Taking careful aim, I burned off one of the Vulbite's two-meter-long legs with it.

Snipping off legs was something I'd seen the Rigellian bears do with Vulbites, and that's where I'd gotten the idea. Vulbites had lots of legs, a hundred or more, like centipedes. When those bastard bears wanted to punish them, they simply snipped off one or two of the extras.

The creature broke off its little speech. It squirmed around like a snake and even made a hissing sound.

"You done?" I demanded. "Do you understand who you're talking to now?"

When it had stopped thrashing around, it spoke again. "You are the master. You are the one-who-must-be-obeyed. But know this, human. In the end, my kind will consume all of your kind. Your young will wriggle in our maws. Your—"

I burned her again, on the left side this time. Another leg fell off, steaming.

Natasha tried to push my belcher down, to aim it at the floor, but I didn't budge. She could hang from the barrel for all I cared. I wasn't going to tolerate any more back-talk from this over-sized swamp bug. She was going to start listening to me.

"You must stop your depredations!"

"I'll stop when you admit defeat."

The creature paused for a few seconds, but then she spoke at last: "I admit defeat."

Smiling at last, I lowered the belcher. The granddaddy of all centipedes watched this closely.

"Okay then, this is how things are going to go from now on."

I proceeded to explain the terms of her surrender, and she never said a word in response. She did do a quite a bit of hissing, however. I decided to take that as a clear sign that she was getting the message.

-61-

The queen was not entirely cooperative. While I got her to agree that she was our captive and would obey us, her troops didn't seem to get the message.

They broke open the main tunnel to the upper levels and came flooding in. We shot down a hundred, then a thousand. Finally, I began to get worried.

"Sir," Adjunct Barton said, "we're running out of pellets in our snap-rifles."

"Shave metal off your kits. That can work at short range."

The truth was a snap-rifle was a very rugged and versatile piece of gear. It could take a beating and pound out a thousand rounds, each of which was about the size of a BB. Such tiny projectiles were able to deliver a surprising amount of kinetic force when accelerated to several thousand kilometers an hour. They struck roughly as hard as a traditional rifle bullet.

Barton shook her head. "We've been doing that, but the juice for the accelerators is about gone, too. We need fresh battery packs."

Compressing my lips into a stubborn line, I suggested they tap the batteries that ran the heavy trooper air conditioning, rebreathers and the like. Harris immediately came up with his own complaints.

"Sir? Did you tell Barton she could leach off my men? We can hardly light up a force-blade as it is. These rigs need every ounce of power we have left to keep the auto-assist exoskeleton working. Without that, armor is just a quarter ton of dead weight."

I thought it over, and I nodded. "You're right. Have the men shed their armor. Transfer all power to weapons and basic survival."

"Say what? Heavy troopers without armor? What's the point?"

I almost reached for him and gave him a shaking, but I stopped myself. We were all tired and frustrated.

"Adjunct Harris, listen up. We're in a bad way. A heavy trooper in armor isn't worth much if he can't fire his weapon. That's all that matters now."

Harris looked around to where a group of techs were working on the broken gateway system. They appeared dejected and toyed with the disassembled parts listlessly.

"It's that bad, huh?" he asked. "I'd hoped Natasha could pull another miracle out of her rear end. But we're not getting out of here, are we?"

"I doubt it," I said. "But I've still got some options."

"Such as?"

I pointed grimly at the towering queen Vulbite. She was quietly watching all of us, and her alien intelligence was obvious even to me.

Harris released a grim laugh. "I say we wire-up that big termite. If we all die, at least she'll die too."

Not answering him, I walked toward the monstrous alien. He wandered off to harass Graves next. I knew he would try to get all my orders changed around, but I didn't care. Right now, I was in charge of the op.

The queen immediately turned and dipped her head to get a good look at me as I approached.

"Your Royal Highness," I said, "can I have a word with you?"

"Speak, egg-thief."

I didn't know what an egg-thief was, but I've been around long enough to know when I'm being insulted. I let that slide right off me and smiled. "What's your role here, Queenie?"

The monster regarded me with the giant black jewel that served as her left eye, then with the right. I was too small and close for both her wide-set eyes to see me at once.

"I am the birth-mother. I am the life-giver. I am the beginning and the end of all things."

"That's real nice," I said, "but why are you down here all by yourself? Why aren't there other Vulbites feeding you and taking away your newborn young?"

The great beast coiled up a little. "Because I'm not producing my precious eggs. I'm resting, as none of my daughters are necessary."

"Your daughters—?" I began, but was rudely brushed aside.

Harris was back, and this time he had Graves with him.

Graves looked the giant Vulbite up and down, then turned to me. "Trying to score, McGill?"

"Not quite like you'd imagine, sir."

As I watched, he hefted up a belcher. He aimed it at the huge alien, who stood motionless.

"Sir, that creature is our prisoner," I told him.

"That's right, but I figure she needs a little encouragement."

"Uh…"

Without a big speech or other preamble, Graves sighted and fired the belcher point blank up into the queen's face. He nailed an eye and it slagged.

The queen reared up and began to buck around the cave. A few soldiers were knocked flat and one light trooper was crushed.

"Dammit, Primus!" I shouted, grabbing onto the belcher. "I was just getting somewhere by talking to her."

"You're too soft on aliens, McGill. They only understand one thing—if you're lucky."

"Scale-mites!" the queen boomed, raging. "Egg-thieves! Cretinous monsters!"

"Uh… I'm sorry about that, queen. Some of the men here are real hotheads."

"I'm your superior officer, McGill," Graves said sternly. "And I'm standing right here!"

I paid no attention to him. The queen's one good eye was still watching me, and she kept me visible at all times by oddly tilting her head. The other side dripped like melted wax.

"Let me tell you how you can be rid of us," I told the queen. "Get your Vulbites to stop attacking for starters. Then, tell them to bring us technicians to repair our gateway posts. When that happens we'll leave your world, and you, in peace."

"That can't be done."

"Why not?"

"I will tell you. Vulbites do not have such technicians. Our gateways are built off-world by others."

I couldn't help but notice that after being shot by Graves, she seemed to be in a more forthcoming mood. "Off-world?" I asked. "You mean by Rigel?"

"Yes."

I thought that over for a second. Before I could finish my thought, a ruckus began at the tunnel entrance, and our men took cover.

"They're coming again!" Harris shouted. "Positions, everyone!"

Another dark wave of enemy soldiers rushed in. They were gunned down without a qualm. They no longer bothered with stealth suits, having either run out of them, or decided they weren't effective like they'd been in the past.

I pointed at the tunnel mouth and the dying Vulbites. "Brave soldiers. Your children are dying to save you. Can't you tell them to stop? To allow us to leave this place?"

"They are doing what they were created to do," she said. "They will kill you all in the end, and they know this. It makes them eager to give up their lives."

"Great... listen, where is the man from Rigel?"

"There is no man from Rigel."

"I mean those little bear-looking dudes. Your masters."

"Those creatures are not in this chamber."

Sensing an opening, I took a step forward. She eyed the belcher in my hands warily.

"Is he in this nest? Someplace else?"

"Yes."

I smiled. "Can you contact him?"

The great queen, with her damaged head still cocked, stared down at me. "I am in contact with him now. He is watching these proceeding with great interest."

"Uh..." I said, looking her over for cameras and the like. I didn't see any, but that didn't mean they weren't there. A camera eye could be the size of a bacterium these days. "Talk to him. Call him, bring him here!"

"There is no need," she said. "He was alarmed by your violent actions toward me, and he is coming here right now to put a stop to it."

She seemed somewhat pleased with herself as she said this. I suspected she was hoping I would get my comeuppance when her master arrived. I didn't say anything else, but left to stand ready at the entrance tunnel.

No delegation from Rigel arrived. I'd hoped they might march down the tunnel, demanding to parlay. Instead, they sent a floating drone.

Fearing it was a bomb, my men shot it down immediately. I had one of the techs rush up and inspect it.

"Any explosives?"

"Negative. It's... I would guess it's a com-link bot."

"It's going to blow up!" Harris insisted. "You're a fool if you pick it up, McGill! A fool!"

Walking forward, I examined the broken drone. It looked harmless. I dropped it in the dirt.

Before I could return to our hastily built wall of earth that provided cover for our troops, another drone came buzzing along.

"Down, sir!" a specialist called out, sighting on the drone.

I got between him and the second messenger. "Just hold on a minute!"

There were calls of "it could be a bomb!" but I ignored all that. If it *was* a bomb, it might be a relief. I was getting tired of this mission, and I wanted to either finish it or die. Either way, it would be over and done with.

Snatching the drone from the air, I examined it. Buttons built for activation were on the side of the unit. Shrugging, I pushed one.

The drone stopped buzzing and began to make clicking sounds. I got my tapper out and activated the translation matrix.

"...recalcitrant criminals..." my tapper said. "...to those without redemption, without respect, without..."

"Shut up!" I told the drone, and it quieted. "Who is this?"

"You are speaking with Viceroy Chaska. I am in charge of the planetary garrison here."

"Is that right? Okay Chaska, let's talk terms."

"You will surrender. You will be expunged immediately for your crimes. There can be no terms."

"Too bad you feel that way. I'm afraid I'm going to have to kill old Queenie here to make a point."

The queen had been listening in. Upon hearing what we said, she slithered away back to her original bed-pile of slippery carapaces.

"It's too bad," I said. "She thinks quite a lot of herself. I bet old Squanto would handle things differently."

"What do you know of Squanto?"

"As a matter of fact, I know him quite well. He's almost a friend of mine."

"How can this be? What is your name, Earthman?"

"I'm Centurion James McGill," I said proudly. "Squanto and I, we go way back."

The communications drone was quiet for a moment. Then, after a time, it spoke again.

"This is High Lord Squanto of Rigel," another voice said. It was familiar to me, despite the fact the translator made a garbling mess of Rigellian speech. "Are you truly the one I seek?"

"That's right, Squanto old buddy! I'm McGill, come here to mend fences. If we've done you and yours any harm, let me be the bigger man and apologize—"

"Silence, beast!" Squanto shouted. "I'm calling over a deep-link pathway, but my word is that of a deity on this planet. You shall be destroyed. Everything in that chamber shall be destroyed."

"Yeah? Even the queen lady I've been romancing for the last hour or so?"

"She is replaceable. All slaves are replaceable. Her loss will be regrettable, but no price is too much to pay to end your existence, McGill."

"I'm sorry to hear that, Squanto."

So saying, I crushed the drone in my hands and dropped it. I walked back to the queen, who had been listening closely.

"You hear that, your worship? Squanto just ordered that you, me, and everything in this place be destroyed. What do you think about that?"

"Improper. Poor decorum. Rule-breaking. Treaty expunged."

"I take it that you're not happy? That maybe Squanto and his companions should be taught a lesson?"

"Instruction would be fruitless with the treacherous and cruel masters from Rigel."

"Right you are. I'll tell you what, if you can get these tunnel-rats of yours to stop attacking us, and maybe to bring a few items we need—I can get you out of this. I can see to it that we all live to see another day."

The massive Vulbite shifted and writhed. It coiled, then uncoiled. At last, it began to speak again.

"What is it, exactly, that you propose?"

Right then I smiled. It was the first honest smile to cross my face since we'd ported into the caverns under Glass World. There was a glimmer of hope—just a glimmer, mind you, but I was more than willing to take it.

-62-

I cut a deal with the big queen to summon her Vulbites in a peaceful way—instead of having them rush the cavern in berserker hordes. We gave her some communications gear, and she made good use of it, contacting her countless people.

After a bit of time, a group of them came worming down the tunnel, shoving aside the stacked bodies. They seemed to care little for their own dead. The hardest part for me was keeping my own troops from butchering these newly docile bugs. No one by this time had any qualms about killing them. It had become downright reflexive.

"Stand down, dammit! Stand down! Hopper, that means you!" My shouting eventually caused the troops to back off. Many were out of ammo and had fixed their blades onto the end of their rifles, using them like spears. That was unusual for legionnaires, as we were normally well-supplied.

The Vulbite procession slithered directly past me, ignoring my speech and the welcoming spread of my arms. They wriggled and rippled along toward the queen herself. My translator box clicked and squeaked, but they barely paid attention.

"Looks like you've ordered up a personal guard for that queen of yours, McGill," Graves chided me.

"Nah, that's not gonna happen." Despite my words, I followed the churning feet and watched as they did indeed approach the queen and line up in front of her.

Then, to everyone's amazement, she began dipping her massive head and chomping on them.

"What the hell?" Harris demanded. "Is she pissed off or something?"

One by one, the queen ate her twenty-odd attendants. We stood there, gaping. I had no idea what I should do.

Walking up to the busy monster, I used the translator again. "Uh... Queen? Why are you eating your technicians?"

She paused after the eighth one and her head began to convulse. To our sick horror, she spat out a pile of loose, nasty-looking skins. They looked just like the ones that filled the cavern, but they were slimy and wet.

The queen regarded me with her one good eye. "These are not my technicians. They are sustenance. I require much food to deal with the stress of your presence here."

"Food? You eat your own young?"

"Heretical! Foul-words! Disgust!"

"Uh... is that a yes or a no?"

"That is an emphatic negative. These captives are the young of rival queens. They've been selected and sent here as a tribute to me. They are for the express purpose of consumption."

Now, as a matter of reflex, I considered the habits of aliens to be baffling, repulsive and even angering. But this one must take the cake. I hadn't even known Vulbites were a cannibal species. Looking around at the hills of dead, I figured this big worm had made quite a lifestyle out of the practice.

"We should put this thing down right now," Graves said, coming up and standing next to me. "If you won't do it yourself, you should give me that belcher, McGill."

"Come on, Primus. I've almost got her right where I want her."

"Nonsense. All you've done is arrange for her last meal. Well, that's over with now. Let's get back to business."

"The business of being cornered, out of supplies, and soon to be wiped out?"

He twisted up his face. "At least we'll be rid of this nightmare."

The queen wasn't helping her case any. She'd gone back to eating her snack. After devouring every Vulbite and spitting out the skins, she looked down at me again.

"Are you going to comply with the terms of our deal now?" I demanded. "If not, you can consider that your last meal."

"What you've asked for will take time."

"No!" I shouted, knowing that was the one resource we were out of. I raised my belcher and aimed it at her dripping snout. "Get the technicians down here to fix our gateway this instant, or I'll blow your other eye out and burn the rest of you!"

"Your suggestion is a non sequitur. An impossibility. A none-such."

Taking careful aim, I focused a narrow beam at her second eye. She twitched and shied away.

"You would not dare. You know not what you ask."

"I sure as hell do. Are you going to comply, or what?"

The giant bug wriggled for a bit, and I tracked her movements, never letting her get close enough to strike.

"I have summoned them. Great pain will be borne by my young... you should feel shamed."

I laughed and lowered my belcher. "You're talking to the wrong human if you want to see shame. How long until they get here?"

"They must overcome the guards first. With luck, they'll succeed due to the element of surprise."

I gaped up at her, not sure quite what she was saying. Harris, who'd been listening in, walked up to me.

"Whoa, whoa, whoa!" he said. "Am I hearing what I think I'm hearing? Did you talk this giant bug-lady into rebelling against Rigel? How's that possible? I didn't even see you diddle her."

I thought about slapping him one, I really did. But my lower jaw was hanging wide and I could hardly think. This wasn't what I'd expected all.

But then, almost as a reflex, I snapped my treacherous, telltale mouth shut and stood tall. "Of course that's what she did. What do you think I've been up here yakking about for the last hour? We cut a deal, and she's delivering on her half of the bargain right now."

Graves was standing to my left. He snorted and eyed me doubtfully, but he didn't burst my bubble. He just watched.

Another ten minutes went by. We heard some echoing sounds of gun-fire coming down the passages. At least we weren't rushed by a fresh horde of Vulbites.

"This is taking too damned long, McGill," Graves complained.

"Listen Primus! The firing has stopped!"

I approached the queen again. "Are they coming? Did your technicians get what they needed?"

"I told you that Vulbites are never technicians."

"Whatever. Where's the promised help?"

The queen consulted her communications gear. "It is done. This is a sad day. A great alliance has ended."

"If they couldn't keep you safe from marauders like me, they weren't very good."

"That was my own reasoning. Rigel not only failed to defend the Vulbite homeworld, they also built a conduit allowing my person to be endangered and physically abused. Why serve such a master?"

"Why indeed?"

Shortly after this exchange, another procession approached down the tunnel passage. These were Vulbites, standing on their rear legs and bearing swords. They were bigger, older creatures. Many of them bore scars and fresh wounds.

In the midst of the group was a lone bear from Rigel. He looked like a cub amongst the bigger Vulbites.

"What is the meaning of this?" demanded the Rigellian. "I am Viceroy Chaska. I will not be treated in this fashion by outlaws and chattel!"

"Well, Mr. Chaska sir," I told him. "In that case, you've got yourself a problem."

I proceeded to explain the situation to the bear. He didn't like it much.

"Impossible! I would no more serve you, ape-creature, than I would serve this moronic insect!"

It took a little wrangling, convincing, and the plucking of six curved black claws, but finally old Chaska was in a more compliant mood.

Looking up at me from the dirty cavern floor, his sides heaved and his one good eye stared. "I will describe the equipment needed. Send your Vulbite slaves to fetch it."

I squinted at him, considering whether I should believe him or try to get it myself.

"McGill," Graves said. "We may not have much time. This isn't the only Rigellian on this planet. They have a spacecraft manufacturing center in orbit, remember? It's only a matter of time until professional troops arrive."

Taking his advice and calling it good, we sent off the Vulbite color guard with the queen's instructions. The wait was a short one—and I soon saw why.

They didn't return with tools or parts. They came back with something much better: two free-standing gateway posts. These were undamaged and they looked identical to the ones we'd used to get here.

A hoarse cheer went up at the sight of this equipment. My legion comrades pummeled my back, and they told me one-and-all that they'd known I could pull this off. I reflected as the gateway was assembled that I wasn't the only terrible liar in this expeditionary force.

My instructions to Viceroy Chaska were clear, and he didn't argue much. He wanted to be free of me as soon as possible. He kept talking about bombs and about the whole nest going up.

"Uh..." I said as he sweated over realigning and reprogramming the gateway for a new destination. "Are you serious about that? Will the Rigellian ships really bomb this nest?"

"Of course, fool. What do your people do with rebellious slaves? In our empire, such insurrections are considered a cancer. They will not be suffered for an hour, much less a day."

"Hmm... in that case, you should get a move on. Even if it's only to save your own skin."

The bear glowered at me over his shoulder. His yellow eyes were as thick with hate as Squanto's had always been at these moments. "Now I know why you are such a priority to our High Lord," he said. "He would risk his own life to take yours."

I smiled. "That kind of hate is the sincerest form of flattery!"

The bear grumbled and went back to work. Soon, he had the coordinates reprogrammed.

"It is done. All you have to do is step through, and—"

Taking him by the shoulders, I began pushing him toward the posts.

"What are you doing?" he cried out in alarm.

"I'm testing your workmanship, of course."

"You promised I would be released! You promised I—!"

"And that's exactly what's going to happen after our little test. We'll walk through and right back again. After we see everything is in working order, I'll send you back upstairs with bells on."

"I want no bells, nor do I want any part—!"

The bear was struggling pretty hard, and even though he was unarmed and beat up, he was still as strong as a strong man. I had to work, digging my gauntlets under his fuzzy armpits to half-lift, half-push him toward the glowing field.

"Stop!" he shouted plaintively. "The gateway is unsafe!"

"What?" I asked in mock surprise. "How do you mean, Mr. Viceroy?"

Chaska quickly explained that the posts had been reprogrammed to terminate on the surface of the nearby star. Most likely, anyone going through would be disintegrated and never reassembled, but even if they were, it would be an unpleasant destination. Dark World's sun was only a brown dwarf and relatively cool for a star—but it was still hot enough to incinerate a man instantly.

"Why, Viceroy!" I said to him in reproach. "I'm surprised at you, trying to trick dumbass monkeys like us! What a mean thing to do. I'm inclined to toss you through to burn, then fix it my damned-self!"

"You could never do it. The process would take too long. You can't be—"

"All right then. You get one more chance. Be quick about it!"

This time, the little rat-bastard bear worked at a frantic pace, and he didn't give me anymore back-talk, either. When he was done, about five minutes later, he sullenly gestured toward the glimmering field.

"The pathway is sound."

"He's right," Natasha said, standing next to us. "I can tell the connection is a good one. It goes somewhere stable."

Grabbing Chaska, I picked him up and tossed him through the posts. He squeaked in mid-air, then vanished.

The others around me looked shocked. "What if it was another trap?" Natasha demanded.

"Then you'll have to figure out how to reprogram it yourself. You were watching him, weren't you?"

"Yes, but... where are you going, James?"

I shrugged and ambled toward the posts. "Someone has to test it. Besides, I got the feeling the boys at Central might not like Mr. Chaska."

Stepping into the field before I would have to listen to any more calls to stop, I vanished. In what seemed like a moment to me, I was instantly reassembled on the far side.

Guns. Lots of gun muzzles. That's what I saw for the most part.

Mr. Chaska was on the deck, face down, with a dozen hogs surrounding him. They'd banged him up a bit, but they hadn't shot him—not yet.

"Hey boys!" I said, happily. "Is this Central?"

The chief Hog turned in surprise and stared up at me. He nodded after a second, and I started to grin.

I was home at last.

-63-

"Hey..." I said to the hogs.

"Stand back, sir!"

They were working over Chaska pretty good. He'd made the mistake of struggling and even biting a few of them. If you really want to piss off a hog, just try biting one sometime.

They were trained to control a prisoner's hands. But for a Rigellian bear-dude, that wasn't even his most dangerous weapon. What's more, they seemed to start off underestimating the furry little bastard's strength. These bears were damnably strong, with muscle density three or four times that of a human. That was common on Earth, too, where most predatory animals and apes were stronger than men, gram for gram. But even so, these hogs were taken by surprise.

After a few bites and some cries of pain, the shock-rods came out. They began to crackle, snap and thud onto Chaska. I almost felt sorry for him—almost.

"Say, fellas," I said after Chaska had spent a solid thirty seconds of growling and scrabbling on the floor. "I don't want to be a wet blanket, seeing as you're clearly having yourselves a good time—but if you give him a heart attack... well, he does have diplomatic immunity and all."

The security chief looked up in surprise. He was panting and beads of sweat rode on his flushed face. "What? Why didn't you say that before?

"I figured it wasn't my place. You boys know your business... don't you?"

Breathing hard through his teeth, he ordered the rest of his men to stand down. They got up and circled the bear-dude. Chaska, hands cuffed and snout dripping blood, got slowly and painfully to his feet.

"I'm terribly sorry about this misunderstanding, Mr., uh... What's his name, McGill?"

"Chaska."

"Really? Well, I'm sorry Mr. Chaska, but you can't just go around biting security personnel. That's frowned upon on Earth." He turned to me again, jabbing a thumb at Chaska. "Does fuzz ball here comprehend Standard?"

"He does if his translator is on."

"I understand, you stinking ape," Chaska said. "You will release me and allow me to go back through the gateway. If you fail to comply, I will see that you're tortured before your execution."

The security hog blinked and smiled. He looked like he was about to laugh, but his laugh died in his throat when he caught a look at Chaska's angry stare. It was clear the bear meant it.

"I'd advise you to keep a civil tongue, alien," he said, "diplomatic immunity only goes so far on Earth."

"That is clear. What a pathetic, barbaric race of cub-stealers you all must be."

I laughed to break the tension, putting a heavy hand on the little bugger. "Let's go home and sort this out."

Automatically, Chaska whirled his face around as if he was going to bite me. I almost flinched, taking my hand off him. It was that close.

But I held on, and seeing it was my hand, Chaska settled down. "Yes. Let's leave this barbaric place."

The hogs weren't sure what to do. They stepped from foot to foot.

"McGill," the security man called after me, "don't you have to file a report or something? Why'd you bring that little mutant here in the first place?"

"To prove the gateway worked."

The hog's face cracked into a smile as he figured it out. "Ah... that's why the bear was walking ahead of you, right?"

I waved for him to shut up, and he shook his head at me.

A moment later, we stepped through the gateway and returned to Dark World. We let Chaska go free. Five minutes later, my people were streaming through the gateway to the safety of Earth. Alarmed, the security people began calling for help. Medical teams, officers, more security hogs and plenty of frowning brass soon swarmed us.

I didn't much care for any of them. They got in the way, mostly. I wanted to find a shower, a hot meal and a bunk—maybe one that belonged to a pretty lady.

My search led me upstairs to Legion Varus headquarters up around floor three hundred. As I had a special relationship with Tribune Galina Turov, I was allowed to enter, despite the fact it was after hours.

I helped myself to Galina's private shower, fold-out bar and her secret stash of diet food. Thirty minutes after I'd returned to Earth, I was snoring on her too-short couch.

The next morning I was rudely awakened by an angry woman. She stood over me, fists on her hips and a confused stare on her face.

"McGill? What are you doing here? What are you doing back on Earth?"

"Uh... mission accomplished, sir!"

She licked her lips thoughtfully. "Where's the rest of my legion?"

I shrugged. "Do you really care? You can always revive the rest."

Her mouth fell open, and her eyes widened improbably. "You mean... Winslade got them *all* wiped?"

"Not all, I suspect—but a lot of them."

I proceeded to tell her my sordid tale of woe. It was long, it was wild, and it wasn't what she wanted to hear.

"That doesn't sound like you succeeded at all! That Winslade... he's a bigger idiot than you are!"

I smiled, and I watched her fume for a while. At last, she wanted to know what the hell I was smiling about.

"It's good to be home, Galina."

"Don't get any ideas."

"I'm not, I'm not. But let me explain—we brought back more than a lot of banged up troops."

"What are you talking about?"

"Let's go down to the barracks and talk to Natasha and Graves."

Warily, she followed me out of the offices. As we exited, I was pleased to see her boy-toy secretary Gary look as stunned to see me as Chaska had looked when the shock-rods had grazed his nads.

Way down a few hundred floors, we found temporary housing for visitors. It wasn't the best, which was why I'd chosen to sleep on Galina's couch.

"McGill... Tribune!" Natasha was climbing to her feet and stretching when we got there. She was still wearing the same crumpled, dirty uniform she'd had on when I'd last seen her.

"You've been here eight hours, Specialist," Galina said, "what have you been doing?"

"Working, sir."

Natasha proudly showed us a series of polygon boxes. They were about waist high.

"What is this?" Galina demanded.

"Didn't McGill tell you? We negotiated a special deal with the Vulbite queen. She let us take several of her best spinners with us."

"Her best what?"

"There are small Vulbites in these boxes, larvae that spin cocoons."

We explained how the armored suits were made, and the necessity of using natural Vulbite silk to adhere the suit together until it was cured. We then showed her the Vulbite spinners, who were docile worker-types, and the partly finished suits we'd taken.

Galina watched all this, her eyes big and darting around as she took it in. "This is astounding. I can't believe insects had anything to do with the process. We'll have to find a work-around, of course, but... yes. You've done well, James."

She beamed up at me, and I grinned back.

Natasha didn't look as happy. She rolled her eyes at us when Galina wasn't looking.

"We'll have to set up a larger work-area," Galina said suddenly a few minutes later.

"But, sir..." Natasha said, "we've got a lot of work to do right now."

"What are they working on? Do you have you got a sample?"

Natasha smiled, and she went to the Vulbite workers. She had to wrestle away a suit that was incomplete, but it was human-sized. They didn't seem to get the idea that she didn't want them to finish it.

Galina grabbed up the suit, but then quickly threw it at me. "Gah! It's sticky and disgusting. McGill, you must come with me to Drusus' office. We must display this find and claim it fully before anyone else attempts to take some of the credit."

Shrugging, I moved to follow her. Natasha reached out a quick hand and hooked me. She looked up at my big, happy face.

"She's going to screw you somehow, James," she hissed. "You know that, don't you?"

"That's kind of a private matter, Natasha. But yeah, I was kind of hoping..."

"No, you idiot!" she hissed. "I mean she'll take all the credit. She's already moving to edge out Winslade."

"But he was trying to scoop her himself..."

"Yes, yes, exactly. That's what the brass does! They ditch failures and glom all the glory for anything that goes right."

"Hmm... You've got a point, there. I'll be careful."

"One more thing..." she said, looking down.

"Uh... what?" I asked warily. We'd been lovers a few times on this trip, and I was worried she'd ask for more. Like... to be my girlfriend again.

"I just worked like a dog for you overnight," she said, "while you slept upstairs on a couch."

I wasn't sure how she knew about the couch, but then she was a tech. All techs were spies.

"Yeah...?"

"You remember your promise?" she asked earnestly. "When we got back to Earth?"

Dumbfounded, I stared at her. I'm a man who makes random promises to women on a near-daily basis. Hell, almost anybody could have said I'd made a promise and promptly forgotten about it. That was part of my charm.

"Give me a clue."

She punched my arm and twisted up her face. Stepping close, she whispered three words: "The casting device!"

"Oh…" I said, feeling kind of relieved. "I'll see if I can get Etta to let you in down there for a quick look later on, okay?"

This seemed to satisfy Natasha, and we parted ways. Holding the armor she'd given me away from my body, I carried the half-complete suit her new-found bug-friends had been spitting on all night.

Following Galina upstairs was a treat as always. That girl could walk, if you know what I mean.

She prattled on about a million plans of hers while we rode the elevator back up to the three hundreds and beyond. It all sounded interesting, but I was kind of sleepy, and I hadn't had breakfast yet. I yawned, and she looked annoyed.

"Are you even listening to me, McGill?"

"I sure am. I heard every word, I swear it."

She frowned in irritation, but then she soon continued to tell me things. I pretended to listen until we got to Drusus' office.

There, I found we weren't the main attraction. We were carrying a sticky, half-cured human-sized armored suit and everything—but no one was looking in our direction.

At the front of the conference table, which also doubled as a powerful battle computer, was a huddle of three people. One was Praetor Drusus. I was happy to see him. The other two… not so much.

On Drusus' right was Praetor Wurtenberger. He was a heavy-set fellow with a euro accent and a gut that pushed furniture around when he leaned forward. His eyes were lit up and full of excitement.

The real surprise, however, was on the left of Drusus. It was none other than that temporary stand-in Tribune Winslade.

"How the *fuck* did he get here before us?" Galina hissed at my side.

"He's quicker than a fox in a henhouse, that's for sure."

"This is fascinating," Wurtenberger was saying. "So, the insects themselves make the armored suits? I can't believe it! Who would have suspected a natural process such as excrement could—ah! I see we have guests."

He turned to look at us as we entered the room. Drusus looked up as well, and he smiled slightly. He was the one who'd told Galina to come here today.

"Tribune Turov, Centurion McGill, please join us at the table." He waved at the numerous comfy chairs. I took one on the Wurtenberger side.

That was partly because Winslade was staring at both of us—eyes sliding side-to-side from me to Galina and back. He reminded me of an outhouse snake that didn't know which ass to bite first.

"I'm... surprised to see you here, McGill," he said. He glanced at Drusus reproachfully, faking a tight smile. "Was this meant to be a surprise, sir? I just reported McGill as missing and possibly permed not an hour ago."

"No surprise was intended," Drusus said. "I simply wanted all the parties involved in this discovery to be present at this meeting."

Wurtenberger was staring at me now. We'd met before, but it was years back, and it wasn't like we were buds, or anything. A flicker of recognition did grow on his features, however.

"Ah! This is the brute you were telling me about, no Winslade?"

"Um... this is Centurion McGill, yes."

"Hmph," Wurtenberger said, pursing his lips in my direction reproachfully. "Disobedience, physical intimidation, frequent conduct unbecoming... I don't know why you brought him to a top-level meeting, Drusus." He turned to raise his bushy eyebrows in Drusus' direction.

Drusus was watching everyone. People thought he was easy to fool because he wasn't a loud officer, but I could have told them different. He tended to figure out what had really happened most of the time—which was both good and bad, from my point of view.

"McGill is unique," he said diplomatically. "For example, as you can see, he's not lost or permed. He's right here, reporting in."

"How *did* you get back to Earth?" Winslade asked, unable to hide his astonishment and dismay on that point.

"I had a little help," I admitted. "Natasha is the best tech around, and it turns out there was more than one set of teleportation gear down there in that termite nest we invaded."

Winslade set his teeth and nodded. He looked at the table for a second, then slapped it with a black-gloved hand. "It makes no difference. In fact, I'm happy you're here, McGill. You can bear witness to a proud moment in my career."

"Yes," Wurtenberger said, looking at Galina for the first time. "Turov, we've been discussing a recent change we made in the Legion Varus roster. Perhaps you'd like to make it permanent?"

Galina wasn't surprised, but she was pissed. Only I could tell that, though, by the way her eyes flashed over her false smile.

The situation was clear to everyone. Winslade hadn't been idle out there on Glass World. He'd tried to perm me, and he was bucking for her job to boot.

"That's a very interesting offer," she said. "I assume I'd be moving back to my previous rank as imperator?"

Wurtenberger and Drusus glanced at one another. In my guts, I began to feel a little sick. After all, Galina was a lousy officer. For instance, she'd run out on us just a week back rather than face a losing campaign. But for all of that, Winslade might be worse from my point of view. He downright hated me most of the time, and he was the sneakiest man alive—with the possible exception of myself.

Accordingly, I figured it was time to intervene.

"Sirs," I said, clearing my throat, "may I make my report? I've got some critical information that you've got to know about right now."

"Very well," Wurtenberger said, "but don't take too long."

I realized right then that *he* was the one running this meeting. He was senior to Drusus, although they held the same rank. It seemed kind of rude that Drusus should be bossed around in his own office, but that was the Hegemony way.

"Excellent," I began, and I slid the armored suit across the table at them.

The three men looked at it like a dead dog. Winslade in particular crossed his arms and sniffed. "We've got lots of those, McGill."

"They're made by the Vulbites themselves," I said.

"We know that," Winslade snapped, and he turned to the others. "If we can continue our previous discussion—"

"Let McGill finish," Drusus said. "I think he's got more to tell."

"Damn-straight I do. Check out this suit—it's not like any of the others you've ever seen."

Sighing, Winslade thumbed the material and fiddled with a sleeve. "Black in color, with a weight and general nature similar to a thousand captured units. Yes, I can see this suit is only half-way through the curing process—and yes, we were able to figure out the Vulbites make them with webbing during your absence. I'm not seeing anything remarkable here."

I stood up, grabbed the suit and held it up. Using my long, long arms, I thrust it high. The legs still dangled on the computerized table, making the screen light up and throw error-icons around.

"Notice, sirs, that this suit wasn't made for a bear from Rigel. It's made for a *human*. In fact, I had it fitted to your size, Tribune."

So saying, I tossed it across the table to Winslade. It flapped up and over his head, and he snatched it down irritably.

"Terribly sorry about that, sir."

Drusus and Wurtenberger were on their feet. They felt the material and examined it with new interest.

"A man-sized suit?" Wurtenberger said. "How many of these have you found?"

"That's the only one so far," I admitted.

"Fascinating…" Wurtenberger continued, "and threatening. Could Claver have been manufacturing these for his troops?

That would make his ham-handed legions much more effective if he could make enough of them. This is news indeed, McGill."

"It's not fully finished yet," I said, "but it will be in a few days after some more processing steps and curing. Then you can try it on, Winslade. I fitted it to your height."

Winslade was still trying to look disgusted, but he was failing. Even he was impressed by my gift, although he wouldn't admit it.

"McGill…" Drusus said, "there's something I don't understand here. If you *found* this man-sized suit, and it's the only one you've got, was it pure chance that it fits Winslade? Or did you manage somehow to tailor it?"

I smiled. Drusus was the smart one, I'd always said as much. He'd finally noticed what I was hinting around about.

Leaning forward with a big Georgia grin, I looked at all of them. "Sirs, I didn't find that suit. I didn't just tailor it, either. We made it, and we can make more. We can even make a suit that would fit you, Praetor." I gave Wurtenberger and his big gut a nod.

All three of them were staring at me for a few quiet seconds. They were feeling up the suit, and it was beginning to dawn on them that I might not be full of horseshit.

"How?" Winslade demanded. "What you're suggesting is virtually impossible. There are no processing machines back on Glass World. Just the raw materials and dead workers."

"That's exactly right, sir," I said, and I nodded to Galina. She woke up her tapper and ran a finger over it, tossing a vid from her wrist to the table we were all leaning on.

There, in full color, sound and three dimensions, a video began to play.

"This is from deep down in the labs under Central. The Vulbite workers you see are cooperating with us. We only have seventy of them at the moment, but they're highly skilled."

Drusus, Wurtenberger and especially Winslade were amazed. Not one of them had a closed mouth. Not one. They were gaping at us like fish, and none of them could struggle out a word.

"You see here?" Galina went on calmly. "This Vulbite is using her mouthparts to spray a sticky residue over the base fabric. This is done in layers, and as far as we can tell, the stardust material is never actually ingested by the Vulbites. It would probably be fatal to them if they did eat it."

"Where...?" Drusus began. "These creatures are *here*, at Central?"

"Yes. We've given the lab people custody, and I must point out that this is a highly classified situation. We had to get permission from Hegemony Labs just to tell you about it. Only the fact it's a defense matter allowed us to get permission to discuss it."

"I don't believe it..." Wurtenberger said. He turned to us, and he really looked at us both for the first time. He was smiling, smiling big. "This is astounding. You've completed the mission. Not just bringing back intel—but an actual manufacturing process!"

"Just so, sir," Galina said primly. "But as the tribune of Legion Varus, I can't take sole credit."

Winslade made a small, choking sound.

"No," she continued. "That wouldn't be right. McGill here was critical, as he's always been our top commando. A miracle-worker who does the grunt work I assign to him with amazing proficiency. Similarly, I can't forget the contributions of Primus Winslade. He held down the fort at Glass World, and it does seem he made discoveries on his own regarding the process. These details have now been rendered obsolete, of course, but nonetheless the effort was commendable."

I had to hand it to Galina. When it came to squeezing the glory out of a situation, she was hands-down the best. Winslade had tried hard, but he was simply out-classed.

"This does seem to put a new spin on things..." Drusus said.

"It certainly does," Wurtenberger said. He was back to fondling the armored suit. "You said something, McGill, about making such a suit for me?"

"That's right sir."

"I would very much like that."

"Then you've got it. As soon as we kick up the flow of crystals from Glass World, we'll put our team of bugs on the project."

The group fell to happy handshakes and congratulations. Only Winslade seemed left out, both in mood and attention.

From a quiet distance, he showed me a line of teeth instead of a smile. He had to be pissed and then some to be upstaged like this. For some reason, that fact made me grin so hard and so long that my face hurt by the end of the meeting.

By the time we left, we had new orders. We were to oversee the construction of several new suits and deliver them to the top brass.

"That frigger Wurtenberger thinks I'm his seamstress now," Galina complained as we left.

"Did you see Winslade's face? His expression was worth dying a time or two right there."

She glanced at me. "You did well, James. Not only on this mission, but in that tight political situation."

I hefted the sticky suit between us. "I had the goods this time out. That's makes it easy."

Galina smiled. "Yes… yes you did. Would you like to report to my place this evening?"

My eyes blinked once. This was out of the blue. Galina was always a woman who could blow hot and cold from one minute to the next, but we hadn't been together for a while, and she'd pretty much ditched me out on Glass World.

Still, as a man, I knew there wasn't any percentage in holding a grudge against a woman in need—especially not one who was as fun in private moments as she was.

I smiled. "Let's do dinner first. I'm starved."

"Certainly, but I'm buying."

"Deal!"

That began a lovely evening that couldn't have gone better from my point of view.

-64-

The next day I was summoned back to Central with fanfare. Galina got herself on the roster somehow, and she showed up with me at Drusus' office at 800 hours. She had her finest uniform on, the one that cinched-up tight in the back. More than one person had asked about it, wondering if smart-cloth was in short supply this year. Galina always met such questions with a frosty silence.

Today, however, she was all smiles. I knew she was planning to cash-in on my success, but I was in such a good mood I didn't even care.

"McGill!" Drusus said, standing and shaking my hand as we entered his cavernous office. He was beaming, and I returned the expression without a hint of my inner surprise.

"Good morning to you, too, sir."

"Centurion," he said, "I can't tell you how wonderfully this campaign went. I'd almost lost hope when I was reviewing what Winslade came back with. He had data, he had samples, but he didn't have the process. We would never have been able to duplicate the enemy armor manufacturing techniques without being able to study these Vulbites in the act of making the stuff."

"Glad to be of service, sir."

"Right, well—"

Galina cleared her throat at that moment. Drusus glanced at her as if only just noticing her presence. That was saying something, as most men couldn't take their eyes off her when she wore the get-up she'd painted on today.

"Ah, Turov," he said. "Do you need something signed, or…?"

A frown flickered over her features, but she stamped that out quickly enough. If one of her underlings had made that suggestion, she'd pound them into dust. But she always knew which side of the bread had the butter on it. She forced a smile and shook her head.

"Not at all, sir. I'm merely here to observe this well-deserved commendation. I've had my eye on this centurion for a long time, and I'm very pleased that my careful tutelage has resulted in real mission success today."

"I've heard that you've kept McGill close at hand," Drusus said, giving her a meaningful glance, "and it's probably a good thing you're here today. Praetor Wurtenberger and I had a few discussions yesterday, and we've come to an agreement in regard to the leadership of Legion Varus."

Turov blinked rapidly and kept her smile firmly planted. "How so, sir?"

"We were considering placing Winslade in command, as you might have known. But… we've changed our minds on that point. You both did well, but there's no reason to shake up a team when they're just starting to gel and get real work done."

Galina's tongue slipped out to wet her lips. I knew she wanted to be an imperator again, and I also knew she wanted to scream at Drusus right now, or possibly physically attack him.

But she did none of that. Instead, she straightened up and nodded. "Very well. I will take my leave then, sir."

Drusus nodded and she turned away stiffly. She walked off, and Drusus and I caught each other watching her go.

"Ah… McGill. Back to the business of the day. I've got an offer for you, Centurion."

"Yes, sir?" I asked, truly having no idea what he was going to say next.

"Yes. I'd like to make you a primus."

My jaw sagged low. I think my chin might have hit my collar. What's more, it stayed there for several seconds.

"Uh..." I said. "Are you sure about that, Praetor, sir?"

He laughed. "You know, you're not the only one who's questioned the idea of pushing you up in the ranks. But I have to admit, James, you get things done. It's never in a conventional manner, mind you—never—but still, things happen."

I nodded, feeling stunned. I couldn't deny what he was saying, but I couldn't own it, either. The rank of primus was a whole different beast than centurion. Sometimes a primus would go into the field personally, the way Graves did, but most of them were staffers. Brass in nice offices. The idea that I might actually fly a desk someday soon... I didn't know what to make of it.

"I can see you're surprised," Drusus said. He was getting out a few glasses and pouring drinks. "Let's talk about it."

"I surely am... to think, I've made it all the way up to the rank of primus. That's not a surprise, it's a shock! Did you know I had plenty of legionnaires in Varus tell me I'd never make it to my second enlistment? Wow... Harris is going to have a conniption. He'll have to salute me if I'm one step under the tribune up on Gold Deck."

"Hmm..." Drusus said, tapping his glass to mine. We both downed our drinks, but a slight frown played on his lips, and he didn't meet my eye.

"What is it, sir?"

He sucked in a breath and studied his empty glass. "About Legion Varus... as part of this promotion, you'll be reassigned."

My mouth fell open again. This time, my expression was one of horror. "Don't tell me, sir... please don't tell me you want me to become a hog. I'd rather blow off the tip of my dick with this here pistol!"

Drusus chuckled. "No, no. It's not that bad. Why would we cage a tiger like you? No McGill, Wurtenberger, Winslade and I did some heavy talking, as I said..."

I stopped listening. My radar was up and pinging away. Before, he'd said something about Wurtenberger. But now we were suddenly talking about a cabal, a trio of officers, only one of whom actually liked me.

The scent of an ornery rodent was in my nostrils. Winslade and his new patron Wurtenberger, were behind this change. I braced myself for the worst.

"Give it to me straight, Praetor. What did Winslade come up with?"

Drusus glanced at me, then looked down at his hands again. "The suggestion has been made that you'd do well in the combat arm of an off-world legion. There is, in fact, one operating as a garrison force on Storm World. They were originally under the command of Armel... but you know how that went. Since then, we've been trying to replace our officers at the post—"

"Wait a second," I said, holding up a hand and showing him the flat of my palm. "Are you saying you want me to play primus to a zoo legion?"

"That's an unfortunate term that we're working hard to stamp out, McGill. Are you aware that most of Earth's legions are now so-called 'zoo legions'?"

"I didn't know that, and it makes me sick to hear it. Who's the tribune?"

"I've got good news there. Primus Fike has become the tribune, and he's doing well."

My mind was whirling, and I felt a little sick. The idea of being sent to Storm World... years of service hundreds of lightyears from home... nothing but stinking Blood-Worlders to tend to... and I bet there weren't six real human women on the whole damned planet. The icing on that nasty cake was answering to Fike and his shitty attitude.

Drusus was still talking, but I only caught snatches of it. He went on and on about how I'd worked with Fike before, and how it would be great experience, and it wasn't going to be forever. He also mentioned how I'd hit it off so well with the native scuppers on my first tour out there.

At last, I raised my hands. "Sir, I really appreciate this. I sincerely do. But I just don't think that kind of post is right for me. I couldn't take it, sir. It would be like putting me in prison."

Drusus looked at me sourly. He wore an expression of mixed annoyance and guilt.

"James," he said quietly. "I know it doesn't seem fair."

"Sir, it's worse than that. You realize Armel quit and went AWOL over this exact assignment, right? Now he's running a mercenary outfit full of Saurians. Did you know that?"

He nodded. "I did. Armel failed us. I think you can do better. But more importantly, James—this isn't exactly an offer. It's an order."

"An order?"

"Yes. Earth needs her best sons today—today more than ever. No one wants to serve out at some garrison on a sunless world. I get that. But someone has to do it, and you've proven yourself ready for a command on the frontier."

I sighed, and I stared him in the eye as I stood up. A moment later, he stood up as well.

"Sir," I said. "I regret to inform you that I'm resigning my commission, effective immediately. As my unit has been deactivated, this shouldn't cause you or Varus much trouble."

As I said these words, I stripped off my centurion insignia and placed them on his desktop.

It was Drusus' turn to look stunned. "McGill…"

I put up a hand. "I'm sorry, sir. I just can't do it. I can't be a sub-primus. If Varus doesn't need me… well sir, I'm done with the military."

Slowly, I turned around and headed for the exit.

"Halt, soldier!" Drusus said sternly. "You haven't been dismissed."

I turned back around and stood at attention. He approached, hands clasped behind his back, and he paced his broad carpets in front of me.

"You've put me in quite a position with this ultimatum, McGill," he said.

"My apologies, sir."

"Are you serious? This is no bluff? You won't take this promotion and serve Earth where she needs you most?"

My mouth worked for a second. I thought of all sorts of bad words to say, but I kept that stuff from coming out—barely. "Listen, sir. This isn't a promotion. With all due respect, it's a spite-filled slap in the face."

"From me?"

"No, sir. From Winslade and his newfound patron, Wurtenberger."

Drusus didn't answer that one. He glared fiercely at the carpet between us. A few quiet seconds passed. I got the feeling he was thinking hard. "James McGill, I'm demoting you back down to centurion. You'll stay at Varus. If anyone asks about this, we never had this conversation."

I almost staggered, such was the impact of those words. My whole identity was wrapped up in Varus. I couldn't imagine fighting and dying with anyone else—much less retiring entirely. I was gladder than I'd expected to be to know I was reinstated.

Drusus threw something at me then. I caught two shiny objects out of the air.

In my palm were my centurion's insignia. I quickly put them back on again and hustled out of the office before he could change his mind.

-65-

That night, I went home to my shack in Waycross and got drunk. I felt like I'd dodged a bullet—but no, it was better than that. A bullet could only kill you once, it couldn't imprison you on a planet for years of misery.

Along about midnight, I heard a tapping at my door. I'd been dozing, and came awake with a snort.

Giving my head a shake, I got up from my couch and padded to the door. Somehow, I'd lost my shoes.

In my mind, I expected to see Galina when I opened that door. After all, we'd been having some nice get-togethers lately. I kind of suspected she'd known about Drusus and his plan to promote my ass off Earth, and I was therefore feeling angry toward her.

Throwing open the door, flinging it wide, I stood tall. My shack was dark inside, almost as dark as it was outside, and I probably cut a scary-looking figure framed in that doorway.

The smaller shape on my doorstep cringed a little. My mouth opened to begin shouting, to start demanding to know if she'd been in on the ambush I'd just suffered up at Central—but then I stopped.

It wasn't Galina. Female, yes. Trim and fairly young, yes. But this girl didn't have the same distinctive shape. I could only see her silhouette, mind you, with the moonlight shining in her hair from behind, but that was enough.

Reaching out, I flicked on the porch light.

"Abigail?" I asked, completely flummoxed. "What are you doing here?"

"Striking out, apparently," she said, and she turned around to leave.

"Wait... hold on. I was expecting someone else."

"Obviously."

"Someone else who kind of pissed me off today."

She turned back slowly and grabbed onto a post on my creaky porch. "Are you glad to see me then?"

"Uh... yeah, sure!"

"You thought I was Leeza, didn't you?"

Reaching up a hand, I scratched my head. Then I recalled that she and Leeza had come to blows not that long ago. The truth was I hadn't seen much of her for weeks.

"That's right," I lied. "She's got me angry."

Abigail leaned away from her post, but she didn't let go of it. "That's good," she said. "I hate that woman."

"Understandable. Come on in."

After a few more moments of hesitation, she followed me inside. I got her a beer that was still sealed from the stack of cans on the coffee table.

"You've been drinking?"

"A little."

We didn't say much for a time, sipping our beers. At last, Abigail broke the ice. I was glad she did, as I was running out of ways to keep things from going sideways.

"Look, you failed to keep up your part of our bargain," she said.

"Huh? How's that?"

"You remember that I told you about Glass World? That I led you to it? That you were just lauded as a hero because of this?"

"Oh... yeah, sure. You wanted access to Earth's markets—but I'm not in control of that part of the deal."

"Exactly. So, I'm not blaming you for Drusus and his denial of my petition."

"That's a real relief to me," I said, faking concern.

She looked at me quizzically. "Sometimes," she said, "you're so reflexively full of shit, I can't tell the difference. Can you?"

"Uh… usually I can."

Abigail laughed. "All right then. The good news is we're officially allowed to make contracts with Earth again—despite Drusus."

"How's that?"

She shrugged. "My brothers and I… we're tenacious people. We tend to work hard to get what we want. We play every angle. In this case, I had another deal going, just like yours. That one has now paid off, so I got the contracts signed."

I stared at her for a few moments. "Another deal? You don't mean with Winslade and Wurtenberger, do you?"

She blinked in surprise. "You knew about that? It was a secret—but yes, that team managed to get the deal done."

"A team, huh? I had a connection to Drusus, so we were a 'team' too? Is that what I'm hearing?"

"That's right. You're not upset about that, are you?"

"No," I lied. "You guys sure are six kinds of tricky, but I don't care one whit."

"Good. Now, let's get down to why I've come here tonight."

She stood up and began pulling her shirt over her head. This took me by total surprise.

"Whoa, whoa girl! What the heck is this?"

She stopped with her bra showing. Her tight belly was shiny in the evening light.

"We had a deal, didn't we?" she asked. "You upheld your end of the bargain, so I'm upholding mine."

"Uh…"

She went back to stripping, and I sat there dumbfounded. This girl was a strange one. She'd grown up off-world, as far as I knew, surrounded by her brothers. She didn't seem to get how to behave in any kind of a romantic fashion.

"Why exactly are you doing this?" I asked her. "I mean… I didn't even get you into Hegemony. Winslade did."

"Yes, but I never flirted with him. I don't even like him."

"Can't say that I blame you there."

"You tried to complete our contract. You acted in good faith. I can't withhold payment on this kind of deal in that situation."

"Payment...?"

"Yes," she said, standing before me in her panties. I had to admit, my eyes were roving, so I might have missed whatever explanatory expression was on her face. I was barely able to hear her words at all.

"You tried, Drusus screwed it up, so I'm paying up."

"But wait... I didn't explicitly demand... this."

"Come on, McGill," she laughed. "I flirted with you to gain your cooperation. I did it for months. Flirting is a promise of future sexual access. Therefore, I made a promise—and we Clavers always keep our promises. You can have me tonight."

"Uh..." I said, staring at her. I was feeling discombobulated. "So... you aren't really interested in me? All this time it's been a pretense to make some money?"

"Not *some* money," she said, methodically baring her breasts. It didn't look like she was stripping down in a sultry way, it was more like she was getting into the shower after a long run. "We're talking about billions, McGill, maybe *trillions* of credits. That's why Wurtenberger got off his butt and pushed for this. He can be motivated by money—but not Drusus. When we offered him cash on the side, he balked."

I thought that made sense. Drusus was a straight arrow. Offering him bribes wasn't the way to get past him.

Giving myself a shake, I stood up. Abigail was plenty cute and all, but she wasn't going about this the right way.

"Abigail... look, I don't want to be rude or anything, but maybe you should put your clothes back on and leave."

"What?" she asked in honest surprise. "You don't find me attractive?"

"Oh no, you're cute and all... but you're kind of freaking me out."

"I can't believe it..." she said, looking crestfallen. She pulled her pants back on and stared at me. "What did I do wrong?"

There. Those were the first honest, hurt words I'd heard out of her. "I don't know... I guess you took the wind out of my sails, girl. I don't want some kind of second-class pity payment. That's not how I do things. When a lady comes to my place, it's because she *wants* to be here. Not because we're executing some clause in a contract."

Abigail gathered her things. Half-dressed, she marched outside without even looking at me. I could tell her feelings were hurt, but the situation just didn't feel right. I'd had women sleep with me because they'd been paid to do so before, and I'd never liked that sort of thing.

When the door closed behind her, I sighed and popped open a fresh beer. The night wasn't all that hot, but it was humid. One of those late spring nights in southern Georgia.

I turned on a game and began to watch, but not one minute later, there was a tapping at the door again. This time, the tapping seemed muted.

Throwing it wide again, I saw Abigail standing there. She looked like she was about to cry or something. She also looked a bit angry.

"Look," she said. "I did it wrong. I don't do this well—I don't really know how to... to interest men. You're not the first who's been intimidated by me."

"Intimidated?" I laughed. "I was disappointed, not intimidated."

"All right then. What do I do? Tell me."

"All you have to do is be honest. You've got to be real—you've got to be yourself. Fully engaged and interested in the here and now."

She blinked a few times. "I'm not good at that."

"I think you are, in other situations. You're a frank person, a girl who says what she means, right?"

"Yes... usually."

"There you go. So... try it."

Abigail looked kind of upset. She tossed her hair a few times, thinking it over. "I do like you, James. I've been interested in you since the first time I met you."

"Same here."

"So… maybe we can make something out of our mutual attraction. What do you think?"

Grinning, I stood to one side and pointed at my couch. "There you go! Was that so hard? Come on in."

Abigail walked by me, and I waved for her to take a seat. She looked like she wanted to complain about my couch, but she didn't. Not this time. She was in the groove.

We finished our beers, then drank another. I didn't grab her, or nothing. I didn't want to make this easy on her, and I also wanted to see what she would do next.

"This is weird," she said. "I'm feeling kind of uncomfortable."

"Why's that?"

"Because I don't know the score. I don't know what's expected from each of us."

I rolled my eyes, and she caught that. She gave me a light slap. "You dick! I saw that."

We laughed, and I finally kissed her, because the moment was right. Timing is everything in these situations.

Hours later, I decided she could be sweet enough when she wanted to be. Sure, she looked like her brothers, and that was a little bit freaky. I had to remind myself of all the times I'd chased the sisters of guys I'd known in the past—their looks hadn't bothered me then, so it shouldn't bother me now.

Abigail wasn't very experienced. Sure, she liked to act like she was sophisticated and worldly and could make a sex-deal like she was swiping credit out of her tapper—but it wasn't true. I'd been with plenty of women, and I knew this girl was nervous and uncertain underneath.

I found that kind of sweet, and I was gentle with her. We made a night of it, and around two am. we dragged out my daughter's auto-scope. Etta had left it behind when she'd moved to the city.

It turned out there was some magic left in the stars for both of us. We were seriously well-traveled people, and it was fun to show one another places we'd been. I was surprised to learn she'd seen more planets and stars than I ever had.

When morning came at last, she departed early, saying she had to go off-world. I was left wondering which star would be shining overhead the next time we met.

Books by B. V. Larson:

UNDYING MERCENARIES

Steel World
Dust World
Tech World
Machine World
Death World
Home World
Rogue World
Blood World
Dark World
Storm World
Armor World
Clone World
Glass World

REBEL FLEET SERIES

Rebel Fleet
Orion Fleet
Alpha Fleet
Earth Fleet

Visit BVLarson.com for more information.

Printed in Great Britain
by Amazon